The Reconstructionist

Nick Arvin

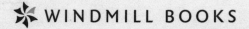

WINDMILL BOOKS

Published by Windmill Books 2012

2 4 6 8 10 9 7 5 3 1

First published in Great Britain in 2010 by Hutchinson

Windmill Books
The Random House Group Limited
20 Vauxhall Bridge Road, London SW1V 2SA

Addresses for companies within The Random House Group Limited can be found at:
www.randomhouse.co.uk/offices.htm

The Random House Group Limited Reg. No. 954009

www.randomhouse.co.uk

A CIP catalogue record for this book
is available from the British Library

ISBN 9780099538073

The Random House Group Limited supports The Forest Stewardship Council (FSC®), the leading international forest certification organisation. Our books carrying the FSC label are printed on FSC® certified paper. FSC is the only forest certification scheme endorsed by the leading environmental organisations, including Greenpeace. Our paper procurement policy can be found at:
www.randomhouse.co.uk/environment

FSC
www.fsc.org
MIX
Paper from responsible sources
FSC® C016897

Printed in Great Britain by Clays Ltd, St Ives plc

For R.G.H. and C.R.A.

A crying of tires erupted from the street.

The two boys in the house froze and waited, listening. A high wooden fence surrounded the subdivision where they lived; on the other side lay what they called *the big streets.* Between their backyard and the intersection of Mill and Main stood only the wooden fence and a hundred feet of sidewalk.

Tires squalled and cried toward the intersection, and Ellis and Christopher waited. They had done this before. Accidents occurred there often.

This was when they were young, and they still played together.

Then the collision ripped the air open for one roaring instant, and the boys startled, and the glare on the television glass trembled. It ended with a lingering metallic sound, like a rolling paint can, that drifted away, and silence resumed. The boys stampeded the door.

They ran nearly a quarter mile until they reached an opening in the fence, then turned into the big streets where a line of unmoving traffic was already forming, car behind car, drivers staring toward the intersection. Ellis wheezed and felt the shortness of his legs relative to Christopher's, but he kept up. A siren's howl drew toward the intersection from the other side of town.

Two boxy American sedans—a Chevy and a Plymouth—lay in unnatural postures, pointed in oblique directions, their black guts exposed, their glossy surfaces crumpled, twisted, torn. An acrid odor filled the air. Radiator fluid the color of green Kool-Aid glistened in an arc on the asphalt. Across the intersection lay a single shining hubcap. It matched the chrome hubcaps on the nearest sedan, the Plymouth, where a fat man and his fat wife stood. The husband peered toward the approaching sirens while his wife glanced at her watch, repeatedly, and Ellis wondered why she was barefoot. Near the Chevy were two women. One, older, was comforting the other, a young woman with heaps of hair who lay on her back on the street and held her hands over her face and moaned and cried out to God for help.

A few people gathered on the corners. Two more boys from the neighborhood arrived and joined Ellis and Christopher. A third. They punched one another on the shoulders.

A policeman picked up the hubcap and directed traffic around the damaged vehicles. Another policeman talked to the women in the Chevy and scribbled on a notepad.

An ambulance arrived. The woman holding her face and moaning was placed onto a gurney and swallowed by the ambulance. A wrecker with flashing amber lights backed up to the Plymouth while the ambulance moved off with its siren alternating yowls, bleeps, and squawks.

The twins trotted in, and they were punched on the shoulders, too.

The sedans trundled away behind a pair of wreckers. A cop remained, taking notes, talking with people. He measured distances with a wheel on a stick that he rolled from point to point. He retrieved a camera from the trunk of his cruiser and took photos.

"Go home," he shouted toward the boys.

They sidled a few steps down the sidewalk and loitered there. Only when this cop, too, had climbed into his car and driven away did Christopher start to saunter off.

The others followed. The short twin was pushed and he stumbled. "Leave me alone," he protested, and the others laughed. They shoved one another and pretended to trip, flailed around, clutched one another. One of the boys jogged backward in front of the short twin and chanted in his face, "Leave me alone. Leave me alone." Christopher veered over and hit Ellis with his shoulder and shouted, "Smash!"

Ellis bounced into another boy, yelling, "Crash!"

Christopher surged into the tall twin and screamed, "Wham!"

The boys tumbled together headlong down the sidewalk, pinballing and roughly chanting, "Smash! Crash! Wham! Bash! Crash! Slam!"

The tall twin screamed, "Boom!" A boy shouted, "Wreck!" Another hollered, "Blood!" And another yelled, "Guts!" They punched one another on the shoulders and shook their fists as if on a team that had won. They began to sprint and strain for speed.

The next day, Ellis rode through the intersection with his mother in her Oldsmobile. The damaged vehicles were gone, of course, and the splash of green fluid had vanished, too. The only indications of the collision were a couple of short dark tire marks on the pavement and, at the corners of the intersection, the shards of glass and broken ruby-colored plastic pushed by passing tires into long shallow piles.

One

One

On his lap Ellis Barstow held the police photographs of Pig Accident Two. He'd sorted them into three groups of about a dozen images each. The first group showed, from various angles, the accident vehicle—a white Mercedes lying a short distance from the large pine tree that had smashed in the driver's door. In the second group was vehicle-path evidence—black tire marks deposited on the asphalt as the Mercedes skidded and yawed before going off-road, and the furrows that the wheels had cut through the soft earth leading to the tree. And in the last group were roadway obstructions—the scattered carcasses of a half dozen crushed and bloody wild pigs.

Ellis also held a rough, hand-sketched diagram of the accident scene. It had been made by the police, and it showed measurements locating the Mercedes, the tree, and the tire marks. He kept turning from the photos to the diagram and back again, with a vague impression of something anomalous. He couldn't identify its origin.

He and Boggs, his boss, had boarded the airplane in the purple darkness of early morning; now, as they banked, the first red light of the sun burst in the window. They were flying from the humid summer of Michigan to the humid summer of Wisconsin, to land in Milwaukee at eight in the morning. Ellis sat on the aisle, and next to him sat a young couple, a woman who wore a hair product that smelled like some obscure fruit—papaya, maybe. Next to her was a man with tattoos all over his arms. The two of them argued in undertones. When the woman's elbow nudged Ellis's on the armrest, he flinched and hunkered down. He didn't want to be distracted. He wanted to see the diagram and the photos completely and, further, to see the physics that they implied.

Boggs sat two rows up, his big hairy head tilted backward, asleep. At the airport that morning, while they'd waited for the flight to board and Boggs clipped his fingernails, dripping little white trimmings onto the airport carpet, he'd declared that he hated waiting and he hated waiting in airports and he hated airports. "The only viable emotion in an airport is anxiety," he said. "You come into the airport and you feel anxious or you feel nothing."

"I don't know. What about irritation?" Ellis suggested. "And boredom."

"Boredom seems awfully close to the feeling of feeling nothing. But, irritation—yeah, I suppose you're right."

"And now I'm feeling the thrill of being right."

Boggs worked at the nail on his thumb. "Even if I were feeling irritated," he said, "I wouldn't admit it."

A couple of the photos on Ellis's lap were close-ups of one particular pig, the largest, a boar about four feet long from snout to tail, with a bristling razorback and tusks as big as a man's finger. Positioned more or less in the center of the lane, it lay on its side with one leg bent back underneath and an eye smashed in. This appeared to be the specific pig that caused the driver of the Mercedes to swerve. Ellis turned through the photos again. It looked like there was room to steer around the pig, through the road's shoulder.

Ellis noticed suddenly that the papaya-scented woman beside him was ignoring her companion and gawping at the photos. Reluctantly, he put them away.

Still, he thought about them.

A man in a white four-door Mercedes C280 driving a rural two-lane road. Alcohol in his bloodstream. At the entry to a long leftward curve, he encountered dead pigs in the roadway. Six dead pigs, scattered over a couple hundred feet. Bristling hair, blood, bone, and viscera. A couple of them had been completely shattered and smeared by traffic down long stretches of asphalt. The driver passed most of the pigs without a problem, but as he came to the big one lying right in the middle of his lane, he turned hard. The driver's-side front wheel bit into the soft dirt of the roadside, and the rear wheels began to pivot around. The car went sideways. The rear legs of another, smaller pig that had been lying well off the side of the road caught under the front wheels and it dragged along; its original position could be traced back along a streak of blood. Driver's side leading, the Mercedes smashed into a pine tree.

The photos showed the driver collapsed into the steering wheel, from which the deflated airbag hung like a tongue, like a large dog licking the dead man's cheek. According to statements in the police report, the driver was an estate-law attorney, four times married. He left behind six children.

The police had talked to his current wife; she said she had no idea what he was doing, drunk, on that road, in the middle of the day, in the middle of the week, far from his office. She had thought he was at work.

"Obviously," Boggs said as they reviewed the file, "he was having an affair. The jerk."

They landed, exited the plane, passed through the beige tunnel of the Jetway, and walked together to the main terminal making pig jokes. "You read *Animal Farm*?" Boggs asked. "Everyone always wondered what happened to Snowball."

"The question is, why did the pig cross the road?"

"A, to escape the dystopian allegory, or, B, to dodge the swerving drunk?"

Ellis stopped at the baggage claim while Boggs went ahead to the rental-car counter. The baggage carousel stood empty and unmoving, so Ellis found a bench against the wall and sat and took out the photos again.

The overall accident sequence was clear enough: the Mercedes had swerved into the dirt and slid sideways into the tree. The issue in dispute was why. A blood test had found that the driver of the Mercedes was at 1.5 times the legal alcohol limit. But the dead man's heirs blamed the dead pigs.

Ellis had never heard of wild pigs before; he'd had to research them. They were the bastard offspring of escaped farm pigs and European wild boars imported for hunting stock. They had started in California and the Carolinas, but in recent years they had spread rapidly all across the lower forty-eight, and they had grown common in northern Wisconsin, where the accident had taken place. At certain times of year they migrated in large numbers across this particular roadway, so that, inevitably, some became roadkill. The dead pigs in this instance had, allegedly, caused the driver of the Mercedes to steer his car into a tree. The logic was, if the dead pigs hadn't been lying there in the road, the man wouldn't be dead. Ergo, the pigs were at fault.

For the plaintiffs, though, there was a problem: the pigs had no monetary assets.

So the plaintiffs had taken aim, instead, at the state highway department. And the highway department, in turn, had hired John Boggs to provide expert witness analysis and testimony for their defense.

The plaintiffs' contention was that the highway department had contributed to a foreseeable accident by failing to dig a tunnel under the roadway to provide safe passage for migrating wild pigs. This sounded ridiculous, until Ellis saw the photos—horrifying images of a half-dozen shattered and flayed pigs scattered over the road, their guts broken open, bodies twisted and flattened. It was hard to know what a jury might think when they saw those photos. A jury might think: *Someone should have done something about this.*

Still. Death by wild pig. It was absurd. To say so didn't demean the man's life. It was just a fact. It wasn't the man's fault that he had died absurdly.

Ellis had been sitting at the baggage carousel for only a few minutes when he became aware of a commotion. A man and a woman were arguing—the same couple that had sat beside Ellis on the plane. Now that they were out of the plane, it was surprising how short the man was. He had short legs under a more normal-size torso. His tattooed arms were long and beefy. He uttered strings of profanity and rubbed at his knuckles. When he subsided, the woman spoke hissing and glaring at the floor. The small crowd waiting for their suitcases watched, but no one interfered.

Ellis bent to examine the photos again.

Multiplying the overall swine-related absurdity, this was the second job he and Boggs had worked recently that involved pigs. They'd started calling the cases Pig Accident One and Pig Accident Two, or PA1 and PA2. "We didn't know One was One until we had Two," Ellis told Boggs. "Sure," Boggs said. "Like World Wars." PA1 had been a fog-induced multiple-vehicle pileup that included a trailer that broke open and spilled live pigs—a domesticated variety—all over a state highway in western Nebraska. But that was completely separate from the matter at hand.

Ellis studied the police diagram—the distances that located the tree, the resting position of the Mercedes, the tire marks on the road, the furrows in the dirt. For some reason, the police hadn't measured out the positions of the pigs. He looked from the diagram to the photos, searching for differences. The cops might have made an error in one of their measurements. Measurement errors were fairly common—people were idling in their cars waiting for the lanes to open again, and the cops had to hurry. One couldn't blame an officer if he made an occasional mistake on a drawing. But where could the mistake be? Comparing the photos to the diagram, Ellis couldn't see that one contradicted the other.

He also retained in the back of his mind the idea that sometimes reality looked unrealistic. In a complex, high-energy interaction among vehicles, bodies, and other objects, sometimes odd things happened. Things bounced in unexpected directions, stuck together, or flew apart counterintuitively. It was a problem sometimes. Juries expected reality to look realistic.

He'd mentioned his unease to Boggs, and Boggs had looked things over and said he didn't see anything unusual. Ellis had a great respect for Boggs's understanding of these things.

Still, he stared at one photo after another, trying to convince himself, at least, of whether or not there was a problem to find.

Someone tapped his shoulder. Ellis looked up and there was Boggs, with a white lollipop stem jutting from his mouth. He held out a second lollipop. "Bowl of them on the counter," he said. Ellis took the lollipop. "Car's waiting across the street." Boggs glanced around. "What's with the lovebirds? I heard them on the plane, too."

"They were sitting next to me," Ellis said. "It began with something about which of them was supposed to have booked the hotel, and then they started throwing around all the dirty laundry. She thinks he might be gay. He countered by pointing out that he'd once slept with her sister."

He and Boggs watched, sucking their lollipops.

"Public displays of emotion by strangers are so awkward," Boggs said. "Is it okay to watch? It seems voyeuristic. But I can't ignore it."

They watched. Then Ellis returned to the photos.

"See anything good?" Boggs asked.

"Not really. The swing to the right seems a bit extreme."

"You think? Looks to me like when the front wheels hit the dirt, they stopped and the back end kept going. It's a classic oversteer scenario."

"Even before that, though, it's a heck of a turn."

"The guy saw a big dead pig in the road. What do you expect? Plus, he was drunk."

"True," Ellis said. But he turned to the next photo, which showed a gruesomely flattened pig.

"Everyone likes bacon."

"If only I were a charcuterie chef."

"Keep looking, you'll see something new. There's so much information in that stack of photographs that you can always see something new if you look long enough. Keep looking until you satisfy yourself."

Ellis turned another photo over.

The couple from the airplane were still yelling and hissing back and forth.

Boggs cleared his throat. He started tapping a foot. Then he stood and walked away.

Ellis turned another photo, but suspicion made him look up. Sure enough, Boggs was headed toward the arguing couple.

Ellis looked at the photos again, but his concentration was gone. He'd seen Boggs insert himself into arguments between strangers a couple of times before, in hotel bars. It baffled Ellis. It would never have occurred to him to do such a thing, to intrude on strangers in conflict, and Boggs's motivation mystified him. He set the photos aside and followed.

Boggs was a tall man, six foot four, not easy to ignore, and now he edged up to the arguing couple, so close that he was nearly bumping the woman's shoulder. They broke off and peered at him.

"If you'd explain the nature of your disagreement," Boggs said, nodding, smiling, holding his lollipop in the air, "I'd be happy to tell you who's right."

Ellis moved closer. The woman's mouth hung open; her nostrils twitched.

"Help you settle things," Boggs said, "so everyone can move on."

The man scuffed a step forward. "What?" His face had turned a color like the pig guts in the photos.

"Put a period on it," Boggs said. He made a chopping motion with the lollipop.

Ellis saw the small man's knees bend, muscles tightening under his tattoos. Ellis jammed his own wet lollipop into his pocket and stepped forward. This kind of thing seemed particularly unwise in an airport. And they had work to do.

He touched Boggs's shoulder. "Forget it," he said. "No one ever said you can't argue in public."

"No, no. Just trying to be helpful."

The tattooed man grunted and grimaced and made mean eyes at Boggs.

"Come on," Ellis said.

Boggs shrugged and turned away.

The tattooed man followed a couple of paces. But then a buzzer shrieked, motors whirred, gears clanked, and everyone looked over at the baggage carousel. It started turning, and the tattooed man stopped and stood alone. "What?" he said again.

Ellis went back to where the photos lay on the bench. His legs shook. He felt exhausted. "What was that, boss?" he asked. He tugged the sticky lollipop from his pocket and threw it at a trash can. "Am I a babysitter now, too? If so, I want a raise."

"I've sometimes wished that someone would step in when my wife and I are arguing." Boggs sat with his hands in his lap, working his lollipop in his mouth. "And don't call me boss. We're colleagues. Partners."

Ellis detected in this a trace of apology. "You don't really wish anyone would step in like that. You'd hate it."

"That's what I mean. It would give me someone else to be pissed at."

How much of this was a joke, Ellis wasn't sure. He didn't ask. He felt very close to Boggs, but he didn't dare let the distance go to zero.

The carousel turned round and round, but still no bags appeared. Ellis worried that the tattooed man might get his nerve up and come swing a fist at someone. He tucked the police photos away and zipped his bag and stared at the baggage carousel.

The plan was, they would complete their inspections of the vehicle and scene today. Then Ellis would return home on a late flight. Boggs would stay; his wife, Heather, was coming the next morning to join him for a long weekend on the shore of Lake Michigan.

Ellis's secret wish, which he hadn't stated clearly to himself—which he barely allowed himself to be aware of—was to still be here when Heather arrived. To see her.

He could imagine circumstances that might arise and cause him to miss his flight, perhaps a breakdown of the rental car, or maybe a case of appendicitis, or possibly he would simply arrive late to the airport due to misremembering the time of his flight. He imagined, too, that he might encounter her in the airport in some inexplicable way, as if airports were reality-bending places in magical suspension between the earth and the sky. Indeed, he had this job because once, years earlier, he had chanced to see Heather in an airport.

But he also knew that when the time came, when none of those things had happened, he would take his flight home. He would do so not least because he liked Boggs very much, and he appalled himself with his own preoccupation with Heather, who was, after all, Boggs's wife.

Inexplicably as a change in weather, pieces of luggage finally began to appear, sliding down a ramp, slapping into one another, gliding around the oval track. Ellis picked up the surveying equipment; Boggs took the hard-shelled equipment case that held their measuring tapes, cameras, plumb bobs, levels, masking tape, pressure gauge, calipers, magnifying glass, walkie-talkies, and light meter.

They found the rental car, a Kia sedan. Boggs drove. Ellis studied a map and called out directions.

Two

From the airport they drove north for ten minutes, turned onto a side street, and rattled over a river on the grated surface of a drawbridge. Lake Michigan lay somewhere just to the east, but they couldn't see it. Down the river stood tall boat-loading cranes, and further off rose enormous concrete grain silos. As they moved down the street, they passed warehouses, old industrial buildings, a new condo building, a few houses, a bar named The Horny Goat. Ellis called out the addresses, then pointed and said "There," and Boggs pulled over.

The highway department's lawyer was waiting for them at the gate of a parking lot surrounded by a cyclone fence. The lot was filled with trailered water-skiing and wakeboarding boats, and in the middle of the rows of boats, under a plastic tarp, was the accident vehicle—the white Mercedes-Benz. "Apparently the plaintiff's attorney's father-in-law is a boat dealer," said the highway department's lawyer, pinching her lips in a minimized smile. She looked young, hardly thirty, and seemed uncomfortable. Her hair was curled at the ends in an oddly old-fashioned style, and she wore a gray pantsuit that looked too warm for standing outside in the sun.

Ellis had on a cheap polo shirt and khakis, and Boggs wore a red-striped button-down with a paisley tie. While Boggs loosened the tie and rolled his sleeves, he asked the attorney about the schedule for discovery and depositions and about her strategy for the case. She was uncertain and terse, then smiled and laughed nervously, and it struck Ellis that she probably hadn't done this sort of thing much before.

They dragged the tarp off the Mercedes, and it lay naked, crumpled, and pathetic-looking amid the ranks of sleek white boats.

From the passenger side the Mercedes didn't look all that bad, except that the roofline bulged up and the windshield was broken. On the opposite side, however, it looked as if someone had upended it and hit it with an enormous baseball bat. The driver's door was caved in, the door glass gone, the fender and rear door distorted, the seat and steering wheel pushed into weird angles, the surface of the dashboard cracked and folded, the driver's-side front wheel bent back with a deflated tire hanging around it.

While Ellis and Boggs began to work, filling out sheets of vehicle data—VIN, tire make and size, mileage, gearshift position—the attorney moved around a little to look at the car from one side and then another, then stood watching and blinking the sweat out of her eyes. She made Ellis anxious. Most trial attorneys were talkers and questioners. This silence was unsettling.

He put down four measuring tapes to box the outline of the car. He wrote down measurements off the tapes. Then he held a plumb bob so that it hung directly above the tape along the damaged side of the car.

"Every six inches?" he asked.

"The damage is so focused," Boggs said. "Let's do four."

Ellis held the bob over the tape measure and Boggs used a second tape measure to read the distance from the bob to the door. Ellis wrote down the two measurements, then moved the bob down the tape four inches, and Boggs measured again.

Boggs glanced at the lawyer, then began a kind of patter. "These are our X-Y-Z measurements. With these, we can calculate how much energy went into crushing the vehicle into this particular geometry. That's the crush energy. When we have the crush energy, then we can calculate how fast it was going when it hit the tree. Because kinetic energy was converted into crush energy as it hit the tree. So, set crush energy equal to kinetic energy; then calculate the one from the other. That gets you velocity. Speed. Miles per hour. We use the tape measures on the ground to establish spatial relationships between the driver's-side damage relative to the passenger side wheels. You don't measure driver's-side damage to the driver's-side wheels, because the positions of the driver's-side wheels may have been affected by the collision. Later we'll track down an undamaged vehicle—this same make, model, and year—to take measurements of the undamaged surface for comparison. We call that vehicle an exemplar."

He read numbers to Ellis.

"Only way to find an undamaged exemplar of an older vehicle like this," he added, "is to search the used-car lots and the classifieds. It makes for funny conversations. 'I'm calling about the car on Craigslist? No, I don't want to buy it. I want to measure it.' You have to explain yourself three or four times before they get it. I told one guy that I was a reconstructionist, and he said, 'Oh, is that what they're calling body-shop work now?' But they're usually happy enough in the end. We'll pay them fifty bucks, maybe a hundred, to look at the car for a half hour. It's free money."

The attorney nodded, looked serious.

Ellis took several dozen photos from all around the vehicle and then closer shots of the damaged components. He stopped and asked, "What happened to the driver's-side mirror?"

Boggs looked. "It's gone."

"Gone smashed, or gone gone?" the attorney asked.

"Totally gone," Boggs said. "Was it in any of the police photos?" he asked Ellis.

Ellis took out the photos and flipped through them. "No."

"What's that mean?" the attorney asked.

"I'd guess it was smashed to absolute smithereens by that tree,"

Boggs said. "Whatever was left of it fell off. Some cop grabbed it and tossed it into his trunk and forgot about it." He crouched down to peer inside the wheel well. "Ooh, lookie," he called. "That there is pig hair."

He lay flat on the asphalt to get an angle, clicked the camera a couple of times, then reached in, grunted, yanked, and came out with a small patch of bristling thick hairs, which he held by just a hair or two, with the tips of his fingers. Ellis retrieved a plastic baggie.

"Do you want to hang onto this?" Boggs asked the attorney. "Or we can file it into our evidence storage system."

"Go ahead," she said, wincing. "Keep it."

Ellis put it away. Boggs walked around the car a couple more times, then he looked at Ellis. "Are we done?"

"I think we're set," Ellis said. He began to pack away the equipment.

"That's it?" asked the attorney.

"The rest is math," Boggs said.

"How do you think it looks?"

"The driver was drunk and he overreacted," Boggs said. "He could have steered through safely. There's no good reason to go veering off the roadway. Pretty much by definition he overreacted. We can calculate his steering wheel angle for you. It'll look ridiculous." Boggs circled his hands, madly spinning an imaginary wheel. "Because of what? A little pig meat in the road? Go around. Or run it over. Other people did."

"One of their claims is that, because the pigs have black fur, the driver couldn't see them against the road in time to react appropriately."

"That's stupid. You can push back on that."

"But it is kind of hard to see the pigs in the photos."

"Only because your average cop is a terrible photographer. When you have the guy on the stand, ask him to explain the difference between aperture and focal length. He can't."

"I don't know," the lawyer said. "It doesn't seem like a good strategy to try to make the cops look like idiots."

"You can gussy it up. Flatter him. Ask him, You're an expert in several fields, aren't you, sir? Expert in criminal law? Expert driver? Expert in the use of firearms? Et cetera, et cetera? But you can't be expected to be an expert in everything, can you? For example, photography?"

The lawyer nodded, but she didn't look convinced.

"You planning to come look at the accident scene with us?" Boggs asked.

"Do you think it would be useful?"

Boggs shook his head. "What we do is boring," he said. "Photos. A survey."

She hesitated, but nodded. She led the way out through the gate, locked up, and drove away. Boggs took the driver's seat, and Ellis sat in the passenger side and took out the map again. "She seemed unhappy," he said.

"Well, she has problems we can't really fix. We can reconstruct from here to kingdom come, we can do all sorts of technical crap, but her basic problem is that when this guy drove up, there were dead pigs lying all over the road. You saw the photos. It looked like a horror movie. One dead pig and you can say, whatever, people navigate past road kill all the time. But here there were six, and a herd of dead pigs is an unusual thing to discover on the road. So the driver sees something really weird there in the road and, sure, he's drunk and he overreacts, but a jury looks at those photos and they could think, 'Holy shit, I would have freaked the fuck out, too.'"

"Especially if he couldn't see it until the last second because the color blended into the road."

"Yeah, well, that's bogus."

They worked in the interstices of geography—when Ellis looked at the lines on a map, it struck him that they worked not in any of the places that the lines led to, but, rather, *on* the lines—where they were often bracketed by lookalike roadside landscapes, malls and strip malls, overpasses and underpasses, gas stations and fast-food outlets, motels and supermarkets, big-box stores and convenience stores. There were always differences between places, of course, but he was often impressed by how many features repeated themselves, varying only in their configuration. Here a McDonald's stood next to a Mobil station; there it stood next to a HoJo. Even on occasions when they visited the locations of accidents on highways out in the countryside, still the foreground was filled by the gray asphalt road surface, painted lines, green highway signs, and roadside weeds, so that the Arizona desert and the Appalachian mountains looked much the same if he forgot to lift his gaze and study the distance. Reflecting back to the assembly line where he had worked, it seemed to Ellis that the invention of standardized parts—making every 5/8" bolt interchangeable with every other 5/8" bolt—had facilitated the invention of the mass-produced automobile, which facilitated the standardization of the landscape. And so standardization was the engineering principle that had come to define the world.

As they drove now, he tried to watch the countryside, but it didn't do much to distinguish itself. The land was flat as rolled steel, the view textured mainly by trees. Sometimes the trees were near and sometimes they stood off across fields, but they always made the horizon into a ragged line. There were many open fields, empty or with a few cows in them. At intervals they came to grim little towns, and each town had put up a stoplight to make you stop and look at the grim little buildings for a minute. Between the towns, the only signs of human population were the occasional little white neighborless ranch-style houses that stood a couple hundred feet back from the road. When the road passed along a small, still, blue-water lake, it was a relief—the water pulled the eye hypnotically.

Boggs had put in a CD.

"*. . . saying there is nothing you are accountable to anymore,*" the judge said. "*You have got no status, you have chucked it away. No* *blame to you for that, Marshal, but it is gone. What I am saying is you can't post those four fellers out. You are no law-making body. You can't make laws . . ."*

It was Oakley Hall's cowboy novel *Warlock*. While they listened they came into National Forest land, and the forest thickened. They drove another twenty miles, then turned onto a narrow side road, and forest pressed close on both sides of the asphalt. Boggs moved slowly along it.

"Maybe somebody will get killed, Judge. But that is between them and me, for who else is hurt by it?"

"Every man is," the judge whispered.

"I like this book," Boggs said.

"It's good."

"Sometimes," Boggs said, "on a long drive with a good book, I feel like my mind reaches a place where my head is the car, and the voice of the story is the voice in my head."

"You have been going on about pride like it was a bad thing, and I disagree with you. A man's pride is about the only thing that he has that's worth having, and is what sets him apart from the pack . . ."

The police report had indicated the accident location a hundred feet past a yellow curve warning sign. When they came to it, Boggs parked on the roadside.

The land here was unusually rocky and hilly in comparison with all the land they had just traveled through. The hills were covered with tall old pine trees, growing close to the road. The trunks were bare up to twenty or thirty feet in the air, where the branches began and made a kind of cathedral roof. The soil under the trees was black and moist, covered by a rough carpet of fallen needles. Moss grew in tattered skirts around some of the tree trunks. Birds called faintly high above. Where sunlight squeezed through the canopy, it fell in thin golden shafts. The road split the forest, opening a stream's width of sky and creating a thick line of sun that shone on the road and glinted on the mica in the asphalt.

The tree that had killed the four-times-married estate-law attorney stood seven feet off the side of the road at one end of a broad curve. Ellis looked closely at the bark, but it didn't appear that the Mercedes had damaged it in the slightest.

The curve was the kind of curve that would cause many drivers to pretend that they were race-car drivers and push the g's. But the driver of the Mercedes had been only beginning to enter the curve, turning left. "He had that long straightaway, as he approached," Ellis said. "Middle of the day. He should have had plenty of time to see things on the road and adjust."

"That's why they want to claim he couldn't see the pig," Boggs said.

They walked the site for a few minutes, orienting themselves. Tire marks could take weeks to fade from a road surface, but this accident had occurred almost a year earlier, and Ellis couldn't see any trace of them now. Nor of the pig gore. Boggs, however, discovered a few gray bones half-buried in the gravel and black earth at the side of the road.

They began with photogrammetry.

The police hadn't bothered to make any record of where the dead pigs were lying, but they could be seen in the photographs of the scene. Ellis had picked out a handful of the photos that showed the pigs, and he'd blown these up to 8.5 x11 inches. He believed that only the large, one-eyed pig in the middle of the lane really mattered for their analysis—but you never knew what might come up, and juries liked thoroughness, so they would do all six pigs. He had put a piece of transparency over each of the photos and, by hand, he had traced the pigs and several of the surrounding features, picking out objects in the fore-, middle-, and background—lines and cracks in the road, shrubs and a large rock, trunks of trees. Then he printed the traced images onto small transparent slides that he could insert into a modified camera lens. A low-tech approach, but it was more accurate than the available computer programs.

Now he held up one of the original photos. It was strange to look at the photo and then at the place, because the photo looked like gaudy death on a shabby set, but the forest itself was a fairytale landscape. He talked with Boggs about the position of the camera that had captured the image, and they moved around until they found roughly the right spot, a location off the edge of the road. They set up the surveyor's station, then the camera on a tripod. Boggs put Ellis's slide into the camera and peered through the viewfinder. He adjusted the camera height, rotated it a couple of degrees, moved it forward, then to one side, then back again, making increasingly minute adjustments.

Eventually he called to Ellis to look. In the viewfinder, the road lines and trees that Ellis had traced on the slide perfectly outlined their counterparts in reality: their camera was now positioned exactly where the police camera had been held when the cop clicked the button to take the photo. The only difference was that, while the police camera had looked out on a road occupied by actual dead pigs, theirs contained the slide showing the ghost outlines of dead pigs.

Ellis carried a surveyor's sighting rod into the road. "Be ready to jump if you hear a car coming around that curve," Boggs said. A couple of vehicles had passed by, but for the most part the only sound was the murmur of a breeze in the needles and branches overhead. Boggs looked through the camera and yelled directions—*left several feet, forward a couple, back up a bit.* He was directing Ellis to get the sighting rod in the middle of a pig traced on the slide. When he was satisfied, Boggs held up a thumb, called, "Don't move!" and went to the surveyor's station and shot the position of the sighting rod.

They repeated the process until they had reconstructed the locations of six long-gone pigs.

Ellis had also prepared slides that showed the locations of the Mercedes' tire marks, and now they started on these. By the time they finished working through all the slides, they had been here for almost four hours, and the day had cooled perceptibly.

They surveyed additional points at the base of the tree, along the painted lines on the road, and on the edges of the asphalt surface. Then Boggs wandered around with the camera, taking one last series of reference photographs. Ellis was returning the surveying equipment to the rental car when a series of snorts and purrs distracted him.

About twenty feet away a two-track dirt trail ran through the trees, and an ATV was approaching along it. The rider was a kid of sixteen or seventeen in jeans, flip-flops, a lime-green T-shirt, and no helmet. He stopped opposite Ellis and took in the rental car, Ellis, Boggs.

Ellis walked over. They didn't have any kind of a permit to be out in the road. This was rarely an issue, and they were almost done anyway. But, still, it would be better if the kid didn't call the police. Or call a mom or dad who would call the police. Or go fetch a gun.

"Hey," Ellis said. "Do you know anything about an accident that happened here, about a year ago?"

The kid shook his head.

Ellis described the accident and explained what they were doing. "You ever see those pigs around?" Ellis asked.

"Shit. Everyone round here hates the pigs. They're vermin. DNR lets you hunt them year-round. Dad shot one just yesterday. They root up the fields. We have land over that way, and we kill them when we can."

"And then, what? Trash them?"

"No, we skin and butcher them. It's good meat. Freeze most of it."

"Do you still have the hide from the one yesterday?"

"It's lying on the garbage pile."

Ellis called Boggs over. "What do you think," he asked, "about putting one of those pigs in the road and taking some high-quality photos?"

"You have one of the pigs?" Boggs asked the kid.

"Think so. The skin."

"How much do you want for it?"

The boy took out a cell phone, called his father, and handed the phone to Boggs. They negotiated two hundred dollars for the pig hide.

Three

Ellis's first job out of college had been in a plant that made truck axles. He began each day at 5:15 A.M. with a journey across the factory floor, where curiosity led him on circuitous routes through rows of drills and lathes, assembly lines, stamping presses, robot arms maneuvering weld pincers, and a heat-treatment area where tubular furnaces glowed and flamed under the care of hunched, thin old men wearing goggles and heavy asbestos gauntlets so that they looked like Halloween demons in an actual hell. Ellis enjoyed these walks, enjoyed the spectacle of a mechanized world where the sprawl of machines spread out of sight to all sides, conveyor systems crisscrossed overhead, and grates underfoot bridged gutters coursing with used cutting fluids, whitish stuff that looked like streams of milk. And he liked how sometimes, as if to punctuate the strangeness, a sparrow swooped down from overhead and worried at a stray Cheeto or muffin paper on the blackened floor.

But little else about the job suited him. He had finished his bachelor's degree in mechanical engineering without developing any concrete ideas about what he wanted to do with it. He had supposed that an engineer should want to work with things that made things, so he had taken a job where things were made. His particular realm was a 10.5-inch differential assembly line with twenty-two manned stations that pieced together a set of gears and then secured them into a housing, called a pighead because it looked like one. The line workers accomplished their work by fitting parts into fixtures, then pressing buttons to engage a hydraulic press or spin down a set of bolt drivers. Then they pulled out the result and put it on a conveyor to the next station. It went station to station this way, gaining parts at each step, until it reached the end of the line, where the assembled pigheads were stacked on a pallet, and a forklift carried them off to another assembly line where axle shafts and brakes were added.

He was, ostensibly, an engineer. He had been given a box of business cards that said, "Ellis Barstow, Engineer." And on his first day a bearing-press operator had come to shake his hand and said, "Great to meet a new engineer." The man grinned. "Know why I like engineers?" He then—while Ellis stared, comprehension lagging—dropped the top half of his coveralls to show his hairy, purple-nippled chest, and did a little hula dance. "Because they suck great dick!" he shouted. Then he pulled up his overalls and went back to work.

There were almost two dozen separate manufacturing areas in the plant: tool-and-die lines, welding lines, heat-treatment lines, and assembly lines like Ellis's. During his interview, the line supervisor job had been described to him as a great entry-level position where he could get experience in how the plant really worked. Then, in a few years, he might be able to move to a facilities engineering position in the front offices. After he began, he did glimpse a couple other young engineers working in positions similar to his, but most of the manufacturing areas were supervised by much older men who stomped around scowling. Many of them were not trained engineers at all but had been promoted up out of the skilled trades, and Ellis had the impression that they regretted the promotion.

Ellis's task was to supervise his line in much the same way that one would manage a franchise restaurant. He needed to schedule deliveries of parts, and he needed to handle the crew. And although he was soon orchestrating the deliveries of parts with reasonable success, he didn't know how to deal with the people. Every one of them had fifteen to forty years on him. They ignored him. He tried to be nice, tried to be funny, tried to be stern. He gave them gifts—donuts, birthday cakes. For Christmas he brought everyone a toy model of one of the trucks that their axles went into. He was basically an introvert, and none of this was easy for him.

And none of it worked. The day after Christmas, he came back to work and found the toy trucks returned in a pile on his desk.

He knew he was doing poorly. His jokes weren't funny. His sternness was tainted with apology. They had been here before him—some of them had black in the creases of their skin where years of oil and dust had collected—and they would be here after he was gone. After a few months of this, he began to spend more and more time at his desk, in a little low-walled office near the line, executing pointless manipulations of columns of numbers in Excel spreadsheets.

From time to time, a loud buzzer sounded to indicate line halts. Several of the machines on the line broke down routinely, and then Ellis had to track down a tradesman and get it fixed. One day, after the buzzer had been clamoring for a full five minutes, Ellis left his desk and found no balky machines, no jammed conveyors, no mechanical problems. Rather, the man who'd pulled down his coveralls was sitting with his forehead against a bearing press, asleep.

Ellis's mind seemed to fill with a sudden, opaque whiteness, and then to sunder itself. Trembling, he grabbed the man, pulled and shoved him, yelling. The man's eyes opened wide, and Ellis pushed him away, and he circled to scream at several others.

The line went back to work.

A few minutes later, when the adrenaline had faded, he sat at his desk, feeling sick. It had felt as much like panic as anger, but he was less concerned with naming its origin than with the subsequent loss of control. In losing that, it seemed to him, he lost everything.

To his surprise, for the rest of the week he had a relatively efficient line. But after a weekend the crew resumed old habits and became, if anything, more uncooperative. It struck Ellis that if the only way to do his job was to yell at people who grew negligent about repetitious, numbing work, then probably he didn't want the job.

The next Monday, he watched a pair of sparrows hop around in his office doorway. They pecked and preened, observed him with one eye then the other, doubting and verifying. Ellis pulled his earplugs, and faintly amid the general unending roar of the plant he heard a chirp.

He stood and edged toward the birds, hoping—hopelessly—to move them in the direction of a building exit, but they only flew into the dark overhead. He peered after them, then turned a circle, and came to a resolution.

He crossed the plant floor to his manager's large, clean, quiet office.

A stamping press accident years ago had taken the ends off two fingers on his manager's right hand—he fidgeted with a micrometer in this hand while Ellis uttered a few irrelevant phrases, then finally blurted, as if an admission of guilt, that he intended to quit. The manager boomed, "Just put in your time! You're smart! You'll figure things out!" He was half-deaf.

"I guess I don't think the whole manufacturing environment feels right for me."

"Okay! What kind of job do you think is right?"

"I don't know."

The manager nodded and stood and leaned on the surface of his desk and looked at Ellis. Then suddenly he smiled and extended his hand. Ellis stared at the two nub fingers, then realized that this was an invitation to shake, and to leave.

He put his things into a box and carried it out a side door.

The sudden sunlight blinded him, and he stood hugging his box and blinking. His idea of himself was vague to the point of invisibility. And his choices so far had only brought him to the edge of a cliff, where he couldn't see any sign of how to move forward.

• • •

As a child he had always done well in school, did so with relative ease. It had never bothered him to sit in his room and do homework, to read and study. It gave him something to do. His mother would look at his report cards and say, "Looks good. But don't get a big head." And no one else particularly congratulated him. There were only a couple hundred students in his high school, and he knew it was a small place, and he had a feeling that real life was going on somewhere else. He wondered if he would ever encounter it.

After he left the axle plant, he still had that feeling. Over several years he shifted from job to job, none of them in engineering. It seemed absurd, as if he'd spent years training as an acrobat, only to finally climb to the high trapeze and find that he disliked heights.

He spent a great deal of time reading. As a child, he had fed on books, and now he continued to read—mysteries, science fiction, Calvino, Eco—books to carry him from his own life to someplace else. He contemplated returning to school for a degree in English, but couldn't imagine what he would do with it. Teach? He doubted whether he could inspire kids, or even control a classroom. He felt he lacked a vocation. For consolation, he read and grew lost in du Maurier, Chandler, Lem, Borges. *The Big Sleep* and "The Garden of Forking Paths."

One winter he spent his savings on a two-week trip to India, which he'd become interested in through reading Rushdie. He was twenty-five years old. He traveled alone, and he found himself anxious and overwhelmed by alienness and sensory density. And diarrheal. At the end of the trip, he could hardly say what he had seen except a swirl of colors, gods over doorways, animals in the streets, ragged clothes, outstretched hands. To beggar after beggar he had given away more than he could really afford. He kept thinking that, but for the accident of where he had been born, their life might be his own.

After landing again in the States, he had to wait for one more flight to carry him home, and he sat in the airport feeling flaccid and ill. His head contained a miasma and the objects around him trailed green auras. As he watched through the windows, snow began to fall and soon gathered into a white, obscuring storm. Flights were delayed. He sat queasy, his bag between his legs.

To make one of the touts in New Delhi go away, he had paid too much for a tiny, soapstone figure of elephant-headed Ganesh. The size of a walnut, fat-headed and coarsely carved, with one broken tusk—Ellis took it from his pocket and turned it obsessively between his fingers.

Delay passed into delay. In the windows, snow fell fast and straight down.

Desperate to clear his head, Ellis stood and began to walk. At the food stalls uniformed employees served the trapped with surly languor. Along the hallways travelers lay propped on bags and one another. The fluorescent lighting blued their lips, yellowed their eyes.

Then he saw Heather.

He stumbled, and stopped. He let the traffic of the hallway push by. He'd last seen Heather Gibson a decade earlier, when he was fourteen and she was seventeen, and his memories of her were surrounded by glinting, uncomfortable emotions.

She sat with her back to a painted concrete wall, head tilted, eyes closed. A small woman. Across her face lay a slight shine of scar tissue; Ellis wondered if he would have noticed it at all if he hadn't been looking for it. Her dark hair, which had been curled when they were in high school, now fell straight and neat around her face. She had one arm propped on a duffle bag and her feet were covered by a small blue blanket. She appeared alone. Memories crowded in, of her, and of Christopher, his half-brother, who had been in his senior year of high school and had been dating her all that previous summer—so many memories and of such varied feelings that they crowded and confused one another. She had been burned in the aftermath of the accident that killed Christopher, and as Ellis stood staring with a sensation of wide confusion his attention returned again and again to the alteration of her face.

Then a passerby struck Ellis's bag and spun him a quarter turn, and his illness suddenly became urgent.

He went to the restroom, then returned to the gate for his flight. The chairs were full, so he sat on the floor, put his bag on his knees, and rested his head on it. He tried to sleep, but couldn't quell his agitation. Finally he stood again.

Heather—still asleep—had not moved. He edged himself into an opening between people seated against the opposite wall, and he watched her in the spaces that flickered between passing bodies. She stirred once or twice but did not look toward him.

He saw suddenly that her eyelids had no lashes. Those, too, had burned away. He still could hardly separate his emotions from his dizziness, his muddled senses, and his abused internal organs, but he knew that he felt, at least, wonder.

Perhaps as much as an hour passed before he moved on again. The snow had slackened, and soon he boarded his flight.

Talking on the phone with his mother about the trip, Ellis mentioned that he'd seen Heather Gibson in the airport.

His mother wanted to know why he hadn't approached her, and he said that she had been asleep, and besides he was sick. He asked his mother if she knew anything about what had happened to Heather in the years since Christopher died. She said she didn't.

He guessed that not knowing would bother her. And two days later she called back—she had talked to a friend who knew the Gibsons. Heather lived in Livonia, part of the same sprawl of southeast Michigan suburbs where Ellis also lived, and she had married a man named John Boggs.

This was information enough; he found an address and drove out. He crossed through Livonia on a wide road lined with colorless strip malls, then turned off into a neighborhood of two-story homes, each on a quarter acre of lawn, each with a two- or three-car garage, each with bits of brass around the front door—knob, knocker, porch light. Maybe a wrought-iron or picket fence. No sidewalks. Snow lay in a scatter of white scraps pocketed in the grass. Near the address, he slowed. An asphalt driveway led to a garage on the side of the house, which was faced with brick on the first floor and wood-sided on the second. The garage door stood open. The winter-brown lawn looked neatly kept. Several trees stood leafless, and from the lower branches hung a few parti-colored birdfeeders made from soda cans. A red Taurus wagon rested in the drive; a sticker on its rear bumper had a few words that he could not read and an image of an Egyptian mask, sketched with simple lines.

Ellis had slowed almost to a stop when he noticed, hidden in the gloom of the open garage, a large, bearded man with a grocery bag in one hand. The man waved.

Ellis accelerated away, determined not to return.

But weeks passed—and still he recalled again and again the interval of watching Heather's face as she slept against the airport wall.

Then, on the interstate, he glimpsed the Egyptian mask, stickered on a Lincoln Navigator. Pulling nearer, he saw it more clearly: an ad for Detroit's art museum.

For half a day he wandered among pieces by Picasso, Bruegel, Donatello, van Gogh. Sarcophagi and medieval armor. A collection of tiny, intricate snuffboxes. A few days later he returned. He came back repeatedly, all through that spring and summer, sometimes two and three times a week.

He often brought a book, and he liked the empty open peace of the place, where he could idle for an hour or two, reading, watching an object of art, in a hush only rarely interrupted by one or two people strolling by. He enjoyed this, but his real purpose was obvious even to himself, and as he read, as he studied a sculpture, as he walked a high-ceilinged gallery, as he edged nearer to a canvas, a fraction of his attention was listening, watching. Sometimes he sniffed the air for the trace of her presence—as he had years before, when she had visited Christopher in their house in Coil.

Then one day, he stepped from a roomful of misty landscapes—*Luminist & Tonalist: Martin Johnson Heade & Frederic E. Church*—into an echoing marbled hallway, and he saw her. A small figure in loose linen clothing, sandals, sunglasses on her head, as she never would have dressed in high school. She knew him immediately; she smiled, and with enthusiasm she hugged him. The scars. False eyelashes. A clotted feeling in his lungs. "Ellis!" she cried. And she looked at him with an expression near amazement, as if she thought he might do or say something extremely pleasing.

But then she looked down, her expression flattened a little, and he feared he had imagined it. He made himself speak. He told her that he had studied engineering in college but had done little with it. Her gaze returned to him, and he mentioned odd jobs, reading books. Now he held a floor job in an appliance store, in the television department.

If that disappointed her, she showed no sign. She said she had majored in art, and since then she'd been working on obtaining her teaching certificate. But she'd also worked in graphic design, shelved books at a library, wrote copy for an advertising firm. "I guess I'm not entirely focused," she said. She had been married almost five years. "He works in automotive stuff," she said.

"An engineer?"

"Forensic engineering," she said. She hesitated. "Car crashes. He looks at accidents, to see how they happened."

"Do you think he could get me a job?"

She seemed startled. Then she inclined her head forward as if they might be overheard. By whom? Ellis wondered. He could only think—by Christopher, perhaps.

"Or maybe," she said, "the preferred term is accident reconstruction. They hire out to insurance companies and attorneys. I don't know. I should have a better sense of it, but I don't really like hearing about it."

She hadn't answered his question, and now she changed the subject and talked of a few classmates and teachers they had known in Coil. Where his mother had kept track of people, Ellis was able to give news; he even made Heather laugh once or twice. Yet even when she laughed, he noticed, her eyes seemed a little impassive. He finally realized that the burns had caused this—the way they glossed the skin. It seemed terrible and sad, and it made him angry.

She glanced at her watch. "Really," she said. "It's good to see you."

His heart fisted. "Wait—" But what had he expected? He thought of all his time here, of finding her then—nothing. The long hallway gyred. He nearly fell down. "Let me give you something," he said. He groped into the backpack he carried, and his hand came on pens, books, a calculator, and then the little elephant-headed Ganesh. He pushed it forward. "For luck," he said.

She turned it over and back again. Ellis feared she would try to hand it back.

"You could talk to my husband," she said. She squinted closely at Ganesh, with one eye. "If you're serious about looking for a job."

"Yes."

"Maybe it's okay, if you can get past the ugliness. He's mentioned that he might want to take someone on to help with his caseload. I don't know if he's serious, but it won't hurt to ask." On a slip of paper she wrote a phone number. At the top she wrote, "Boggs." She said, "Everyone, except for me, calls him Boggs."

Four

A large aqua-blue SUV lay in a corner of the parking lot, terribly mutilated—windows broken out, front and rear lamps gone, bumper covers hanging, grille missing, wheels settled on flat tires, doors twisted out of doorframes, hood bent like a potato chip.

Other than the damaged SUV, the place looked like an ordinary suburban office building, with ordinary cars clustered in the parking spaces nearest the front door.

Ellis had arrived early for the interview and sat in his car looking at his résumé. It seemed a document built from scant and shabby materials.

"*He is in the old labyrinth*," said a deep voice. "*It is the story of his gambling in another guise*."

A shining green Volkswagen convertible had come into the parking lot, top down despite the cool weather. "*He gambles because God does not speak. He gambles to make God speak*." It took Ellis a second to connect the voice to the convertible and its stereo. A preacher on a Christian station? No, it seemed to be the level tones of a professional reader. An audio book, perhaps. "*But to make God speak in the turn of a card is blasphemy. Only when God is silent does God*—"

A large bearded man in a dark blue overcoat stood out of the Volkswagen and stalked toward the office. His sand-colored hair held itself out from his head like frayed hemp rope, and he carried a bright orange bag stuffed to overflowing with papers and binders. Ellis guessed that this was Boggs. He felt pretty sure it was the same man he'd seen in Heather's driveway.

He glared at his résumé a little longer, until he was startled by a knock on his window. The man from the Volkswagen peered down. "Ellis Barstow?" he called.

"Yes, sir."

"You're early! I'm Boggs."

He had vivid blue eyes. Ellis stood out of his car, and Boggs shook his hand and grinned. If he recognized Ellis or his car from the drive-by half a year ago, he showed no sign of it. He only tilted his head. "Come on."

He led Ellis to the battered, aqua-colored SUV and asked, "What do you suppose happened?"

"Hit by an avalanche."

Ellis meant it as a joke, but Boggs only shook his head, as if he'd met a few avalanche-struck vehicles in his time, and this wasn't one.

The terrible dents and tears, the missing windows and lamps—Ellis looked at it studiously, but he didn't know how to begin to make an intelligent guess. "Um—" he said.

"Rollover damage," Boggs said, "at highway speeds. Happens every day, more or less. The left rear tire blew out, and the causes of that are being argued, but whatever the reason, it blew out and induced a leftward drift. The driver attempted to steer back to the right, but he overcorrected. Very quickly the vehicle had turned almost sideways. Then the driver's-side wheel rims bit into the road surface, both passenger's-side wheels lifted, and the whole thing vaulted. After that, it spun and bounced along like a punted football."

"How many people were inside?"

"Five occupants. Two fully ejected, three partially ejected. Five fatalities."

"All of them were killed?"

"Probably dead before the vehicle stopped moving. A matter of seconds."

"That's horrible."

"It is. It really is. And now it's part of a very expensive lawsuit." He put a hand back through his hair, and it stood out yet more from his head. He held himself with a loose confidence. Ellis was immediately fascinated by him. He remembered later how, from the very beginning, he had wanted to please him.

"So," Boggs said. "Let's say you're a reconstructionist. You've been asked by an attorney involved in a very expensive lawsuit to examine this vehicle. Could you tell him how many times it rolled over?" After a second he amended, "*At least* how many times."

Ellis touched a scarred door, the metal chilly, abrasive. He stepped back and examined the forms of the damage, the denting, scraping, and tearing. It looked as if it might have been spun inside a concrete mixer. He admitted, "I really have no idea."

"Look at the scratch patterns."

Ellis wasn't sure what he meant by patterns. Random scratches seemed to be everywhere—single long scratches, scratches in pairs and threesomes, groups of light scratches, and areas that looked as if they had been attacked with a power sander. Boggs pointed to an area on the passenger's-side fender. "Like these."

Here were scratches of the power-sander variety, gouged deep into the sheet metal, while above and coming down at a slight angle ran a second set of scratches, longer, less deep. Ellis moved a finger over them. He crouched to get out of the sun's glare and saw running almost perpendicular to the longer scratches a third set, very light, little more than minor disruptions in the paint.

"Three?" he said.

"Three?" echoed Boggs.

"Three rolls?"

"Three rolls? Why three?"

Three sets of scratches. Could that mean three rolls? Why?

"Think about it," Boggs said. "Let me know."

Stacks of cardboard banker's boxes filled the corners of Boggs's office and paperwork sprawled over the desk. Littered among the papers, as if stranded in snow drifts, were toy cars—a Ferrari, a Land Rover, a GTO, a milk truck. A bookshelf was lined with textbooks, technical manuals, collections of conference papers. They talked through Ellis's résumé in about fifteen minutes—college engineering classes and projects, and the supervisory job at the axle plant, which Ellis glossed. He ticked through other jobs: a lawn service, a coffee shop, running deliveries, selling appliances. The conversation began to wallow, Boggs seemed subdued, and Ellis grew embarrassed. He had an engineering degree that he'd hardly applied and no useful skills. A life of clowning. He sat here only because years ago his now-dead half-brother had been the boyfriend of a girl who was now this man's wife. Absurd.

Yet he wanted this job. He saw an opportunity for a new path. He badly needed a new path.

From the clutter on the desk he picked out the toy Land Rover and turned it, like a bouncing football.

A thought came.

"At least three times," he said. He rolled the Land Rover slowly over the desk, touching it down, turning it, then touching it down again. "Each time this corner hits the ground, it picks up new scratches." Growing excited, he elaborated: a vehicle couldn't slide in two directions at once, so each set of overlapping scratches indicated a different time that that part of the vehicle had been on the ground. He'd seen scratches running in three different directions in the area Boggs had pointed out, so the fender had hit the ground at least three times.

Boggs smiled. He took the toy and showed him something else: how the angle of a scratch indicated the direction the vehicle had been traveling as it struck the ground. One could also draw conclusions, he said, from the depth of the scratches; for example, that deeper scratches were made when the vehicle hit asphalt while the lighter ones were made as it hit softer soil off the roadway. And, looking closely, one could often determine the sequence in which scratches were made, because the cutting of a new scratch pushed paint into the existing scratches that it crossed.

"We do a lot of reports for our clients," Boggs said. "Can you write?"

"I won a prize for something I wrote in college."

"Really? Why isn't that on your résumé?"

"Well, it was fiction. And it wasn't really so much an award as an honorable mention. And, in retrospect, it was terrible."

"You like to read? Have you read Coetzee? I've been listening to him on CD."

"In your car."

"Yes." Boggs grinned. "I like to listen to books." He talked happily for a few minutes about books, of Dostoyevsky, of *War and Peace*. He said his father had majored in French literature, but ended up working as a construction contractor in Ohio. Boggs, though, disliked French literature, with the exception of Simenon. "I like the Russians," Boggs said. "Do you know this one?" he turned to his computer and clicked, and a voice began: "*. . . why, where in the world has his character gone to? The steadfast man of action is totally at a loss and has turned out to be a pitiful little poltroon, an insignificant, puny babe, or simply, as Nozdrev puts it, a horse's twat . . .*"

"Poltroon!" Boggs laughed happily. "Did you know that Gogol could pull his lower lip up over his nose?" He grew distracted in straightening the vehicles on his desk. "This job," he said suddenly, "is emotionally odd. Are you okay with that? It's analytic, and you sometimes have to remind yourself: people died."

"I don't know if—" Ellis stalled. He let the sentence lapse.

"Well, there is no way to know. I'm just saying, it's odd. You look at terrible events and analyze them minutely. It's not normal. It's strange. Then, after you've done it for a while, what's also strange is how you get used to it, and even how much you forget. It seems a little indecent to forget. I've worked a lot of cases, and, some of them, all that I can remember is a fragment or two. Wisps. It's as if, if I were a better man, I'd go back to tour the old accidents from time to time. Like an old soldier revisiting Somme or Gettysburg or Khe Sanh. Austerlitz. But no one remembers Austerlitz anymore." He looked hopefully at Ellis, as if he might be the exception.

Ellis admitted that he didn't remember Austerlitz.

By the time he left, Boggs had offered him the job, and Ellis had accepted.

Walking to the door, Ellis asked, "Wouldn't it be unusual for a reconstructionist to drive a convertible?"

Boggs laughed. "People take a significant risk every time they take a car out of the driveway onto the roads. But they don't really understand the chances. There's risk no matter what you drive, unless maybe if it's an M1 tank. There's so much driving in life, I want to enjoy it. Besides, that vehicle is safer than a lot of others. The center of gravity is low. Many of the vehicles that people think are big and safe might protect you in a collision, but then they trip and roll over and kill you anyway. Like that SUV. You can't avoid risks." He looked out at the parking lot, then turned and touched Ellis on the elbow. "I'm sorry about what happened to your brother."

"It's all right," Ellis said. It seemed a stupid thing to say, but he didn't have anything else.

"You think you'll be okay with this work?"

"Yes."

"Good."

In the parking lot Ellis stopped to look again at the aqua-blue SUV. He scrutinized a few of the scratches, then leaned through the vacant space where a window had been. A strand of gleaming purple and green Mardi Gras beads were wrapped around the gearshift. Black tire shards and an empty can of diet soda littered the cargo area. Dry leaves lay on the backseat, along with a yellow receipt that was, he saw, from Babies "R" Us.

He returned to his car and sat, lightly touching his hands together, hesitating now to drive into traffic, onto the streets, the interstate. But after a minute he started the engine, and he drove.

• • •

Ellis had largely fallen out of touch with his father, so that was easy. He spoke regularly with his mother, but he waited until he had already accepted the job and begun working before he told her. He worried that she might think of Christopher's death and disapprove of this work; perhaps she would articulate certain objections that he had not yet articulated to himself. But she only asked what his salary would be. He told her, and she sounded happy, and soon she was complaining that the neighbor's cottonwood was dropping branches onto her lawn, and Ellis thought, Maybe that's all it needs to be—a job.

On his first day, Boggs handed him a stack of technical papers—"A Comparison Study of Skid Marks and Yaw Marks," "Physical Evidence Analysis and Roll Velocity Effects in Rollover Accident Reconstruction," and "Speed Estimation from Vehicle Crush in Side Pole Impacts." He sat at a desk in a cubicle with five-foot-high foam-core walls, two shelves for books, two file drawers, a computer, and a telephone. His cubicle was one in a grid of twelve, each occupied by an engineer. "Eggheads in a carton," Boggs called it. Around the periphery of the room were a handful of walled offices where the senior engineers sat. At the rear of the building a wide door accessed an underground garage where items of physical evidence were stored: car seats burned down to their internal steel frames, pieces of exploded tires, dismantled disc brakes, windshields glittering with crack lines, a fuel tank cut into halves for examination, a Honda motorcycle improbably twisted, a Dodge pickup truck blooming with front and rear collisions.

Ellis occasionally had projects with some of the other engineers, but for the most part he worked directly with Boggs, and he acquired the skills of the job by doing the job with Boggs. Boggs was boss, mentor, and co-worker. Talking with him, Ellis learned the nomenclature. When Boggs, as testifying expert, went to have his opinions taken outside of court it was at a deposition, which was called a *depo* or *dep*. The pillars connecting a vehicle's body to its roof were named alphabetically from front to back: *A-pillar*, *B-pillar*, *C-pillar*, sometimes a *D-pillar*. The people in a vehicle were *occupants*. Anyone thrown from a vehicle in the course of an accident was *ejected*. The dead were *occupants* or *pedestrians* who had sustained *fatal injuries*, or simply *fatalities*.

And he learned techniques. The mathematics of crush energy analysis and momentum-based analysis, how to calculate speed loss during braking, and how to incorporate perception-reaction time into a time-space analysis. He learned photogrammetry for identifying the locations of objects that appeared in photos, how to examine tires and brakes for evidence of defects or improper maintenance, how to look at light bulbs and seatbelts for indications that they were in use at the time of a collision, how to document the damage to a car, how to build computer models of vehicles and terrains, how to generate data describing motion and impacts.

There were slow days, and days spent reading maddeningly useless depositions, days spent working out some trivial but necessary problem of mathematics or physics, days spent trying to find a source for obscure information on decades-old frame rails or fuel-tank designs, days spent traveling between depopulated towns amid empty plains in order to take a few photos and measurements of dubious utility. But even these days held at least a possibility of discovering something of significance, of newly seeing a problem or coming upon some small, critical, overlooked evidence. The work reminded Ellis of the books he enjoyed, stories of sharp-eyed detectives, stories of worlds a little separated from the normal.

At intervals, he did come across an accident-scene photograph—a blood stain on the pavement, a solitary tooth on a car seat, a body burned past recognizing—that turned him cold in his bones. That reminded him of his reservations, that this might be the last job on earth he should have.

But he also felt that the work suited him, and it began to seem to him almost as if he had always been a reconstructionist. He recalled, as a curiosity, that the work had once been new and strange to him, that it had felt like entering an obscure nation with its own language, customs, and peculiar manner of thinking, that even the word *reconstructionist* had once felt odd in his mouth.

Five

They drove the rented Kia up a long driveway toward a gray, metal-sided pole barn and a faded blue ranch house. A rusting old Ford tractor stood surrounded by weeds, tires, and antiquated devices of mysterious purposes. To one side of the house, several cows grazed in a pasture bordered by rows of apple trees. In the other direction, corn grew in strict rows, running out to touch the forest in the distance.

The kid's mother met them as they stepped out of the Kia. Her smile and the wrinkles in her face cut through dense freckles. She led them into the pole barn, through a dark clutter of implements and odors of manure and mold, and out the other side, to a wide heap of dirt, weeds, cut brush, and trash. The pig hide lay atop this stuff, bristling with thick hairs and rimmed with blood. Flies moved on it.

Boggs winced. "Have to admit, I was imagining it'd be a little more cleaned up. I hate actual blood."

Ellis bent and lifted a corner of the hide with a finger and thumb.

"And we can't just take a picture of that thing lying on the road like a bear rug," Boggs said. "No one will believe that's what it looked like to an approaching driver."

"We can build a rig to fit up inside of it."

"That will take hours."

"I can postpone my flight," Ellis said.

Boggs looked at his watch. "Here's the problem. I'm anxious about monkeying with the travel schedule. This is supposed to be like a trip into the repair shop for me and the wife. Top the fluids. Replace the brake pads. New battery. Her idea. Good idea."

"We could come back next week," Ellis said, "but I don't think the attorney will be happy about expanding our travel expenses. She was pretty concerned about the pig visibility issue, but she's still on a budget."

"The pig visibility issue." Boggs put his hands on his head and tapped one index finger.

Ellis looked at him, waiting. Hoping.

Finally Boggs put his hands down. "Okay. We build the rig tonight and take the photos tomorrow," he said. "You'll have to call and reschedule your flight."

Ellis felt a vast, dumb, tidal mixture of thrill and regret. He would have to reschedule his flight. He would be here when Heather arrived.

He said only, looking down at the pig hide, "This one has more blond color than the dead ones in the police photos."

"Some pigs are black," the mother said. "But this one's what you call piebald. If you don't want it, we can call when we get another. We've been getting them pretty regular recently."

"No way," Boggs said. "We're doing this thing now. I'm not going to fly out here again for some pig pictures."

"We can paint it," Ellis said.

"That's ridiculous," Boggs said. But he began laughing. "But why not. Let's put paint on the piebald pig. Why the hell not. Let's cover the whole pig with black lipstick."

They wrapped the hide—stinking, bloody, greasy, and dirty—in a piece of burlap and carried it to the back of the Kia rental and closed the trunk lid over it and its flies. Boggs wrote a check, then asked to use the bathroom.

The mother smiled steadily, and her smile reassured Ellis. Things would be fine. She led them into the house and pointed

Boggs to the bathroom. Ellis milled in the living room while the mother worked on something in the kitchen. Photos hung on the wall over the sofa. In one a man held a boy upside down by his feet. Another frame held the ghostly ultrasound of an unborn child.

When Boggs came out, the mother, smiling, presented them with two thick sandwiches wrapped in wax paper. "Pork roast. The fresh is good. It makes a real difference."

Boggs laughed. Ellis could smell the roast, and it smelled good. He looked at the woman's freckles and her smile. He said, "Thank you."

They ate as they drove. The meat was delicate and rich, and the thick-cut bread had been slathered with pesto. Boggs chewed and turned on the stereo.

Billy Gannon had looked back over his shoulder and seemed to be trying to dodge when the rifle went off. It sounded to Blaisedell as though he yelled, "No! No!" and when Billy turned back to face him he thought that Billy was going to put his hands up. But then Billy changed his mind, or else it had been a trick, and made his move . . .

When Ellis finished eating, he took out a pad of paper. He began sketching a rig design.

At a Home Depot, they bought several lengths of two-by-twos, a selection of bolts, nuts, and screws, four caster wheels, some plywood, duct tape, screwdrivers, wrenches, a handsaw, an electric drill and bits, several pieces of Styrofoam, a can of black spray paint, and a waterproof tarp. They drove with the windows down to combat the odor of rot seeping from the trunk.

They checked in at the hotel, then returned to the Kia, wrapped the hide in the tarp, and carried it in by a back door. They proceeded three floors up a gray stairwell, then along an empty hallway to Ellis's room.

They cut and bolted the two-by-twos into a crude frame that mimicked the shape of a pig lying on its side, then they cut a rectangle of plywood, screwed the caster wheels onto the four corners, and bolted the frame onto the plywood. They pulled and tugged at the hide, which still oozed blood—Boggs held his breath and made monkey faces—but it didn't fit. They had to yank it off again and rework the frame a couple of times, until finally the hide fit, more or less. They stuffed pieces of Styrofoam up inside and closed the belly of the thing with duct tape. It was two in the morning by the time they had finished, and they were smeared with sawdust, grease, and blood.

"This," Boggs said, grinning, "is awesome."

"It'd be more awesomer if we'd done it in your room," Ellis said. The room was rank with the sawdust and pig scent. Ellis looked down at himself and at the pig and giggled.

"I give you a good job doing interesting work for decent pay," Boggs said, "and all I hear is complaints."

They pushed the pig rig onto the balcony. Boggs shook Ellis's hand and headed into the hallway, toward his room. Ellis heard him call to a passerby, "Don't worry. It's not my blood."

Ellis undressed and lay in bed. Only the short end of the night remained, but he felt restless. He stood and went to the balcony door—there in the gloom the rig looked like a pig-zombie. Finally he sat in his underwear in an armchair in a corner of the room. His knees twitched up and down.

Due to overbooking or perhaps a clerk's whim, he had been upgraded to a large room with a sofa, chair, and a small fireplace with a gas log. The fireplace and hearth were covered with green marble tiles, and the fireplace opening held a framed screen surrounded by brass trim—a style two decades out of date. It depressed him a little. Whatever you might build now to look classic and timeless would inevitably look dated later. It seemed that it should be possible to create designs that were ageless and appealing in any era, perhaps by designing to some equations. But he suspected that it was impossible, that humanity was too fickle. It was bothersome.

But while he thought about this, or, tried to think about this, he really thought of Heather. He had hoped to see her, but now—he despised himself.

Six

A knock on the door startled him awake. He was still in the chair. Groggily, he looked at his pants and shirt on the floor. He hadn't brought a change of clothes. Instead, he fetched the hotel's white terrycloth robe.

The knocking had turned to hammering. Ellis yanked the door open, and there stood Boggs, with Heather. She was small beside Boggs, wearing jeans, hair in a ponytail, eyes hard to read. "Oh my God," she exclaimed, and Ellis thought at first that she was offended by his naked legs. But she was staring at the room behind him—the sawdust, scattered tools, wood scraps, dried blood. "What have you been doing?"

"Animal sacrifices," Boggs said, "and Pinewood Derby cars."

"You haven't told her?" Ellis asked.

"I told her we have some work still to do today."

"You killed someone," she said.

Ellis retreated. "I should've put on pants."

Boggs said, "Pants are overrated."

Boggs went out to the balcony while Ellis yanked on his pants and socks and shoes. Boggs pushed the pig rig into the room.

Heather said, "I'm having trouble imagining an explanation for this."

"It's art—a concept piece," Boggs said. "A sort of Damien Hirst thing."

"Ha," Heather said.

"We're going to spray-paint it," Ellis said.

"Day-Glo orange?" Heather said. "Hot pink?"

"We might need your help," Boggs said.

"Spray paint's very easy to use," she said.

"Not painting. Traffic spotting," Boggs said. "That's all."

She looked unhappy at this, but she said nothing.

Ellis still had on the hotel robe. He went into the bathroom to wash his face and pat at his hair. He put on his shirt and did his best to wipe away the stuff on his clothes with a wet washcloth. He came out and found Boggs and Heather both sitting on the bed, silent. They looked at him. Had they been arguing about something? Ellis said, "We can take it out by the back stairs."

"I'm too lazy," Boggs said. "Elevators were invented for exactly this kind of thing."

"I wouldn't say exactly *this*," Ellis said.

"You don't need to make a spectacle of yourself," Heather said.

"You want to carry it?" Boggs asked.

"I'd rather not touch it," she said.

"Elevator," Boggs said.

Ellis gathered his things and put the tools that they wanted to keep into a bag. Boggs went down the hall, bending to push the pig rig. Its eye sockets gaped, the mouth hung, the hide of the legs dangled, the shape bulged strangely with the Styrofoam inside. "Let's name him Wilbur," Boggs called.

Ellis helped him shove the pig rig onto the elevator and stepped in with him. Heather stood outside looking at them. "Go ahead," she said. "I'll get the next one."

Boggs held the door. "Come on. Godammit."

"No."

Boggs glowered. When the doors had shut, he glowered at them.

"Probably not quite how she imagined her vacation," Ellis said.

"But this is exciting. Isn't this a hell of a lot of fun?"

Ellis shrugged.

"It is." Boggs grunted. "But she doesn't like our work."

The doors opened, and Boggs cut straight across the lobby, pushing the pig rig. A group of men in dark suits fell silent and watched.

Ellis held the door for Boggs. Heather came out of the elevator, and Ellis waited for her, holding the door, and he went out with her.

The hotel had a parking lot the size of a football field. Running alongside the parking lot was a busy four-lane road, and across the road stood an office park of low, anonymous buildings with tinted windows, distinguishable from one another only by white five-digit numbers displayed over the doorways. Ellis glanced at these, then looked at the painted lines in the parking lot, then at the sky, the platter-shaped clouds there. But his attention was consumed by the soft tap of her step beside him.

"I love this," Boggs called, as he pushed the pig rig clattering through the parking lot. "Don't you love this?"

"Something like that really does make him happy," Heather said.

Boggs had traded the rental car for a pickup truck. They put their bags into the bed of the truck, and Boggs took out the can of black spray paint that they had bought at Home Depot and shook it so that the agitator inside clattered. He bent down and painted onto the side of the pig a word: *PIG*.

"This is not a pig," he said.

"It is not a pig, but it was a pig," Ellis said. "Part of a pig, anyway."

"Cute," Heather said. "Couple of hams, you two."

Boggs sprayed the paint over the rest of the hide, and then the wooden base of the rig. The paint made the animal seem a bit less tortured, though perhaps more demonic. They waited a few minutes for the paint to dry, and then Ellis and Boggs lifted the pig rig into the bed, covered it with the tarp, and tied down the edges.

"Let's get breakfast," Boggs said. "The accident time of day wasn't until eleven. We'll want to have the right sun position for our photographs."

Boggs's feet lay up along the booth seat, and he had out a couple technical papers from the Society of Automotive Engineers. Heather frowned at Boggs's feet when she returned from the bathroom. She sat beside Ellis. "Guess what we had for dinner last night?" Boggs said.

"What?"

"From the farm. Free-range."

"What?"

Boggs grinned. She looked at Ellis. He blushed. She looked again at Boggs, and Boggs nodded.

"Oh, Jesus," she said. She laughed. "That's terrible. You're terrible. Whose idea was this?"

"We were just good guests. We ate what we were given."

"I mean, the whole idea of putting a dead pig in the road."

"This was my colleague's ingenious scheme," Boggs said.

Ellis made a pained smile.

"We were going to go to that restaurant in Door County this afternoon," she said to Boggs. She glanced at Ellis. "There's a Swedish restaurant with grass and the goats on the roof."

"The goats won't fall off the roof before we get there," Boggs said. "Don't be sulky."

"We had a whole weekend planned."

"This will be fun. Pretend it's an art project."

"It's more like I landed in the middle of a Monty Python skit."

"Just another one of your fabulous art projects."

"What kind of art are you doing now?" Ellis asked her.

She ignored him. "I can't—" she said to Boggs. She shook her head. Then she stood and moved between the tables, past the cashier, opened the door, and walked out of the restaurant.

Presently the food came, on three big oval plates. Boggs began to eat. Ellis watched him and poked at his food. After a few minutes he ventured, "Will she come back?"

Boggs shrugged. He forked eggs and ate them. He seemed undisturbed, except, perhaps, unusually quiet. Heather's meal—a muffin and a bowl of oatmeal—lay cooling at the corner of the table.

They finished eating, Boggs paid the check, and they walked out to the pickup. Heather was sitting on the rear bumper, fidgeting with a few red flexible straws she'd apparently found on the ground.

The pickup had two bucket seats in front and a bench seat in back, with about six inches of legroom. Heather pointed Ellis to the front passenger seat, but he ignored her and crammed himself into the backseat. Heather sat in front of him. "This isn't about my art," she said to Boggs.

"This is about my work," he said.

"You attacked my art."

"You won't take it seriously, but you want me to."

"This is great. Great beginning to a vacation. Love it. Thanks." She sat silent for a while as Boggs drove. "Did you bring my muffin?"

Boggs reached into his bag behind the seat and took out the muffin.

While she ate, she talked about her flight—a man in the seat beside her had made clicking sounds through the entire flight, like a locust. Ellis could see the top of the back of Heather's head and, sometimes, a part of one or the other of her shoulders. She touched her neck with her hand, then rested the hand again in her lap. He tried to detect a trace of her smell.

An hour along the road, and coming up, all alone at a desolate intersection, stood a yellow house with a white-railed wraparound porch, a gravel parking lot, and a sign out front that said SHANON

Realty alongside silhouettes of a deer and flying ducks. Parked on the gravel was a single car, an old model, red with a black hood, two round headlamps, fastback.

"You see that?" Ellis asked.

"What?" Boggs asked.

"I saw it," Heather said.

"It looked just like his."

"What?" Boggs asked.

"The *airlane*," Ellis said.

"Excuse me, what?" Boggs said.

"Forget it," Heather said.

"Forget what?" Boggs said.

"That's perfect," she said.

"Different color, but it was the same," Ellis said. "They only made that Torino-style Fairlane for one year—"

Heather turned and glared at him.

He stopped.

"Anyway," Boggs said. "What were we talking about? I forget."

When they reached the accident scene, Boggs and Ellis unloaded the pig rig. "We should have a technical name for this thing," Boggs said.

"It's a swine facsimile device," Ellis said.

"A prototype porker exemplar." Boggs took out the camera and the walkie-talkies. He handed one walkie-talkie to Ellis and the other to Heather, and he asked her to proceed around the curve and radio a warning when vehicles approached.

She strolled down the road and disappeared where it turned behind the trees. Boggs moved off in the other direction with the camera. He waved, and Ellis pushed the pig rig into the roadway.

He and Boggs were yelling back and forth about where exactly to set up the pig rig when Boggs stopped, looking at something behind Ellis.

Heather was coming back around the curve.

Ellis pushed the pig rig off the road and walked back to the truck. They all came together again at the truck.

"I'm sorry," Heather said. Her jaw worked.

"It's a matter of safety," Boggs said. "Ellis could get run over."

"It's all right," Ellis said. "I'll be fine. I can hear the cars coming."

"You think that," Boggs said, "until a Prius comes round that curve with the engine shut off and turns you into a fleshy speed bump. Or, more likely, you'll jump out of the way but leave our pig rig in the middle of the road, and the driver will try to swerve around it and run into a tree and get killed, and we'll get sued, and won't that be great."

Heather looked at the ground and worked her jaw, her face red and splotching white at the scars.

Boggs sneered. " 'Mr. Boggs, you are a professional accident reconstructionist. You were working on an accident caused by a driver swerving around a pig in the road. And you put a pig into the middle of the same road. Surely you were aware that you were duplicating a situation that had already caused one accident? A driver approaches your pig rig, tries to swerve around it, and an accident ensues? Wasn't this a foreseeable event? Don't you feel responsible?' "

"I'm sorry," Heather said. "But I feel ill."

"We need a spotter," Boggs said.

"Can't you find another spotter?"

Boggs threw his arms out and turned a circle to encompass the pine forest.

"I can't do it," she said. "It's just the feeling I get."

"It's not safe," Boggs said. "We'll have to stop working."

"You know how I feel about this," she said.

"Is it the pig?" Ellis asked.

Heather looked surprised. "The pig?"

"She doesn't like what we do," Boggs said. "She thinks we're cannibals."

"You can do whatever you want," she said. "For God's sake, I don't care what you do. But this makes me uncomfortable."

"The client is expecting these photos," Boggs said.

This was a lie; they hadn't spoken to the attorney about this. Boggs, however, made the claim with perfect calm.

Heather said, "I've said I'm sorry. What else do you want me to say?"

"I just want to understand," Boggs said. "It's just a matter of standing by the road down there. Not even near where the accident was."

"I don't have anything against you."

"You know that there have been accidents everywhere. You just don't know about them. You can't avoid places where there have been accidents."

Ellis said—just to say something, to try to break in—"I can manage it by myself."

"I didn't realize your mindset against this was so complete and irrational," Boggs said.

"You never asked me to help you with your work before."

"It's not safe." Boggs stepped into the road and stood in the middle of the lane, looking to the direction where traffic would come.

"I'm sorry," Heather said.

Boggs turned and shrugged. "We'll pack it in, then."

"I can stand off to the side," Ellis said, "and I'll reel it in if a car comes."

Boggs squinted at the pig rig. "Reel it? We don't have a fishing pole. We don't have a rope."

"I'll use the string off the plumb bob. I'll take the alternator out of the pickup and pull the wire out of it. I'll strip down and use my shirt and pants for a rope."

"Dear God. Please. Forget it. We're done."

"Give me the camera." Ellis opened his hands. He had grown angry.

"Why?"

"Because I'm going to roll the pig out there and take some pictures. It was a pain in the ass putting that thing together. I want to get this done."

"Damn it," Boggs said. He kicked the pig rig, and it skittered away a little. Boggs lifted his foot and rubbed it. "That hurt more than I expected."

But he then took up the camera.

"Let's go. Bring the pig rig into the road. Right there in the middle of the lane."

While Ellis pushed the pig rig out, he saw Heather starting away into the dark of the woods. Wanting to say something, he called, "Don't get lost." Which seemed ridiculous after he'd said it.

She bent to lift something small off the forest floor, then went on.

"Middle of the lane," Boggs repeated. He had moved up the road with the camera. Ellis shoved the pig rig into position, then moved to the side of the road.

"Hide behind that bush," Boggs called. "So we don't have to Photoshop you out of the picture."

He was right; it would save time later. Ellis crouched behind the bush and listened to the soughing pine branches overhead. To summon him out again, Boggs made shrieking, off-key pig calls. "Soo-eee! Ee! Ee! Ee!"

Ellis laughed. He ran out into the road again. "She was right," Boggs yelled. "This is like Monty Python. Turn it a little, will you? Counterclockwise."

As he was adjusting the pig rig, Ellis heard, faintly, the chirpy shriek of a car attacking the other end of the curve.

He tugged the pig rig back toward the roadside, but one of the wheels caught in a crack in the asphalt, and the shrieking closed on him surprisingly fast. He had to jerk the pig rig the last few feet with an off-balance movement that landed him facedown in the dirt. "Stay in your lane, asshole!" he yelled as the car flashed by. The car wouldn't have been close to him at all, except that the driver was straddling the double yellow line.

"You all right?" Boggs called.

Ellis brushed dirt off, and he dragged the pig rig back into the road.

They took several series of photos, with the rig in different locations. Then Boggs said, "We're good."

They packed away the camera. Together, they loaded the pig rig into the bed of the truck.

"What should we do with it now?" Ellis asked.

Boggs shrugged.

Heather had not yet returned. Boggs climbed into the driver's seat. Ellis couldn't read how angry he was. He'd joked while they worked, but his humor seemed to come and go in flashes. He lingered over the camera equipment, fussing with the lenses.

Minutes passed. Eventually, at the corner of his eye, he saw Heather come quietly from the woods. She stopped beside him, cupping her hands. She narrowed her gaze at the pig. "Is your job always so absurd?" she asked.

"You really don't like it?"

"Look what I found," she said, opening her hands. "A crow's feather. A bit of river-rock quartz. A bottle cap."

The bottle cap shone a peculiar, brilliant green. The quartz had the white color and shape of a gibbous moon. Ellis never would have noticed any of them, but singled out and held in her hands they were made pretty.

"Take it," she said, lifting the quartz and putting it in his hand. "For good luck."

As they drove back toward the hotel, they sat again in the same seats. Again no one spoke.

After some miles Heather turned on the radio, and it sang:

You're gonna cry ninety-six tears
You're gonna cry ninety-six tears
You're gonna cry, cry, cry, cry . . .

"Oh my God," Boggs squawked. "You know I'm going to ask you to turn that off."

"That's Question Mark and the Mysterians," Heather said gleefully, as if a ridiculous band name could defeat any objection.

"Please turn it off."

Heather turned it off. "John doesn't like music," she said.

"You don't?" Ellis said. He had always let Boggs run the radio as he liked, and now it struck him for the first time that during all their driving to look at accident vehicles and scenes they had never listened to music, only news radio or audio books.

"I don't like bad music," Boggs said.

"And you think all music is bad."

Boggs glanced back at Ellis. "The problem is that most music is terrible."

"Name some music you like."

"Early Miles Davis and John Coltrane are listenable. Some Bach. Late Beatles. Frank Sinatra did some decent tunes."

"You never listen to any of that."

"I said it's not bad. I didn't say I wanted to listen to it."

"I like music," Heather said.

"It could be that the music part of my brain is faulty," Boggs said. "Most music gives me a headache. It's just a vibration in the ear. I don't see why it should be considered pleasurable."

"John just has to have strong opinions," Heather said. "It doesn't matter if they make sense."

Boggs glared at her.

"You two looked pretty awesome out there," Heather said. "Pig herder and pig portraitist."

"This is the work that Ellis was born for," Boggs said.

Then Heather was quiet, and Ellis waited for more anger, but there was none. No energy at all. They were all quiet. The radio was quiet.

• • •

Some twenty miles from the hotel, Boggs pulled into a rest area. He directed Ellis to help him lift the pig rig onto a picnic table. "A statue on a plinth," Heather said.

"A local hero of the Civil War," Boggs said. He asked her to take a picture of himself and Ellis, sitting on either side of the pig rig.

They left it there, and Ellis watched through the rear window as it dwindled and disappeared into the distance, the terrible black undead pig alone on its plinth in a grassy field.

"Let's meet here in half an hour to go out for dinner," Boggs said in the hotel lobby.

"I'll beg off," Ellis said. "Your vacation has been interrupted long enough."

"No," Boggs said. "You don't understand. We like you."

"Won't you please?" Heather said.

He said yes.

As he stood in the elevator, the closing doors framed Boggs and Heather in the middle of the lobby. Their postures reminded Ellis of the arguing couple at the airport, and he felt sorry, felt an impulse to help them. But he didn't know how. And the idea was followed by a strange sickness of apprehension.

Heather looked over, as if to call to him. But the doors shut, and he rose upward.

He went to his room and lay on the bed. He felt feverish. He perceived himself as an object of heat on the cool of the sheets, subject to the laws of thermodynamics, the energy of himself conducting and convecting away, increasing the entropy of the universe. But then Heather appeared in his thoughts, despite his best efforts, and he felt his feeling about her.

He groaned. He stood and paced the room and tried to analyze his situation.

He was drawn to Heather. Heather was married to Boggs. Boggs was his boss and his friend. Between these constraints, his own position was impossible. There was nothing he could do. He needed to leave. His situation and his feelings were abominable.

He called Boggs and told him that he couldn't come to dinner. He said his stomach was upset.

Which it hadn't been, but saying it seemed to make it so. He didn't eat that night, except for ice from the ice machine. It cracked between his teeth and then seemed to disappear.

He took a shuttle early the next morning for the airport without seeing either of them again.

Seven

At the office, Ellis downloaded the survey data. He plotted the tire-mark locations from the photogrammetry that he and Boggs had done: the results matched up with the police diagram. So they had merely validated the police measurements. Except that now they had the positions of the pigs, too.

He spent the rest of the week working on the case. He located an exemplar Mercedes and spent an hour taking photos and measurements of it. He compared these measurements against their measurements of the damaged vehicle to calculate crush depth. Using reference data from controlled collisions with similar vehicles, he developed estimates of the crush energy in this collision. From that, he calculated the Mercedes' speed as it struck the tree. Then he applied friction calculations to work backward through the Mercedes' previous speeds: 47 mph as it hit the tree, 51 mph as it left the road, 54 mph when the driver first slammed the brakes. The road had a 45 mph speed limit, and a recommended speed of 35 mph posted ahead of the curve.

He created a scaled diagram of the roadway that included the pigs and the tree and an outline of the final position of the Mercedes. He imported the diagram into PC Crash and created a vehicle model to run on top of it using the undamaged Mercedes parameters—dimensions, wheel locations, rear-wheel drive, weight distribution. A coroner's report listed the driver's weight, and he put that into the driver's seat. He simulated the tree with an immovable pole. He set the friction factor on the road surface and created a strip of higher friction for the dirt along the road shoulder. He set the vehicle at the beginning of the tire marks, dialed the braking to 100 percent, gave it a velocity of 54 mph, and started the simulation. The simulated Mercedes skidded over the outline of the pig and off the curve of the road and came to a stop out in the middle of where the forest would be, if he had put all the trees into the model. But he hadn't, because only one mattered.

He started adjusting the steering angles, aiming the vehicle toward the tree.

He worked at it for hours, making minute adjustments of steering angle and braking, but it was difficult to make the vehicle track the tire marks into the tree in the correct orientation. He rechecked the scene diagram scaling and the vehicle parameters, but they were fine.

It began to grow dark in the office windows, and the car still wouldn't track over the top of the tire marks. He decided to try a different approach and put down a couple of patches of varying friction at locations on the road and shoulder leading to the tree. It was the equivalent of putting a swath of soft dirt in one place, an oil slick in another.

These helped a lot.

He looked at the photos again, focusing on the places where he had put the friction patches. He didn't see anything in the photos that he and Boggs had taken, but in the police photos there was, maybe, something. A dark bit of something on the road, and the other area, on the shoulder, had a strange texture. It might have been sandy. In addition, there were surely bits of pig guts and gristle scattered all around. It was hard to say what exactly he was seeing; the photos were of poor quality. But he experimented and tweaked the friction numbers a little more, and soon he had the vehicle swinging and sliding with all four wheels moving neatly across the tire marks. Most often the evidence pointed you to the physics, but sometimes the physics pointed you to the evidence. And sometimes the physics was the evidence.

He looked at the photos again, but he couldn't be certain what was there. He wished they were of better quality.

Then he created a new simulation in which, instead of crashing the Mercedes, it steered gently around the pig and on down the road. This was easy. It took only a few minutes.

Friday afternoon, Boggs came into Ellis's cubicle and sat. "So. How are we doing?"

"Could be worse."

"Can't you say something more confident than that? Ideally, something that will also make me laugh? Some kind of pig joke? We're not already out of pig jokes, are we?"

"I've been working on the Mercedes' motion," Ellis said. "To get it to follow the tire marks and end up in the tree, I had to put down a couple of additional friction swatches."

Boggs watched the simulated vehicle movements. "Well, that's it," he said. "That's what the evidence shows. Those are the tire marks. That's the car. The car made the tire marks, and they show you how it went from A to B." Boggs checked the scaling, the model parameters and vehicle dimensions, things that Ellis had already checked three times already. Then he looked at the friction numbers. "I don't have a problem with these. These aren't outrageous. Could have been blood and gore anywhere on that road. And who knows what he bumped into in the dirt."

"I didn't say it was crazy. I just wanted to point it out."

"There's always some margin of uncertainty."

"I just wanted to make you aware."

"Who knows what the friction was really like on that road that night? Police didn't measure it."

Ellis said, "It's also true that the entire concept of friction is a ridiculously simplistic reduction of a complex interaction."

"Yes, yes. Let's not get into the subatomic interactions. We do the best we can with the evidence we have. We just reduce the margin of uncertainty as much as we can."

"I know. But you're the one who has to testify to it."

"But you're the perfectionist. It looks okay to me."

"I don't know what else to do."

"The perfectionist has accomplished all that he can. Show me what the driver should have done."

Ellis played the simulation of the vehicle steering smoothly around the pig.

"Fabulous," Boggs said. "See how easy it should have been? If only he had been sober. No one would have had to sue anyone. Let's wrap this up. We have to move on. You have to move on. I have attorneys calling me and asking about three different jobs that we haven't even started." Boggs slapped Ellis on the knee. "Giddy-up, friend."

Eight

"I don't really know what an accident is."

This—or a version of this—was one of Boggs's themes.

"Everything," Boggs would say, "depends on the contingent and the adventitious"—Boggs, liking that word, drew it out—"and if some people make some decisions that result in the physical interference of one vehicle with another in an intersection, and that can be called an accident, then what can't be called an accident? Where my footsteps fall, where I place my hands, where I sit, where I stand, how I appear in the world, who I speak to, the kind of work I do, who I befriend, who I fall in love with?" Boggs pouted. "*Accident?*"

It had taken Ellis a long time to realize that Boggs didn't generally keep friends. He could be too overbearing, too blunt, too indifferent, too chatty, too silent. But somehow, because Ellis worked for him and because Boggs loved the work, Ellis was shielded from the worst of these traits. Moreover, by the nature of the work they were often seated side-by-side for long periods—in airports, airplanes, rental cars, and hotel bars as they traveled to inspect accident scenes and vehicles—and the demands of the work curtailed other relationships even as the two of them were pushed together. They talked about books, and they joked easily, and they could be silent easily.

They developed a habit of late, fitful conversations called from desk to desk when everyone else had left the office. Sometimes these seemed to Ellis almost a reflection of Boggs's ideal of a book on CD in a car: a dream of voices in the head.

"One of the problems between my wife and me," Boggs said once, late in the office, "is over kids. What do you think about kids?"

"Kids are okay, aren't they? They're pretty cute. I guess sometimes I get tired of their noise on airplanes. You?"

"Don't like them when they're little. Little village idiots. You can't have a real conversation."

"Cute, though."

"Cute, but they don't even know how to wipe themselves. Who wants to spend day after day hanging out with a roommate who can't wipe his own butt?"

"Someone did it for you."

"Bless her. No idea why. Look at what she got out of it. You know I once sent her a case of beer for Christmas? In cans. Not to mention the times I forgot to send anything at all. I'm a horrible offspring."

"We're a result of mindless propagation of the species."

"You're being sarcastic, but you're right."

"You're being sarcastic."

"Nope. The other thing is, I'm sure any kid I have will die before I do. Hit by a bus, drowning in a pool, SIDS, finding a gun in the neighbor's closet, leukemia, drafted into some dick-swinging war, whatever. How can a child possibly survive? Most do, somehow. But I'm stuck inside my own lizard brain, and whenever I think about having some idiot kid, I get chills. Dead kid. I'd hate every day with the kid, and then the kid dies, and I'd feel even worse. I would go to the nearest steel foundry and jump into a blast furnace."

Ellis looked at the gridded tiles of the office's drop ceiling and said nothing. The silence went on a minute. Then Boggs emerged from his office and came to Ellis's cubicle.

"I'm sorry." Boggs frowned. "I wasn't thinking of your brother. I hadn't made the connection. I'm the idiot."

"My dad's life did go pretty much straight to hell after that," Ellis said. He looked at his computer screen, trying to give nothing away. He already knew Boggs's position on the topic of children, through Heather, because he had begun his affair with her.

Nine

Was it an accident? An accident, that Boggs created the opportunity for it to begin?

Boggs was away, giving his deposition in Pig Accident Two. Ellis's phone rang, and Boggs, in a growly tone, said, "Do me a favor?"

Heather, said Boggs, was stranded in her father's RV in a grocery store parking lot. The engine wouldn't start.

"Do you know what it costs to get an RV that size towed?" Boggs asked. "And I wouldn't be surprised if it's just a bad connection at the battery."

Ellis went.

The RV, a Coachmen Leprechaun running a Ford V8 under the hood, lay at the edge of the parking lot, big and rectangular as a fallen megalith. The problem was just as Boggs had suggested. Ellis retrieved pliers and a wire brush from a hardware store down the street, cleaned the battery connections, tightened the leads, and the engine keyed on.

Heather, in the driver's seat, clapped. She climbed down and peered at the murmuring engine. "All good," Ellis said. She was small—he was surprised by this every time; she seemed larger in his memory. The sunlight caught out a few strands of copper in her dark, straight hair.

"Want some iced tea?" she asked. "Want to come in? Let me show you my sometimes lakeside, sometimes mallside, always roadside studio?"

Marbles, rolls of toilet paper, electrical wires in many colors, stones and seashells, dryer lint, blackened sheets of aluminum foil, quartered tennis balls, Dixie cups, images of children cut from magazines, molded-plastic zoo animals—these were gathered in coffee cans and shoe boxes all over the floor. A camera tripod rested in the corner. On the small dining table lay a large set of watercolors and an old anatomy textbook with holes drilled through and plastic flowers sprouting from it. She cleared a seat for him and poured iced tea in repurposed yogurt cups.

He sat, anxiety bobbing inside.

A few strange objects stood on the bit of counter space beside the sink. A pair of little alien creatures—assembled from pen caps, wires, pieces of cell phones, bits of shining broken glass for teeth—looked at themselves in dollhouse mirrors. A spiky ball of cigarette butts had been painted an unnaturally bright yellow, making it a sunny little object. And flooding from the double door of a plastic toy barn came a bloblike collection of pieces of things, arranged as if oozing into all directions. Looking closer, he saw that the blob-thing was made of many plastic soldiers, or pieces of plastic soldiers, assembled to present a surface of weaponry—pistols, rifles, bazookas, mortars, machine guns, aiming everywhere.

"Don't touch!" Heather said. But then she reached with a finger and prodded it. "It's too delicate. Someday I'll hit a pothole and destroy it." She apologized once more for the clutter. "Dad doesn't use the RV anymore, so he let me borrow it." She searched in a pile of construction paper on the table. "I was experimenting with popsicle sticks for a Halloween ornament project for my class." She held up a star-shape, decorated with glued bits of colored cellophane. "The trick is to remember to pretend that you have the clumsy hands of a child."

He fidgeted, looked around. The rearmost several feet of the RV were sectioned off by a rough partition of drywall with a narrow door, painted red. Ellis pointed at it. "Storage?"

"Darkroom." She opened the door to show him a small space, carefully arranged—the passenger side was stacked with a vertical system of shelves holding trays and jugs of chemicals, and the driver's side was occupied by a crane-necked enlarger and photos suspended from a network of wires and clips. Mounted to the ceiling was a red light on an extension-cord reel. "I can take photos and develop them and go right back to shoot again if I don't like them," she said. "I use pinhole cameras." She showed him three: one made from a box for kitchen matches, another in a round Quaker Oats carton, and the largest in a simple box of unfinished wood. "I can put six-by-nine-inch plates in the big one," she said. She handed him a stack of photographs. They were black-and-white and generally blurry, with odd areas of crisp focus, flares of light, and erratic black splotches. They seemed to examine aspects of a scene that usually would be ignored—the upper reaches of a tree, a corner of a billboard, a portion of a bridge where the concrete had eroded and exposed the rebar, a shot from behind an empty wood-slatted bench that stood near the edge of a road where traffic streamed. Oddly graceful images, with an aura of nostalgia. She had printed certain shots again and again with variations of cropping and exposure. "Almost all of them are taken from inside here," she said, "inside the RV, through the windows."

This was obvious, once she pointed it out. Often, a portion of the window framed the view.

"Why?" he asked.

"Well, there are a couple of ways I might explain it. One is, this is how people see much of the world. Through a car window, on a road or in a parking lot."

"A vehicular viewpoint," he said.

She repeated this phrase, pleased. "I'd like to take some photos while the RV is actually moving," she said. "But the pinhole requires long exposures, so I might just get a lot of blur. And it'd be sort of dangerous to do it myself, while driving, obviously."

He turned through a few more pictures. "I've never really known an artist before," he said.

"I'm not much of an artist," she said. "I don't feel like one."

"But these," Ellis said, holding up the photos.

"I like seeing things. I just want to see everything. Maybe this sounds schmaltzy or something. But I want to see and see and see. I don't mean by traveling around the world. Just seeing what's here." She gestured to the floor. She held out her hands. "I feel like sometimes I can go around for days without seeing anything at all. So I make these things to trick myself into seeing."

"My work is like that at times, too," he said.

She looked at him with surprise, then bent and fussed with the cellophane-and-popsicle-stick stars. She seemed embarrassed and kept her eyes down. She wasn't wearing false eyelashes, and the naked eyelids somehow made her eyes seem aged. "That would be explanation number two, for the photos. That I'm trying to access your work. Or maybe trying to access something of what you access in your work. Even though I hate it. Your work."

"I never did thank you," Ellis said, "for helping me to connect with Boggs, for the job."

"Should you? You do like it?"

"It's always interesting. It's beautiful, sometimes."

"Beautiful? The dead pigs and all?"

"When the evidence . . . Sometimes the math comes together. Sometimes you find something surprising. There's a particular feeling."

She said, "John's glad to be working with you. He likes you."

"I like him, too."

"But don't you wish sometimes that he'd just shut up?"

Ellis laughed. But she didn't. She made a small adjustment to the position of the pitcher of iced tea.

"It wasn't a coincidence, exactly," he said, with a feeling of abandoning the shore, "when I ran into you at the art museum." He told her about seeing her at the airport, about driving by her house, about going week after week to the museum.

"Why didn't you say something, at the airport?"

"My mom wondered the same thing," he said. He hoped she would laugh, though, having now said it, he couldn't imagine why anyone would laugh, and she didn't. "I was surprised," he said. "I suppose I was scared."

She looked at him. Was she waiting for him to go on? He couldn't go on. He ached and jittered and looked down at the stack of her photos. The topmost showed a white fencepost holding out white rails. He found himself thinking of Boggs.

Abruptly he stood and said goodbye, and he fled. He saw that she was surprised, and he went too quickly to see if it became disappointment.

For days afterward a pain worked in his chest. It was the physical working of his heart, its mechanical contracting and relaxing, paining him. Why should that be? His heart wasn't doing anything different or new. It was a muscle, working as it always had. But now it hurt. Something about her presence. He'd felt the same way years before, when she was Christopher's girlfriend, before he died.

The deposition for Pig Accident Two had been unremarkable—Boggs and the opposing expert agreed on the overall accident sequence, although Ellis and Boggs had the Mercedes going 19 mph over the posted recommended speed, while the opposing expert had it only 10 mph over. Much of the deposition was spent on questions around this discrepancy, but it was familiar ground for Boggs. Reasonable assumptions could be taken across a certain margin, and each side took the end of the margin that favored their own client. Presumably a jury would split the difference.

When they turned to the photographs of the pig rig, the plaintiff's attorney had asked Boggs whether a painted pig would reflect light in the same way as a real pig. Boggs took out the thatch of pig hair he'd found in the wheel well, set it beside a photo of the painted pig rig, and suggested that they looked pretty darn close. Then he developed a long explanation of the visible spectrum of electromagnetic radiation, the properties of absorption and reflection, and the physical mechanisms for detecting color and white and black by the cones and rods in the retina—and he basically bored the attorney into dropping the subject.

He told Ellis that he expected the case would settle out of court. Most cases did.

But as the court date approached, there was no settlement. The highway department's attorney gave the impression that she, too, was surprised that the case hadn't settled yet. She arranged for a mock trial, immediately prior to the actual trial, to test-drive her arguments, and she asked Boggs to participate.

Ellis reviewed the file and spent two full days with Boggs prepping testimony, reviewing their animations and presentation materials, raising and answering every question and objection that they could think of. Then, Boggs caught a flight to Wisconsin.

He thought, I'll tell her I found myself dialing—

No. Precision mattered to him, and he didn't "find" himself dialing, as if awoken while sleepwalking. As if it were an accident. He didn't want to dial, but he also did want to dial, and he allowed himself to dial.

"Hi," Heather said.

A great void opened in his chest; he could feel it sucking emptily. "It's Ellis," he said. "I just decided to dial. I mean, to call you, to see how things are going."

"I'm glad you called."

"Yes. I decided to."

"I just bought this really big bookshelf. It's still in the car."

"Oh."

"John is out of town. I'm glad you called. Do you think you could help me move it?"

"It?"

"The shelf?"

"Oh. Of course." He was an idiot. But amid the blood-rushing clamor in his head he could barely manage even to be an idiot. "I'd like to help. Yes. Right now? Your house?"

She said nothing for several seconds. Then, "If you can."

He parked in the driveway in front of the garage where Boggs had stood waving at him as he slunk by years before. Heather came out and smiled at him. After he had carried the shelf into the house, they looked at each other, and finally he said, "Can I help you take some pictures from a moving RV?"

He drove the RV down the road while she set up the Quaker Oats camera. She put the tripod between the driver's and passenger's seats, pressed a lump of modeling clay on top of it, and pressed the camera onto the clay. At the front of the camera was a flap of black paper hinged with a piece of tape; to expose the film, she lifted the paper, revealing a tiny hole in a piece of aluminum foil. While Ellis drove the interstate at 70 mph, she held the paper up for a two-second exposure, then closed it again. She carried the camera back to the darkroom to change the film.

They took several more. "Into the sun!" she called. He exited onto a county road and drove squinting. He'd never driven such a large vehicle before; it felt like he was sailing a large boat down a narrow creek. "Keep it straight," she called, and he said, "Aye, Captain, keeping her straight," and she laughed and said, "Don't make me laugh, I'll shake the camera," and he said, "Aye aye, no merrymaking, Captain."

They went on this way until the sun had set, then circled back to the east.

And that was all. He stopped in front of his duplex and climbed down to the street. She moved over to the driver's seat, smiled, waved, and drove away.

He wondered if it had been settled, that they would only be friends. But his other emotions came around on him again like a club to the head.

He called again that night. She answered with sleep thick in her voice. "Sorry," he said. "It's too late."

"No. It's all right."

She didn't seem surprised that he had called. "Did you develop those photos we took?" he asked.

"They're terrible. The RV jiggles too much."

"We could build an isolator with gyroscopic positioning."

She giggled. "Go for it. But it might be more trouble than it's worth."

"Can I see you?"

Two

Ten

In France, late in the reign of Louis XV, a man named Nicolas-Joseph Cugnot invented the world's first automobile. Cugnot called it a *fardier á vapeur.* With wagon wheels, a kettle-shaped steam generator, and a tiller-style steering mechanism, the *fardier á vapeur* could accelerate to speeds as high as 2.5 mph. Perhaps inevitably, having invented the car, Cugnot also invented the car crash, when he drove the *fardier á vapeur* into a wall. Although no one was hurt, Cugnot lost his research funding.

Or so Ellis reported to Boggs during a plane flight.

"Thank God," Boggs said, "the name *fardier á vapeur* never caught on."

Ellis had started this research out of simple curiosity, but Boggs encouraged him; a good anecdote might be useful in court. Ellis went on: More than one hundred years elapsed before the first fatal automotive accident occurred. In 1896 a woman named Bridget Driscoll was strolling with her daughter on the grounds of London's Crystal Palace when she was struck and killed by an Anglo-French Motor Car Company vehicle. Witnesses reported the Anglo-French vehicle was traveling at a "tremendous speed," later estimated to be 4 mph.

"You're kidding," Boggs said. "Is it even possible to be killed that way? Four miles an hour is barely a fast walk."

"It's a bit like letting yourself be trampled to death by a marching band," Ellis said.

"I don't know if I can use that in court. It might kill my credibility."

Prosecutors alleged, Ellis went on, that the automobile had attained such an impressive velocity only because the driver had secretly modified the engine to provide more power. Nonetheless, a jury determined that the death of Mrs. Driscoll was not the fault of the driver. Instead, the jury called the death *accidental*—the first use of that term for an automotive collision. Ellis quoted from the testimony of the coroner who examined Mrs. Driscoll: "This must never happen again."

Boggs chortled. "And here we are."

At this time, Ellis only had been working for Boggs for a bit more than a year. They were returning from an inspection of the collision damage to a Mitsubishi SUV that had crashed into the back end of a trailered yacht at a closing speed of 55 mph. Stored in a field behind a gas station, the Mitsubishi had filled with rainwater, its contents rotted, and a family of rats lived in the dashboard. Boggs uttered spectacular blasphemies while they worked, and Ellis held his breath until he nearly passed out.

Boggs bought two mini-bottles of Scotch from the flight attendant and drank the first neat from a transparent plastic cup, a dainty object in his large hand. They were flying above a smooth white cloud surface like a perfected landscape.

"Christopher was your half-brother on which side?" Boggs asked. The question startled Ellis; it was the first time Boggs had asked about his brother since Ellis had first interviewed with him.

"My father's," Ellis said.

"What was his mother like?"

"Skinny, tight pants, too much makeup. Smoker. I never saw much of her. Whenever I heard about her, it seemed she was moving into a new place with a new guy in a new town. I couldn't figure out the understanding she had with my dad. But every so often he told Christopher to get ready to leave. Then she turned up and took Christopher away for a night, or a week, or whole summers. The longest was nearly two years. When Christopher came back from that one, he was fifteen. He had become much more withdrawn. He couldn't bear to look at us, to speak with us. It was as if our family made him physically ill. He literally refused to speak to me."

The plane banked. They were approaching the Detroit airport, the clouds had broken, and the earth was covered with the miniature streets and buildings of an industrial city absent industry—houses lay gutted with constituent elements strewn into overgrown lawns, factories crouched amid empty parking lots.

"I was excited when Dad said Christopher was coming back. But then it might as well have been a stranger who moved into the house—" Ellis lifted his hands. "It was confusing."

"Sounds like adolescence. And he probably resented you, for your more stable home life."

"Actually, I always thought that, fundamentally, he was just not a very good person."

Boggs looked over. "Well," he said, "the dynamics of a family are pretty much the most inexplicable, anti-analytic thing on earth."

As they descended, the city's empty apartment towers presented faces of glassless window openings, black voids repeated in ranks. Few cars moved on the street grid; traffic surged in large numbers only on the lanes of the interstates, en route to other places.

Eleven

Ellis did later observe that *the big streets* of Mill Street and Main Street were actually not very big. But they were the only through streets in Coil, a town stuck out among the corn and sugar-beet fields a hundred interstate miles north of Detroit, a town with a one-block brick-fronted downtown, several bars and churches, and one supermarket, one movie theater, one middle school and one high school, and more or less one of everything else that people really needed. It had begun as a railroad town, a stop on the line carrying timber and ore out of the north. Eventually the trains vanished, but when an interstate was built a couple of miles to the east, the town found new service as a bedroom community for men and women who worked in automotive factories in Flint. But those jobs had begun dwindling before Ellis had even been born. People in the area began to take on makeshift, odd jobs, drew unemployment or disability, moved away. All the while that Ellis was growing up, the town around him seemed to be fading like an old photograph.

Although Ellis's father had rarely held any kind of a job for long, he did for a few years manage to keep a position in sales for a concrete contractor. He had a strange passion for this product, and when business was slow, he drove around looking for gravel driveways and cold calling at front doors, hoping to talk a homeowner into beautiful, solid, maintenance-free concrete. Eventually he was fired, but at their own house the job had already been immortalized: the summer that Ellis turned eleven, the entire lawn had been covered with concrete. For the rest of his childhood, the house stood on a small hard plain of gray, graded for runoff, gridded by expansion joints, the driveway marked by two shallow gutters on either side. Sometimes his mother put a few flowerpots along there for color.

To Ellis, the main consequence of the concrete was that in the summer the yard grew so hot that he could hardly bear to be outside. The house itself was a boxy, two-story structure built sometime in the 1970s. It looked much like all the neighboring houses: aluminum siding, faux shutters bracketing the windows, a TV antenna stuck up over the roof, every room carpeted, cottage-cheese texture on the ceilings, pink tile in the bathroom, green appliances in the kitchen, and an unfinished basement that was his father's refuge. When the concrete began to gather the summer heat, they put box fans in the doorways and windows and ran them on high, so that loose papers and magazines lifted and fluttered and everyone yelled to be heard.

Ellis and Christopher had always been separated by a certain incomprehension, and Christopher had always treated Ellis with a measure of disdain, but he had also granted enough blithe kindness to pull Ellis's guard down before eventually hitting him with something from his arsenal of understatement—the stare, the sneer, the too-childish compliment, the narrow glance, the unanswered question, the joke not laughed at. Even this treatment, at least, represented a kind of attention.

What exactly had changed in the two years that Christopher was away never became clear to Ellis, and he could hardly even mount a reasonable theory of an answer. His only evidence was a series of long, low-voiced telephone conversations that his father had held during that time, slumped, staring down at the kitchen table, wary of being overheard. Years later, when Ellis asked his mother, she claimed to be unaware of any change in Christopher's manner. It surprised Ellis, and it took him some time to realize that her sense of permissible gossip was limited to the living.

When Christopher returned, he couldn't bear, it seemed, to talk to Ellis or his parents or even to look at them, as if to see their faces would give him hives. He made concessions for his father and, to a lesser degree, his stepmother, but he literally refused to speak to Ellis. Days passed before Christopher allowed Ellis so much as a chance meeting of eye contact. Ellis would have liked to return the disregard, but he wasn't as good at it, he couldn't entirely avoid, dismiss, or forget his half-brother who, after all, lived under the same roof and ate at the same dinner table. He didn't know what to do about it, and so he lived with it. Like a needle in his skin, it pained and pained.

One day he heard a voice over the fans, his mother's, outside. From the window he saw his father, his mother, and Christopher standing around a large black coupe. When he came outside his father was placating, "Darling—"

"We can't afford it!" his mother cried. "He's too young!"

Dad's gaze didn't quite meet Mom's. He turned and paced back and forward on the concrete yard. Tall and thin except for a bulge at the belly, he walked with an up-and-down bob, like a towering bird. While they argued, he looked bewildered and said over and over, "It's only an old Fairlane," as if an old Fairlane weren't a car, exactly.

Then he suddenly added, with fresh excitement, "And the radio only gets AM." As if a lack of FM made the Fairlane a go-kart.

Mom stared, then set her head back, held her arms straight and fisted at her sides, and made a long, thin wailing noise.

Ellis and Christopher and their dad watched her. Dad showed his yellow teeth, grimacing. When she breathed, he said, "Gosh, Denise."

She did it again.

Dad slouched, and when she stopped, he said, "Christopher's sixteen."

She took a breath, but Christopher broke the cycle—he opened the car door and slid into the driver's seat.

Mom said, "You're not driving that."

Christopher closed the door and stared at her. After a second, Dad said quietly, "Sure, you can go for a drive."

Mom shook her head, but hopelessly. Then she moved, at a run, around the car to the passenger's-side door, as if to get inside. But she turned to Ellis. "Go with him." She leaned to peer at Christopher. "Take him."

Ellis wasn't sure of her logic. Perhaps she felt that granting the car should in turn require greater generosity from Christopher. He felt like a pawn, but he climbed in. Christopher started the car and adjusted the rearview mirror. Cigarette burns scarred the dash, and from somewhere flowed a nauseating odor of turned milk.

Mom closed the passenger door. Christopher glanced at Ellis, in the thinnest possible acknowledgment; then he put the car into reverse and backed into the street, and they went away into *the big streets*.

They bore west. "Where are we going?" Ellis asked. Christopher had his left arm in the open window and his right hand draped at the bottom of the steering wheel as if he had been driving this car for years. He said nothing.

"Do you like it?" Ellis asked.

Christopher frowned.

Ellis put a hand out the window to cup the torrents of air. After some minutes he reclined his seat. He said, "Even with the windows open, it stinks."

Christopher's eyes never left the road. His hair licked around in the wind. They traveled over two-lane roads through a landscape of open fields of corn and potatoes. Beside the fields stood old barns, silvery grain silos, and tri-level houses with lawns polka-dotted by dandelions. For a couple of miles they traveled through a shadowed wood, then broke suddenly into expanses of empty furrowed fields wafting the odor of manure. Christopher slowed when entering the towns and accelerated out of them. Some of these towns had names Ellis recognized, although he was certain he'd never driven through them before. Then, eventually, they began to encounter towns with names he'd never even heard of: Hubbardston, Pewamo, Smyrna. They drove on without speaking, but Ellis felt happy. They covered distance without any intention that Ellis could discern, and to drive without purpose seemed original and exciting.

Hours later, when they got home, the sky was a lavender field spread with rough tatters of blazing yellow and red, as if gasoline had been thrown there and set afire. Christopher took the keys from the ignition and went into the house without looking back. Ellis stood a minute looking the car over. It was big for a two-door, painted black, with pits of rust on the doors and fenders and a broken nameplate on the passenger's side that said *airlane*.

Soon everyone called it the *airlane*. The *airlane* hooptie. The limo d'*airlane*. The Jefferson *airlane*.

Ellis never rode in it again.

Twelve

One day Ellis had come downstairs and found something strange in the living room. It lay on the coffee table, and it was built out of Legos. It was built out of his Legos, but he had not built it. It was impossible to say what it was, except that it was strange, and it was made of his Legos. A large, strange thing spread across the coffee table. He couldn't decide what it was.

The Legos had rested for years in a cardboard box in a corner beside the sofa. Ostensibly they were kept in the living room, rather than Ellis's bedroom, so that Christopher could also use them, but Ellis had only seen Christopher pull them out once, years ago, and then all he'd done was arrange the little yellow-headed knights and astronauts so that they appeared to be sodomizing one another. But Ellis had spent many hours with them, building spaceports and spaceships, castles and siege weapons. He had mostly outgrown them, but the previous winter he had pulled them out again and spent a couple of days creating his own design for a car with a little electric motor and a working manual transmission to gear it into higher and lower speeds. Once the car worked to his satisfaction, he'd yanked it apart again and dropped the pieces back in the box. And they had lain there since.

Now someone had taken them out and covered the coffee table

with this shambolic architecture of arches and bridges, spires and cantilevered extensions.

He'd never seen anything like it before, and he was annoyed. This wasn't any way to use Legos. Legos were for building forts, fire engines, moon rovers, rockets, and race cars. The little yellow-headed men were fitted with armor, helmets, and space suits; they came with swords and ray guns: their professions were clear enough, and your task was obviously to provide those little men with the equipment and vehicles that they needed to do their jobs.

But this! What was this? It was impossible to say what it was. Even the little yellow-headed men themselves had been disassembled and their body parts incorporated into the unruly thing: a yellow head here, a pair of blue legs there, haphazardly attached to the structure—if it was a structure. What kind of structure was it? Nothing like a building or a bridge. More like a smashed spider web or a pile of bones.

But there was—he sat a long while, examining it—there was a peculiar intelligence implied. The pieces were assembled in long chains that rose up to create interwoven arches and a radiating series of spires. Translucent blocks had been gathered in gleaming clusters. The overall form was impressively compact and dense and complex and intricate.

He had never imagined such an approach to Legos before, abstract, organic. The longer he sat looking at it, the more he appreciated it. As if this were a bit of alien technology. As if aliens made their technology out of Legos.

It wasn't the work of anyone in his family. Probably it had been built by one of Christopher's friends. Christopher was popular within a certain crowd at high school, and he often had friends in the house.

Elis wanted to know who had built this. But how might he find out? He couldn't really watch Christopher and his friends directly. He was afraid to do so. Christopher had a couple of buddies in particular who, whenever they could catch hold of Ellis, would give him

Indian burns, pin him down and dribble spit in his eye, pull his underwear up until it tore, knock him down and kick him in the ribs. And Christopher didn't even bother to watch.

Ellis imagined obtaining a fingerprint kit to pull partial prints off the Lego blocks, then comparing them with Christopher's friends' prints, gathered from drinking glasses and doorknobs. He imagined watching them from outside a window with a kind of periscope made with mirrors and PVC pipe. Or drilling a hole in the wall to view them. Or installing a two-way mirror. Or a surveillance camera.

Instead, the next evening he opened the door of his parents' room and left the lights off. He positioned himself deep in the room with a pair of binoculars. From here he could not see downstairs. But he had set a small piece of mirror at the top of the stairs, angled to reflect a view to him, which he could examine through the binoculars. His mother was out working; his father was in the basement. If someone came upstairs, he could hide in the closet until they were gone. He'd taken the Legos apart and left them scattered on the table.

Christopher and several friends turned on the TV and VCR to watch a horror movie. The movie glowed over them with writhing shades of green and blue.

He had to move around the binoculars, examining tiny bits of view and mentally assembling them together—a finger, an elbow, some shoulder, hair, a chin.

It was a girl. This surprised Ellis. He'd assumed the Lego builder was a boy. It was a girl. While he watched, she built steadily with the pieces on the coffee table. She wore her dark hair permed into curls, a white V-neck T-shirt, shorts, flip-flops. Ellis could see faintly the pale forms of her legs, extended forward, crossed at the knees. She sat beside Christopher, and when she sat back from her work at the coffee table, she interlinked one hand with his.

His mother mentioned that Christopher's girlfriend's name was Heather Gibson. Ellis had seen her around the school, and he knew—it seemed the kind of knowledge that simply hung in the air of the high school—that she was a favorite of the school's art teacher. Ellis also had the impression that she was a little aloof, but nearly every upperclassman seemed that way to him. She lived on one of the long straight roads a couple of miles outside of town and bussed into school.

Everyone also knew that Heather's father was a cop. One evening he came to the house in his squad car to introduce himself, using his handshake to crush fingers. No, he didn't want to sit. Yes, he would take a glass of water. He drank, and under his heavy moustache his mouth clamped and winced as if he had a tack in his shoe. He grunted and waited until all of Ellis's parents' attempts at conversation had suffered and died, and then he turned and sauntered out again.

Heather hung out with Christopher on the sofa, or in his room, or rode with him in the *airlane.* The others began to come to the house less often. Many days, Christopher's only visitor was Heather. She no longer touched the Legos that Ellis left on the coffee table. Still, he was fascinated with her. But to talk with her in Christopher's presence seemed impossible, and Ellis's internal default position held that he didn't want to anyway.

He might have never known any more about her, except that every once in a while she walked to their house from school, and one evening he met her alone in the early darkness. His mother had sent him to buy double-A batteries at the gas station at the corner. When he came out with the batteries in his pocket, he found her there on the sidewalk, waiting for the light.

She said hello.

"Christopher isn't home," he said.

"Oh," she said. Then, "My dad's working the night shift tonight."

"I liked that Lego thing you built at our house. A while back. You built two of them, actually."

"Dad says I fidget too much." She shrugged. "I don't want to go home."

He nodded.

"It's your neighborhood," she said. "Let's not stand here."

He stared at her until he realized what he was doing and grew embarrassed. He looked around—the park lay cattycorner from them. He said, "The park?"

They crossed the street, stepped onto the soft grass, passed under a row of poplars. They threaded through picnic tables to a small playground—swings, a merry-go-round, a set of monkey bars. He hesitated here, and Heather stopped beside him. The darkness was thick. A little further ahead the land sloped downhill to the creek, and Ellis could hear its happy burble. "That's a good swing set," he said. Below the vertical parallel lines of the chains and the U's of the seats lay a series of scalloped holes where the earth had been eroded by the passing of feet. Growing up, it had been his favorite because the swings hung from an unusually tall frame and he could fling himself to alarming heights.

Heather sat in one and began twisting side-to-side. A minute passed in silence.

"Do you think that Christopher and I are a good match?" she asked.

"I don't know," Ellis said.

She swayed forward and back. "Guys never tell you what they really think."

He spent some seconds considering this. He asked, "Do girls?"

"I try."

"Do you think that you and Christopher are a good match?"

She pulled her legs back, kicked forward. Soon Ellis had to step out of her way. At the furthest point of her motion, Ellis could hardly see her, then she appeared from nothing to rush at him, passed upward, returned backward, slipped away, vanishing. "I like him," she said. Her voice changed pitch with her motion, and Ellis recalled a word: Doppler.

He edged forward and held himself as near to her path as he dared. Her hair collapsed around her face and hid her eyes as she receded. "He doesn't talk to me anymore," Ellis said.

"But he's pretty sensitive inside."

"Maybe everyone is, I guess."

She laughed. "You two are a lot alike."

"I don't think so."

"It's true."

"Like what?"

"For one, you both look that same way when I say something that you disagree with. You tighten your eyes like that. And your nostrils."

He concentrated on relaxing his face.

"Do you think it's possible to think too much?" she asked.

"Sure," Ellis said. "Sometimes all I want is to be able to stop thinking."

"Dad says I think too much about things like my mom did. My mom is dead, you know."

"From thinking too much?"

"She had cancer. In her boob."

He said, "I'm sorry."

"I hardly remember her. How old are you?"

"Thirteen."

She said nothing. A set of flashing lights moved down the street. The siren was off, so the lights passed silently. Ellis moved an inch or two nearer to Heather's path of motion.

Rising, she said, "I don't want to kick you."

He stepped back again. Then he sat in the swing next to hers, pushed off, pumped his legs. He tried to move side-by-side with her. The chains of his swing squealed where they were bolted to the cross-bar, a noise that paused at the swing's suspended zenith of motion. "I haven't been on a swing in a long time," he called.

Stars then trees then earth. Earth then trees then stars.

"Do you have a girlfriend?" she asked.

He swung to and fro once before he admitted, "No."

"That's what I thought."

She slowed, then hopped off her swing in midair. Her silhouette floated against the stars before dropping.

"Should get back," she said.

He went backward and forward, liking the cool of the air. He felt he didn't want her to leave. He pulled hard and swung his legs.

"Are you coming?"

He pushed off at the top of the swing's motion. The air felt dense. Then he landed suddenly and tumbled forward onto his hands.

"Are you all right?"

"Yes." But his hands and knees were scuffed, and remembering what she said about boys, he revised. "Not hurt bad, anyway."

She started toward the street. "Smells like rain," she said.

The air did offer up a faint mineral odor. As they passed under the poplars, he watched the vague form of her back, the pendulum swings of her arms. They were nearly to the street, where they would be under the streetlamps, out of the concealing darkness, and he felt a dread that caused him to reach out to touch one of her swinging arms.

She stopped to peer at him. "What?"

"Want to hear a joke?" He had recently gotten hold of a book of risqué jokes, which he had studied a little obsessively.

"I guess."

"Knock knock."

"Who's there?"

"Fuck."

"I can see where this is going."

"No, it's grammatical."

"What?"

"Just say it, 'Fuck who?'"

"All right." She smirked. "Fuck who?"

"No, it's fuck *whom*."

She angled her head. "I guess," she said, wonderingly, "that's actually not the worst joke I ever heard. Pretty close, though."

She laughed. He laughed, relieved.

"Do you really want to know what I think?" he asked.

He could not see the expression of her face clearly. They both stood as if waiting for the other, until finally she said, "Okay."

"I like you a lot."

He feared she would laugh again, but she did not. She did not move or say anything, and that perhaps was worse. The trees made soft noises, and cars moved by with throbs of sound.

"Thanks," she finally said. "But I have a boyfriend."

"Yeah," he said.

She laughed. Then she stepped close and pressed her face into his shoulder and turned her head from side to side, a warmth and movement so unexpected that it hardly seemed credible. Clumsily he reached to the back of her neck, but already she was stepping away.

When they reached the entrance to the subdivision, she said goodbye as though she expected he would go in, and he did. He glanced back, and she was walking quickly away. Yet as he continued around the curve of the street toward home, he had a slippery sense of accomplishment. He glanced up and saw clouds obscuring the stars in the west.

In bed, he lay turning his thoughts and waiting to hear the rain. He lay awake until late, but he didn't hear any rain, and then he slept.

Thirteen

Boggs seemed to be oblivious, which was good. That was important to Ellis. And to Heather, too, he assumed.

In great caution, they didn't meet very often. Sometimes he didn't see her for three weeks, four weeks, and he grew anxious. Then despairing. The architecture of his life was lunacy.

Affair: the word astonished him every time it appeared in his mind. All he'd done was rediscover and fall for a small, dark-haired, scarred, slow-smiling woman.

She spoke with an emotional directness that startled him. "Sometimes you seem to even forget that you're in the world at all," she said to him once. "We see you, you know. You don't disappear."

That she happened to be married wasn't a part of the equation. That she happened to be married seemed simply strange. That she happened to be married to his boss seemed strange to the point of unreality.

He met her in cars and motels and in the duplex where he lived, but most often in her father's RV, in strip-mall parking lots and highway rest stops. Sometimes he helped her set up pinhole photos through the windows. But when they were in bed, the RV's little windows were always shut, the lemon-yellow curtains drawn, so nothing outside could be seen, and no one outside could see in.

He watched her working meticulously as she took and developed her photos; he watched her at the RV's dining table playing with experiments for her classes or some of her own work—an Elvis bust made from peppermint drops, small gold Christmas tree bulbs glued together into a crashing wave. She worked for weeks or months on these things; then they sat around for a while until she threw them away. She only persisted at the pinhole photography, and that erratically. When Ellis suggested some of her work could be displayed or sold, she scoffed, as if this were patent flattery, as if he'd suggested she could be a concert pianist or a Bolshoi ballerina.

Nearer in memory, however, were the movements of Heather's ribs as she breathed, the touch of her fingers on his skin, the minty odor of her shampoo and her own human scent. She called his penis Detroit; her vagina was Los Angeles. And they called it a *recreational vehicle* in a way that made it a double entendre. In memory, the RV meetings washed together warmly and settled into a few singular, wondrous impressions—movement against movement, minute action and response, vibrations and hums, vibrating, humming, crying, and shining like gods. Feeling as if this might extend infinitely.

"Tell me something you don't like," she'd said once, lolling beside him.

"*Moment.*"

"What?"

"Just the word, *moment.*"

"Okay." She laughed. "Why?"

"It might mean a fraction of a second, or it might mean minutes, or days, or weeks. In a history book it might mean years. It's completely imprecise. The only thing that's worse is 'a moment or two' or 'a few moments.' I don't know how anyone ever understands anyone else when we use words like that."

"You should let your inner dork out more often," she said. "It's cute." She rolled over and grabbed his penis with both hands. "Just don't get cocky about it."

"I think Detroit might be on the verge of an urban renewal."

Smirking, she climbed on top. "What if joking is a substitute for real communication?"

"Detroit doesn't know what you're talking about, and Detroit doesn't care."

Time drew on. Eight, nine, ten months.

Sometimes she said that things needed to change. On a couple of occasions, she grew angry. "We all need to grow up! We're not infants!" she cried. "I'll just tell him it's time for a divorce. It's actually not such a big deal. A divorce."

It made Ellis fearful. He wished he weren't, but the fear rose fierce and unwilled. He feared sabotaging Boggs, feared Boggs's reaction, feared losing his job, feared the end of his present life. He could hardly imagine doing this work without Boggs. He wished the break could be done in some way that would not hurt Boggs. She spoke of *soon*, but *soon* remained undefined. He had decided that if she asked him to give up his job and his friendship with Boggs, he would. But finally she didn't ask, and he wondered, what did *she* fear?

The covert nature of the relationship amplified, he saw, its excitement. The sense that they were getting away with something, that they should be ashamed, that no one else knew the emotions between them, that they created and inhabited a hidden world. When their relationship became public, it would become something different.

Shouldn't he want an ordinary life with her? He did. He did. And he had an obscure trust that it would come.

And nothing changed.

She said that her husband had closed away the essential parts of himself. Once, as they sat in the RV, she said, "John patronizes me because he decided that he's smarter than I am. That makes me pitiable. He's interested in you because he hasn't decided yet if he's smarter than you."

"He doesn't like your art?"

"He likes art in a theoretical kind of way, but he dismisses mine because he doesn't think that I work hard enough at it. He thinks that you have to choose your work and make it your life."

She stared at the RV's vinyl flooring.

"He's disconnected in some way," she said. "He doesn't quite touch things. Everything he does is, on some level, a game, or play-acting. What is that? Is it cynicism? I don't know. What's terrible is that he knows that it's not how it should be. He knows. He tries to find it. A connection. I used to think I could help him."

"But now?"

"It's who he is, is all."

"I don't really understand," Ellis admitted. "Maybe I don't know him as well as you."

"I don't know. I don't think I know him very well anymore. Maybe you know him better, in a lot of ways." Her voice had dropped, to almost a whisper. "Maybe I'm wrong."

"I hardly know anything about anything."

"Just, be careful."

Ellis liked Boggs. But he had no doubt that being married to the man would be a different thing from being friends with him.

There had been entire days on the road when Boggs spoke not a single unnecessary word. And when they examined the result of some inexplicable driver action—a driver who attempted to pass in a blind curve, or ran a red light, or pushed a grocery cart full of concrete mix down the street with the front bumper of a Camaro IROC-Z—Boggs could display a daunting misanthropy. "Seems like the only thing that makes humans different from animals," he said once, "is that humans can be *creatively* stupid."

There had been a salient event on the night that they finished working the scene at the other, earlier pig accident, PA1. They had spent twelve hours at the foot of a hill topped with groaning tri-bladed windmills, documenting evidence on the interactions of numerous pigs and eleven vehicles in a long, fog-bound pileup. They had finally gotten back to the rental and returned to civilization along a nearly empty highway, gliding between gently sloping hills faintly glowing under a half-moon. Boggs, driving, had hung several car lengths behind a semi trailer for a dozen or more miles. A small sign on the trailer doors said: *THIS TRUCK MAKES WIDE TURNS!*

At some point—Ellis didn't notice exactly how it began—Boggs started to edge nearer to the semi. He crept closer and closer, whittling down the gap, moving in ever more tightly. Soon the front bumper of the rental car was running scarcely two or three feet behind the blunt steel beams of the trailer. At 75 mph.

Ellis could see each textured ridge in the truck trailer's tail lamps' translucent red plastic. He glanced at Boggs; Boggs only reached down to adjust the volume of the CD where a voice was reading *Lord Jim*.

"*The rain began to fall again, and the soft, uninterrupted, a little mysterious sound with which the sea receives a shower arose on all sides . . .*"

"Boggs," Ellis said, gently. "You're doing what, exactly?"

Boggs didn't say anything.

"Something you'd like to talk about?" Ellis asked.

Boggs didn't say anything at all. He looked quite calm.

Ellis reached and turned off the CD. "Anything?" he asked.

Very slowly, Boggs began to ease away from the semi.

"You're okay?"

"Just got a little distracted," Boggs said. His tone was not that of a man who wanted to discuss it further.

Ellis said no more. He intended to bring it up again later, at a time when Boggs seemed more clearheaded.

But Boggs never did it again, and nothing, really, had happened—there had been no collision. There was no physical evidence.

The lack of evidence seemed almost to imply he might have imagined the incident. He had seen in his work that memory was strange stuff, that people often had firm recollections of nonexistent and impossible things. Not that that had happened in this case, but it wasn't impossible that the closeness of the semi had grown exaggerated in his memory.

And after all it was a tricky topic to raise with a man who was his boss.

There was another thing that Ellis recalled later, after the chaos that soon overtook his life, after everything had changed, after Boggs's strange effort had reached its end:

On occasions when they visited an accident location near a casino, Boggs always made time in the schedule to go gambling. He didn't talk about it. He simply announced, "We're going to the casino," and they went.

There—inside the windowless buildings, amid the endless mesmeric flashing dazzle, the clamoring of buzzers and bells, the gamblers in comfortable chairs—Boggs spent an hour or two loitering at the periphery of the roulette, craps, and card tables. All he did was watch. Until, eventually, he obtained a few chips. He put them down for one spin of the roulette wheel, one roll of the dice, or a single hand of blackjack. Then, win or lose, he walked away. Whether he won or lost, his attitude was calm, quiet.

Ellis had no previous experience in casinos, and he watched Boggs do this a couple of times before he learned to interpret the colors of the chips and realized that Boggs was gambling large sums in this manner.

One afternoon in an Indian casino in Colorado, Boggs set his chips on black, watched the roulette turn and slow, watched the ball drop on black. Then he took his chips and walked away. He was more than five thousand dollars ahead.

Seeing so much wealth materialize in an instant, as if by sorcery, made Ellis giddy. "Holy crap," he said, slapping Boggs on the shoulder. "You're rich. You're rich!"

Boggs walked on.

"You should convert it all into ones!" Ellis said. "Throw them into your room, and roll around naked on them."

Boggs grunted and stopped. He looked, very briefly, angry. But then he glanced away and became almost embarrassed. "It's hard to explain," he said. "But I want to understand something. It's hard to define. It's embedded in risk, I think. It's in the instant of transition between wondering and knowing. But you can't observe it, really, unless you have enough money on the line to make the event significant, to make yourself feel it." He looked at the chips in his hands, his expression tight and spiteful. "I prefer it," he said, "when I lose. That cuts into the thing I really want to get to."

He cashed out, and they went on.

Fourteen

Then Heather's father died.

His health had been in collapse for years, but that hadn't stopped his habit of burning and inhaling three or four packs of cigarettes a day. Ellis learned of the death in a brief phone call from Heather. She had not seemed especially close with her father, but he had been her only parent from the time she was four. Ellis couldn't go to the funeral, couldn't see her, couldn't comfort her. It was terrible, and he went through his days thinking of her with a trembling guilt.

When he did finally speak with her after the funeral, on the phone, she said that she was all right, more or less, that her father's lengthy illness had prepared the way for the end. But she was angry with Boggs; he had sold the RV.

"Does he know about us?"

"No," she said. "He doesn't."

"Really?"

"He always hated the RV. He thinks it's a distraction, a waste of time and money. He wanted to get rid of it a long time ago. This just gave him an opening to bring it up again. We'd have to transfer over the title and insurance and whatever. The problem was that I didn't dare to tell him he couldn't sell it—I was afraid I'd become too emotional, that I'd give us away. I wanted to cry as soon as he suggested it. I didn't dare argue."

"He could have been testing you."

"No, he just sees the whole RV thing as one more example of my arty flakiness."

Nothing more came of it. June passed into July.

Pig Accident Two came back into the office.

The four marriages of the driver of the Mercedes had resulted in a complicated family tree of step- and half-relations, and a new branch of claimants had appeared who had been excluded from the original settlement. They were attempting to reopen the case. "Can they do that?" Ellis asked.

Boggs shrugged. "That's a lawyer question." He told Ellis to pull out the file and verify their findings.

That weekend was the annual company picnic, which everyone in the office anticipated with feeble dread—a vaguely ritualized event where cold catered food lay on picnic tables and Ellis's colleagues stood drinking beer from cans or shepherding their smaller children through the adjacent playground equipment. Michigan's humid July heat made everything—even the air itself—seem over-alive, moist, fleshy. The company's COO, a man named Fasenden, stood on a cooler before his employees to give a speech. Fasenden had a big, bald, lemon-shaped head, and as he spoke he made small, pointing gestures that seemed to bear no relation to what he was saying. He complained that he had a cold, and after that he was hard to hear: *Teamwork . . . mumble, mumble, growth, but efficient . . . lessons learned, mumble—Improvements—Mumble goes to your paycheck ha ha mumble— Enjoy yourselves, that's why we're here, the company paid for this so let's enjoy ourselves— I will personally enjoy very much at least two helpings of dessert ha ha mumble—Enjoy yourselves, please mumble. Thank you. You're welcome.*

Ellis had never seen Heather at one of these events—she also skipped the company Christmas parties—but this year, to his surprise, here she was.

He smiled at her, careful not to smile too broadly, and said, "Hello," and, "Boggs told me about your father. I'm very sorry."

"Thank you," she said.

Then he avoided her. Her presence made him anxious and wretched and a little ecstatic with secret knowledge.

Boggs came to him with cans of beer. Ellis already had a soda in his hand, which Boggs silently took from him and replaced with the beer. Then he led Ellis a little distance away. "That job with the logging truck?"

"The logging truck hit by the Hyundai."

"The attorney fired us."

"He did?" Ellis was confused. The logging truck was a new job. "Why did he do that?"

"I don't know."

"We'd hardly gotten started."

"Exactly! We're trying to help him. We're on his team. He kept asking why the truck didn't move more. Well, obviously, because it's so heavy. Inertia. Hit it with a Hyundai and it won't move. It's not that complicated. I couldn't understand why he kept pushing the question. I blew it, Ellis."

"What did you say?"

"I got all worked up, and I explained who was the expert in these matters. And he explained who paid the bill for the expert."

They both stood quiet, looking at the cans they held.

This was, actually, not a complete surprise. A couple of clients had recently stopped bringing jobs to them. It worried Ellis. The world that they worked in was small. Reputation was important and fragile.

"I could try talking to him," Ellis said.

Boggs didn't answer.

"I'll pretend I didn't know you'd talked to him already, because one of us was out of the office, the weekend, whatever, and I'll talk him through it, just start talking before he can cut me off."

"No. Forget it."

"What could it hurt to talk to him?"

"He won't take your call. And if he does take your call, and he figures out what's going on, he'll sue us for harassment or something."

"I doubt it."

"That's what lawyers do: sue people."

"Just seems like we shouldn't give up work without a fight."

"Drop it."

"Okay."

"We can't give these people any openings," Boggs said. "If you talk to him, God knows what kind of a can of crap it will open up. They can always find a reason to drag you into court."

"I said okay."

"We're just fucked. That's all. I fucked it, and now it's fucked, and we have to move on."

"Okay, boss."

"Don't call me boss."

They returned to the party. There were about thirty people on hand, most of the company staff. Ellis talked and joked for a while with the other engineers and the administrative personnel. He helped set up a volleyball net and hit the ball over a few times. He ate cold barbecued ribs, potato salad, and coleslaw with too much mayonnaise. People gathered in cliques of three or four, talking for some reason in hushed tones. A half dozen played volleyball.

Ellis did not see Heather; she had somehow vanished. Boggs had wandered off and stood at the top of a grassy hill, alone, hands in pockets, looking away.

When he had finished his food, Ellis started up the hill, trying to think of something to say that would make Boggs laugh. Boggs seemed to be looking at his feet.

"Hey," Ellis called, and Boggs looked around, with a peculiar twist in his lips. Then he smiled, but too widely. And Ellis saw that Boggs wasn't alone, that Heather lay in the grass.

Ellis wanted to veer away, but it didn't seem plausible that he'd been heading anywhere else. Heather raised herself. "Hi, Ellis," she said. "I was telling John he should lie down and look at the sky with me."

"She claims I've never seen it before," Boggs said.

Heather settled back into the grass. "I'm just saying."

"Come on," Boggs said to Ellis, grumbling, lowering himself. "Lie down. So I don't feel like I'm the only idiot."

Lying side-by-side on the grass at Ellis's feet, Heather and Boggs looked as if they'd fallen from an exploded airplane. Boggs twitched his legs around. Ellis glanced back toward the picnic site, but then he lay down, beside Heather.

"I haven't done this since I was seven," Boggs said.

Heather said, "Just, *quiet*. Watch."

The grass bristled coolly on the back of Ellis's neck, and the air at ground level smelled wormy and coppery. In the south a head of cumulus expanded rapidly, changing form with unnerving speed. Below it, and all across the sky, scrims of haze moved from west to east. After staring at it a couple of minutes, the entire sky seemed to pulse slightly, advancing, receding, advancing.

"You can't paint it or photograph it," Heather said. "Canvases aren't big enough, and it's all about the third dimension anyway. If you two-dimensionalize it, it becomes a completely different thing." She moved her arm slightly, and the back of her hand came into scarce contact with Ellis's hand.

After a minute Boggs said, "Hey Ellis, you've read Chekhov?"

"A few of the stories," Ellis said.

"His plays are better," Boggs said. "*Uncle Vanya* is on the schedule in Ann Arbor in a couple weeks, three weeks, something like that. I'm going to make Heather come with me. You want to see it? For you, it's optional."

"I don't know—" Ellis said. Then he began coughing, to make time to formulate an excuse.

"Inhale a grasshopper?" Boggs asked.

"It would be great if you'd come," Heather said. "It's running for a couple of weeks. I'm sure we can find a day that works."

Ellis, set aback, said, "Okay."

Then he lay transfixed. With shallow breaths, he waited for the next thing. Heather's hand still touched his.

"Good," Boggs said.

A grass blade niggled Ellis on the ankle, a breeze shifted over his face, but these were only background to the touch of her hand, the point of pressure and warmth.

"I'm still pissed off about that depo last week," Boggs said. "Have you read the transcript?"

"Not yet," Ellis said.

"I'll let you try to guess the point in there when he threw his pen at me. The fucker."

Ellis pressed her hand. She pressed back. The grass clutched at him while the hillside careered.

Boggs said, "When the wind shifts, I can smell the stink of that barbecue." He sat up. Heather's hand departed. "I need to stop at the office for a file," he said. "I'll see you at the airport tomorrow?"

"Tomorrow's Monday already," Ellis said.

From the ground, he watched Boggs and Heather rise. Their faces appeared against the sky. He couldn't read Heather's expression. "I'm going to stay here," he said. "I like this."

"Right on. Sleep here if you want," Boggs said. "Just be sure to get up in time to meet me at the airport. We're only doing inspections. You don't need to change clothes or anything."

Heather gestured with one hand. Ellis listened to their steps in the grass until even that faint sound was lost.

His inspections with Boggs the next day went fine. One of the accident's victims had been killed by a burning semitrailer loaded with Life Savers candy, which inspired a few jokes. Life Takers. Life Enders. Life Whackers.

Boggs claimed that the name, Life Savers, and the idea of a candy with a hole in the middle, had been developed by a bereaved confectioner whose child had choked to death on a mint.

Fifteen

As Ellis slanted down the on-ramp, flashed his turn signal, merged left, and joined with the interstate's great flows of red and white lights, his phone rang. "Where are you?" Heather's voice asked from the tiny speaker.

"I'm coming."

"Are you going to be late?"

"I won't miss the start," he said, although, when he glanced at the clock in the instrument panel, he wondered. "I have my ticket. You and Boggs can go in."

"John isn't here either. His flight was delayed."

"Then why are you yelling at me?"

"I'm not yelling. I just hoped to see you first."

"Okay. I'm sorry. I'm sorry."

As they hung up, he ramped off the interstate. His nerves felt thin and tight. When traffic slowed, he made himself keep away from the bumper of the car ahead.

Chekhov.

Ellis didn't care about the play, and he didn't like this arrangement—his sense of guilt was hot and bright at the prospect of seeing Boggs and Heather together. But Heather had repeated that she wanted him to come, and when he thought of skipping the event entirely his guilt sent out a flare that wrapped around and urged him onward. As he passed a cluster of large, rectangular dorm buildings cast into tones of orange and sepia by sodium lamps, his phone began ringing again. He thought it would be Heather again, but when he looked at the screen he winced. On the third ring, he answered. "Boggs, are you with Heather?"

"She's already at the theater," Boggs said. "We drove separately. My connecting flight was late. Actually, I think she probably could have given me a ride, but she said she wanted to stop at the store."

"I could've picked you up. I can't believe we're all driving to the same place in separate cars."

"Welcome to America. Where are you?"

"I'm just passing Geddes Ave." He had almost reached the theater, but he would have to circle past to reach the parking lot. "Should I be wearing a tie for this?"

"I hope not. I'm not wearing one. You're running a little behind me. Look for us in the lobby."

"Sure."

"Bye."

"Yeah."

"Oh, wait, wait, Ellis," Boggs said.

The light turned yellow, and in front of Ellis an older model C/k 1500 pickup started braking. Mud was spattered over the rear of the truck, so that the brake lamps glowed a strange, irregular pattern through clumps of earth. Ellis cursed under his breath and glanced to the right lane for an opening. Then the driver changed his mind, and the pickup accelerated. Ellis, muttering again, followed through the intersection as the light went to red.

"What are you mumbling about?"

"Traffic," Ellis said.

"On the Matteson job," Boggs said, "I was asked if we can calculate the Volvo's speed at the time he passed that thing, the warning sign—"

In later memory the temporal dimension now began to stretch, as if someone had gently touched a turning phonograph.

On either side of the street, people moved along the sidewalks in clusters and pairs, and, although Ellis didn't see Boggs's tall shape, through the phone he heard vehicles passing near Boggs. The columned face of the theater imposed itself into view on the right. The mottled brake lamps of the pickup lit again. Ellis grunted, "Turn signal, jerk."

He glanced again over his shoulder and swung into the right lane to pass. His car hesitated for a few tenths of a second before it gave a rush of acceleration. In the left lane the pickup continued to slow.

Then Ellis glimpsed, ahead, an unusual motion. Unsure of what he'd seen, of size or shape or location or direction, he lifted off the gas.

"—with the flashing—" Boggs said. Traffic noise whispered behind his words.

Ellis still trailed to the right of the pickup when the motion appeared again, ahead and on the left, nearer now, on the edge of the pattern of pale light cast by his headlamps, a moving object, a figure, hunched, walking rapidly into Ellis's lane.

A sudden sensation of hopeless drowning—Ellis fumbled for the brake pedal, turned the wheel to the right—not too hard, aware of people on the sidewalk. He could see that he didn't have nearly enough distance to stop. But there remained a chance, if the shape in the street stepped back.

But the figure moved head down, with deliberate speed. A tall, thick male figure in dark clothing—Boggs. Wasn't it Boggs?

"—light—" Boggs said.

"Boggs!" Ellis screamed into his phone, as at last he managed to get his foot down on the brake pedal. "Move!"

The figure in the street faltered, his head turning, his mouth glinting. The ABS kicked the brake pedal up against the pressure of Ellis's foot. He dropped his phone while reaching to put both hands on the steering wheel and fought down against the ABS. The pedestrian in the street leaned back the way he had come, but nothing could be done now. Ellis already could not see the man's feet, obscured by the hood of the car.

With a crack of breaking bone and plastic and a slight shudder of the car—amid the continuing ABS-driven stutter and squall of the tires—the pedestrian swung sideways.

He pivoted unnaturally at knee-height, and came down on the hood, striking sheet metal with hip, elbow, shoulder, a calamitous metallic noise, and he balanced there an instant that went long, one leg up in the air, ribs and shoulder on the hood, an arm thrown sideways, his head approaching the windshield. Ellis shut his eyes. He also began to scream. But over his own scream he heard the violent pop of the windshield, chased by the patter of glass on his hands and chest. A shard bounced off the closed lid of one eye.

An impact sounded on the roof.

He looked. He could see ahead only through a vertical area of unbroken glass on the left and a small, sagging, jagged hole where the pedestrian's head had struck, and there the pedestrian pinwheeled through the space lit by the headlamps. Hair on end, pant legs and jacket aflutter, flinging dark blood from a wound in the knee.

The legs came down against the pavement one after the other and crumpled, and then he was out of sight. Cool air streamed through the gap in the windshield, and Ellis felt a painful straining of his leg against the brake pedal and the shape of the pedal underfoot while it jerked with animal movements, then chattered a last time, and the car lurched and halted. Ellis sat gasping, hands still on the steering wheel, foot still hard on the brake pedal. Through the hole in the windshield, he saw that he had stopped at an angle, with his right-front wheel against the curb. When he closed his mouth, he gagged. He coughed, worked a chip of glass forward, and spit it. "Boggs?" he said.

He reached into his mouth to drag out another fragment and looked at the shape of it—a tiny shining cube on the end of his finger—with a sense of incomplete comprehension. He thought: Boggs Boggs Boggs. Boggs up on the hood. Boggs pinwheeling.

He heard a horn droning. He gasped, gasped. Then, frantically, he unbuckled his seatbelt and stood out of the car. An SUV had struck the rear of the muddy pickup, and presumably the interminable horn was the SUV's. The SUV had begun to turn in an attempt to avoid the pickup, and it sat at perhaps a 35-degree angle to the lane lines. That collision didn't look very severe. Vehicles were stopping behind the SUV, while in the opposite lanes cars moved by slowly. Ellis saw all of this in a glance, along with the many stark lights along the roadway, and on the sidewalk an elderly man who gazed at him with an expression of curiosity. A stranger, who had just witnessed an accident. Ellis watched the man watch him, until he recalled again what had happened—the figure in the street, the sound of traffic behind Boggs's voice on the phone. He ran forward. At first he saw nothing, only the open lane, and he had a surge of hope, that perhaps he had somehow imagined matters to be much worse than they actually were.

But then he looked further ahead. He hadn't understood how far the body had been propelled by the collision. It lay beside the curb in a shadowy interval between the overhead lights, alone, legs inhumanly twisted. Centrifugal effects had thrown his shoes from him and pulled his socks halfway off.

Ellis approached at a staggering run, anguished.

But as he came closer, seeing now the man's form and clothes, he began to think that this might not be Boggs. The dark made it difficult to be certain, but the man's hair looked lighter than Boggs's, he looked thinner through the trunk of the body, and Ellis hoped, *Let it not be Boggs.* This was the only thing he wanted.

The man's face pressed the concrete gutter. Ellis fell to his knees. The man had a beard, but more closely trimmed and again of lighter color than Boggs's. Grayed. This man was probably twenty or thirty years older than Boggs. Ellis nearly laughed.

A woman crouched beside him. She had round spectacles and small fat hands. Ellis said to her, "I think he's dead."

"I'm a nurse." She edged him aside.

He sat on the grass between the curb and the sidewalk with his knees to his chest. He rocked forward and back, his sense of relief already gone. A broken body lay on the ground, and it seemed clear to him that in his impatience he had killed a man. He tried to recall the decision to pass the pickup on the right—it had hardly been a decision. He had seen the situation and responded.

Watching the nurse as she touched and manipulated the man, he felt a great deal collapse on him until it seemed he should be blinded or deafened, or perhaps the world should cease altogether.

"He's breathing." The nurse glanced over. "Can you find a blanket? Something to cover him?"

Ellis stood and took a step backward. He turned. On the sidewalk a number of people had gathered. One moved toward him, and Ellis looked at the approaching figure with a curious fractional delay between perception and understanding: Boggs, wearing a dark blue jacket and a white shirt open at the collar, reaching toward Ellis.

"I thought it was you," Ellis said. "I thought I hit you."

"I'm fine." Boggs gripped him on the arm and came close. But then he glanced away. "Although I might be sick. That poor guy's legs. I hate real blood. Are you okay?"

"I went to pass on the right, and when I got on the brakes it was too late. I hit him pretty hard. Probably thirty-five, forty miles an hour."

"I saw the damage to your car."

"There's a nurse. She wants something to put over him."

Boggs pulled off his jacket. "Here," he said. "Take it. Excuse me. I'm really sorry, but I'm going to be sick."

Ellis took the jacket and moved toward the fallen man, but several people now huddled and crouched there. "Give us room," the nurse said.

Ellis tapped a young man on the shoulder, and the jacket was handed down. Ellis stood peering, but because of the others he could see little. "How is he?" he called.

No one replied. He tried to press in, but an elbow nudged him away, and he lost resolve.

Traffic moved in the opposite lanes, people walked by on the sidewalks. The continued progression of time was surreal. Where had Boggs gone to be sick? He looked down at himself, at the clean, unmarked length of his clothes. The muscles of his right leg ached from pressing the brake pedal.

He returned to his car and stood next to it—a hole smashed into the windshield, a shallow dent in the hood. The laminated glass shaped itself around the hole like a stiff, glittering fabric. He felt as if a kind of error had been made in putting him into the center of this accident. If only he could work out the origin of the error and remedy it, he would be transported into his real life, in the theater, where he would sit watching a play, a little anxious, a little bored.

The SUV's horn—which had continued to drone on and Ellis had forgotten—finally stopped. A police car sidled up beside the broken pedestrian, lights orbiting.

Peering into the glare thrown by the headlamps of waiting cars, he could make out small intermittent markings made by the pulsing of his ABS.

He moved back along the street, counting paces. He estimated that he'd braked for almost 30 feet before the approximate point of impact, and then for another 80 feet before coming to a stop. Using these distances and a standard friction factor, he mentally calculated that he'd been traveling at about 45 mph when he began braking, and around 40 mph when he hit the pedestrian, assuming that he'd correctly estimated the location where his car met the pedestrian—no physical evidence of that impact showed on the roadway, and he could only make a guess from memory.

The measuring and calculating helped to calm and structure his thoughts. He stood at the open door of his car waiting for the police, examining a shallow dent on the roof, where the man's leg or arm or hip had struck before he was thrown forward.

Then he heard a short shrill warble, an alien sound difficult to connect with anything in the field of reality. It frightened him a little, and only after it had sung out repeatedly did he realize: his cell phone. He discovered it on the floor of the car. "Heather?"

"Ellis? Is Boggs there? Where are you?"

"Heather—" he said. He felt a dread of speaking, as if doing so would make events irrevocable.

"Looks like there's an accident. Are you stuck in traffic?"

"Where are you?" Ellis said.

"There, I see you. Is that your car?"

He looked from face to face along the sidewalk and saw her as she stepped into the street. She wore a black skirt and a black jacket, clutched a purse with one hand, held her phone to her ear with the other. He had a strange awareness of her tininess on the vast face of the planet. "Are you okay?" she asked.

Dark hair cut straight at the neck, teetering a bit on tall heels, she looked large-eyed, confused. Ellis examined her with an aching uncertainty. Where was Boggs? "Wait there," he said. He hung up the phone and put it in his pocket and hesitated, recalling how he had nearly laughed when he understood that the man on the ground was not Boggs. He thought, Perhaps I am not sane. Then his muscles moved and carried him toward her.

"You're all right?" she said.

"I thought I'd hit Boggs. But it wasn't Boggs."

Her mouth open, she peered up at him, and he was a little glad to see her stunned. At least he wasn't crazy to be stunned.

He asked, "Have you seen Boggs?"

"No."

He stepped back to look around. "I hit a pedestrian," he said. "I was on the phone with Boggs."

She moved to put her arms around him, and he felt off-balance, and then his legs lost strength altogether: he collapsed to the ground, and because she would not let go she came down with him. He sat on the street crying, the asphalt rough under him, a pair of headlamps pressing him with white light, and Heather still clinging to him. "Careful," he said, weakly. "Boggs is around here."

Then a police officer touched his shoulder.

• • •

The rear seat of the cop's Crown Vic smelled of soap, bleach, and plastics. Heather bent at the window and gestured with her fingers, back and forth. Ellis attempted to smile, but on his face it felt mangled. "I'm going to look for John," she called and waved again and turned away and glanced back and turned away.

The cop had already gone. A wire barricade blocked off the front seats, where a CB radio blurted numbered codes.

After a time he glanced out the window and saw, down the sidewalk, Heather running and—it seemed, faintly—Boggs's tall shape moving away in the distance. And Heather ran after her husband until she vanished.

She must have taken her heels off, Ellis thought. He examined the door, but the handle was inoperative. He watched the place where they had gone, but saw only the night, and eventually set his elbows on his knees, closed his eyes, and waited, listening to the world's small unimportant sounds.

He could still smell the odor of tires scrubbing against asphalt. Although he rarely thought of the accident that had killed Christopher—avoided the memory—the smell made that memory inevitable.

He knew that Heather would also think of it.

Christopher, his half-brother, too, had lain ruined in the street. Here, however, there was not the smell of burned flesh.

Three

Sixteen

After the accident, released by the police, Ellis went home. He tried to phone Heather, then Boggs, without success.

He lay awake late with a seething mind. His thoughts wouldn't move away from what had just happened.

"It's not illegal to pass on the right," the cop had said. He didn't look up from his paperwork. "On the other hand, jaywalking? Illegal." Ellis asked if he could ask the name of the man he had hit, and the cop peered at his notes and said, "James Dell."

Ellis rose and paced. The rooms of his duplex were haphazardly furnished with a mix of antiques and items from Target—the long, battered wooden dining table had only two cheap plastic chairs, and in the living room an ornate grandfather clock and an imposing writing desk stood over otherwise modern furniture. It was nearly four in the morning. In the windows he could see nothing but the darkness and his own reflection. He switched on the TV, hoping to distract himself. But the people on the screen looked like ghosts, and they spoke in such banalities that he couldn't bear it. He shut it off and moved toward the books on his shelf, but the uniform ranks of authors and titles seemed to glare at him with accusation. In his bag were several files from the office—he spread them on the dining table.

Here was PA2. He took out the familiar photos and turned through them, again. Dead pigs.

He thought of Heather and he thought of Boggs, of pushing the absurd pig rig in and out of the bushes. Heather had taken that photo of it on the picnic table with himself and Boggs, but she'd refused to help them with their work of taking pictures. That car had come around a curve and nearly hit him, making the sound of tires straining against the turn as it came, straddling the double yellow line.

And he had an idea.

He took out the photos that he and Boggs had taken of the Mercedes, turned through them again. This time he knew what he was looking for, and he saw it.

In the damage to the driver's-side door, at the leading edge of the door, along a vertical length of six to eight inches immediately below the rearview mirror, the sheet metal was folded toward the rear of the car—very faintly, just a folding of the first couple of millimeters of metal. But it was distinct. Something had caught the front edge of the door and pressed it toward the *back* of the car. Then, the impact with the tree had pushed the entire door severely *inward*. The damage caused by the tree had obscured the backward-folded edge. But now that he looked for it, he could see it in several different photos.

He took out his laptop, opened PC Crash, and ran a new simulation with a second vehicle. He set the second vehicle up and ran it around the curve on a trajectory designed to give the Mercedes a little sideswipe. With only a few minutes of tweaking, it worked—the second vehicle nipped the Mercedes, and the Mercedes went spinning off into the tree. He didn't have to use any of the dubious friction patches that he had used before.

He looked at the photos one more time and felt the pleasant relief of a lingering doubt settled.

But the feeling didn't last. It curled and fell as the name came again into his mind—James Dell.

• • •

As the sunlight in the windows began gathering strength, he was sitting in a stiff-backed armchair, listening to the clock ticking, ticking, and staggering him forward through time. He still hadn't slept.

Heather never called, and that worried him.

When the clock struck noon, he finally stood. He needed to see what he had done, and he did not want to hesitate. The police had impounded his car, so he phoned for a taxi. He asked the driver to take him to the hospital.

Sweating, he went through sliding, quiet, automatic doors and between white walls to a desk where he asked for the room of James Dell. The clerk looked into her computer. "Are you family?"

Ellis whispered yes, and she told him that Mr. Dell was in critical care, room 312.

As the elevator ascended and Ellis leaned in the corner, two stout nurses in teal scrubs complained to each other about their shift schedules.

Three hundred twelve stood open, but a curtain suspended from a curved track on the ceiling obscured much of the room's interior. Ellis knocked at the doorframe, and a woman with a flat, reddish face peered from behind the curtain. "Are you here for lunch orders?"

He shook his head. "I'm sorry." He moved around the curtain. The woman sat on a stool at the foot of a bed that held a man with a respirator on his face, an IV line in his arm, bandages on his head and arms. A white sheet concealed the rest.

"Are you a doctor?" the woman asked.

Ellis still wore the clothes he had put on the day before—slacks, a belt, a pale blue dress shirt now badly wrinkled. "I'm afraid not," he said. The heart monitor beeped in slow rhythm. Where skin could be seen between the bandages it was dry, pale, and darkly veined.

"You're crying," the woman said.

"I'm sorry," Ellis said again. He raised his hands and pushed the tears off his face. "I'm the driver."

"The driver?" She looked at him out of her flat face, then swiveled—her stool creaking—to the bed. The heart monitor counted time and Ellis stood, not moving, fearful of moving, of time, of the woman, of the man in the bed, of sound and smell, of air and light.

"I couldn't stop," he said.

"No," she said. "I'm sure." She looked at him. "Please. Don't let it bother you too much. I'm sure it was an accident."

Ellis, in his surprise, said nothing. The only sounds were of faint voices and clangor up and down the hall, of the heart monitor and slow breaths in the mask. The man's lidded eyes barely showed amid the bandages.

"Both legs were broken," said the woman, "with multiple fractures. And three ribs, punctured lung, cracked vertebra, internal bleeding. They're not sure yet how hard he hit his head."

Ellis recalled the pop of the man's head striking the windshield.

"There are more operations to do. But they hope he might show some alertness today." Her gaze drifted. "All there is to do is wait."

He found more tears on his face and pushed them away. Suddenly, the woman caught Ellis's fingers in her own hot, soft hand. He had expected her to rage at him, expected her to curse, to claw, to send him away, and now he had to ask himself, What did he want here?

"Are you—" he began. But the questions that came to mind were either empty or heartless.

After a minute he pulled away. "I think I had better go."

But he stood while the woman sat as if she had not heard, gaping at the bed. Eventually a nurse entered with a plastic apparatus in her hands. When she glanced at Ellis, he nodded and turned and stepped out of the room. For a minute he stood against the wall, letting it prop him, dizzy and gasping.

Seventeen

Another taxi. He watched the side window as it carried him home. Children with baseball bats stood on a corner. A handwritten sign taped to a streetlamp advertised a weight-loss plan. He passed a series of wide paved fields populated with ranks of glittering vehicles—car dealerships.

"Nice day," the cab driver said.

It was. The land lay ablaze with sunlight, as if some power wanted to be sure that nothing would be left unrevealed.

But soon traffic slowed, and they halted in the darkness beneath a thundering interstate overpass. Ellis's phone rang, Heather's name on the display. "Hey?" he answered.

"Ellis," she said.

He heard a trace of fracture and guessed that, somehow, things had gotten worse.

"I'm sorry that I didn't call sooner," she said. "John and I were up late. Ignoring each other. Yelling at each other."

"I went to the hospital to see the man I hit."

"You did?"

"He's bad. He looks terrible. I broke his legs, his ribs, vertebra, everything. He hasn't woken up. His wife said they weren't sure how hard he hit his head, but I remember. It hit the windshield. The laminated glass. Hard."

"It's not your fault."

"If I had stayed in my lane. If I'd had some patience."

"If he hadn't been in the middle of a busy street in the dark."

For some time neither of them spoke. Houses flashed by the window of the cab.

She sighed. "Have you seen John?"

"What's he done?"

"He hasn't called you?"

"No."

"He was very emotional," she said. "I'm worried. He got a lot of papers from his desk and spread them on the dining table. All of our financial stuff. Insurance. The mortgage. Our wills."

"Wills."

"The papers for the cars. He labeled folders and filed everything into neat stacks, wrote down a list of phone numbers—our lawyer, our financial advisor."

"He did all this last night?"

"Then he got on the computer and set up folders on the desktop for all of the financial files in there. I'm hysterical, and he says, 'That should be everything you'll need.'"

In the window streamed a mall and a thousand empty parking spaces. Ellis closed his eyes against them, but only gained the impression that they would go on forever. "One of his funny jokes, maybe?"

"He's upset about you and me."

"He knows?" Ellis hunched forward and pressed his fist into his eye. "How? We didn't do anything last night."

"I don't know."

"And he's leaving."

"I'm not sure that's his plan, exactly."

"What do you mean?"

"The lawyer. The financial advisor. The wills. He was turning everything over to me."

"He's leaving you?"

"His attitude was more final than that."

"You think he'd, what? Do something to himself?"

"I don't know."

"Someone should talk to him."

"He won't answer his phone for me."

"I mean someone other than you or me."

"Who?" she asked.

That was the problem. Boggs didn't keep friends. Ellis suggested a couple of men at the office that Boggs might, conceivably, be willing to talk to. Then, after an exchange of vague murmuring, they hung up.

Home again, he collapsed on the sofa, and there might have been a seepage of sleep. The grandfather clock ticked unvaryingly. Then it stopped: he had forgotten to wind it. He lay in the silence, watching the thousandfold flickering of the leaves of a locust tree in the window, sweat slipping sideways down his forehead. He had agonized over his actions with Heather. His affair with her. Yet knowing what he was doing had been different from fully apprehending its terribleness.

When Heather phoned again, the ring startled him badly.

"John called," she said.

"Okay."

She said nothing.

He would have liked to leave it at that. But he said, "And?"

"He's—" She laughed roughly. "He talked about me, mostly."

"He was trying to make you feel guilty."

"Yes."

"What did he say?"

"I don't know. Nothing, really. What a terrible person I am."

"He's horrible. He's ridiculous," Ellis said.

Silence.

He asked, "You really think he could kill himself?"

She said, "Last night he looked—older."

"What do you think we should do?"

"I can't even guess."

"I'm trying to think where he could be."

"He said something about the lake."

"What?" he said. "What lake?"

"I don't know. I was crying, I was yelling at him, and in there, with the crying and the yelling, he said something—a lake, the lake."

"Could be any lake in the world."

"There's a camping spot on Lake Michigan where we used to go, when we were first married. He went alone a couple of times more recently. He always liked it."

Ellis remembered. Boggs had taken a long weekend, and Ellis had met Heather in the RV while he was gone. When he got back, Boggs talked about the pebbled beach on the lake.

"I'll go," Ellis said. He wanted to take action. "I'll talk to him."

"Should I come?"

"Both of us together is maybe not a good idea."

She offered her car, but he said he would buy one.

Eighteen

Under an afternoon sky whitened by haze he walked the roadside past low houses, past square graceless apartment blocks, past gas stations, past a strip mall. An adult-entertainment cabaret named Lavender. An Applebee's. A sallow office complex with tinted windows.

After a mile and a half he came to a used-car lot. He walked among Fords and Pontiacs and Buicks and Chryslers and Jeeps, disliking all of them without particular reason, until he found a gray Dodge minivan—six years old, 87,349 miles. He looked at the interior, looked at the underbody, looked at the engine, then started the engine and looked at it again. Light scratches marked the hood, a crack vertically spanned the passenger's-side mirror, something orange had stained the carpet behind the driver's seat, but otherwise it appeared to be in good shape. A goateed salesman in a blue blazer with anchors stamped on its shining buttons watched. "You have a family? Kids?"

"No."

"Well, it's terrific for hauling cargo."

"Minivans are pretty safe," Ellis said. "You don't see a lot of fatal accidents involving minivans. Some, but not a lot."

"Huh," said the salesman. He thumbed and twisted his anchor buttons.

"At least I haven't," Ellis said.

When he had written a check and transacted the paperwork, he sat unmoving in the driver's seat a minute, then started the engine, let it idle, did not touch the controls but stared at them. He took out his phone and dialed Boggs, but Boggs didn't answer. He set his hands on the steering wheel to absorb the engine's tremble.

He had not driven since coming to a stop as James Dell flew into the darkness of the street ahead.

He thought about driving. In some gentler world empty of cars and highways and stoplights and parking lots and accidents, he wouldn't need to keep driving.

But that was a fantasy.

When he lifted a hand it shook, but he put it to the gearshift. The minivan lurched from reverse into drive. But otherwise the process of crossing the parking lot and turning into the street was routine.

He bought a map at a gas station, and with the map and his phone lying on the minivan's passenger seat he drove to the interstate and joined the westward flow. The broken white line flickered beside him, the odometer wheels rolled, the sun moved down.

He phoned Heather. "Is this a terrible idea?" he asked. "I find him—then what do I say?"

"Tell him that he's—" She stopped. "A friend. Tell him that he's loved."

Ellis laughed. "I'll be lucky if he doesn't kill me."

"You'll know what to say. You'll think of it." But her voice was uncertain.

"We could be overreacting. Do you think he could kill himself? I never would have imagined it before."

"He used to say that if I were to die, he'd kill himself. But he hasn't said that kind of thing in a long time."

Seconds passed. Ellis said, "What did you say?"

"When?"

"When he said that."

"I don't know. Why? I probably told him he was morbid. But I did kind of like it. At the time. But now I'd really like to be done with morbid. Do you know that John didn't tell me about his job until after we were married? He talked about his work in these very general terms. He said it was technical, said it was boring. I believed him."

"You never told me that."

"I was young. I met him in a bar. Some girlfriends and me, with fake IDs. We were nineteen, twenty. I was twenty. I remember he told me about Shakespeare's sonnets, how they were addressed to an unknown lover. He quoted some lines. He was older than me, he was an engineer who quoted Shakespeare, and I thought I'd met the most unique man in the world. Among my friends I wasn't the pretty one, but he only looked at me. I was drunk. I told him about Christopher that night, I remember, crying. I think that's why he didn't tell me about his work."

Ellis hated to hear this, anything of the detail and reality of their relationship, which felt like gasoline on his guilt. But he said, "I never asked how you met him. I should have asked."

"I worked at the desk in the library at that time, and he started coming in to chat me up. And he checked out lots of audio books. Audio books. He's been doing that for as long as I've known him. I thought it was quirky and charming."

"Well, I think so, too."

"It fit with the idea of himself that he wanted to project. Like that convertible, a terrible thing to drive in a place like this, with a real winter, and he has to explain it in court all the time."

"He does a good job of explaining it. Accidents are the results of driver actions, enjoy the road if you're going to be on it, so forth. He can go on and on."

"I'm sure he can."

They were quiet for a time. On Ellis's left a Jersey barrier ran between the opposing lanes of the interstate, and he passed a section that had been broken wide open, apparently by some massive collision. And further down, a long black marking ran along the barrier.

He passed a series of middle-size cities with big box stores by the interstate exits, then ramped off the interstate and passed white-clad homes and the dark vertical lines of telephone poles and reaching trees, the lowering sun flickering yellow in the leaves. He traveled northwest, slowing in the limits of little towns with a block or two of storefronts. Pizzeria. Barber shop. Bar. Pharmacy. Bank. Auto-body shop. Between towns, small ranch houses squatted over flat, aggressively green lawns. He passed a bar with a painted sign, THE CLOVERLEAF LOUNGE, a vinyl-sided structure with a couple of high, small windows and a sagging banner: "Bud Light $1.50." He came down a gradual hill to an intersection where, off to the side, a swath of raw earth lay leveled and heaped beside two enormous yellow machines. Ellis waited under a green light for a semi to clear the opposite lane, then turned left toward the lake.

He traveled a couple more miles before it struck him that he'd been in that intersection before. With Boggs. They had done an accident-scene inspection there—an old motel had stood on the ground now scraped down by the yellow machines. They had come to it from the opposite direction, from a vehicle inspection in a storage yard to the north. He remembered that the neon had been gone from the motel sign, its lawn had been untended and overgrown, but a handful of cars had stood in front of the rooms, and a shirtless man had been loitering in the parking lot, scratching his thighs while Ellis and Boggs dodged in and out of the intersection with measuring tapes and cameras. Three years ago? More or less.

A sign pointed at the park entrance.

Narrow, high-crowned roads led to three different camping areas, and Ellis drove through the loops of each, past RVs, SUVs, pop-up campers, pup tents, fire pits, tiki torches, lawn chairs, and a few couples, children, solitary men. None was Boggs, and none of the vehicles was Boggs's convertible.

He phoned Heather to be sure he'd come to the right place, to see if she had any ideas, and she directed him back to the most remote of the camping areas. He circled through it twice more. Then he drove the others again, then turned at the sign for the boat ramp, followed a short road to the water, and found the area empty.

He parked and walked down to the lake edge, where wavelets tongued the beach's small round stones. Above him, forest loomed and reached toward the water and the spectacle of the setting sun. Haphazard on the stones lay bits of pale rounded driftwood, a plastic milk bottle, a bicycle tire. Seagulls rose and fell. To the south a man and two children were prancing in the water's edge. In the other direction, smeared by distance into anonymity, a single figure moved. Impossible to say that it wasn't Boggs.

Ellis started that way. The sun balanced on the horizon and cast a street of dazzle over the water, and the distant figure resolved into a woman in a bikini top stooping to collect stones. Past her the beach lay empty. Ellis turned back, and a wind began to gust from the lake and pull his clothes out against his body. Inland, campfires glowed amid the trees, faint and skittish.

When he had come back to the boat ramp, he stood looking at the water, indigo under a cavernous twilight. The waves clicked stones against one another. Ellis thought of what he'd done to the stranger, James Dell, and to his friend, Boggs, and he felt that the condition of his soul, if he granted that such a thing existed, was wretched and very possibly beyond repair.

He drove away from the lake, out of the park, through the murk of the forest, between the open dark fields. At the intersection where the earthmovers had rid the world of the motel that he remembered, a rabbit bolted and raced toward the piles of dirt.

He turned through the intersection, but then stopped on the shoulder. The night had absorbed the twilight and stars glowed. He attempted to phone Boggs, but there was no answer. He sat with a gnawing in his chest, and when he could not bear to be still any longer, he stepped out of the minivan.

A single overhead streetlight cast a thin, pinkish illumination. He studied the asphalt, the painted lane lines, the timing of the stoplight suspended overhead. Little traffic moved through. A black pickup. A silver SUV. The drivers glanced at him and went on.

The accident that had occurred here, three years ago or more, involved a Mercury Grand Marquis—a chromed, civilian version of the big Crown Vics that the police liked. The Mercury had crashed into a tiny Ford Fiesta. The Ford was stopped, waiting for the light, when the Mercury impacted it from behind and sent it careering diagonally through the intersection, hitting two other cars along the way, then sliding off the roadway. It began that way, but the end duplicated Pig Accident Two: the Ford stopped with a telephone pole enfolded in its driver's side and the driver—a young woman, a cosmetology student—dead in her seat.

Witnesses reported that the Ford had been waiting at a red light. The timing of the stoplight relative to the collision was impossible to verify, but even if the light had been green, the driver of the Mercury had an obligation to attempt to slow and stop, and there was no evidence that the driver had touched his brakes. Also, the driver admitted fault. In fact, he told police he'd accelerated into the impact. He said he'd been *possessed by demons*—an assertion the police recorded without comment alongside driver's-license numbers, scene information, and vehicle descriptions.

At issue had been whether the Ford should have protected its occupant better. Through an evaluation of crush damage Ellis and Boggs had calculated that, at impact, the Mercury was traveling at about 70 mph, far exceeding any government test standard.

Ellis, with Boggs, had documented the tire marks that swooped across the intersection toward the telephone pole. Ellis followed the memory of those lines to the telephone pole, and at about waist height he found an impression of crushed and splintered wood where the Ford had struck. He remembered photographing it the last time he'd been here.

Scuffing at the base of the pole, he found bits of glass—maybe from the Ford, maybe from some other collision. He watched several cars move by. None was Boggs's.

Although the case had never gone very far, he and Boggs had referred to it often. *Possessed by demons.* The notion of demonic possession came in handy when faced with inexplicable driver actions.

He drove up the road to the Cloverleaf.

Inside, the dimness made it impossible to discern the color of the walls or the tables or even the tie of the short, broad bartender who stood projecting an attitude of everlasting patience. Ellis ordered a beer. When it was set before him, he asked if anyone had come in who looked like Boggs—tall, big, with blue eyes and a brownish beard. The bartender, studying a point behind Ellis, shook his head.

Ellis hunched at the bar, sipping his beer, looking around whenever the door opened. He wished he'd brought a photograph of Boggs. He felt tense with futility. He drank up and ordered another. The dark space of the bar was narrow as a railcar and filling with men in blue jeans, boots, and bas-relief belt buckles, slouching, laughing, turning from time to time to stare at a TV in the corner where a baseball game played.

"You lose something?"

Ellis discovered at his side a man with a circular face and quarter-circle shoulders, from which hung a sacklike T-shirt.

"Me?"

"Saw you standing around on the corner like you'd lost something."

Ellis hesitated.

"Maybe you found it," the circle-faced man offered. He smelled of armpit and peanut butter.

"There was a bad accident there," Ellis said. "Years ago."

"Sure, there's been plenty of accidents there." The circle-faced man grinned—tiny, even teeth with gaps between. "My girlfriend and I met in an accident there."

Ellis stared.

"Love works in mysterious ways."

"I guess so," Ellis said.

The man introduced himself: Mike. He said he knew a guy who'd accidentally shot some woman's dog while deer-hunting, and that was how he met her and fell in love. He knew another guy who broke into an apartment to steal a stereo and was surprised by a woman coming out of the bath, so he ran his mouth like crazy to keep her calm, ended up marrying her.

Mike talked on like this and led Ellis to a table under the little TV, where a woman with heavy shoulders and breasts and gleaming wide eyes sat over a glass of cola. Mike said her name was Lucy, and she said hello. When Ellis glanced around everyone in the bar seemed to be watching him—but it was the TV overhead. He searched the faces, and when he began listening again Mike was saying that after four years he and Lucy still had not married, which was his own fault. "I just can't seem to settle into the idea of being a claimed man." Lucy sat sipping her cola. She peered at Ellis as if he were a figure atop a far hill and she was trying to decide whether she had anything worth saying, considering the distance to be crossed.

A sheen of sweat flashed on Mike's forehead in time with the TV. He asked Ellis what he did, and Ellis explained and described, for an example, the accident that had occurred just down the road. As he spoke, an image pressed up out of the past: a police photo of the Ford at its point of rest, with the cosmetology student torqued toward the passenger seat, eyes closed, skin pallid, blood seeping from her mouth and ears.

"Sure," Mike said. "That's the same one. That's the crash where I met Lucy."

Ellis looked at Mike, then Lucy, and she did an odd thing, curling herself as if she hoped to fit into a crate.

"I was turning left," Mike said, "and Lucy was turning right and that first car was hit by a truck and came spinning through and whacked Lucy then me and she spun and I spun and we came together—" He clapped his hands and held them. "My door against hers. Our windows were broken, and I looked over and said, 'Are you all right?' and she said, 'I think so. Are you?' and I said, 'Except for my heart. My heart! I'm in love!'" He grinned at Lucy. "Anyway, the truck turned turtle in the ditch. I knew the guy that was driving the truck, too, by the way, my step-uncle. When I was a kid he carried worms in his pockets to scare me." Mike giggled and showed his teeth.

"It didn't roll into the ditch," Ellis said. "And the driver was demon-possessed."

"Demon who-what?"

"And it was a Mercury Grand Marquis, not a truck. I think we're talking about different accidents."

"No, no," Mike said, with the slow enunciation of a gentle man speaking to a moron, "the first car was stopped and hit from behind and came bang into her and me and then the first car went flying off the road. Killed a girl."

"Well, that is similar."

"Sure it is. What did you figure out about it?"

"We had the Mercury going seventy."

"A truck all right, a GMC. I know that because it was my step-uncle's. Seventy? No. I don't believe that."

Ellis shrugged—he was frustrated, but it didn't seem to matter. "Step-uncle?" he said.

"Banged the bejeebus out of my old Monte Carlo. Never aligned right again. And my uncle's still getting his tighty-whities sued off by that dead girl's family. Some good came of it, though, since we met." He winked at Lucy.

Ellis shook his head. He said he was looking for someone who might have been through that intersection recently, and he described Boggs and Boggs's convertible.

"Gonna be tough to find the guy," Mike said, "if that's all you've got to go on."

Which was right, Ellis knew. He wished everyone in the bar weren't looking toward him. He felt small and suspect, and the image of James Dell kept coming up before him. The air here smelled like urine. He had not eaten all day, and the beers were moving in him.

"Could be I saw him," Lucy said.

"You did not," Mike said.

"It was a blue car."

"It's green," Ellis said.

Mike laughed. But Lucy said, "Sure. Green. He had the top down."

"A convertible."

"He was playing the radio real loud."

"Did you hear it?" Ellis asked.

"Someone talking," she said. In the crowd noise and the noise of the television and the thud of a jukebox, they were now leaning close over the table, and Mike's little, bright teeth stood only inches from Ellis's face. "I saw him pulling out from the corner there," Lucy said. "Went north."

"Did you notice the license plate number?"

She only stared.

"Anyhow," Mike said. "Another drink?" Ellis shook his head. Mike pressed his fat hands on the table so that they flattened, and the table rocked as he stood and walked away.

Ellis asked, "What do you mean, he was pulling out?"

"He was pulling onto the road there."

"From off the shoulder? He had stopped? What was he doing on the shoulder?"

She shrugged.

"Went north?" Ellis said. She nodded, but her gaze was fixed over Ellis's shoulder. "How did he look?" he asked. "Happy? Sad?"

"Mike didn't ask if I was okay after the accident," she said. "He just sat there. He was crying pretty hard. The airbag broke his nose." She aimed her glare at Ellis atop his distant hill. She was drunk, he realized; her drink wasn't just Coke.

"That green convertible, was it dusty? Clean?"

"You worked for that awful lawyer."

"My boss and I worked for an attorney, but it wasn't the accident that you're talking about."

"Mike's uncle's been sued broke, so he's living with Mike now. Mike would've married me if it weren't for what happened."

"It was a different accident. And we just present a side of an argument, that's all. It's not personal. We operate in an argumentative, oppositional legal system."

"Mike would've married me by now, except for what's happened to his uncle and all that that's put onto Mike. How can he afford a wife, when he's paying his uncle's debts? Since the accident, his uncle can't hold a job, gets really bad headaches. But his uncle's the one who gets blamed, gets sued. It was an accident. He didn't want anything like that to happen. But you people come after him, and you take his guts out and throw them around the room while he watches. It's still going on. He has no money, but people keep calling."

"I never worked a case like that. It's a problem of memory. People misremember things all the time."

"It must be the same. How could it be so much the same but different? It was this kind of car or that, whatever. You weren't there. I was there."

Ellis cringed a little. He had been certain, but now he admitted to himself that it had been a long while, and this would not have been the first time that he had misremembered or transposed details between cases. Yet he kept referencing his memory, and the only vehicle he found there that had been driven in a demon-possessed state was a Mercury. He wanted to know if he was right—but did it matter? She wanted to put yet more guilt on him. He hated the idea. He felt as if his vessel for guilt were already full.

He tried to think of some evidence to corroborate his version of the accident, but all he had was the certainty of the vehicle. And then that certainty began to seem strange. Where could that certainty come from? Could he say how such a thing had gotten into his mind? It could be wrong.

It was a problem of memory. He hated such problems, because they implicated the mind, and thereby implicated everything. He wanted facts and analysis.

"You don't recall any other details?" Ellis asked. "At all? About the convertible?"

"You can't help," she said.

"I don't think so."

"You could get them to drop it all. You could talk to the family."

"You want me to talk to the family of the woman who crashed into the telephone pole and died?"

"Not the telephone pole. She hit the sign for the motel that was there."

He was relieved. She was certainly talking about a different accident. He remembered the damage on the telephone pole, and he remembered the police photos of the car next to the telephone pole. Then he had a suspicion.

"You said my friend went which way?" he asked. "This way, toward the bar? Or the other way?"

"This way."

"This way is south. You said north."

"South, then. I never was good at east-north-south-type direction. Are you going to help?"

"Why is Mike supporting his uncle anyway?" he asked. "With due respect, you ever wonder if Mike's just feeding you a line? I mean—his step-uncle?"

She opened her eyes and gazed at him with liquid, hopeless hate. And then Ellis felt a meaty hand on his neck. "What's that?" Mike said into his ear. "Say that again?" He sounded sad.

"I'm sorry," Ellis said.

"That's all right. I heard you." Mike pulled out his chair and sat. "My heart is large. I'm just doing the best I can, like you, right? Like anyone. Right? That's okay. It's all good." He peered at Lucy. "So you'll talk to him, but you won't talk to me?" He laughed. To Ellis he said, "I'm in the doghouse."

Lucy said, "Mike's a good man."

"Really, everything's beautiful," Mike said.

"I'm sorry," Ellis said, standing.

Lucy stared at him, but Mike said, "See you 'round," and then Lucy's expression suddenly turned melancholy. " 'Luck finding your friend," she said. Then, looking at Mike, she said, "If everything were beautiful, it wouldn't be so hard, I don't think. You should stop saying that."

Ellis started shouldering by people. In the parking lot he felt an impulse and ran to the minivan. A mile down the road he stopped on the shoulder and sat in the dark breathing heavily. He watched the mirror as if Mike's white shirt might reappear.

He calmed slowly. He had felt strangely terrified. It had to do with the idea that there were no answers to be found in these people. That she could be wrong about anything. That there were possibilities of error that could be pursued infinitely, into a madness of never understanding.

By force of effort he put it aside and convinced himself that the important thing was that someone had seen Boggs. He believed he had gotten the right direction out of her at last. He switched on the dome light, spread the map over the steering wheel, and looked at the line of the road he was on and its route south, the branchings of that line, the branchings of those branchings. Occasionally a car came up with a whisper and a light that slowly filled the minivan, then flashed past, replaced by dwindling red tail lamps and the chirring of insects.

He felt his face with his fingers and weighed his exhaustion and his options. He was very tired and the beer had fogged him. He decided he had to try to sleep a little.

He drove back through the intersection and into the park, turned into the boat ramp area, then eased into a swath of tall grasses at one side. A wind pushed at the tops of the trees, and the lake made a great open space where moonlight sparked on the waves. He reclined his seat and crossed his hands over his stomach.

The noises of the insects were apocalyptic. The day had been hot but now a chill settled into him. Despite exhaustion, he slept poorly. The figure in the road—James Dell—approached out of the darkness and made noises of impact as he broke at the knee and then came down on the hood with a leg up in the air, and Ellis thought also of the sheet-obscured figure on the bed, the noise of the breath in the respirator, the wife's hand gripping his own.

Nineteen

He opened his eyes and examined the tangled dark shapes of the trees, then stirred and looked at his watch. 3:11. He brought out his phone and dialed Boggs. Four rings, a click, and the quality of the quiet on the phone changed. Ellis waited.

"Hello?"

"Boggs."

"Who is this?"

"You know who this is."

"Well, to hell with you, too," Boggs said. "It is the middle of the night."

For perhaps an entire minute neither of them said anything. Finally, Ellis said, "Boggs, I'm really sorry."

"Great apology. Good job."

Another silence, and in the darkness Ellis had a sensation of the minivan floating, as if the lake had risen to bear him away. "Heather says she thinks you're on the brink of killing yourself."

"Do you know," Boggs asked, "why I answered the phone when I saw it was you calling?"

"No."

"Me either."

"But here we are," Ellis said.

"I don't think I said anything about killing myself. But death is a part of it."

"Part of what?"

"You can just leave me alone."

"Not if death is a part of it. What the fuck, Boggs?"

"I don't think I want to talk."

"But you answered the phone."

"I can't explain it."

"Where are you? Let me come see you."

"I've got hold of some things. I won't say it was a lifting of a darkness, but more like reaching the end of a road and saying, 'Now I see, this road doesn't go through. It ends.'"

"I don't know what you mean by that, but I'd like to."

"Please, don't talk that way. Have some dignity. And maybe the road ran off the top of a cliff. Maybe it ran smack into the sea. Maybe it was a road done up in gold brick and candy and banners and whiskey bottles, and when I say it ended, maybe I mean that I woke up."

Ellis smiled. "Maybe you're talking nonsense."

"Maybe. It's late. I can't seem to sleep. Here's what it is. I feel as if I'm trapped by the action of some huge machine, a complicated arrangement of motors, gears, shafts, all turning and grinding, and what's worse is that the machine is me, and its design is my own, which caused me to give you your job, to give you my wife, and finally to give you even my own job. To give you, basically, my life."

"I'm not qualified to take your job, Boggs. I don't want your job—" Ellis stopped. Having said this, he regretted how it implied the truth of the rest.

"Stay in it a couple more years and you will have my job, and you will be better at it than me. I loved the work, but I wasn't really very gifted at it. I piss off my clients on the soft side of things, and on the hard side I miss things."

"Everyone is going to miss something from time to time. Your knowledge of the field is incredible. It's not true that I was better at it. I haven't even done a deposition."

"You should. You'd do fine with the depos. They're just a matter of managing the flow of information. The reconstruction is the work. In that, your instinct is great."

This should have been flattering, but it only opened another hole Ellis didn't know how to fill. He said, "That guy I hit isn't doing well."

"I'm surprised he's alive."

They were quiet, and it seemed a mutual feeling might begin to seep into these intervals between speaking, but Ellis detected none.

"I've been thinking about risk," Boggs said. "Accidents are inevitable, so our relationship with them is a matter of managing risk. Actual and/or perceived. Everyone has his own relationship with risk and chance, his own choice when chance rises to look them in the eye. Sense of risk, of course, is a construct, partly a cultural phenomenon. The idea that bicyclists should wear helmets would seem absurd in many countries."

"I spent a few days in India once. The roads were insane. People drive the wrong way on divided highways."

"You understand. It's also an individual matter. Some drivers will take risks that others won't. And it can change from moment to moment. If you have a kid in the car, you might not gun it for that yellow light, for example. Everyone has a relationship with risk, flirts with it, tries to hide. Mostly hide."

"Sure."

"It's strange. There's this variable in the equation, for how much of a chance on your life you're willing to take to, say, get under that yellow light, but no one is ever much aware of it or quantifies it."

"And?"

"It's just a strange thing."

"I talked to this couple tonight," Ellis said. "They met in a car accident."

"That's lovely. I like that. You ever talk to Heather about your brother's accident?"

"Not really. Why?"

"Ever look into it? Pull up the old police report?"

"That's the last thing I want to do."

"Yes. Yes. Just curious. Found myself wondering."

Confused and wary, Ellis turned from this. He said, "That accident with the driver who was possessed by demons—what was he driving?"

"Something big. I don't remember."

"Come on."

"Really, I don't," Boggs said. "Why?"

"It's too easy to be glib over the phone. Meet me. Tell me where you are."

"No."

"I know you drove to the lake. Then you turned south. Didn't you?"

"I'm just seeing the sights. I'm engaged in a program of self-actuation and self-improvement."

Heather had interpreted the comment about the lake through her frame of reference, but if Boggs's interest was actually the accident site, then the correct frame of reference was the one Ellis knew.

"You're going to the sites again, aren't you?" Ellis said. "The ones we worked."

"Like a dog lifting his leg," Boggs said. "Like the old hunter in the leather chair in his den, looking up at the furry heads with their teeth and antlers mounted on the wall."

"I'm going to find you."

"Go back," Boggs said. "Let's don't have me make it about you."

And the line died. Ellis looked at the phone until the screen's backlight went dark.

He reclined in the seat.

It seemed to him that making it about himself might be all that he could really provide—to give Boggs a focus of anger sufficient to distract him.

The feeling of sleep never came, but suddenly he woke to a sky stained crimson.

He unfolded his map again and contemplated it. He recalled an accident they'd worked on a couple hundred miles or so to the south of here. Another somewhat to the east of that. Another south of that. Touring accident sites. Over the years, once or twice, Boggs had mentioned the idea.

He stared at the map, unsure of what he should do. Whether he should pursue this sudden veering. He wanted to help Boggs, but this driving around looked like a kind of madness. Or it might be a kind of baiting. It might be that Boggs only wanted to lead him away from Heather. Ellis wanted to return to Heather. But, he thought, it might be that he deserved to be led away from Heather.

He tried to set aside his guilt. He wanted to help Boggs, and he remembered the incident with the couple arguing in the Milwaukee airport, and how Boggs had ended it by drawing their emotion onto himself. But he did not want to be duped into a vain pursuit. He did not want to be a strange kind of one-man posse. But he thought of his admiration for Boggs and his friendship with Boggs.

He tried to analyze. One, he wanted to return to Heather. Two, he wanted to help Boggs.

It would not be fair to Heather to leave her; it would not be fair to Boggs to abandon him.

He feared to go after Boggs, feared entering a kind of irrational vector space. He told himself he should not act out of fear. But perhaps he feared, a little, too, to return to Heather.

He didn't know what he would do, but at the same time he suspected he would go after Boggs. Discovering that he suspected this, he immediately urged himself against it. He told himself that he should not act from fear, and that he should not act from guilt.

He wanted to set aside his guilt, but it could not be set aside, and he saw, with fear, the possibility that it would only grow, heedless of his choice now. He could feel the enormous force of his guilt acting on him—it seemed almost as if its force and vector could be calculated by a set of Newtonian equations. He thought of how, in situations involving extreme forces, things sometimes went flying in surprising directions.

He stared at the map, but it made no sense. He had to concentrate for a long while to make it make sense again.

Twenty

Waterfront cottages. A solitary and vast weeping willow. The cars on the road had their lights on. One by one they switched off, while the sky's first dark blush retreated before a more forceful blue.

Ellis pulled over for gasoline, a bottle of orange soda, a package of Pop Tarts. The stop, though short, sparked anxiety—if Boggs was on the road, he was gaining distance.

He skirted Lake Michigan southward, passing little towns and marinas full of idle white boats. A gift shop advertising seashells far from the sea. The outspread water was the color of rolled iron. In the distance dark clouds dangled wraiths of rainfall. As he began to move away from the lake, he crossed a terrain of flat reedy marshes where only the road seemed solid. At a light he waited behind an SUV and watched through its rear window a small screen that played a cartoon that involved computer-animated insects. He merged onto an interstate and passed between broad ditches and lines of wire fencing, while further out stretched cornfields, and here and there a house and sometimes a road running parallel to the interstate, a car there moving in near-synchronization with himself. The mile markers fled by. A white pickup tailed him for thirty miles; then he glanced in the mirror and it was gone.

He watched for Boggs's car, not only among the vehicles around himself but also in the traffic across the median. But traffic went by constantly and fast, his thoughts wandered, and he caught himself watching only the lane in front of him. A black tire mark arced toward the median. Another extended straight ahead, stuttered, then stopped. Another showed the doubled wheels of a semi.

When the phone rang, it startled him, and the body of James Dell leaped again onto the windshield—he answered breathlessly.

"Where are you?" Heather asked. "Are you coming back?"

Ellis told her about his conversation with Boggs the night before. He told her that he was going to look at a couple of accident sites. "I think I can find him."

"Why would he go to those places?"

"He told me before that he wanted to look at these places again."

"But why would he do that?"

"He has his sentiments."

"He's sentimental about his work, you mean."

"His work," Ellis said, "is what he would fall back on. He once told me he bought an old Camaro when he was a kid—not because he really cared about the Camaro or the parts but because it gave him an excuse to go look around in the junkyards. He loved looking at the smashed vehicles. He even took measurements of crush damage and made crude calculations."

"Do you suppose that's true?"

"You don't?"

"He told me that, when he was a kid, all he wanted to do when he grew up was buy a bunch of chickens and run an egg farm."

"He said that?"

"He likes eggs. Over hard."

"Maybe it was a joke."

"Who knows?"

"I've been trying to figure out if we should have seen that this was coming. Is it just one day he puts some files on the table and leaves?"

"Could be that it's been so long coming I stopped seeing it coming. It's hard to explain how disconnected he and I have been."

This was actually relieving. "Okay."

"I'm not sure this is a good idea," she said. "Chasing around after him. He's only going to try to hurt you."

"I'd like to come back."

"Come back, then."

"But I can't not try to help him," he said. "And I don't mind the driving right now. I could use a little time alone, to try to think and clear my head."

"I don't know," she said flatly, in a way that might have been bitterness. He wasn't sure. "I've known him such a long time, but the problem finally was that I never really felt like I knew him. It's funny how, in time, it seems like all the aspects of a relationship can invert themselves."

Faintly, he heard her breath catch. He said her name softly a few times.

Twenty-one

While Ellis drove, a series of calls came from the office, mostly from the cell phone of the COO, Fasenden.

Fasenden went around the office saying things like, "Ellis— Hi— Hey, just wanted to mention, you know, I saw you printed out that deposition in Tahoma font, and it's just a good idea to use Calibri instead, because, as you may know, Calibri requires considerably less ink than Tahoma. Which saves us money." In Boggs's and Ellis's absence the client calls on their cases would be routed to Fasenden to deal with, but Fasenden had no idea how to deal with them, and he was probably frantic.

Ellis didn't answer. He drove on. He was in Illinois already.

Finally he left the interstate and came to a stop on an empty north–south road between fields of low soybean plants. The landscape here was immense and flat, except for the bunches of trees that grabbed the horizon here and there. Electric wires ran between triple-armed wooden poles beside the road. Out to the far north stood a couple of large, metal-sided barns. In the south, a half dozen mobile homes lay clustered together.

Ellis stepped out of the minivan and walked the road's edge. He knew the place he wanted by the bent lip of a steel culvert that spanned under the road. A Thunderbird, trying to gas it on a rain-wet road surface, had veered off and hit the culvert, tearing open the gas tank. The occupants lived, but in the fire one boy lost 30 percent of his skin, lost his ears, lost his eyelids. His deposition had been an interminable accounting of medical conditions and complications—a life that might have been Christopher's if he had lived. Or, at least, that had been the thought that had edged into Ellis's mind before he forced it away.

The state highway department had been sued for leaving the sharp edge of the culvert exposed, but the case had settled out of court, and it appeared that the state hadn't bothered to make any changes to the culvert. Ellis stooped to peer inside: darkness, a trickle of water moving through. He walked the road shoulders, looking for a sign that a car—Boggs's car—had stopped. Cumulus cluttered the sky. Sweat traced slow paths down his skin. When he'd begun working for Boggs, he hadn't anticipated how very many of their cases would involve fires. But burn victims made juries sympathetic, so car fires attracted lawsuits.

It had been autumn when he and Boggs had inspected and documented the accident scene here. A lean mutt, white in the muzzle, had trotted across the harvested fields and stopped to watch. Then it wandered over to their equipment case and lifted a leg. Boggs had shouted and sprinted toward the dog, and when it ran off, Boggs went after it, grabbing clods of dirt from the fields and throwing them while the dog trotted ahead. The chase was hopeless, but Boggs ran until he became a small figure far away. He returned slowly, laughing. Later, as they drove off, Boggs said, "I read the other day that maintaining a pet dog generates as much carbon dioxide greenhouse gases as driving an SUV. And it crossed my mind that you could create a carbon offset business model that involves dropping labradoodles and chows with a sniper rifle."

Ellis moved slowly, peering at the ground. Looking for what? The knack for looking without knowing exactly what you were looking for lay in guessing where to look for what you didn't know. Was *here* or *here* or *here*, then, where to look? But it was impossible to say.

A solitary vehicle, a large old Lincoln, passed by, rattling, the driver's gray sexless head hardly higher than the steering wheel, wavering in the lane. It startled sparrows from the weeds at the edge of the road, and then the car was gone, and Ellis stood alone again. Nothing here but a culvert and a memory of a dog joke. Nothing. Nothing, and what had he really expected? There were a lot of places like this. He decided to go on, but he felt as a chill the notion that he might now be compounding any number of mistakes.

A strange insect of stunning size met its end on his windshield, and over the miles its parts lifted away. He entered again the hurly-burly of the interstate. A little Toyota with glistening rims flashed by in the left lane—it had to be moving at near 100 mph, and Ellis expected to watch it oversteer and begin barrel-rolling, bodies flying out the windows. Energy increased with the square of velocity. But the Toyota only dwindled into the distance and vanished.

That afternoon, he walked back and forth over an intersection of two gravel roads. To get here he had crossed an old, single-lane steel truss bridge with wooden decking and entered into a scrappy wood of weed trees. This was the place where he had found an unopened package of lime-green boxers abandoned in the weeds, and he and Boggs had spent a few minutes prancing around with underwear on their heads. It was also the place where a Honda had propelled itself deep into the side of a Jeep Wrangler and fractured the spine of the Jeep's driver. He could see traces here of any number of vehicles, but the tire patterns were disorganized by the gravel, and Ellis couldn't think of a reason to connect any of it to Boggs.

When he sat again in the minivan, he discovered that most of the day's hours had already been destroyed. He wondered if he should give this up, now, before going too far. He thought, I should give this up.

But he went on. He phoned Heather and talked once more about the idea that Boggs was traveling between accident sites, as if to keep the idea warm by the chafing of repetition.

She was quiet and didn't acknowledge what he'd said. He heard a TV in the background. "I keep thinking that this is my fault," she said. "I can't bear to touch his things. These folders he set out. His shoes. His magazines. His skim milk in the fridge. His mug that says, '*You know you're OLD when gettin' lucky means finding your keys.*' I hate that thing. I've been trying his phone number every few hours. Since you got him at three in the morning, I'll be up all night trying him."

"I'm not sure that's a good idea. You'll drive him crazy."

"Crazier?"

"He's looking at these places. It's about his work. His work. I feel like it would help, maybe, if I had a better understanding of what the work means to him."

"He loves his work. I don't know why. It's interesting, I guess." She didn't sound very interested. "He's an only child. Maybe that's it. That can explain anything."

"Have you met his parents?"

"They're normal people. He hardly ever talks to them. He has no real relationship with them, as far as I can tell. His mom taught high-school English. His father was a contractor. Built houses. Nice people. They're both about a foot shorter than John. He stood over them like they'd spawned some kind of yeti. You could just leave him alone."

"I can't turn from Boggs and let him destroy himself. I keep thinking of the guy lying in the hospital bed. Wrecked. Because I was inattentive."

"You're never inattentive. That's not a fault you have."

"Everyone is inattentive. The mind is an error-prone mechanism."

"So, you see, it's not your fault."

"You mean, accidents are inevitable."

"That's why people aren't supposed to be crossing the road in random places."

"Outside a theater, a driver should expect it."

"If you want to blame yourself, no one can stop you. But it doesn't mean that John is doing anything but needling you."

"If he is, I think it's a secondary consideration for him. He'd still be doing what he's doing."

"Maybe he's just lost his mind."

"I don't think so."

"What I mean," she said, "is maybe there's nothing to understand."

"It makes sense to him, I'm sure." Ellis passed a semi pulling a long tank with a polished surface that drew the world into shining horizontal lines. "Enough about him," Ellis said. "Tell me how you feel."

"I'll tell you what I feel." She was silent for a long while before she continued, in a rush of exasperation. "I'm sad."

He laughed. "I'm sorry," he said. But she laughed, too. "We're a couple of clowns," he said, "crying on the inside."

"I hate self-pity," she said. "I hate it. It's useless."

"Go on."

"But it's a cruel, cruel world. It's a darkness."

"Last one out turned off the lights."

"I was once in a bathroom stall," she said, "and someone turned out the lights as they left."

"What did you do?"

"Nothing happened. I calmed down and felt around to find the wall and I followed it out. But it was terrifying! A dark restroom is the archetypal darkness."

"Life is a dark restroom full of blind clowns crying on the inside."

"Is it a crime if a blind clown shouts fire in a dark restroom?"

"If a clown falls in a forest of deaf clowns in a dark restroom, does he cry on the inside?" He was laughing. "What are we talking about?" he said. He tried to stop his laughing, but it only grew worse.

"Send in the clowns," she said.

His diaphragm hurt.

"All right," she said. "It's all right."

"The crying leading the crying," he said.

They were silent a minute.

"I can't believe we're not together," she said.

"We'll be together."

"Really?" she asked.

"I'll be back soon."

"But will we be together, really? A couple?"

"Of course. I will come back. And there's no reason to hide anymore. Is there?"

"Do you want to?"

"Very much."

"It's going to be hard for us," she said. "To be together."

"No."

"I mean, to explain to friends. To suddenly now be a couple. When all that we've had until now were snatches of moments and everyone has understood our relationship to be something different from what it actually was."

"It might be hard at the beginning," he said, "but then it will be easier. Everything will be better."

"Are you placating me?"

"I just want you to be happy."

"No. Not happy. Listen, I need to be angry, and you won't give me any room to do it. I'm losing my mind. And you're out there. Why are you out there, when I'm so furious?"

He was silent.

"Say something."

"Do you want me to say I'm sorry?" he asked.

"No, no. I don't know. Maybe, I want you to say you're angry, too."

"I am. I'm very angry."

"You don't sound like it."

"I'm angry!" he shouted.

"I'm angry!" she cried.

"I'm fucking pissed!" he shouted.

Heather laughed, chokingly. "All right," she said. "We're both losing our minds. You will come back?" she said. "I feel like everyone has left me."

"Of course I'll come back."

"I'll hold you to that. I can be ruthless."

"You know—" he said. He stopped, debated, went on. "Boggs said something about Christopher, and it made me wonder what you remember about the accident when he died."

"What do you mean?"

"What do you remember?"

"Let's not talk about that now, for God's sake."

"We should've talked about it a long time ago."

"Maybe, but we didn't. Now John says something, and suddenly it's urgent?"

"You were at the Exxon station when it happened, right?"

"A Mobil station, or whatever it was. I don't want to get into this."

"Exxon, I think."

"I remember a Mobil," she said.

"A red sign. I remember it was red."

"Yes, Mobil."

"Exxon is the red one," Ellis said.

"Really?"

"I drove past one a few miles ago."

"I guess I could be mixed up."

"But you were there, right? Were you actually looking directly at the intersection when the collision occurred?"

"Stop it," she said.

"You don't want to talk about it."

"John is trying to get his fingers into your brain."

They said a few empty things. Gaps opened between phrases. She said goodbye.

He then phoned the hospital and asked about James Dell. Dell was still in 312, the receptionist said, but no one answered the phone there.

He put the phone in his pocket and bit down on his tongue until it bled.

Twenty-two

Later he caught the minivan drifting over the white line and into the rumble strip. He startled awake, but soon he was struggling again with his eyelids, and he had to defer to a staggering exhaustion. He took the next exit and followed a two-lane road until he came to an abandoned Gulf station, graffiti-tagged, windows boarded, pumps gone. He parked behind the building and reclined the seat to sleep.

His watch marked creeping minutes. A haze softened the moon. His back ached. He dialed Boggs a couple of times, without success.

Screaming, he woke from a dream he couldn't remember. Nor did he want to; to prevent its return, he kept his eyes open and sat feeling stunned and wishing the night over. But accidentally he slept again, this time in a deep oblivion.

He bought breakfast bars and orange juice and ate in the minivan, watching vehicles move between gas pumps, watching drivers talk on their cell phones with mirthless expressions. James Dell's pallid, desiccated skin suddenly hung before him, as if in a curtain, with the choking antiseptic odor of the hospital—he remembered that these had been elements of the dream that woke him the night before.

He started the minivan and began to drive.

• • •

He drove two hours, road to road to highway. More than three hours. He had in mind an accident site in eastern Iowa. He was sure Boggs would remember it. During the vehicle inspections, Boggs had found a triangular fragment of a man's skull embedded in a radiator. Gagging a little, Boggs had extracted it with a pair of pliers. They'd stored it in a plastic baggie.

On a state highway, he drove through land that was as flat as a concrete floor and planted with corn from one horizon to the other—ahead, behind, to either side, mile after mile, as if to meet a need of infinite magnitude for corn.

Nearing an isolated rural exit, he let off the gas, rolled past the ramps, and edged over to a stop. Here the land on the opposite side of the highway was planted with corn, but beside Ellis the land ascended slowly uphill. The ground below the hill was covered with milkweed, grasses, and patches of sumac, but up above rose a wood of great old maple trees. The single, lonely structure within view was a rectangular brick building just a few hundred feet off the highway exit. It was covered with extravagantly flaking white paint, and on one wall were three large, blue block letters: VFW. A red Chevy pickup, at least twenty years old, rested beside the building. In front stood a vintage howitzer, also painted white, weeds brushing the bottom of its barrel.

Ellis stepped out of the minivan on the gravel shoulder and walked the taper of the acceleration lane to the point where it vanished into the traffic lanes. Then he turned and strode into the milkweed and grasses and weeds, some of which offered clusters of small yellow flowers. When he turned, he could see the trail he had cut, pressing down the plants as he walked. He looked for a similar trail that Boggs might have left if he had been here, and for several minutes studied a couple of weeds he found broken, but he had no experience in this kind of tracking and could make no conclusions.

An hour passed, and more, as he searched. He stopped after each step and examined the ground and its objects. The delicate pale bones of a bird. A pizza box collapsing into the earth. An oval sink basin, strangely. Then, half-buried in the dirt, he discovered a wooden shingle.

He recognized the shingle. It was from a homemade camper, sided with wooden shingles, that had been carried on the bed of a Toyota Tacoma pickup. In the midst of a winter storm it had slid off the roadway and mired here in snow. A tow truck had come out to help. And the tow-truck driver had been killed when a semi came off the roadway, slid through the snow, and pulverized the tow-truck driver's upper torso against the back of the Toyota—like a finger in a stamping press. It was in the radiator of the semi that Boggs had discovered the piece of skull.

In the police photos nothing could be seen of the dead man, except for the blood smeared over the two surfaces that had killed him and a single booted foot extended from beneath the semi. "I thought that kind of thing was only supposed to happen in Oz," Boggs said, "to witches."

Police photos had showed distinct tire marks in the snow from both vehicles, and the tire marks showed clearly where the tow truck had parked when it was backed into place to extend its winch hooks. But the driver of the semi claimed that the tow truck had been parked partially in the right lane of the highway, and the snow on the road obscured the painted lines, making it hard to judge whether that was true or not. Ellis, however, had spent hours analyzing the police photos, and, using some photogrammetric techniques, he was able to prove that the tow truck had, in fact, been parked fully on the shoulder, out of the lane. It had been utterly satisfying to him that he could derive such a simple and direct answer to a problem. It was faintly pleasing to him even now to recall it.

After the shingle, finding nothing more, Ellis drifted into abstraction, staring at a runnel-fed low place, full of cattails. Redwing blackbirds moved in bursts and called in trills. The humid atmosphere resonated with the sun's yellow-white downward hammering.

Finally he walked up the acceleration ramp and to the building with the howitzer.

Crabgrass flourished in the dirt and gravel parking lot. Here and there lay a few scattered cinderblocks. A plastic lawn chair tilted on a broken leg. The building's windows were glass block, and Ellis could see nothing in them. He knocked on the door.

A stout, green-eyed man opened the door immediately—as if he had been waiting—and said hello.

Ellis said hello and the man nodded and shook hands earnestly and said hello again. He looked about seventy years old. "I'm sorry to bother you," Ellis said.

"Name's Tommy," the man said, shaking Ellis's hand again. "So you know, this hasn't been a VFW post for the fifteen years since I bought it from the VFW. I never have gotten around to painting." He scuffed a head of crabgrass with his foot. He wore a T-shirt marked with the logo of Harvey Mudd College and a pendant oblong of sweat. He said, "My wife, now in heaven, always said a man alone would forget how to live in the world. But I don't give a damn, I don't have anyone to impress." He had his hands in the pockets of his jeans and held his elbows flared out.

"A while back," Ellis said, "I did some engineering work on an accident that occurred down there by the ramp."

"You're an engineer? I used to design ball-peening systems. I designed ball-peening machines for GM and ball-peening machines for Ford and ball-peening machines for Boeing and ball-peening machines for the National Mint. Do you know about the famous eleventh-century swords of Toledo—not Ohio!—Spain? They could be bent almost double and they would spring right back, good as new. Guess how they did it?" Tommy stood happy and flexing his hands.

"Ball-peening?"

"Ball-peening!" the old man exclaimed. "The guys who knew how to do it took the secret of it to their graves and the idea was lost for a thousand years, until GM tried blasting their springs clean with steel shot instead of sand. They lasted longer! Ball-peening!" He bounced on his feet and leered. "I saved the Feds millions of dollars when I got them to peen the money-printing dies. I told them that they could take it out of my taxes. Guess what happened to my taxes."

Ellis felt his feet sweating in his shoes. "What?"

"Nothing!"

"I'm looking for a friend of mine," Ellis said.

"The gentleman in the convertible?"

Ellis lifted his hands but stopped short of grabbing the man. "When was he here?"

"Yesterday afternoon, stereo blasting talk radio at top volume."

"Maybe an audio book?"

"Never took to books, myself, audio or regular."

"What'd he look like?"

"I'd say like a man in a convertible—sunburned, windblown. He asked about this accident, the one you mentioned. The guy, Chuck, who died there, was someone I'd seen a couple of times. At the Cracker Barrel at breakfast. He was a grits-and-gravy guy. Personally, I hate grits." He sucked his lips and looked around as if he regretted this last comment. The great old maples behind the VFW building rattled under the pressure of a breeze. Traffic ran steady and fast on the interstate lanes. "I didn't know what happened at first. From here, all you could see was the flashing lights, the red and the blue, bouncing off the falling snow, coloring that part of the sky. The snow had been coming and going all morning. So I walked a little closer. It was a horrible mess. I stood above it, and I didn't know exactly what had happened, but an ambulance came, and I could see it was bad. I remember thinking it seemed strange, that mess, someone dead maybe, I didn't know yet, and all around it was a really beautiful morning. The air had that edge in it, that cleanness, like you should bottle some for later. A clear blue sky coming out of the clouds, sky the color of those original powder-blue Ford T-birds, the ones with the porthole side windows. And this land is pretty in winter, white all the way out. I never get tired of that. My footprints in the snow looked like the footprints of the last man on earth. I remember I thought, It's bad down there, but it's nothing to do with me. Nothing to do with me and I feel fine, just fine, I thought, By God, I'm happy. I hadn't had a clear feeling like that in a long time. 'Course it turned out it did have something to do with me, as I knew Chuck a little, and I felt pretty bad about it then."

They stood looking at the traffic. A convoy of five semis. A Prius.

"Funny how you think things like that," Tommy said.

Ellis made himself speak and asked a few more questions about Boggs—had he seen which way Boggs had gone, or paid any attention to the condition of the convertible?—but learned nothing. "I explained to your friend that ball-peening is badly neglected at most of the major engineering schools."

Ellis excused himself and returned to the accident site. He'd not noticed anything beautiful about it, which made him think he might have missed something. He scuffed around until a thought came, and he went back up the ramp and knocked and asked where Boggs had parked the convertible.

"About there," Tommy said, pointing.

The tires had made distinct impressions in the soil. The rear tires were both nearly bald; the front tires had four deep longitudinal grooves to channel water, and a pattern of hexagons between the grooves. With a pen, on the back of a receipt, Ellis sketched the pattern, then tried to brand it into his mind.

When he returned to the minivan, he took out his map again. He knew that Boggs had been here, but he didn't know where Boggs had gone. He thought, I'll never catch up by following him.

He thought, I need to jump ahead.

He began to drive again.

Corn plants covered the world. He drove under the double white line of an airplane contrail, as if his direction were being echoed, or affirmed, overhead. In the long quiet of driving, his mind turned again to what Boggs had asked. *You ever talk to Heather about your brother's accident?*

Twenty-three

After their conversation on the swings, Ellis had still felt blockaded from speaking to her by Christopher's presence. To go through him to Heather seemed as implausible as building a V8 from the contents of his bedroom—the task made a mockery of his resources and his tools.

He listened to them from his room, but he never could make out words. Their laughter upset him; he could not think what they might be laughing at, unless it was himself.

The Legos lay jumbled in their box. Now he found only a few doodles she had done, on a corner of a magazine, on the back of a piece of junk mail. They depicted random objects. A shoe. An egg. A hand. He stared long at these.

At the places where he knew she had been—the living-room sofa, a chair at the kitchen table—he put his face to the surfaces and smelled for her.

Then one day he went up the antenna. He had no particular intention of spying: he didn't even know that anyone was home. His father had had cable TV installed a couple of years earlier, and the antenna hadn't been used since. To try to grab the station signals out of Detroit, it had been put up on a 30-foot tower made of steel tubes. It had crossbars that formed a kind of ladder, and Ellis liked to go up to see the horizon and watch the traffic in the street, to be alone and above things.

A rain had fallen earlier in the afternoon, leaving the crossbars cool and moist. He paused at each rung to be sure of his grip. At the second floor, at Christopher's window, a narrow gap remained between the shut curtains, and in this gap he saw a movement, the color of flesh, perhaps an arm rising. He looked away, to the concrete below. A low chorus of engines muttered at idle in Main Street, on the other side of the fence. He listened for a few seconds. Then, leaning precariously, peering through the opening between the curtains, he saw Christopher, shirtless, facing him, and he was afraid that Christopher could see him, but Christopher made no sign of doing so. In front of Christopher stood a desk chair. His attitude and posture seemed odd. He twitched. Also, someone sat in the desk chair with a head of permed brown hair, Heather's, and she leaned toward Christopher. Briefly, Ellis thought they were talking, but then he saw that this was incorrect. Heather faced Christopher—who faced Ellis—with her head at the level of his hips, and he had his shirt off, and his pants were down. Heather moved slightly, put a hand on his naked hip, and he rolled his head. Ellis adjusted his hands, looked again down at the concrete. She was giving Christopher a blowjob. Ellis felt a weird laugh rising but swallowed it. Christopher made a meaningless vowel sound, loud enough to be heard through the window, and Heather's head inclined. Christopher took a small step backward. Heather turned and moved and Ellis couldn't see her any longer. Then Christopher, too, moved and could no longer be seen. A soft muted sound of Heather's voice came through the window as Ellis pulled himself back to the frame of the antenna's tower, arms trembling.

He moved down, stood breathing, examining his fingers—they had set into clawlike hooks, and to make them move and straighten required peculiar concentration.

After a minute he walked to the front of the house. He wandered down the driveway between the flowerpots—two rows of containers of empty dirt—and returned up the driveway. He went in through the door and closed it behind himself noisily, carried his algebra homework to the sofa, peered at the symbols without comprehension.

Had he believed that Christopher's relationship with Heather was immaculate? No, and yet he had not imagined the other either. He had even, in fact, tried to imagine it, but he saw now that his imagination had failed him. He also felt aware that his announcement to Heather in the park—*I like you a lot*—had been rendered pathetic.

He heard Heather coming downstairs, her steps entering the kitchen. Water ran. Chair feet rubbed on floor tile.

Soon Christopher came down the stairs and joined her. In a low voice she said something.

Ellis left his algebra and went to the kitchen.

The two of them sat on either side of the small kitchen table, Heather giggling. Ellis went to the cupboard and took down a beveled glass for milk and observed them sidelong. Christopher cracked a knuckle. Heather traced shapes on the table with the tip of her finger. Christopher looked over. "Ellis."

After being ignored for so long, to be addressed by him was stunning, as if the refrigerator had started yodeling.

"Ellis!"

Ellis sipped his milk, watched the floor.

Christopher walked over and stood before him, so that when Ellis looked up he saw his half-brother grinning.

"What are you looking at?" Christopher said. His tone turning soft-hard with insinuation, he repeated himself, "What are you *looking* at?"

He had known—Ellis realized—that Ellis had been at the window, watching. He had known, and allowed it to go on.

Christopher reached forward and shoved Ellis on the shoulder, hard enough to snap his head back against the cupboard. The milk glass hit the edge of the counter, fell, and broke.

Ellis nearly cried out and took a wild swing, but with an effort he held still. He wanted to be cold, wanted to make a comment that would wither Christopher's superiority—but his mind failed to propose one.

"Christopher," Heather said. "Don't be a jerk."

"Yeah," Ellis said. This seemed insufficient. He added, "Back off."

Christopher nodded. "Okay," he said. He grabbed Ellis by the shoulder and swung him around and pushed him toward Heather. "Go get her, champ."

Ellis stumbled to a stop in the middle of the floor. He hoped she might say something to aid him, but there was only an awkward—nothing. Silence. She didn't look at him.

"Hey," Ellis said, suddenly grown bitter. Still, she didn't look at him. "Here's a joke," he said. "Do you know the difference between a cheeseburger and a blowjob?"

She stood and walked past Ellis to the door. "Come on," she said to Christopher. Christopher grinned at Ellis, and left.

Twenty-four

Ellis avoided them, hid himself in books and earphones. He was unhappy, but he saw no solution to it.

Only a few days had passed when he heard, even through his earphones, the mallet blow of a collision in the intersection behind the house. Minutes later multiple sirens were converging there.

But he had heard a lot of accidents there over the years—he listened to a couple more songs, before finally deciding that he was intolerably bored and that the results of a collision this loud might be worth seeing. He left his room and passed through the living room, where his father and mother were watching TV. Without looking up, his mother said, "Don't be out late."

Autumn, late in the day, and the overhead lamps were flickering into feeble luminescence as Ellis followed the curve of the street and then passed between the collapsing brick posts that marked the entrance of the subdivision, into a stench of burning rubber, plastics, and other petroleum products.

The traffic idling on Mill Street included two semis that obstructed his view until he moved closer to the corner: a rear-ended station wagon on the curb had burned black from the rear bumper to halfway along the hood, and at the far side of the intersection lay a black coupe wrecked aslant over the front. The fire had been extinguished, but a haze of smoke still hovered and stank. Policemen and firemen stood around the burned station wagon, and several prone figures, evidently injured, lay here and there in the street. The scene looked familiar, like other accidents here, though certainly worse than average. Ellis regarded it without focus, almost in a state of daydream, until one of the people on the ground sat up and screamed, a woman's scream.

A cop held a bandage to her face and urged her gently down. "Calm, honey, please, please—" Ellis knew the cop: Heather's father.

And then, with that element of familiarity established, his sense of what he saw flickered and surged. He ran forward.

He had not imagined that the wrecked coupe might be the *airlane*. But it was, and the person screaming was—Ellis saw—Heather. A figure beside her lay under a gray blanket and did not move, and Ellis dreaded everything ahead.

He called Christopher's name, feeling the syllables in his mouth, their rhythm slow and clumsy, tasting of smoke and chemicals. One of the firemen caught him across the chest, but with a sudden fierce motion he slid under it and lunged forward. He pulled away the blanket: a hardly recognizable face, a horror—a mass of blisters, blood, and blackening, lips burned off white teeth, eyes and nose bloody holes—a blackened shirt, and the jeans on the unmoving body might have been anyone's, but he knew Christopher's white-and-blue leather sneakers. Someone drew the blanket over again, and a hand grabbed Ellis's arm, restraining him. Heather screamed, and the bandage fell and exposed her face, blistered and bleeding. Awkwardly she swung herself so that she landed against Ellis's chest. Terrified, he closed his eyes, but he filled with the smell of sweat and blood and burn and the sound of Heather's incoherent voice.

Her father pulled her off, and someone else dragged Ellis back. He wanted to run away, but he could barely breathe and the grip on him was too strong.

He was led to a curb, where he sat with his face in his arms, and let time pass. He couldn't understand this. He tried to let understanding come to him. He felt that his perception of it must be mistaken. Yet when he looked around again, nothing seemed to have changed. Christopher had been burned, but Christopher's car wasn't the one that burned, because Christopher's car was not a station wagon, and the burned car was plainly a station wagon.

People moved around him, and he tried to understand, and then he saw that the sky had fallen off and revealed the dark and the stars. He was still seated on the curb. The gray blanket shaped by the form of his brother remained in the street. But Heather was gone.

Heather's father crouched down, hat gone, hair smeared. "What happened?" Ellis asked. He shook, thinking of how his parents would react.

"Breathe, okay? Concentrate on breathing."

"That's not his car," Ellis said, gesturing at the burned station wagon.

"He blew through a red and hit the wagon, and it exploded. Then he went in to help them. Heather wasn't in your brother's car, thank God." Heather's father glanced around in agitation. "I couldn't pick her up until my shift ended. So she had walked over from school to the gas station to buy a Coke, but she saw the fire, and she ran over. She tried to help your brother. I'm sorry. Breathe, that's all you need to think about now. Breathe. I need to go be with my girl."

She hadn't been in the car. She had been at the gas station. Ellis worked to understand this. And then his mind, exhausted, gave up.

Later, with a feeling of waking, he startled upright in his bed. From another room came a series of small strange sounds. Ellis listened for several minutes before he realized that these were the whimpers of his father's weeping.

After Christopher's accident, Ellis scarcely left the house for several days. In the autumn cool the box fans around the house were quiet. Ellis hated the quiet; the time would have passed more easily in the summer, when the noise and wind filled the air.

He did wonder at the chances of it, because they knew of so many accidents in the intersection, and yet he'd never thought of it as a particularly dangerous place, never heard his parents or anyone else describe it that way. No one advised special caution there. Maybe—he thought—if one actually worked out the statistics, it would have seemed no more dangerous than an average intersection with the same traffic load. Maybe he'd seen so many accidents there only because it happened to be near home. If accidents tended to occur in intersections, and that was the intersection he saw most often, of course he would see plenty of accidents in that intersection. And if Christopher drove most often through that intersection, then it would be the intersection where he would be most likely to have an accident.

His mother cried unpredictably in sobs that took her like a seizure, up to and through Christopher's funeral. But the next day she said to Ellis, "We have to move on," and she resumed her old routines and sent Ellis back to school. She carried boxes into Christopher's room and began packing things. Dad, however, looked ten years older, and his sense of focus—never a strength—seemed to vanish entirely. At dinner he looked at his food until it lay cold. At night, Ellis found him standing in the living room, staring at the wall. He slept until noon or later. Often, at all times of day, he wandered into Christopher's room, looked around, then wandered out.

One day a ruined car appeared in the backyard, a thing crushed and bent across the front by enormous forces. Ellis stared at it from the kitchen window and again it took him some seconds to recognize the *airlane*.

He went down into the basement. His father was working sandpaper over a cylinder of wood. Ellis scuffed his foot, and his father stopped sanding but sat considering his hand—as if it were a little machine that he was unsure about operating—before he looked at Ellis and asked, "What do you think?"

"Mom won't like it," Ellis said, and then he went back upstairs.

Despite the collision, the broken *airlane* nameplate was still on the side of the car. Ellis tried the driver's-side door, but it wouldn't open. The passenger's-side door, however, opened. He crawled in and slid over to the driver's side. The damage to the car had pushed the dash and steering wheel close to the seat, so that he had to squeeze in. Setting his hands on the steering wheel, he imagined the traffic, the stoplight ahead, nearing the intersection, a car crossing there, the dusk sky beyond.

When his mother came home and discovered the car in the backyard, she went into the basement and began yelling.

She argued and pled for days, but his father would not allow the *airlane* to be moved. It was critical to him in some way that he could not articulate. "Christopher died in there," he said.

This was not true, Mom pointed out: Christopher hadn't died in the *airlane*, he died in the other car, the car that had burned.

Dad shook his head. He offered to build a shed around it.

In the weeks that followed, Ellis's father wandered around the house moving the furniture—never far, only a few inches in one direction or another, in a way that made entering a room vaguely disorienting. He began to go through several shirts a day and running laundry for shirts he'd worn only a couple of hours. For a while Ellis's mother complained, and then she ignored it, coldly.

Ellis and his mother moved out a little more than six months after the accident, and on his last night in the house Ellis spent a long while at the window, studying the *airlane*. It still lay in the backyard: under the moon the concrete of the lawn glowed a little, and in the middle of that space the black car sat absorbing light, perfectly dark.

His father was out of the house, no one knew where, when Ellis and his mother departed in an orange-and-white U-Haul. The latch of the small, hinged vent window on the passenger's side was broken, and the wind pushed in with a snickering noise. His mother made a three-mile detour to avoid the intersection where Christopher died. Winter had dragged to a muddy end, and they passed stubbled brown-gray fields, stands of leafless trees, an occasional barn and silo. The truck's engine rumbled and rattled and grunted, as if straining to the limits of its power, as if the things they were leaving behind exerted a gravity that could be escaped only by an immense physical effort.

Four

Twenty-five

Why, he wondered as he drove, was he especially cursed with a life marked with car crashes?

Well, there was the work, which was full of them. But even though vehicular collisions were the nature of the work, he was involved in those collisions only secondhand—with their evidence and aftermath. He was not a participant. And if that was a curse, then it was a curse that he had chosen for himself.

There had been the many collisions in the intersection behind the house growing up, where he had chanted, "Smash! Crash!" But those, too, were secondhand. Moreover, stoplight intersections were dangerous places. A driver had to observe the lights, check the oncoming and cross traffic, and also simultaneously manage velocity and directional changes. A lot of accidents happened under stoplights. He happened to live near one. Young boys were drawn to anything related to violence. A coincidence of circumstance.

Which left the accident that killed Christopher, and his own collision with James Dell. Those were the two accidents that had impinged directly on his own life. Although he hadn't actually seen the accident that killed Christopher. And it hadn't even been the accident that killed Christopher, but Christopher's own rescue effort.

But, even granting that one and adding the collision with James Dell, it was hard to say that two collisions in a life was an unusual number.

Perhaps it was only his chosen work that had led him into this mirror maze of accidents.

And why had he chosen the work? Because it suited the structure of his mind. Because it had come to him by circumstance. If he hadn't chanced on Heather in an airport, he wouldn't have entered onto this path.

Boggs had impressed upon him that, just as the mind's recollection of events was fallible, the mind's application to chance was error-prone. The mind constructed patterns—curses, luck, fate—where there were none.

No one lives an average life. He'd read that somewhere once, or heard it on one of Boggs's audio books, something by Jim Harrison or Richard Powers, perhaps.

He remembered Boggs talking about miracles. First, Boggs said, define a miracle. Let's say that a miracle is a million-to-one chance, i.e., odds of 1:1,000,000. How frequently then, on average, is one likely to encounter a miracle? But let's invert the question and ask: How frequently does one encounter the mundane? More or less continually, as we pass the days. So let's say that one makes an observation of the phenomena around oneself about once per second. This seems conservative, since while awake we have several senses operating continuously and simultaneously, and we are certainly able to make more than one observation per second—but, for argument's sake, assume one observation per second. Further, let's say that a person is typically awake and making observations for sixteen hours a day. Sixteen hours is 57,600 seconds. Multiply that by 30 for the number of observed seconds in a month: 1,728,000. That's a number well over a million. So, statistically speaking, one should easily encounter a one-in-a-million, i.e., *miraculous*, observation once a month.

The miracle, Boggs said, is that there aren't more miracles.

And what were the chances if he stayed in one place and watched for Boggs, that Boggs would parade before him? Well, if he picked the right place, the chances were high. But he feared he still didn't really understand very well what Boggs was up to. A miracle wouldn't hurt.

The place he had picked lay in southern Minnesota, six hundred miles from home. He came down a state highway on an east–west line that sagged and rose through a series of gentle hill slopes, then slumped into a lowland where bright signs and flat buildings appeared—a pair of strip malls, a supermarket, an Olive Garden, a McDonald's, gas stations, and various others, all accessed by a road with a lane in either direction and a center turn lane—a three-lane.

Along the access road he found a two-story motel, of 1960s vintage, seemingly the oldest structure here, facing the three-lane with a discordant ensemble of pastel yellow, aquamarine, and, on the second-floor balconies, salmon pink. Ellis parked under a semicircular scallop-roofed canopy in front of the lobby and walked to the back of the motel to check the view: the rooms here gazed without obstruction at the highway. He went inside and asked for a second-floor room, in back.

He stepped into the room and frigid air gripped him; mounted into the opposite wall was a roaring air-conditioner unit. Next to it stood a sliding glass door onto the balcony. A watery green-and-blue wallpaper flowed from the ceiling to a plum-colored carpet bearing a history of spills and heels. A bed covered by a polyester blanket, two wooden side tables, a dresser, a desk, and two hardback desk chairs crowded against one another. On the dresser stood a TV, and over the bed hung a little framed picture of a jumping swordfish—it looked as if it had been cut from a magazine. Ellis stepped onto the balcony.

To one side of the motel Ellis could see a Jiffy Lube; on the other side was a drive-thru bank. Ahead, across the highway, lay a golf course where people in twosomes and foursomes took practice swings, hit balls, watched them fly, settled into golf carts to drive a hundred yards, then stopped again, searched for balls, took practice swings, hit little spurting chip shots, stood around on the green talking, took practice putts, putted, all of this at a leisurely pace that contrasted oddly with the traffic's incessant flurrying. The highway had two lanes in either direction, separated by a wide grassy ditch. Once, a Suzuki Samurai had been stopped in that ditch, and the Suzuki's driver happened to look in his rearview mirror just in time to see a semitrailer sliding crazily, perpendicular to the lanes, like a chef's knife working sideways to gather crumbs. But not perfectly perpendicular—it was veering off the lanes, right toward the Suzuki.

He stood for some minutes on the balcony, watching the highway traffic, then went back into the room and retrieved one of the desk chairs. He sat and watched the road.

As the afternoon passed, the traffic in the westbound lanes clotted and dragged into a low-speed crawl. It was just starting to clear a couple of hours later when his phone rang. It showed a number that he didn't know. He started to set it aside, but suddenly it occurred to him that Boggs might call from a pay phone or a motel.

"Hello," he said.

"Ellis— Hello— Good day—"

During an instant of discombobulation, Ellis knew he knew this voice, but to access the knowledge seemed impossible. He knew he knew but couldn't know what he knew. It was like knowing that he had dreamed the night before without any hope of recalling the dream's content.

But then, just as inexplicably, suddenly it appeared—this was Fasenden, the COO.

"Are you okay, Ellis? We haven't heard from you, you know."

"Hi, Fasenden."

"Are you coming in tomorrow?" Fasenden asked. "Or Monday? Do you think you can come in Monday?"

"What is this number you're calling from?" Ellis asked.

"My wife's cell phone. Why haven't you been answering your phone? How are you? Are you doing all right? Are you ready to get back to the old routine?"

"I don't know."

"You don't know how you're doing?"

"I don't know when I can come in again."'

"Boggs sent an e-mail that said he was quitting. Are you quitting?"

"I haven't really thought about it."

"I am glad you haven't quit. You know—just so you know—I mean, you should be aware—you only have a couple of days of vacation left. Actually, three point five days of accumulated vacation time remaining."

"Put it down as sick time."

"Well, as you know, sick time is only to be used in time of illness. You'd hate to use it on a vacation and have it gone if you get really sick in the flu season. Especially since you're using up your vacation time."

"This isn't a vacation."

"No? What is it?"

"I don't know."

"Where are you, anyway?"

"Middle of nowhere. I have to hang up now."

"Wait, please, I have to tell you. Here's the problem—the real problem that has come up that we are trying to deal with while you're gone. I hope you can come in Monday, at the latest. The problem is the job with the pigs. It's reopened."

"I know."

"The attorney is pushing us for our work product. The stuff you did before and some new stuff she wants us to do. I can't even find all the old stuff."

"It's in the files. But it doesn't matter. That analysis isn't right."

"What isn't?"

"Our analysis. There's a second vehicle. It was a hit-and-run. I only figured it out the other day."

"Hit-and-run? No, the lawyer said it's a single-vehicle accident with some pigs."

"That's how the police reported it, and we followed along. But it's not right. It was a hit-and-run."

"It was?"

"Yes."

"Oh my. This is why we need you here. You know this stuff. You know, you left us in a bit of a lurch. All these cases open, and we don't know what's going on in any of them. We'll have to go back and re-create your reconstruction, basically. To really understand it, you know. To be able to testify on it. But we can't bill clients for the time to redo everything! So what do we do? It's a bad spot. The firm's reputation could be destroyed. We can't just drop these clients, we have to figure it out, but it's basically impossible. And who's going to do the work? We can't just grab engineers off the street to do this work. You know that. We need you back."

"I can't make any kind of promises."

"But you'll try? Will you tell me you'll try to be here on Monday?"

"Oh, sure." Ellis felt giddy. Fasenden's voice was making him giddy. It hardly seemed to matter in the slightest what he said to Fasenden. Fasenden existed in some other universe. "I'll try."

"Great. Fabulous."

Ellis hung up and laughed.

Soon the sky was hung with a scatter of white stars, and the traffic had thinned to a swift motion of lights pressing the speed limit. He phoned Heather and told her where he was, what he was doing, described the motel. "Do you think it will work?" she asked.

"Driving, I could miss him by a minute, I could pass him in the night. Statistically, my chances have to be better in one place."

"It sounds more healthy. Downtime."

"I guess."

After he'd hung up, he wondered if Boggs might come here at night. He thought it unlikely. No one visited old battlefields in the dark.

Hungry, he stepped back into the room and then stood looking around, a little dazed, after so much driving, with the shock of still being in the same place. He went out the front of the motel to the three-lane and walked on the shoulder. At a Target, he bought a bag of new clothes—two pairs of jeans, four T-shirts, and a week's worth of socks and underwear—then crossed the parking lot to the Olive Garden and consumed penne and chicken. When he finished, his stomach complained against the quantities, and he sat watching his glass of beer, the tiny bright sparks there that rose straight upward.

His waitress stopped to comment on his sunburn, and when he told her he'd had his arm hung out of the window of his car for a couple of days, she talked about her car, a Buick that smoked when she started it.

He set himself out on the balcony again as the sky, still sunless, began to brighten. Boggs will come, he assured himself.

On the morning of the accident the highway had been glazed by a light rain. When the man in the Suzuki in the ditch looked at his mirror and saw the jackknifed, overturning semi—like fiery crashes, the deep-pocketed hauling companies were beacons for hopeful litigants, so Ellis and Boggs had often been involved in cases with semitrailer trucks—coming broadside toward him, he ducked. The roof of the Suzuki was crushed flat, and the driver had to be cut out using a Jaws of Life, but he walked away. The semi, however, continued into the opposing lanes, flipping. Even more fortunate than the man who walked away from the Suzuki were the occupants of a Ford Taurus that passed under the trailer at the apex of its flight: police photos showed the Taurus parked beside the road, undamaged, except for the radio antenna, which had been hit by the flying semi and bent at a right angle, like a crooked finger.

Then the semi flopped onto the roadway behind the Ford and a fifteen-year-old Dodge pickup pulling a pop-up camper trailer crashed into the trailer's roof. Several seconds passed before a Toyota Highlander, traveling at approximately 64 mph, struck the pickup from behind, smashing the pop-up camper to pieces and forcing the trailer hitch into the Dodge's gas tank, igniting a fire that spread rapidly forward and backward. The pickup burned, the Toyota burned, the semi and its load of discount brand furniture burned. Two fatalities in the pickup and three in the Toyota. Only the driver of the semi, who extracted himself from the overturned cab with broken arms, survived.

Boggs was contacted just days after the accident by an attorney associated with the manufacturer of the pickup. After landing at the airport, Boggs and Ellis had driven to look at the Toyota. This had been one of Ellis's first cases, and the Toyota was held in a vehicle storage yard of a kind he'd never seen before, a collecting place for vehicles involved in potential or ongoing litigation. Towering racks held vehicles atop one another, three high, and each rack ran five hundred feet or so, ended at an aisle, and then began another set of racks, and these rows of racked vehicles ran out to a distance of a half-mile or more. Every one of the hundreds of racked vehicles bloomed with unique damage; the place was like a strange museum of roadway catastrophe.

Amid the rows roamed big trucks with long lifting forks, roaring as they accelerated and spun at high speed around the corners. When Ellis and Boggs found the Toyota, Boggs hailed one of these forklifts to pull the Toyota from its second-level rack and set it on the ground. The forklift then went away, diesel engine gnashing. Through the stacked vehicles, more of the lifting trucks were sometimes visible, charging around like beasts with great horns. Ellis looked at the vehicles to either side of himself—a Yukon with the front end flattened as if a slab of concrete had landed on it; a Ford Excursion with the circular imprint of a wheel in the damage of its grille; a Mini with the sheet metal ripped off one side as if it had run into a big planing saw.

"Ellis, hello?" Boggs said. "Still with us? What's going on in your noggin?" He was unwinding a plumb bob. He had already laid four tape measures around the Toyota.

"Just looking."

"And thinking?"

"Not really."

Boggs grinned. "Now that's a talent." Boggs shuffled and kicked his feet, still grinning. "As for me," he said, "my dancing frightens children and makes adults nauseous."

When they came to the scene—here, the place that Ellis now sat watching—the tire marks had been still visible on the pavement, though faded. The vehicles had skidded straight ahead, leaving longitudinally striped patterns on the roadway. Ellis had compared these with the tires themselves, and he noticed that the police had confused the tire marks of the pickup and the Toyota. Which was bad for their client, the defendant's attorney, because it meant that the Toyota had braked longer than the police had assumed, and hit the pickup at a lower speed, which made the breakout of a fire seem less reasonable.

"Of course," Ellis said, when he showed the error to Boggs, "we could pretend we didn't notice."

Boggs cocked his head. "That would be a little unscrupulous, wouldn't it?" He held Ellis's gaze a second, then shrugged. "Anyway, when you start doing stuff like that in this business, it catches up. The other guys are smart, too. Usually they figure it out, and we end up looking stupid."

He'd forgotten that incident, until now, as he sat looking at the place. Recalling it, Ellis experienced a regretful guilt that felt also like anger. He wished to say to Boggs, you *taught* me how to do this. As anger, it mounted in him, and then, during the slow passage of time on the balcony, subsided into its own feeble uselessness.

The wide field of hurt that had been stretched through his mind seemed to be weakening a little. He'd never understood the use of idle vacations, of endless sitting under the sun, but maybe this was it.

Behind this thought, however, regret suddenly flipped itself back into view. With a sense of compulsion he took out his cell phone and called the hospital and asked for room 312. The fifth ring cut off as the phone picked up. "Hello?" Mrs. Dell said, tentative.

Ellis hesitated.

"Hello?"

"I'm Ellis Barstow. I stopped in a couple of days ago."

"Yes?"

"I was wondering if there's any change in your husband's condition."

"They cut him open, did some things, to alleviate pressure, I think. And tests. Scans. He looks—" She was silent. "Not good." She breathed. "They say wait. Wait and see. They try to be kind, but they make me feel like a child."

"I'm sure they're doing their best."

"Sometimes when I ask a question there's a strange look. Maybe they don't like to say, 'I don't know.' Sometimes I wonder if they know anything, really."

"They're doing what they can," he said, without conviction.

"Fifty percent," she said. "I asked if he would live. Thirty, said another. Percent."

"I'm sorry." A pickup glided over the highway in front of him, pulling a camper trailer painted shining red, the sun dancing on it.

"As if we were talking about the humidity."

"It is meaningless," he said.

"I can't even think about it." She added, in an odd tone of complaint, "He loves me."

"Of course."

"He loves music. He's an excellent dancer. I doubt if he'll be able to dance anymore."

"I hope so."

"I should ask what percent they have on dancing."

Ellis laughed but caught himself and said again, "I'm sorry."

"No, no. You're kind to listen to me."

Some seconds passed.

"Are you still there?" she asked.

"I am."

"I'll let you go."

Twenty-six

That night he returned to the Olive Garden. He had the Buick-driving waitress again. She was heavy from the waist down and her face sagged with fatigued skin, but her smile was broad and earnest. She interpreted his return as a compliment to the food. She said the cooks here took greater care than at the Red Lobster where she used to work, and she tried to talk him into a dessert. He said no but ordered another drink.

The restaurant emptied, he sat contemplating his beer, thinking his work with Boggs had made him strange. No one except Boggs saw the road and the world as he did, so that they seemed to live in a world of the same stuff as everyone else, but terribly rearranged. No wonder Boggs had become his friend.

No wonder he didn't know what to do now except to look for Boggs.

His waitress brought him a piece of chocolate cherry cake, whispering, "Free free free!" It would just be thrown away, she said. He started eating only to placate her, but the stuff tasted marvelous. He forked through it slowly, then worked the crumbs up one by one, thinking to himself that it might be as good as anything that he had ever eaten. This idea made him teary-eyed.

The waitress stopped to pat his wrist. "It does that to me, too."

• • •

Late the next morning as he sat on the balcony, his phone rang. He answered, and Heather said, "I'm here."

"You—where?"

"The guy at the desk won't tell me which room you're in."

"How can you be here?"

"By the miracle of the Dwight D. Eisenhower Interstate Highway System. Will you tell me your room number?"

"I'm just surprised!" He told her the room number and sat waiting. Giddy. Anxious. She seemed to take a long time. And then even longer, so that he began to worry that he had hallucinated her call, that he had been alone for too long with his own brain, and now some of the synapses were firing up false echoes and distortions.

When a knock sounded at the door, he flung it open. Heather stood there—small in the dim hallway, hair pulled back, eyes red, tired, intent on him.

"Please—" he said, reaching. They clung to each other and soon were talking energetically, nonsensically. Suddenly Ellis lifted her and dropped her on the bed.

They made love with the clumsiness of delirium, then lay cupped together and watched the sky in the window.

When finally Ellis stood and dressed, they talked and joked about her drive, about the weather. She talked to the ceiling. Ellis drifted around the room. He came to the balcony door: although it was a Saturday, the traffic had started thickening again and slowing in the westbound lanes. He hoped that Boggs hadn't come and gone.

"I was a little afraid you'd send me away," Heather said. She laughed. Without leaving the bed, she was pulling on clothes.

"That's why you didn't tell me you were coming?" he asked. "I'm glad you're here."

"Everyone loves a surprise?" she said.

He laughed. "I don't care."

She went into the bathroom and ran the water. He opened the

balcony door and stepped out. A couple of crows hopped in the grass between the highway and the motel. He heard her emerge from the bathroom. "Is John out there?" she called.

"Nope."

A few seconds passed. "Hey," she said.

He turned from the highway to look at her. She sat on the foot of the bed, and she seemed to be looking at the highway behind him. He glanced over to see if something were happening there.

She said, "I'll go if you want."

"No, no." He hesitated, then moved into the room to stand in front of her. He knew enough to wait for her to go on.

"What are we doing?"

"What do you mean?" It had been a mistake, apparently, to go onto the balcony. But she knew why he was here. "We're in a motel room, talking."

"Really?"

"Yes."

Her gaze collapsed to the floor. "Could you possibly stop calculating what you say to the third decimal place?" She gripped the edge of the bed with her hands, then straightened and stood and moved and touched the bed, the wallpaper, the TV.

He said, "I'm sorry—"

"No," she said. Her face blushed, splotching white in the scars. "I just sometimes keep wondering," she said, "if there's anything more between us than shared disasters. What are we doing? What kind of fucked-up catastrophe of circumstance are we?" She laughed, not happily.

His breath shook. "We're just two people in a room."

"You're the brother of my dead boyfriend. You work for my husband, and you're his friend, and he's gone insane. It's not a good situation. It's a very complicated, very awkward, and very bad situation."

By now a liquid and opaque dread had filled him. His glance strayed between the tension in her neck, the highway, the swordfish. "You drove out here to break up with me?"

"We're just bonded by trauma," she said.

"It was a terrible accident," he said, "and I'm glad Christopher did something noble, if stupid, and tried to help someone at the end. But he never did anything to help me, and I never did like him very much. If you think that accident is all I have invested in this—"

A diesel went by with Jake brakes thundering. He glanced toward it, and she said, "Okay, go back to your balcony seat. Go look for your buddy."

"You know I came here to watch for Boggs."

"Okay," she said. "Go ahead."

He went outside and sat. He locked his gaze onto the roadway.

Some minutes passed.

In the room, something crashed.

He went back in as she pulled over the two bedside tables, then the desk. She pushed over a desk chair and then yanked the bedclothes to the floor. She turned and stood before him, gasping, her face strained.

"Calm down," he said.

"*Stop that!* I haven't slept in days. I don't know what's happened, to my life, all of a sudden. What happened to our lives, Ellis? Things were a mess, but they weren't like this— I can't stop crying. I don't know what anyone wants. And you say *Calm down*."

"I'm sorry," he said.

"Don't say that."

Then he didn't know what to say.

In the silence, she reached up with curious gentleness, as if grasping at a butterfly. He braced for her to strike him. But she brought her hand to her own face, gripped her cheek, and pulled down, clawing, nails trailing blood.

In surprise, he shouted and lunged, and they fell together onto the bed. "I hate you," she said, while he fumbled to restrain her arms. A small woman, but strong.

Finally he pinned her. She said, "I hate everything."

He panted. Blood trickled from her face. "Stop this," he said. "Stop this." She only stared at him, and he cried, "Stop this! I didn't ask you to come here."

"No. You didn't." But the resistance had gone from her arms.

He discovered he was squeezing her harder than he needed. He rolled away, stood flexing his hands. She lay unmoving except to breathe irregularly, staring at the ceiling, eyes streaming. His body shook, bright and hot. He sat on the floor. "You okay?"

She said nothing, went into the bathroom. When she came out, holding a washcloth to her face, his adrenaline had drained off, leaving him sagging. She sat beside him.

His heartbeat slowed.

She touched his hand. "I'm sorry," she said.

"Let's not use that word."

She giggled a little, weakly, or nervously. He shook his head. Then, in a loss of control, he laughed too.

"Go watch for John," she said. "I'll join you in a minute."

He sat moving his fingers experimentally, then stood and went onto the balcony.

Time passed, and when he looked back into the room, all the furniture had been set upright again, and she was gone.

He felt a rustle of panic. To find a clear thought was difficult. He'd never seen her do anything like this before, and he couldn't guess what she might do now.

He sat, then stood again. He tried to think. He tried to think clearly. Now, particularly, when everything and everyone had turned strange, it seemed important to be exact.

He tried to analyze, to review the variables of the problem. Heather had been his half-brother's girlfriend. She had liked his half-brother. Ellis, however, had not liked his half-brother. This difference had been obscured behind the fact of his half-brother's death, which made liking him or not into an abstraction. Then she had led Ellis to his job, and thus to his boss and friend Boggs. He liked Boggs. Heather, who was married to Boggs, did not like Boggs; or, at least, she did not love him. Not anymore. And now, having learned of the affair between his subordinate and his wife, Boggs drove and talked of death and risk.

The shape of the relationships was not a triangle but a square bisected along a diagonal:

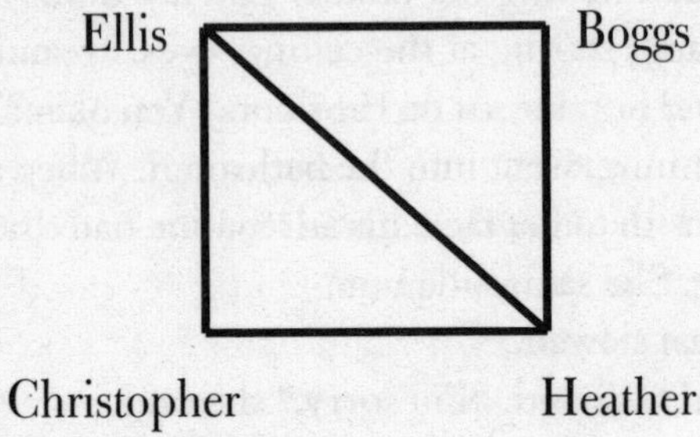

This failed to adequately capture the problem, because it also had a temporal aspect, which extended along a third dimension. He tried to visualize a shape for the events on that axis—but his mind couldn't focus on it, the shape eluded him.

But then, he thought, the situation was not a technical problem. Perhaps to try to understand it as such would only lead to insanity.

How then to understand? To see clearly? How to prevent everything from being contaminated with guilt, doubt, resentment, anger? Was that why she was gone? Was she gone?

A half hour later, she knocked on the door. She came into the room with two cold bottles of Chardonnay and a package of plastic cups. She offered one.

He took the cup, but set it aside and rubbed his face with his hands. "Was that you?" he asked. "Before?"

"No," she said. "I don't think so." The marks on her cheek amounted to three small scratches, in the place where the fire had scarred her years before. "This has been hard."

"It made me feel like I didn't know you."

"It's over." She fidgeted with the wine bottle. "Water under the bridge?" she said. "Or did I burn it?"

"No, you didn't burn it," he said. "But you really scared it." He held out his plastic cup. They sat with their wine, watching the road. After some minutes he said, "I figure he won't come here after dark, when he can't see anything."

She refilled his cup.

Into the evening they talked about inconsequentials and trivia, and he found himself laughing hysterically as the day's end came with the sun cutting under clouds boiling in from the west, so that the fading light and the arriving cumulus appeared like a massive collapse, an avalanche of glory pounding down.

When the sun had gone from sight he suggested the Olive Garden, but she wanted to walk farther, to a family-owned Mexican restaurant in one of the strip malls. The piñatas nailed to the wall were dusty, the carpet filthy. A pudgy girl of five or six wandered in and out of the kitchen gripping a naked Barbie doll. But the margaritas tasted strong, and the salty, greasy food filled him. He touched Heather's leg lightly under the table.

"How long will you stay here?" she asked.

"How long will you?"

"Why can't you answer a question?"

"A week." He said it and felt strings and cords all through him jerk tight. Why a week? He had no idea. And what would he do then? But he had announced it; he let it stand.

"Today is Saturday. You got here on Thursday? At sunset Wednesday, we go home?"

He said yes.

Twenty-seven

The next day he sat on the balcony, and Heather sat with him, or she went back into the room and turned on the TV, or she slipped out of the room without notice. She returned once with a change of clothes, a magazine, chewing gum, and then a second time with food and wine. With the TV on, she called out comments on a home decorating show. On the room's desk she accumulated a little pile of things she found along the road and in parking lots—buttons and dimes, several bluish pebbles, a few coffee stirrers, a pocket-size calendar.

He watched the wind striking the eighth-hole flag. A man stood on the balcony two rooms over and shouted into his cell phone about estate planning. "No, no! There are springing and *non*-springing powers of attorney!" For a long while in the mid-afternoon Ellis heard nothing from the room behind him except for the grunts and subdued voices of a tennis match on the TV and the fainter noise of ice crunching between Heather's teeth.

He asked, "You play tennis?"

"I've made things out of tennis balls. You?"

"No."

"It's kind of sad."

"Tennis is sad? Tennis is love and matches."

"That we don't know these things about each other."

She came to sit on the balcony with him, and through the remainder of the afternoon they talked in a lazy, intermittent, negligible way. It resonated in him differently from their conversations in the past, and it struck him that they'd never before had time like this. The sun might track over the sky, from its first appearance to its end, and the two of them remained together, not hiding, not racing the hour. The traffic always looked the same, more or less.

"Maybe we should stay here forever," he said.

She smiled.

The sun hung a couple of fingers above the horizon, and a fine layer of dust, or pollen, or pollution, had settled over his skin. "When we leave here," Heather asked, "what'll we do?"

"Live together," he said. "Get married?"

"If John just runs away and we never hear from him again, I'm not sure how hard it'll be to get a divorce."

He wasn't sure either. "Should've done it a long time ago," he said.

She stood and went into the room.

The horizon line began to eat into the sun. When he went back into the room, she was lying on the bed, watching him. "Why didn't you say something?"

"What?"

"If you'd said something, I would have divorced him a year ago," she said. "You pursued me, you found me. You knew what you wanted. I liked that. But then nothing. And me, I should make that jump alone? Me? I've never succeeded at anything. Never. And now I'm supposed to leave everything, with no word from you? When I've failed at my marriage. I've failed as an artist. I try to teach art to little kids, and the kids hate me." The left side of her lip twitched. She looked toward the room's door. "I couldn't pull your brother out of that car."

He crossed and uncrossed his arms. He lowered himself to the bed. He said, "I'm sorry." She groaned. "I am," he said.

• • •

They lay in opposite directions on the bed, his head at her feet, with a hand gripping her ankle. They were naked. Streetlights threw pale slants through the half-drawn windows. A yellow light on the ceiling advanced, strained to reach to the ceiling's middle point, held there, then collapsed back in a rush, only to return and work to reach the middle of the ceiling again. He watched this cycle several times, with empty fascination, like the action of waves on a beach, until eventually he became aware, too, of the traffic noise and realized that the light on the ceiling was made by the passing of vehicles' headlamps. He turned from it and moved his other hand to her other ankle, so that he held both.

"Your kids don't hate you," he said.

"A few do."

"You're not a failure."

She said nothing.

"I didn't know," he tried, "that you felt your art was a disappointment."

"Well," she said, shifting a little, "I don't take it seriously, which is the problem. I don't have the confidence to take it seriously."

"I think the pinhole photos are fantastic."

"I'm not very creative or interesting. I'm not very smart. I don't have confidence. I don't know what I want." She laughed. "Should I go on?"

"You don't believe any of that, I hope."

He heard the sheets shift as she shrugged. "I'm just telling you how I feel. I think some of my problems are just a part of growing up without a mother. No one taught me how to live as a woman in the world. I hate this kind of talk. Let's talk about something else."

"I'm sure you can be a great artist if you want. I'll insist. I'll lock you in a dungeon and bring you pieces of trash and Legos to work with."

"Maybe I just want to paint kittens and rainbows. Flags and eagles."

"Eagles and kittens?"

"Kitten-eating eagle flags," she said.

"Sounds more like your style."

He clung to her ankles and felt her settle a hand between his thighs. Eventually they slept that way.

The next day, she came and went again, returning with food, then with vanilla-scented sunscreen. He waited for the times when she was out before he used the bathroom. For some reason he didn't like to admit that he had to abandon his post even for that. And he hurried in and out of the bathroom because, while he felt sure Boggs would actually stop to look at the site, he couldn't guess whether it would be for an hour or just a minute.

Later, Heather came out onto the balcony with a motel pen and pad of paper. She drew a delicate scene in miniature of the highway and the eighth fairway and flag in blue ballpoint, crosshatched for texture. Looming over the scene and looking down were giant flower heads with elaborately realistic human faces. Heather rolled the sleeves of her T-shirt to her shoulders and turned her face to the sun. "I always wanted to live on a beach."

"We can do that," he said.

People on the golf course played with flashlights that night, hitting green-glowing balls. Ellis and Heather left the room and walked to the Olive Garden for dinner. The waitress who had given him cake sat in the booth with them to tell an incoherent story about her husband's hair plugs. Back at the motel room, they joked of Detroit and Los Angeles, muscle and glamour, steel and lights, blue collar and cleavage.

He arose before her the next morning, and he sat outside in the early cool, thinking pleasantly of sleeping in the same bed with her through a night and rising and not leaving, of talking lazily with her, of watching her step from the shower towel-wrapped and hair wet, of detecting the scent of her in the bed and in her towel, of watching her stretch in the morning, up on her toes. Of domestic intimacies that he seized and understood without complication. Much in his life seemed unmanageably complicated, but these things were simple and granted him a knowledge of her that he had lacked.

She sat on the balcony toying with the matchbooks, folding and fitting their flaps together in various schemes of assembly. "What are you trying to make?" he asked.

She shrugged. "I don't know." She pulled them apart and began again and again, sometimes working in a couple of Marlboro cigarette packs she had also found. She created something like a spiral staircase, then took it apart and worked out a swanlike creature. She had a few pieces of broken mirror as well, which she tucked into the crevices of the matchbook sculpture, so that here and there it shone. She hunched over the matchbooks for a long while, making tiny adjustments with small, sure fingers, and she looked absolutely capable, as if the making of small new curiosities signified the skills to do anything, to move the world.

Little scabs had formed where she had scratched herself. Eventually he took her feet onto his lap and massaged them, and she slouched in her chair and fell asleep. Watching her, he recalled the airport where they'd met years before, recalled his misery and awe. And now? Now he was moved to happiness.

Later that afternoon she went into the room. Two golf carts in the seventh fairway had collided in a way that bent a rear wheel. Several men in shorts and polo shirts gathered around. Then, one by one, they wandered off, abandoning the damaged golf cart in the middle of the fairway.

"Golf cart accident," Ellis called to Heather. "I should go over and offer to reconstruct it for them. Then blame it on a wild pig."

Heather didn't reply. He peered into the room, but she had gone.

He went in to use the toilet. A pair of red panties that Heather had laundered in the sink were hanging over the shower-curtain rod.

He ran a finger over the seams, then washed his hands, splashed water on his face, and dried it away. His phone rang.

"Chinese?" Heather said.

"Where are you?"

"I'm just wandering around. I found a bag of water balloons."

He returned to the balcony. An iron shot rose off the seventh fairway and fell and dribbled onto the green, still far short of the pin. "I'll walk over to that Chinese place for takeout," Heather said. "All right with you?"

Ellis said okay. He leaned on the rail and looked over the traffic. Away to the right something snagged his attention, a person on the edge of the highway.

Ellis knew at once that it was Boggs—Boggs bending to look at the ground, then striding along. Ellis's breath caught.

"What?" Heather said.

"He's here."

"John?"

Boggs straightened, turned his face to the sky, and raised his arms outward. Ellis still held the phone to his ear but had forgotten it when Heather clicked off.

He was watching Boggs and didn't see her until she was already running across the lanes of the highway.

The traffic gapped and she crossed quickly. Boggs didn't appear surprised to see her. She stopped maybe ten feet from him. Boggs lifted a foot and looked down at it. His lips hardly moved as he spoke. Heather advanced stiffly. She looked like she might hit him.

Ellis crashed through the room, downstairs, past the reception desk, around the building. By the time he reached the side of the highway, Heather and Boggs seemed calmed. They were talking. Ellis rushed through a break in the traffic. "Hey!" he called from the median. The two did not glance at him. They looked almost as if they might be conspiring against him. As he waited for an opening to cross the remaining two lanes, he burned. At the same time, he was aware that he stood in the same ditch where a man had barely ducked a semi.

When traffic opened and he could move forward, his frustration grew confused. Heather stood downcast. Boggs studied the golf course. He looked well-tanned, rested, and sad, like a man in the midst of a disappointing vacation. "What happened to that golf cart?" he asked.

"You're all right?" Ellis said. But having said it, he was unsure who he meant, or what *all right* could possibly mean.

"Say something," Boggs said. He seemed to be ignoring Ellis's question, to be talking to Heather. She didn't move or respond. The three of them stood in silence. This wasn't what Ellis had expected, and now his strongest temptation was to turn away and run from it.

Boggs said, "Okay then." He smiled at Ellis. "We were just rehashing some history." He glanced at Heather, but she stood silent. Ellis circled in order to see her face—but she wasn't looking at anything: her eyes were shut. She seemed pale, and when Ellis touched her she was trembling.

"Did you hit her?" he asked Boggs, furiously.

Boggs set his hands in his pockets. "Of course not." He started away, into the golf course.

Ellis took a step after him, but stopped and went back to Heather.

"What did he do?"

She shook her head.

"Let's go back to the motel."

"Are you going to go after him?" she asked.

"Do you want me to?"

"Don't ask me that!"

He stared at her. "I couldn't see as I came down from the room—"

"You didn't miss anything."

"Then what—"

"Go," she said. "He's going crazy, isn't he?" She motioned as if she would shove him, but she did not touch him.

Boggs was already at the far end of the seventh fairway. Ellis looked from him to Heather. "Are you sending me away?"

"No," she said.

"No." He studied her gaze a second, but she was now steady and opaque. He turned, ran.

Boggs had nearly reached the golf course parking lot. Ellis sprinted through the rough along the seventh. He remembered that Heather had been married to Boggs for years; in comparison, he hardly knew her.

By the time he reached the parking lot, Boggs, in his convertible, was pulling away. Ellis ran behind, with little hope.

Boggs, however, had to pause for an SUV backing into a parking space. Ellis thought he might actually catch up. And then—what? Vault into the passenger seat?

Boggs approached the street with some speed and made a screeching turn into traffic that terrified Ellis—vehicles from both directions braked loudly, swerved, blew horns. But Ellis, running hard on an angle through the parking lot, had managed to come up beside him. He could hear Boggs's car stereo. It sounded like *Notes from the Underground*—a favorite of Boggs's, although Ellis had a bit less enthusiasm for misanthropy, however well-rendered, and had found it unreadable, nearly unlistenable. He yelled, "Boggs!"

"You all right?" Boggs asked, driving slowly.

"Yes." Ellis had to fight for breath.

"Are you sure? I mean, in a bigger sense?"

"I'm fine."

"You don't have to follow me, you know."

"Let me help you!"

Boggs shrugged. He accelerated a bit. "What do you want?"

"To talk!" Ellis shouted.

"Just say it!"

"What!"

"What you have to say!"

"Let's sit somewhere!" Ellis gasped; he couldn't run like this much longer. Boggs kept just ahead.

"What!"

"This is stupid!"

"What is!"

Ellis cried hoarsely, "This isn't a joke!"

"No joke!"

"No!"

"Okay!" Boggs called. He was accelerating.

"Boggs!" Ellis ran as hard as he could, his lungs feeling scorched.

"What?"

Ellis cried, "There was a second vehicle!"

Boggs slowed a little. "What?"

"Pig Accident Two!"

Boggs called something back, but it was lost in engine noise and tire noise and space. Soon Boggs had vanished.

Ellis stopped and bent, hands on knees. After a minute he turned and began walking back along the road and into the golf course. He watched a threesome in visors and sunglasses hitting off on the seventh tee; a shining white ball popped off the ground in front of him, and caromed forward. Ellis waved to the men and trotted across the fairway. He didn't know what would happen next. He wondered at Boggs and at Heather with distress, but at the same time his mind took tangents—he marveled at the close-cut uniformity of the grass underfoot. It seemed as artificial as concrete.

Then his phone rang.

"Oh my God," Boggs said. "You're killing me."

"A second vehicle," Ellis said again.

"What are you talking about? You're torturing me. You might as well stick a knife in my gut."

"There was a second car." He kept walking beside the fairway. "The Mercedes was sideswiped by a second vehicle. You can see the damage in the photos. The leading edge of the driver's door was lipped backward, just a little. We didn't see it because it was buried in the impact damage from the tree."

"You didn't tell me that."

"Someone in the opposing lane came around that curve too fast. They were over the center line, and they sideswiped the Mercedes. That's why the turn seems so severe."

"It could be that the edge of the door just warped around the shape of the tree."

"No. It's bent *back*. It's *folded backward*. Something caught that edge and turned it back. Slamming sideways into a tree didn't bend the metal backward."

"You're sure?" Boggs asked.

"I checked the dynamics. It works. I put a second vehicle into PC-Crash and simulated a sideswipe collision. It worked perfectly. I didn't have to do all that goofy stuff with the friction factors on the asphalt. The Mercedes just naturally spun toward the tree."

"What about tire tracks in the gore on the road? Could you see a second vehicle there?"

"Those pigs had been hit and spread out by any number of vehicles. I couldn't really pick anything out. Maybe with more time."

"Did you look for a paint transfer? If there was another vehicle, don't you think it would have transferred some paint onto the Mercedes?"

"I didn't see that," Ellis admitted. "But there isn't always paint transfer. You know that. Or it could have gotten lost in the damage."

"Huh."

He believed that he had found the key, that through their work he might open Boggs, change his course. "I think I can prove it," he said.

"You can."

"Meet me there."

Boggs hung up.

Ellis ran out of the golf course and dodged across the highway lanes. When he reached the motel parking lot, Heather's car was gone. This made him feel guilty. Then, aggrieved.

He didn't bother to return to the room. He climbed into the minivan, started it, and turned it onto the road. The site of PA2 was about three hundred miles away.

He pulled into the flow of traffic and phoned Heather. She said she was driving home. "Go ahead," she said. "Go on. You're doing the right thing." Her voice sounded mechanical, maybe even rehearsed. "You know," she said, fading, "you—" She began again, "You know why I called him John, not Boggs, don't you?"

He waited for her to go on.

"Because he hates it."

"Sure," he said. He was surprised by the sympathy he felt for Boggs.

Twenty-eight

He drove fast down the long straight roads through the wide flat landscape. It would take more than five hours, at normal speeds, to reach the site in Wisconsin. He slowed going into the towns, but then as he came out he jammed the accelerator. For a time he was slowed by a pickup pulling a horse trailer and prevented from passing by a stream of oncoming traffic. Ellis cursed and kicked the underside of the dashboard with his shin. Finally he pulled left and passed and scarcely returned to the proper lane in time to avoid an oncoming, honking F-350. Grimacing, he accelerated.

His attempt to find Boggs by following him had failed. His attempt to find Boggs by getting ahead of him had succeeded in finding Boggs, but failed because Heather had been there and things had turned weird and complicated and he had failed to shift Boggs off his course. But now this idea was better. He wished he had thought of this long ago. Finally, he was dictating the itinerary to Boggs. If anything could put a hook into Boggs and pull him back, it was the work. He should have realized that sooner. The work was at Boggs's core, as it was for Ellis. With the work, he could find Boggs, and they would have something—the work, a reconstruction—to talk about, something to anchor into and bring Boggs back to reason. He drove fast. He passed small blue lakes. Trees appeared small and slow in the distance and accelerated toward him and snapped by on either side. He stopped for a light in a small useless town, then barked the minivan's tires as he regained his speed.

His phone rang.

"Where's the proof, then?"

"Where are you?"

"I'm here."

"No. You can't be there already."

"I'm here."

"I don't believe it. I'll be there in fifteen minutes."

"Tell me where to look. What am I looking for?"

"It's just a guess. It might not be there."

"What? Where?"

"I'll be there."

"Tell me what to look for right fucking now."

"It's just an idea."

"Or I will find a place where you'll be driving by and I'll run out in front of your car and see what happens."

"Jesus."

"What am I looking for?"

Or maybe this, too, had been a mistake. It occurred to Ellis that he might have been a little too proud of himself. That maybe the idea of bringing Boggs back to PA2, to show off his clever analysis, had been rooted in vanity.

"Okay," he said. "Start at the tree. The one that the Mercedes hit. Cross to the opposite side of the road. Look there in the weeds while walking back in the direction that the Mercedes came from. I'd guess about a hundred fifty, two hundred feet back. It's hard to say. I'll be there in a few minutes."

"What am I looking for?"

Ellis didn't answer. The rasp of Boggs's breath came through the phone. Ellis was working the minivan as fast as he dared, and it was loud with wind noise and joints and panels rattling on the road's cracks, but he could hear the working of Boggs's breath, and even the clashing of undergrowth as Boggs kicked around. It might not be there. He hoped it wasn't there. This had been a mistake, this showing off, this vanity. He should have directed Boggs to the wrong place, but the idea hadn't even occurred to him.

"Actually," Ellis said suddenly, "it might be on the other side of the road."

"No," Boggs said.

"No?"

"Hey, hear that car go by, a little fast around the curve?" Boggs asked.

"Yeah."

"I'm standing about ten feet off the side of the road and about two hundred feet back down the road from the tree."

"Yeah."

"What do you think is lying here on the ground?"

Ellis was silent a second. "A side mirror."

"A no-shit driver's-side mirror with a white casing. Power mirror, same style as the passenger's-side mirror on the Mercedes. Something coming the other way swiped this thing off the Mercedes and carried it or threw it way the hell down here. Second vehicle. You're right. Christ. Christ Christ Christ. You're right. How did you figure this out? I didn't think you were right. But you were right."

"It just suddenly appeared in my brain."

"Well, you were right."

"What are you going to do now?"

"When did you figure this out?"

"That night. After I hit James Dell in the street."

"That night?"

"I couldn't sleep."

"I was in a state of self-torture, and you were figuring this."

"I didn't really know what I was doing. And, Boggs," Ellis hurried on, "it's good for our client. This accident didn't have anything to do with the pigs. This was due to someone in the opposing lanes who drove carelessly, sideswiped the Mercedes, caused a fatality, and fled the scene."

"You're something."

"I'm what?"

"Yes. I have to go."

When Ellis arrived, he was alone.

He felt vastly alone with, again, the forest around him, its innumerable vertical trunks, the thin light spiking through the branches high overhead and the sun spilling down through the gap over the road. And the deep quiet, which seemed much greater and more permanent than himself, as if he were no more than a dewdrop or a fallen pine needle.

He hunted in the weeds beside the road for a while, but the mirror was gone.

He went to the tree that had killed the driver of the Mercedes, and he punched it. He punched it again, looked at his bleeding knuckles, then punched it once more.

He returned to the minivan and rolled the windows down and sat looking at his knuckles, and then at nothing. The trees stirred and creaked. He looked up at them, and saw that the sky's color was deepening. The day was at its end. He didn't know what to do.

He looked at the woods, at the trunks and the shadows, and he couldn't seem to think anything except that he didn't know what to do or to think.

He saw a deer there, back in the trees. The deer had twitched one ear, drawing his eye. He had been looking toward it for some time, but he had not seen it. It stood maybe a hundred feet away. A doe, no horns, ears like a pair of big radar dishes pointed at him, bright white in the ears and under the chin and under the belly. Her eyes were luxuriously black.

Suddenly, startling him, she leaped high and away. Branches snapped and crashed as she came down. A white tail flashed. And then he was looking at the woods, and it was as if she had never been there.

A car was coming. He heard it now: she had heard it before him.

It leaned hard through the curve, the tires crying, and Ellis turned to watch it go by.

It was a convertible. Boggs.

Boggs looked over and waved as he slipped by.

Ellis started the minivan and turned it around and drove as fast as he dared.

He drove this way for five miles, but he didn't see the convertible, and then he came to an intersection. In the distance, left and right, he saw no one. He beat the steering wheel with his bleeding knuckles.

Then his phone rang. He answered it. Boggs said, "Right." And hung up.

"No no no!" Ellis shouted. But with a sensation of internal flailing, he turned right and drove as fast as the minivan allowed.

A couple dozen miles passed with no sight of Boggs. He dialed Boggs and listened to it ring several times. Then, to his surprise, the line clicked open. Boggs said, "This jerk in front of me keeps tapping his brakes. Going uphill for God's sake."

"I guess we're back at this," Ellis said.

"It's a little hill."

"You're on a little hill. I don't see any hills."

"Look at him! Keeps tapping the brakes. I guess anyone who wants to gets to be a jerk."

"Where are you?"

"Just drive and drive."

"You must be driving like a lunatic. You'll kill someone."

"People out here know the risks. If you've put yourself out on the road, then by implication you've accepted the associated risks."

"I doubt that most people think of it that way."

"People do all kinds of shit without thinking."

"You're not an asshole. Stop it."

"The problem," Boggs said, "is that you still want to think we're friends. Look at what's happened. Look at where we are. What does friendship mean? This isn't it."

"We don't have to be friends. We don't have to be anything. Just go home."

"You don't really want me to go home and inject myself into Heather's life again, go in and stir the situation you've got."

"Do whatever you need to do."

"It would be a mess. I'm just thinking of your interests, Ellis."

"Sarcasm is the lowest form of humor."

"No, really you have to agree that puns are lower. I'll take bad sarcasm over a good pun any day."

"You can joke, Boggs. Life can't be so bad."

"Not really. What's the one got to do with the other?"

Ellis shook his head. He needed to avoid being led into distractions. "You're going around to these places again," he said, returning to the one thing he thought he knew.

"It'd be nice to get hold of something to stuff back into the void."

"I have to say, from an outside perspective, it looks morbid."

"No. Life happened in these places. And when you're in a darkness and you see a few points of light out there, of course you tend to go toward them. And if you've lost something, you go back to the last places you can remember having it. Don't you think people must have learned something from these accidents they were in? Couldn't we learn it, too, if we weren't so obsessed with the evidence and mechanical dynamics?"

"Heather told me once that, basically, she thought you were detached from life, struggling to bring it closer."

"She never told me that. Could be. But I always thought, actually, that I felt things too closely, and so had made the habit of pushing things away."

Ellis was still looking to all sides for a hill. "You said *right*, right?"

"Right, wrong. Left, right."

"What?"

"Wright. With a W."

"Oh. Oh." Jacob Wright was one of their clients. Ellis pulled to the shoulder and stopped the car.

"Now we're getting somewhere, huh? Get it? We're driving, getting somewhere. It's a pun, pretty low."

"We're not getting anywhere." He wasn't. He had stopped on the shoulder.

"Now, that's what makes it funny, because it's sarcasm, too."

"Boggs," Ellis said.

"Boggs. Boggs, Boggs, Boggs. *Boggs, can I have a job? Boggs, can I have your wife? Boggs, can I have your sympathy? Boggs, can I save your life? Boggs, can I feel good about myself?*"

"I'm—"

"*Boggs, will you accept my apology?*"

"Shut up."

"Am I bothering you?"

"You can talk a circle right around me. Good for you."

"Okay. Talk to the Dostoyevsky." Ellis heard an audio book playing. "*That I should cast a dark cloud over your serene, untroubled happiness; that by my bitter reproaches I should cause distress to your heart, should poison it with secret remorse and should force it to throb with anguish at the moment of bliss. Oh, never, never!*"

"I can't believe you had that cued up just for me," Ellis said. But the phone had gone dead.

Jacob Wright had been their most reliable defense client, a fat, affable attorney representing a manufacturer. Including everything—even the jobs they spent only a few hours on before everyone agreed the case looked bad and should be settled—they must have worked for Wright on more than a dozen different jobs. Maybe twenty. Maybe more.

Ellis took out the map. The nearest Wright job that he could recollect lay—like a confirmation—180 degrees off his current course.

He turned around.

Night had now taken the world. He passed an array of towering antennas with blinking red and white lights. Then fields where large numbers of fireflies were flashing.

The fireflies made pale green sparks in great numbers all across the landscape, and they glowed only as they flew upward, so that they appeared to be always rising. Some rose over the road, and the ones that struck the windshield flashed brightly into green smears of phosphorescence that slowly, slowly faded. They began to mass in swarms that pelted the minivan—three, four on the glass at a time, startling him with every impact, dead and luminous and beautiful.

Then the fields ended with an eruption of residential housing developments, and the fireflies vanished.

Twenty-nine

Everyone drove every day; everyone passed accidents from time to time; everyone was involved in accidents and knew family and friends who were involved in accidents; everyone passed, every day, the tire marks and broken glass of recent accidents—it was only that circumstances had attuned him to these particulars. While others drove around obliviously, the calamitous nature of the roadway assaulted him constantly.

He recalled Boggs's contention—that the word *accident* was meaningless, that either everything was an accident or nothing was.

He feared to think that he had somehow brought a special fate down onto himself.

His headlamps ghosted an interstate with a narrow median; a flavor of metal gathered in his mouth; cars came down the opposite lanes like fists. He drove until late, then slept in the minivan off a side road in a rutted open space. In the morning he drove past glowing sunflowers, the endless bright heads peering upward. Black-and-white cows trundled over rolling terrain, drank at the foot of a madly spinning windmill. A haze filled the sky with the color of weathered aluminum, and he stopped at one of the more memorable Wright accident sites, a place where a woman driving her daughter home from choir practice had stopped while a goose and four goslings crossed the road. A pickup crashed in from behind, and the daughter in the backseat died. Ellis spent more than two hours scrutinizing the ground, moving up and down the road, but he could find no trace of Boggs, so he went on.

Boggs wouldn't answer his phone, and he put off calling Heather. He despised himself a little for this, but he was angry with her, too. What had passed between her and Boggs on the golf course?

He examined the place amid alfalfa fields where two SUVs had met head-on, at a combined speed of 115 mph, and burned. One of the drivers died with his head resting on the window sill, the police photos showed, his eyes rolled and exposed like a pair of eggs. Ellis stood on the road shoulder and scrutinized its gravel. After a time he moved forward a half-step. He tried to give attention to each individual stone. Moved forward another half-step. For this accident he and Boggs had developed an elaborate analysis involving Conservation of Momentum, Conservation of Energy, and Taylor Series expansions, but he could remember none of it, only the photos of the dead. Limbs burned to stumps.

He could find no sign of Boggs.

That night, clouds on the south horizon shone auburn with the reflected light of a city. Still, Boggs didn't answer his phone. Now he called Heather, but she didn't answer either. He felt sent away from her. Was that true? Was that why he went on? No. He was Boggs's friend, so he went on. Was that why he went on? Yes. Yes?

Exhaustion came abruptly, like a blow to the head, and sleeping in the minivan now felt habitual and natural. So it seemed foolish to push to look for motels. He slept at an abandoned construction site, obscured from the road by a section of six-foot-diameter pipe.

While he drove the next morning, heat lightning began to glint in the distance. He was in Missouri.

That morning, he phoned the hospital. Mrs. Dell answered in a hoarse voice. "He's worse," she said. "A lot of—worse. I believe he's going to die. They won't say it, won't tell me, but I can see it. His heart stopped this morning. They used the paddles. He looks bad."

"I'm so sorry," Ellis said. "I can't even begin to say."

"Can I tell you something? His heart stopped—" She clucked her tongue. "And something had finally happened. A part of me was glad for the excitement. They had to pay attention again. And it's been so dull, and I get so bored. I don't know what to do. Sit, wait. Patience. Look at him, don't look at him. Think about him, then don't think about him. Talk to him, or don't talk to him. I don't know if he can hear me. They say it's possible he can hear, so I feel that I should talk. But it's hard. It's not like talking to him."

"Tell me about him."

"He's not well."

"I mean, tell me how he was when he was—" Ellis stuttered; he'd nearly said *alive*. "—he was well. What did he like to do? What kind of person was he?"

"He loves dogs," she said, "but he never allowed himself a dog. He isn't allergic. He just didn't allow it. He denies himself things. He can be difficult. He never is who he wants to be, I don't think. None of us is, I guess, but it bothers him especially. He loves sweets and never eats sweets. He hates the theater, but he went. Maybe I sound bitter."

"He loves you, though."

"Oh, yes, yes. But, well, we fought terribly." She laughed. "We've never really had the life we should have. He denies that, too." She coughed. "I don't mean to talk about this. I don't want to."

"It's all right," Ellis said.

He stopped for lunch in a Subway decorated with a yellow that worked in his eyes like needles and paid for a sandwich served up by smiling young people. He felt like wreckage before them, unshaven and unwashed, and he sat at a corner table obscured from sight. She'd said her husband always wanted to make life harder, which made Ellis think of Boggs. But no, he thought, no. Boggs had his particular obsessions, which were sometimes difficult, but the difficulty was incidental. Then Ellis wondered if, perhaps, it was his own problem—making things difficult.

He only swallowed two bites of his sandwich before he left.

Still, he went on. What he was doing—whatever he was doing—seemed to be necessary.

He drove between more sites where they had done work for Wright. An Aston Martin that broke in half. A woman run down by a trash truck. A shuttle bus with faulty brakes. At each, Ellis examined the ground minutely. If there were houses or businesses nearby, he went to ask questions.

He sensed the danger of wafting away on an empty kind of slant life. When he didn't have the flow of the road before him, his thoughts seemed especially disorganized. He stood too long staring. He handed the gas-station attendant his keys instead of his credit card.

The time in the motel with Heather already seemed vague and unreal. When she finally called back, he was enormously glad, but then also taken by a terrible uncertainty. He could hardly speak. He didn't ask about what passed between herself and Boggs by the side of the highway, hoping she would raise it. She didn't.

"You're still driving," she said. He said yes. Soon she said good-bye.

He approached an accident site near Kansas City that had been marked in his mind by an Outback Steakhouse, so he watched for an Outback. But he saw no Outbacks for miles, only T.G.I. Friday's, Olive Garden, Red Lobster, Lone Star, Black-eyed Pea, Chili's. Years had passed since he and Boggs were here, and nothing on the roadside resembled the images in his mind. He began to mistrust his memory, and he had nearly decided to turn back when the Outback's red neon suddenly came into view.

He parked along the fence of a salvage yard where he could see bits of wrecked vehicles between the fence slats and jogged across an access road to look down at the interstate. He took a breath, then stepped heavily down the embankment, to the narrow margin beside the lanes.

The passing vehicles moved in long streams and flows, sucking a wind that fluttered on him. He studied the shape of the embankment, the location of the acceleration and deceleration lanes, the proximity of the overpasses at the exits ahead and behind. Here, on an early morning in winter, after a nighttime snowfall, a Dodge Durango had parked on the shoulder. Its occupants were a family of five Bangladeshi immigrants who had abandoned a rental apartment two days earlier and started driving west.

The driver of the semi that had destroyed the Dodge and killed everyone inside began to lose control after passing the previous exit. For a distance of several hundred feet, the semi swerved back and forth—a little, then more and more as the driver struggled to regain control of the trailer swinging behind him. Ellis had modeled the dynamics. When the driver got on the brakes, it caused the trailer to jackknife. It was traveling at—Ellis had calculated—46 mph when the rear corner ripped open the Dodge and hurled it down the shoulder, spinning in a complicated trajectory that Ellis laboriously reconstructed by an analysis of a stack of police photos of tire marks in the snow. Long ago, that work. He marveled at it, and felt jealous of his former self, oblivious amid his equations and four-by-six-inch photographs.

When the Dodge came to a stop, it stood empty; the five occupants lay in little heaps here and there on the road. Scattered around were cardboard boxes, duffel bags, Fritos, a pair of flip-flops, and a small charcoal grill.

Ellis and Boggs had identified the accident location by walking the shoulder with a book of police photos, watching for the shape of the embankment and a bit of fencing that showed at the top. Or had it been a guard rail? Irritated, Ellis returned to the place where he had come down the embankment and continued on in the other direction. Maybe he had the wrong Outback, the wrong exit, the wrong interstate, the wrong city.

At a break in the traffic, he ran across to the center median, to look for furrows in the grass. He remembered photographing the tracks of still-raw earth with Boggs, and it didn't seem likely that the highway department would have made any attempt to fill them. But he couldn't find them.

The day was darkening, and headlamps began to turn on. Then it started to rain; the noise of the wheels on the road shifted tone as they hit the wet surface. And he was stuck in the median.

He stood waiting for a break in the traffic, watching the moving columns of vehicles. The cars and trucks were moving close upon one another at forty or fifty mph in the rain. His hair plastered down, his shirt grew soaked, his pants. Plumes thrown by passing semis landed on his ankles.

He stood thinking that eventually the traffic must break. It had to. Nothing was infinite, certainly not this. But the traffic was incessant.

If he waited here long enough, he supposed, he'd inevitably see an accident.

His hands trembled in his armpits. It had grown very dark. Confounded, he wandered up the median a short distance, then returned and waited. Eventually he bowed his head and looked at the gleaming wet ground. Eventually he shut his eyes.

Suddenly the sound of the traffic changed. A course of rear lights brightened, cars slowed. He was a little stunned. He realized he'd lost faith that the traffic would ever stop; to see it now seemed a flouting of nature, as if a river had suddenly stopped flowing.

He returned up the embankment and sat in the minivan next to the salvage yard with the heat on. He remembered Boggs's story about wandering around junkyards when he was young.

In the rain he climbed on top of the minivan to reach a leg over the fence, and jumped over onto the roof of a Lincoln Town Car.

Overhead lamps glowed at the periphery of the salvage yard, and puddles shone in the gravel paths between rough rows of vehicles lying side-by-side, just far enough apart to allow the doors to swing a few inches, cars and trucks caved, twisted, pierced, masticated, or freed of doors, hood, wheels, trunk lid, roof, or fenders. Rank on rank, like bodies gathered after battle.

A pile of rusting wheels. A pile of drive shafts. Drops of rainwater clung to the sheet metal, puddled in the dents.

Somewhere a train moved, pushing vibrations that caused the entire field of vehicles to shimmer.

He stopped before a Monte Carlo. The paint gleamed, the tires held air. But the passenger's-side door had been forced deep into the vehicle, as if staved in by a battering ram. He peered inside. A clutter of paraphernalia covered the dashboard and an enormous blotching stained the passenger seat, which was distorted by the impacted door. The stains appeared to be blood. The rain was slowing now, but he was very cold.

The driver's seat held him as softly as a plush sofa. Braid and tassels ran around the windshield glass; cards printed with the images of saints hung from the ceiling; figurines of crudely painted plastic stood on the dash holding swords, scepters, or birds; faux leopard skin wrapped the steering wheel; a bust of a weeping Virgin dangled from the rearview mirror. The leopard skin was soiled at three and nine o'clock. A small stain of, again, blood marked the chin of the Virgin.

He was wet and cold in his clothes. It was easy to imagine that in any slightly different life he would never have come here.

"Where is Boggs?" he said aloud. "How do I find him?"

Silence.

He wondered what he was listening for. The person or persons who'd been in this car—voices from all the accidents he had reconstructed—voices from all the accidents everywhere, ever, from Bridget Driscoll at the Crystal Palace and onward— The accidents in this way became a mathematical progression past counting.

He crushed the palms of his hands into his eyes. There seemed to be a noise skimming the edge of his awareness, a modulating of frequencies, a havoc of tempo, a fire in the ears. Before him hung shining pinwheels, depthless drifting auroras.

He remembered his conversations with Boggs late in the office, talking about how, to be a good forensic engineer, you had to be able to be analytical, had to be able to present a chain of reasoning that defined what you knew about an accident. Beyond that, Boggs suggested, if you wanted to be more than mediocre, you also had to have what was called intuition, which would tell you where to look for evidence and suggest to you the meaning of that evidence. Later you could cobble together the steps of analysis, and if you did it right, it would seem obvious. A leads to B leads to C. But at the beginning it was never obvious. It was only a few tire marks and some banged-up vehicles.

For most engineers, Boggs said, the hard bit wasn't the analysis, but the intuition. Many engineers didn't even care to acknowledge the intuitive part. Which was silly, Boggs said. It wasn't magic. It just occurred outside the limited illumination of consciousness.

Ellis trembled. If time could fall away, if he could look in all directions, where would he look? But he couldn't even keep his thoughts focused on Boggs. Instead he thought of Heather, with an aching.

Boggs had been impressed by Ellis's intuition, and Ellis had been prideful of it. But now he couldn't say what it was, where to find it, or how to use it to find his friend. It gave him access to nothing. Even after allowing himself to be brought this far, his mind shaken and emotional, he couldn't make the part of himself that might offer a revelation do so. He asked it of himself, and there was only nothing.

A breeze hissed on the sharp edges of the car. There seemed a rhythm in it, too. Whisperings. A warble of metal ripping in the faint distance.

Thirty

"Human factors analysis."

"What?"

"People don't assess speed, it's hard to assess speed. We assess the gap. The gap between vehicles, the gap available to cross or turn."

Darkness. "Boggs?"

"Are you happy?"

"No. No, I'm not happy."

"Are you depressed, Ellis?"

"I'm not happy."

"Are you sad?"

"What is this?"

"Do you have feelings of guilt?"

Just before, the pallid, wrecked face of James Dell had been declaiming on the perversity of fortune; as he spoke, his left eye swiveled strangely with a cheerful ringing noise, then popped from the socket and hung on its nerve bundle. Behind James Dell, Christopher stood guffawing and freshly burned. But that had been a dream. "Boggs," Ellis said.

"Are you feeling self-conscious? Self-doubting?"

Ellis had responded automatically to the noise of the phone, fumbled and answered still half-asleep, confused as to place and time. He began to register how complete the darkness around him was. He put a hand forward and felt a fur-wrapped steering wheel.

"It's been interesting to drive and think," Boggs said. He sounded tired, although not as tired as Ellis thought he should sound.

Ellis waited, but Boggs said nothing more. Ellis finally said, "All right. What are you thinking?"

"Oh, I don't know. I guess that the road is a place where you know you might die at any instant. Right? It's a part of the nature of driving. On some level we're always aware of death as we drive. It's actually one reason we like to be on the road. The possibility of an accident, of drama, of death, which is absent from our lives otherwise. Modern life is deathless; we expect to grow old and shuffle away to a facility where we can expire in obscurity. But is that really what we want, deep in our brains? Maybe something will happen on the road, now, or now, or now. You see? It provides an element of risk, and we desire that. How many thousands die each year? I'll tell you: more than forty thousand, just in America. How many of them might be saved if only the speed limit were reduced ten miles an hour? But we don't."

"Boggs, where are you?"

"It seems less interesting that we slow to rubberneck the car crash on the side of the road than that we speed up again as soon as we're past it. That's what I've been thinking about. Tick-tock-tick. In our marvelous machines. Seventy-two in a sixty-five zone."

"That's what you're doing now?"

"Let's allow a perception-reaction time of, say, two point five seconds, to get on the brake. And then braking. I'll be a full football field and more down the road before I can stop this thing. Where are you?"

"In a junkyard. What time is it?" Ellis asked.

"It's almost four thirty."

"A.M.?"

"Is something wrong?"

Ellis let the question float. He could see now the faint glow of a couple of lights far away. "Boggs," he said again.

"Witnesses are unreliable. The car flipped six times, went fifty feet in the air, did a triple lutz! Always prefer the physical evidence over testimony, Ellis."

"Right. Right. Sure. Why are we talking about this?"

"Still following me?"

"I'm trying to," Ellis said, staring at the darkness.

"You do love your subtle distinctions."

"Tell me where you are," Ellis said. "Wright? Wright twenty-nine eighty-two? Wright thirty thirty-five? The one with the hood ornament in the eye?"

"Go home."

Ellis knew he was unlikely to get from Boggs anything that Boggs didn't want to give. He tried to listen for background noise in the phone, but he heard only a faint high whine that seemed to be the sound of Boggs's engine. "Let's step back," he said in aggravation. "Let's be straight about what this is all about."

"By all means."

"I slept with your wife."

"You do realize, there are good reasons why people usually don't say the things that they don't say," Boggs said. "And I've known about you and Heather for a long while."

"You have?"

Boggs said nothing.

Ellis said, "How long have you known?"

"Does that puncture your self-importance?"

"You really knew?"

"Come on, any asshole would have known. I *should* have known the minute you sat for your interview and you didn't dare mention my wife's name, even though she was the only reason you were there. But I thought you were too shy to do anything."

"You wanted us to see the Chekhov, with you."

"I wanted to force something. I wanted a crisis, but the crisis I got was not the crisis I wanted. That accident was such a strange thing to happen."

"I caused that accident."

"After that, it was necessary to make a break."

"You didn't cause that accident."

"You wouldn't have been there otherwise."

"By that logic, the line of causation could go all the way back to the Big Bang."

"Well, sure."

"You really let Heather and me go on, after you knew?" Ellis said. He was angry. He knew he had no right to anger, but he was angry. "You've always been a fraud, Boggs. Self-absorbed, concerned that people will think you're insufficiently unusual."

"Have you ever noticed that freckle behind Heather's left earlobe?" Boggs asked. "Lift the lobe and check it out. It's an exceedingly fine freckle."

"You're a coward. A quitter. A loser."

"When you wash her laundry, be sure you don't fold any of her shirts. She hates that. They must be placed onto hangers immediately. She also dislikes those softening dryer sheets. She's very particular about the whole laundry process. But the folding of shirts is the biggie."

"Your calm is a mask. Your indifference is a mask."

"You've probably noticed that the iris of her left eye is slightly darker than her right. I've always wondered if it was the fire that somehow caused that."

"You're a self-absorbed jerk, you're running away, and what're you trying to do? Poison the well? Salt the fields? We'll be all right, Boggs. You need to help yourself."

Boggs laughed.

"How about a fistfight?" Ellis said. "You can beat the crap out of me and then call it a day."

"Talking to you is such an effort. It kills me. Here, I've been on Kundera, *Unbearable Lightness*. Listen."

"The goals we pursue are always veiled. A girl who longs for marriage longs for something she knows nothing about. The boy who han-

kers after fame has no idea what fame is. The thing that gives our every move its meaning is always totally unknown to us. Sabina was unaware of the goal that lay behind her longing to betray . . ."

"Boggs!" Ellis shouted. "Hey!"

But Boggs hung up.

Ellis sat for a long while before he stepped out of the car. He was alone with the devastated vehicles. The black sky lay close. Even the lights at the periphery of the yard were off. The nearest lights glowed over the interstate.

He found the yard gate, but it was locked. He moved along the fence until he came to an old Suburban, climbed onto the roof, dropped over the fence. He would not have been surprised to find his minivan gutted, its parts spreading across the city. But it stood as he had left it.

He listened for some minutes to the bluster of the traffic. Light had begun to come into the eastern sky. He walked along the top of the embankment, looking again for the accident's specific location, without success.

Sliding in the mud, he went down and searched along the shoulder once more. The clouds had cleared, and as he walked with the traffic he squinted into the rising sun. He recalled that the driver of the semi that had struck the Dodge had talked to the police about the sun in his face before he jackknifed.

But the accident had occurred in the P.M.

And therefore he was on the wrong side of the interstate.

He scrambled up the embankment, drove to the access road on the interstate's opposite side, and parked in front of a Shell station. He remembered this Shell: when he and Boggs were here, they had parked in the same place. Boggs had gone inside and bought a hot dog from the rotating rack. Ellis had laughed at it, and Boggs had said gravely, "Sweet porcine flesh."

It scared Ellis, this slippage of the mind, confusing his directions just like the glassy-eyed woman in the bar back in Michigan.

He crossed the access road and studied the ground. A pen cap. A black plastic garbage bag. A dirt-crusted wine bottle.

And then he saw a gleaming, white thing shining in the weeds—a side mirror. He knew as he bent to pick it up that it was the mirror from the Mercedes, the one that Boggs had found at PA2. But as he picked it up, he found that it had concealed another thing lying on the ground—a broken, weathered plastic nameplate that said *airlane.*

Ellis dropped the mirror and picked up the nameplate. He stood turning it in his hands for a long while, confounded. It *looked* just like the one that had been on Christopher's car. But how could that nameplate have gotten here? Boggs. Of course Boggs had done this.

As far as Ellis knew, his father still had the *airlane* stored somewhere. Boggs could have found it and taken off this nameplate.

But why? What had Boggs been doing with the *airlane*?

Eventually he carried it to the minivan and put it into the glove box.

He tried to phone Boggs, but Boggs didn't answer.

He pulled down onto the interstate and drove fast in the left lane. He needed to find Boggs. Boggs had been here, which meant he was now somewhere else. And, because he was angry and velocity seemed to be the only thing in his control anymore, he needed to accelerate.

Thirty-one

That evening he stopped in an empty corner of a Walmart parking lot. He phoned Heather. "Love," he said wretchedly, when she answered.

"Don't say that," she said.

"What?"

"I don't think you know if you love me."

"Why are you saying this?"

She was crying. He was glad that at least she was crying.

"You're cold," he said.

Somehow, it sounded like a joke, and she laughed. "Then I wonder, what do I want?" she said. "Is it that I can't even have love without questioning it until it becomes something else?"

"Questioning," he said. "Yes."

"You know."

He said, "I'd like to suggest that we need to talk about Christopher."

"I'm going to hang up now," she said, "but you understand that you deserve it, right?"

"Please, I don't—"

"I can't now." She hung up.

He dialed her again, but she didn't answer. He lifted the cell phone and brought it down, smashing it against the top of the steering wheel. He beat it there repeatedly, until it had broken into several pieces.

Then he looked at the pieces and regretted it. He gathered the pieces and put them in a cup holder.

When he closed his eyes, his thoughts clawed at one another in a kind of terrible dreaming.

A tap on the window woke him. A security guard peered in and shouted at him to go on. Ellis asked about the RVs parked nearby, and the guard said, "RVs allowed! Cars not allowed!"

Ellis stared at the young man, but the absurdity didn't seem to penetrate. "This is a minivan," Ellis said.

"Minivans not allowed."

He drove on, down an unknown road, into darkness, trees flickering at the periphery. He saw no good prospect for stopping. His eyelids trembled.

The asphalt ended and he continued on gravel and jarring washboard ruts. A glow appeared in the distance. A hand-painted sign, illuminated with floodlights, said, THE CRICKET BAR. The bar itself was little more than a hut of weathered wood. A bar seemed like a good place to rest: if he were questioned, he could claim to be sleeping off his drinks.

He stopped in a far corner of the rutted parking lot, nosed into some brush, away from the handful of cars and trucks clustered around the building, where a couple of windows showed small, dim light. Cicadas in the trees were screaming like the cutting of a lathe. He could faintly hear voices. No music. No one came or went from the building.

Sleep was a swift fall through perfect darkness, and he awoke remembering nothing. Clouds moved overhead like a flight of giant apricots. The parking lot lay empty.

When he started maneuvering the minivan, it felt and sounded strange, but he gassed it out of the parking lot and into the road before he understood what was wrong. He stopped. The left rear tire was flat. The right rear tire was also flat.

He studied them and found that both had small punctures in the sidewall. Perhaps from a pocketknife. The entire vehicle slouched back, and he wondered how he had failed to notice the flats sooner. His mind's abilities—to remember, to perceive—were failing him. He stood looking at the tires as if with sufficient attention he might discern that they were not flat after all. The minivan had a spare, but it was not helpful because he needed two tires.

He walked over to the Cricket Bar, knocked, and when no one answered, tried to open the door. Locked. He circled to the back and found another door, which gave the same result.

He returned to the minivan, locked it, and started walking.

All he'd been able to see from the road the night before were the trees on either side, but now he saw that the trees on his left fronted a vast field of goldenrod, the flowers dim at first but soon blazing as the sun elevated. Then the goldenrod ended at a wood of birch, and the boles made stripes of vertical white that crowded behind one another into an obscure distance while ferns spread underneath. Dust rose from the road as he walked and powdered his pant legs and clung to the sweat on his neck. He'd been walking for maybe twenty minutes when he heard a vehicle approaching from behind. He walked on the grassy edge of the road to let it pass, but it slowed and idled at his back.

A red Jeep Cherokee.

Ellis did not glance at it again. He moved faster, and it stayed with him. He looked over toward the birch wood, and behind him gravel spurted; the Jeep roared up and drew even. A young man in the passenger window—pale hair shaved to stubble, face long and freckled, eyes wrinkled with smiling—said, "Your minivan back there?"

"Two flats."

"That's some bad luck. Need a ride?"

"No thanks."

The young man grinned with big white teeth, straight as bricks. "It sure looks like you could use some assistance."

"I figure it's a nice morning."

"Just trying to be helpful."

"Thanks anyway."

"We're just trying to help a guy out. You don't have to be an asshole."

Ellis said nothing.

The Jeep accelerated ahead, then skidded to a stop. The passenger stepped out, then the driver—a heavier young man with a ball cap down almost over his eyes. Ellis looked again at the birch wood, but he felt tired and slow and it seemed likely that they could run him down easily, and then it would only be worse.

The young man with the white brick teeth kept smiling—an earnest, likeable smile, a smile that was hard to doubt. But the driver scowled with fat arms hanging like hams, and the two arrayed themselves so that Ellis could only face one of them at a time. The license plate on the Jeep was mudded over.

"Two flats. That is some bad luck. How does that happen?" the smiling one asked.

"A statistical fluke." Ellis felt adrenaline and a fearfulness that annoyed him. "It could happen to anyone." He expected a blow from behind, but expecting it did not help when it came: an exquisite pain at the upper rear of the head. The world chunked with black. He fell to his knees. His vision slowly cleared, and he watched the smiling man shape his lips around incomprehensible syllables. Beside him, the fat one held a short length of pipe. Then a flashing movement, and nothing remained but a monumental pain and the impossibility of movement.

• • •

Shades of white. These gradually tinted blue, then green.

Objects pressed—the graveled earth. Dry, toothy weeds.

A faint shallow rasping noise intruded. He understood this to be his own breath. For minutes he focused on it.

Then, sitting up, he gasped and the black returned, but he strained and kept himself up. He felt a long, soft welt near the top of his head and alongside it an open wound, with blood clotting in his hair. His wallet, his watch, and his keys were gone. His cell phone was gone.

No, he remembered, he had broken that.

When he shifted his gaze to the birch wood, the white trees trailed rainbow images. He felt like sitting down and abandoning the difficulties of the world and waiting, waiting a long time, until his body merged into the rough earth, until he was consumed into something larger, something without self-awareness or memory.

Instead he walked, stumbling with confused balance, back toward the Cricket Bar.

The minivan stood in the same place he'd abandoned it at the side of the road, doors open. The keys lay on the driver's seat. A hole gaped in the dash where the radio had been. But in the armrest console between the seats, under a clutter of receipts, he found his credit card where he'd left it.

He locked the doors, took up the keys, and started walking again. He was paced by phantoms at the edge of vision, white things and red things and black things. They scrambled forward, only to retreat as he turned to see them better. The sun stood high and felt hot on the wound in his scalp. The heat grew as he walked, until it pressed like a blade.

A vehicle approached from behind, and he held himself from turning to look at it. A pickup, it went by scattering gravel from the tires, not slowing.

He did not see another vehicle until miles later when he staggered into an intersection. More cars went by without stopping, and he kept on beside buzzing high voltage lines held aloft by enormous steel armatures. He came to a gas station with a garage attached. A mechanic, sitting at a large accounts ledger on a grease-blacked tabletop, looked at him for some seconds before asking, "What happened?"

Ellis looked at himself, his clothes soiled and bloody. He said, "I'm not sure."

The mechanic laughed.

Thirty-two

He found:

. . . the rural stretch of interstate alongside a pasture full of roan Arabians where a Nissan Armada swerved into the median, overturned, rolled into a Toyota Corolla in the oncoming lanes, and bounced onward, killing three in the Nissan and two in the Toyota; later a piece of human flesh was discovered in a windshield wiper of the Toyota, torn from one of the occupants as he was flung through the window opening.

. . . the two-lane in front of yellow, spiraling water-park slides where a semi struck a Honda Pilot, which struck an Oldsmobile, sending it into the opposing lane to meet a Firebird head-on; everyone walked away except the driver of the Firebird, who was dead by the time anyone thought to check on him.

. . . the highway between slouching hills planted with soybeans where a Toyota Land Cruiser caught a wheel rim and rolled. Centrifugal forces pulled the driver's head out a window opening, and the ground came up and decapitated her. Police photographed her head sitting upright on the earth, as if she had been buried to her neck by children.

And while he stopped only at the places of accidents that he knew, he passed others all the time: he saw tire marks on the asphalt and rutted into roadside gravel and earth, paint transfers on the Jersey barriers, dents in the guardrails, broken glass and plastic glittering on the asphalt.

For a few miles he giggled at himself. It was becoming impossible to see backward and understand how his life had come to be this.

He spent an hour, two hours, with his map spread on the steering wheel, gazing at the X's where he had marked the Wright jobs, trying to see a pattern or approach that would bring him to Boggs. He could see no pattern. He had no intuition.

He noticed, without much interest, that the minivan looked bad. He wiped the windshield from time to time with a gas-station squeegee, but the bodies of insects lay across the leading edge of the minivan in a continuous crust. He shoved receipts into the toothless mouth where the radio had been.

He slept one night in the open empty parking lot of a half-abandoned mall. The overhead lights pushed a glow that woke him repeatedly, thinking that he saw the sun again and again, so that when the sun did actually rise it seemed a delusion. He circled the parking lot in the minivan and discovered a six-lane interstate below him where a thin mist had settled and the vague shapes of commuters moved slowly like great herds of murmuring animals.

At least a dozen days had passed since his collision with James Dell. Maybe more? He wasn't sure what day of the week it was, and as he fingered the stitches in his scalp, he couldn't remember how long they had been in. He was aware of losing his grip not just on time, but also on what he was doing, as if all he was doing was relenting to the movement of the road. Visions of James Dell still occasionally startled him. He recalled Heather and a swirl of intense feeling came. "Heather," he cried aloud. Perhaps he hadn't even heard his own voice for a couple of days. Here on the road, he thought, it doesn't matter what I say. "Heather Heather Heather," he repeated until, over a score of miles, it became gibberish.

He called her from a dusty pay phone in a moldering 7-Eleven parking lot. "Where are you?" she asked.

He told her he was in western Nebraska.

"My God, you're halfway across the country."

"I feel like everything is just kind of coasting downhill."

"You need to rest."

"No. I'm okay."

"It's no good pushing yourself to complete exhaustion."

"I'm all right." The phone in his hand trembled. "I get some sleep. I eat." He thought of the starving old man in *The Old Man and the Sea*, dragged around by a giant fish. The book was one of Boggs's favorites.

The day happened to be beautiful. For miles uncountable, wheat spanned everything not the road, a wind roiling it like water. A flock of starlings dove and wheeled. An odd half-timbered building stood alone, set off from the world by a rectangle of picket fence. A man worked over a fallen tree with a chainsaw. A retailer of farm equipment offered machines, green and yellow and shining. On the interstate, he had the pleasure of accelerating again, moving among semis like a fish in a pod of whales. Bright billboards came up out of the distance to meet him.

The trembling in his hand had spread; he looked at his legs trembling and felt muscles twitching in his face and in his hard, empty stomach. His grip on the steering wheel seemed to flutter.

He turned off the interstate and went through a little clapboard town, and then twenty miles later another town that seemed so much like the first that he spent a while trying to decide whether he'd inadvertently circled. He turned onto a smaller road. There was nothing out here but the narrow road and wheat growing on gentle hills. One gentle hill after another curved him up and down. The clouds overhead rushed eastward in a frenzy.

A narrow gravel road teed out on the left, and Ellis stopped with his turn signal flashing, checked his mirror, then turned, in the same place where a Pontiac Grand Am had slowed to do the same thing and was struck from behind by a semi pulling a load of hay. An oncoming Chevy Lumina had swerved to avoid the collision, went off-road, and overturned, killing its occupants, a family of four that had traveled six hundred miles to visit grandparents who lived two miles from the accident site. In the police photographs a scatter of toys in primary colors described the path of the rolling Chevy. Ellis recalled a photograph of the driver of the semi standing by his rig, bowed. And another photo, of the body of an obese child facedown on the earth.

He could hardly stand the thought of all the people who had been destroyed, the tragic people who had been hammered into his mind by his work, and yet whom he hardly knew. How could anyone bear such knowledge, except by ignoring it? But Boggs was causing that knowledge to unbind itself and shoot fire and fog through his mind.

After scuffing in the grass for a while, he found a green pacifier, half-buried. He had forgotten that the youngest was so young. Earth clung to the plastic and it shook in his hand.

He sat by the edge of the road, huddled. A mouse skittered through the grass. A grasshopper stood a minute on his thigh, then leaped away.

He picked a piece of asphalt from the crumbling edge of the roadway and let it rest heavy and warm in his hand. He set both hands on the road surface, to feel its absorbed heat. Then he lay down in the lanes, on their warmth, and watched the sky.

His mind suggested to him the passing observation that what he was doing was lying in the middle of the road. Why was he doing that? Wasn't this the sort of behavior that led to negative outcomes? But he didn't pursue these questions.

Bright, low clouds scudded across his field of vision. They seemed to be fleeing from a calamity that Ellis was ignorant of. There was no traffic, none at all, and he wondered at the terrible chance that three vehicles had met here. He heard the wind sifting through the grasses beside the road, but he could not feel it. The wind in the grass made a simmering, gorgeous sound. I am learning something important, he thought. But if so he could not describe it to himself, and then he thought, Perhaps I'm not learning anything. Perhaps I'm only following deeper and deeper into a vacant delusion.

A vehicle approached—he felt it in the road before he heard it, a low vibration that gathered to itself the whisper of tires turning. In sudden panic he rolled out of the road just as the car, a Chrysler Sebring, barked its tires, swerved, and passed him without stopping.

Ellis lay in the gravel for a while. When he finally started pushing himself up, there—right in front of his face, faintly pressed into the dirt beside him—was a tire mark. It had four deep longitudinal grooves and a network of hexagons between the grooves.

He scrambled up. Just behind him were the flat markings of the nearly bald rear tires. The same pattern of tire marks that Boggs had left outside the VFW hall. They looked recently made.

Ellis walked over the site again, and he found further traces in the dirt and grass beside the road. It appeared that Boggs had stopped on the roadside, then backed the car into the grass, making a two-point turn to reverse direction, returning the way he had come.

Or he could have been headed for the gravel side road.

Ellis walked to the gravel road and then tramped along it for a couple hundred feet, until he could identify more of Boggs's tire marks.

In Ellis's stomach a ball of snakes writhed. Here was a new point of data. He took out a map, and he found that the gravel road linked over to a rural state highway. And, going down that highway a hundred miles to the west, he would come to—

Thirty-three

He drove until he came to a curve of roadway under a hill that rose forty or fifty feet in the air and then suddenly leveled into a plateau.

He was near the end of the Great Plains: the croplands had disappeared miles back and the earth had turned to brown grasses and rock. He could see no dwellings, no buildings; no one lived anywhere near this spot. The sky overhead seemed excessively vast. Even the bits of hill that stood up in places, like the one here beside the road, only seemed to serve to emphasize the enormousness of the sky they failed to fill.

He stepped out of the minivan, and the air immediately began pressing itself, hot and dry, against him. Yet a lake lay not far away. He couldn't see the water from here, but he remembered it from aerial photos of the site. The hill stood on the north side of the road, and the water lay to the south, below a little rise in the land. He could just see the top of a dead, leafless tree out there that probably stood next to the lake.

His chest ached vaguely. Tremors moved through his hands and arms, into his jaw and eyelids. His eyes, too, felt dry.

He and Boggs had spent most of a day working here, surveying, photographing. Not far away, perhaps half an hour by foot, stood a mate to the hill, a little taller, with three windmills rising off it. Eight months after working below the first hill, they'd been brought out to work a second accident, which occurred at the foot of the second hill, with the windmills. That was the accident they later deemed Pig Accident One.

But Ellis had come first to the other accident location. The soil near the road was sandy with tufts of grass, and he scuffed around with his foot until he found an area full of broken glass. He picked up a piece the size of a housefly and felt its edges, watched it catch the sunlight. By examining the thickness and laminated qualities of a piece of glass it was possible to determine whether it had come from a windshield or a rear window or a side window. This appeared to be windshield glass; he was probably standing where the front of the van had come to rest. How many years ago now? Two? Three? The van, a rental, had burned, killing five of fourteen inside. They were grandparents, aunts, uncles, cousins, children, out on a weekend holiday. With so many dead and burned, some of them children, large amounts of money had been at stake. He and Boggs had worked a long time on this case and came to know it in great detail. They had never uncovered anything unexpected; after the first day's work, they probably could have predicted their ultimate findings to within a couple of mph. But they had produced innumerable reports and diagrams and animations, and Boggs had provided hours of deposition testimony.

Traffic now moved on the two-lane road at about 60 mph, rattling the brush around Ellis. A double yellow line indicated a no-passing zone on the curve around the hill, but a small silver Plymouth had nonetheless been passing, and so came head-on toward the rented van. Both drivers swerved, too late—the front-left corner of the Plymouth struck the front-left corner of the van, and the left side of the van pushed upward, as if it had hit a ramp. It fell onto its right side and slid into the dirt and grass. Deformed sheet metal punctured the fuel tank. Gasoline pooled under the van and began to burn.

Ellis sat sifting sand and shards of glass. He picked out the shards and examined them one by one. He kept thinking he needed to call someone, then losing track of the thought.

On the hill across the road a sign advertised Texaco gasoline, which contained useful additives.

He started looking at the sand, wondering if he could examine the grains individually. He turned the sand a little one way and then another to see how the sun played on it. Certain grains were black, others red or orange or white, their size inconsistent, and some were nearly pebbles.

Finally he rose and walked down the road to a fading two-track trail that disappeared into a wire fence. At the time of the accident, there had been a gate. Two men had been sitting in a pickup in front of the gate, talking about a possible cell-phone tower, to be placed on the hill; Ellis saw now that it had never been built. One of the men in the truck, an ex-marine, had run to the burning van, found a window broken out of the rear doors, and reached in. Fighting through the smoke and flames thickening in the van, unable to see, grabbing hands or legs or shirts or belts, he dragged out seven people.

He was a hero, but in his deposition he was taciturn and grim and spoke at length only of the screams of those he had to abandon.

Two more occupants kicked through the windshield and crawled out on their own. The rest died.

A wind hummed in the fence, and Ellis put his hands on it to feel for the wind's vibrations, but his hands only shook the wire. He walked back to where the van had come to rest and scoured again, from habit, for evidence of Boggs. He worked his way through the weeds until he came again to the fence. From here he could see a few bright glimmers of the lake surface.

He climbed the fence and pushed through brush. The water lay further away than it appeared, and the brush caught him as if to drag him back. His legs started to shake. He had to stand waiting until it passed.

Finally, after bulling through a margin of tall, sharp-edged grasses, he came to an open place along the shore. He crouched. The water was clear, faintly rippling, shallow. He cupped a handful and smeared it onto his face. The opposite shore was also enclosed in reeds and grasses, and the narrow lake stretched away to uninhabited distances right and left. A few ducks moved on the water.

A short squeal of tires startled him, but no noise of impact followed. He stood to look toward the road, and as he did he glimpsed a human shape to his right, near the water. He stepped through some weeds, wetting his shoes in mud. Someone lay face down at the water's edge—someone drinking from the lake or washing in it, as he had just done. But the figure didn't move.

"Boggs?" Ellis called.

He stood watching, waiting for Boggs to raise up. The trembling took him so absolutely that he could hardly move for fear of toppling. After a minute he managed to shuffle forward a few steps—and he saw it wasn't Boggs. Too short, too thin, wearing clothes that Boggs would never wear.

Ellis stepped from one thatch of grass to another, until he stood over the body of a long, thin man, perfectly dead. Waves came across the lake to jostle it.

After a time Ellis crouched. Then he sat. The splayed feet wore white tennis shoes scuffed and grayed by use. The legs wore khaki slacks. A bit of exposed flesh could be seen at the ankle, vaguely obscene. A dark blue sweatshirt, soaked with water. Thick, dark brown hair, wet and plastered to the head. The arms extended loosely, hands dangling in the water. The hair had no gray in it, so the dead man seemed not to have been very old, but it would have been hard to say how young or old he was. A few hairs on his neck bristled out of the water. The noise of the road gathered volume for a time, then diminished.

The day turned to evening and the air slowly cooled.

A pair of coots swam the shoreline and shied from the body and moved along. A magpie landed in the brush nearby, then startled away. Ellis looked up and saw, in a leafless dead tree some distance down the shore, several large black motionless cormorants. One fluttered its wings and glared at him, then stilled again.

He fell asleep—knees drawn up, head on knees—and woke in the cool night. In the distance, as vehicles rounded the curve of the hill, their headlamp beams revolved spasmodically forward and back. The sky glowed magnificently with stars. He was cold. A breeze touched him and jostled the grasses, and he became aware of someone seated a few feet away.

The dead risen—this was his first thought—from the lake water to sit there and ruminate on him.

But the stars made light enough to see that the body still lay where he had found it, face in the water, feet on the sand. And as Ellis studied the form of the person seated beside him, a car arced past and he saw the eyes gleam.

He moved a dry tongue in his mouth and felt an eyelid twitch. "I suppose you think you're stealthy and clever as a ninja or a Comanche or something," he said.

"You look awful, Ellis."

Even in the dark, Ellis could see that Boggs did not look well, either—his eyes watery, his clothes rumpled, his posture poor. But his hair was trim, and he looked like he'd been eating more than Ellis. Ellis turned, in a sensation of daze, uncertain of import, toward the body. "I thought he might be you."

"You keep doing that. Who is he?"

"I have no idea."

"Have you looked in his pockets?"

"I don't want to touch him."

"There might be an ID." Boggs looked at the sky as he talked. "There might be a medical alert bracelet or a bottle of pills."

The water rustled against the body.

"Anyway, now you found me," Boggs said.

"You found me."

Boggs shifted and the sand under him made little mouse squeaks. "It comes to the same thing. Now that we've achieved physical proximity, what do you want to say?"

"I want to say that I'm sorry."

Waves came and made a sound like the intermittent clapping of a child.

"That's it?"

"I betrayed you," Ellis said.

"It's what's happened."

Ellis let that wander over the water into the night. He didn't feel capable of the inquiry that it implied. He hardly felt capable of breathing. The twitch in his eyelid grew worse. He said, "*airlane*."

"Hmm," Boggs said.

"Where's the car? My dad still has it?"

"Not my bailiwick now. But I think you should look into it."

"What did you find?"

"I'm not involved. It's none of my business."

"You steal a piece of my brother's car and drop it on a roadside halfway across the country, and now you won't talk about it."

"Half-brother, right? Not full brother."

In frustration Ellis hit the ground with his fists. "You asshole," he said. "And here's another thing—did you slash my tires?"

"I noticed that your rear tires looked fresh. Nice deep tread."

"Middle of nowhere. And as I walked out, I was jumped by two thugs in a Jeep."

"That's terrible. Makes you wonder why anyone even leaves the house anymore."

"Did you cut my tires?"

Boggs's brow contracted. "No. I have no idea what you're talking about. I have to say, this is a disappointment."

He stood. He grabbed the body by an ankle.

"Come on. Help me."

Ellis stared.

"Let's get him out of the water. I can't stand looking at him like that."

"The police won't want him disturbed," Ellis said.

"I don't care." Boggs lifted the other ankle, stood between the two, and heaved.

"You're nuts," Ellis said, but with a sense of obscure obligation he stood, shaking, and clasped a leg—thin and clammy cold, making him glad his stomach was empty—and together they dragged the man onto shore.

"He sure is dead," Boggs said.

Ellis very gently put down the leg that he held. "Someone might be looking for him," he said. "He could have kids."

"We should roll him and get a look at his face."

"Don't do that. Let him be." Ellis felt close to weeping.

Boggs didn't reply, but neither did he move toward the body. "Might be that no one even knows he's gone," he said. "A solitary guy, wanders out here, dies, and no one notices. The universe as he understood it is extinguished, and it's the passing of a mite."

"You really don't know anything about him?" Ellis asked.

"How would I?"

"It seems strange that I'd stumble onto him here. And then you turn up."

Boggs laughed. "You think I planted a dead guy here?"

"What's your explanation?"

"It is the circumstance that has presented itself."

"You have to admit it's unlikely."

"That never stopped anything from happening."

"That's not true."

Boggs scoffed. With the point of his shoe he prodded the dead man's foot. It was difficult to look away from the body. The man's shoelaces were still tied.

"If you did set this up, I don't expect you'd admit it."

"No. That's true. I'm too smart for that."

Ellis laughed. "All right. Fate put him here."

"Absolutely not. I'm not sure why you think it's so strange. People die all the time."

Ellis laughed again. "You know, it's good to see you, Boggs."

The shirt had ridden up as they pulled the body from the water, showing a thin, pasty waist.

"Maybe he fell from an airplane," Boggs said, scowling.

"What are you going to do now?" Ellis asked.

"Maybe he'd hitched a ride in the bed of a pickup truck, and he flew out on that curve, and in disorientation he crawled here to die of internal hemorrhage."

Ellis was silent.

"Maybe this is just a place that had some meaning to him and he walked over here and ate a handful of pills and waited for an end. Some connection here. You remember that guy who climbed through the windshield? Maybe this is him. The passenger seat occupant. The one who said the hero guy was a liar."

"Really?" Though he'd forgotten it, it did seem that Boggs might have told him this back when they were skimming through the witness testimony. None of it had really mattered to their work. Their area of concern stopped when the van stopped moving. Other experts had dealt with the fire, and the human aftermath was even further beyond their scope of concern. Which seemed insane. Their work had been insane.

"He said that the ex-marine hero man actually didn't do much," Boggs said. "There were a bunch of people helping, and this guy said he pulled several people out himself, and it pissed him off that this other guy was made out to be the hero with the help of some cop buddies."

"His saying that doesn't prove anything."

"That's true."

"I read the marine's depo. Dragging people out and dragging people out. He talked about the screaming. His hand was burned, he went to the hospital, there's documentation."

"No one said that he didn't burn his hand. No one said that he didn't hear screaming but felt that the fire was too intense."

Then, with unexpected finality, as if on a signal, the conversation stopped.

Time ran a murky passage through the dark. Boggs sat quiet, and Ellis worried that disturbing him might initiate terrible consequences. He slept for a spell and woke feeling no less tired. When he searched the sky, he saw that any number of stars had winked away, as if the universe itself were dying. The lake water lay quiet. A few redwing blackbirds began to lurch around, reeds rattling in their wake. The sun cracked bright over the horizon. He forgot the body and then saw it again and then he did not want to look, but neither could he move his gaze away. The man's sweatshirt held a peculiar and slowly changing pattern of dark and light where it was wet and dry. It seemed difficult to believe that the dead man might not move now, while the hair bristled from his naked ankles and the pores there appeared as if they could begin to sweat.

"Don't you think," Boggs said, "that if you weren't in love with my wife, you could come up with something a little more compelling to say? There must be a part of you that would be happy to see me gone. Maybe only subconsciously. Your brain throws up some ideas, not others. What are the constraints on their formation?"

"You're trying to guilt-trip me."

"Yes." Boggs suddenly stood. In the pale early light he towered over Ellis. "Let's go."

"Leave him?"

"Yes."

"We can't do that."

"Actually, we can."

The body's flesh was bone pale. The skin of the neck held two creases, the cumulative effect of years of life.

"You're welcome to stay," Boggs added.

One of the body's hands still extended to the lake, and tiny waves teased the fingers like a cat.

"How can we leave him?"

"You want to put him on a picnic table somewhere, like that pig rig? We just leave him. We don't know anything about him. Later you'll probably wonder if he even really existed."

Ellis didn't know which was more terrible—that he didn't know anything about the man, or that this meant that he might leave him. But Boggs started away and Ellis moved in his trail.

The world around Ellis seemed to unsettle and shift as if composed of tiny swarming insects. He followed as best as he could, but his foot caught in a hole, he fell, and he lost sight of Boggs.

He ran then, but when he reached the road Boggs had gone, and even the road lay empty.

Thirty-four

He drove south a mile, then turned onto a divided highway with entry and exit ramps and a grass median. It was a state highway, but it had the scale and styling of an interstate. He stopped below the windmills.

Right here: Pig Accident One. But Boggs was not to be seen.

Ellis stepped out of the minivan, then after a minute he climbed back inside. He felt at a loss. He doubted whether he had the energy to pursue Boggs further. He didn't know what he should have said to him, but he felt he hadn't said it. Perhaps Boggs was right about his subconscious. Perhaps he really only wanted Boggs's spontaneous and unjustified forgiveness.

Eventually he left the minivan again and walked a little ways uphill, aimless and impatient. Wind ghosted the grasses, and sweeping over them were the long-limbed shadows of the turning windmills, shadows that came toward him and passed over him; he had to fend off a sudden vertigo. The traffic bellowed and shone in the sun. There had been no shining sun at the time of PA1; the accident had occurred in a thick fog and involved three semis, five cars, two SUVs, a minivan, and a pickup towing a pontoon boat. Witnesses described an aftermath of smashed and overturned vehicles haphazard on the road, two of them burning, the pontoon boat on its side, injured people wandering and shouting, the sirens and lights of police, fire, and ambulance vehicles drifting in the fog, and the bodies of the dead pigs—one of the semis had been pulling a trailer full of them—scattered over asphalt and into ditches and fields, and all of this overlaid with the awful screams of the uncomprehending, writhing wounded pigs, and the occasional report of a police pistol silencing one.

But when he and Boggs had come here to conduct their scene inspection a year later, it had been a bright day just like this. And there had been another stray dog, a black-and-brown mongrel, old and white in the muzzle, that sat a short distance away from them and barked dolefully. While the two of them worked up and down the road, dodging in and out of traffic, Boggs had left the rental car's stereo on, declaiming Tolstoy's "Master and Man" through open windows, so that the sound of certain words floated in the air like wallowing balloons.

. . . cob . . . sledge . . . drift . . .

They wielded cameras and surveying equipment, sweated and shouted down the open distance of the roadway over the roar of passing trucks. For most of the afternoon the dog sat scratching itself at the edge of the ditch, occasionally sniffing and doddering around.

. . . ravine . . . mittens . . .

And then this one, too, came to their specially outfitted, hard-sided equipment case and lifted a leg. Boggs looked at the dog, looked at Ellis, then shrugged, yelled, threw a measuring tape, and ran the dog off with his arms upraised, yipping, shrieking, chortling. To Ellis he had appeared absolutely happy.

But then, while they drove back to the airport, Boggs had pulled that stunt of driving just a couple of feet behind a semitrailer.

And now, on the opposite side of the highway, Boggs's green convertible slowed and parked.

Boggs stepped out, gripping a white paper bag, and without hesitation he stepped into the lanes. A car swerved violently around him, honking. Others braked hard.

Ellis shouted and started down the hill.

Boggs walked across the lanes and into the median, while traffic beside him came to a standstill, a chorus of horns blaring. He moved into the other set of lanes the same way, but there happened to be a gap in traffic and the effect was less dramatic. As Ellis came up, Boggs frowned at the minivan. "Don't they make some kind of a man's version of that?"

"Boggs—" Ellis said.

"I brought donuts." Boggs held out the white paper bag. Ellis pushed it away. Scenting the sweetness, he felt sick.

Boggs began climbing up the hill, and after a second Ellis followed. Now and again he stopped to gasp and to yank burrs from the cuffs of his slacks.

He caught up with Boggs at the base of a cyclone fence that surrounded the windmills, and they sat. The windmills swished and squeaked overhead, and the rumble of the highway rose from below. In the distance they could see the other hill and the Texaco sign about additives and the road that curved at its foot and the lake where the dead man lay. With the sun behind them, the lake waters appeared black. It was part of a chain of lakes stretching out behind a reservoir in the far distance. Nearer, a hawk spiraled on a thermal.

"In the fog, you couldn't have seen anything from here," Boggs said. "All there would have been were pig screams and shots." A semi, entering the fog, had slowed. A second semi, following the first, had not slowed as quickly as the first and hit it. Other vehicles piled up behind. A man in a pickup had survived a collision with an SUV and climbed out; as he stood in the roadway, a semi ran him over. To explain how he ended up where he did—seventy feet down the roadway—was tricky, and after a lot of modeling and calculating Ellis and Boggs had concluded that a semi had simply dragged him along until it jackknifed and overturned. It was the same semi that had hauled the doomed swine.

"What are you going to do?" Ellis asked. "Will you quit this driving around?" He'd spent all this time chasing, and still all he could think to do was to ask him to quit it.

"I'm thinking maybe a little hut near a beach in California," Boggs said. "Maybe sell juice and smoothies to girls in bikinis, and I'll have a small apartment upstairs, and I'll learn to surf."

"Are you serious?"

Boggs grinned and shrugged. "I'd like to see these windmills at sunset. Something about windmills has always reminded me of the end of things. Sunsets and windmills and Ragnarok. Nothing so large should be moving like that. It's like we're trying to engineer the world into a freakish final image before we destroy ourselves."

"Yeah. I'm tired, Boggs." He loved Boggs. He wanted to help Boggs, but he didn't know how. He asked, "Are you going to kill yourself or not?"

"I've told you I'm not going to kill myself."

"Talk to me about your decision process about what you're going to do."

"Jesus," Boggs said. "There's no process. I'm devoid of process."

"You're just doing nothing."

"I've been thinking that, on some level in my poor brain, I was probably just giving it all to you. I never felt I was good at anything except work. She was my only other success, and I'd screwed that up. I didn't know what to do, and I didn't know what to do, and it became doing nothing, and it became a gift. I was giving her an out. And giving myself one, waiting for you two to take it from my hands. But you know what got into me and twisted? The way you dragged it out. How long have you been fucking her? A year and a half? Longer? You couldn't just run away with her? I thought I had decided to wait it out. But I broke, I guess."

Ellis shook himself. Leaning forward, not looking at Boggs, he said, "I won't take everything on myself."

"That's the difference between your cognitive experience and mine," Boggs said. "You feel guilty; I feel nullified. I feel the absence of feeling." He laughed. "Am I a robot? No. Sure. I have my own volition. Awareness of my own volition has been eating me alive. Terrible stuff. Maybe none of us really wants responsibility for our own volition. Maybe that's why we call them accidents. Let me tell you about an accident: one day I get out of a depo sooner than expected, go to the airport and put myself on standby for an early flight. We catch a tailwind, and I land on the ground almost five hours early. I get home, and Heather doesn't usually leave her work around in the house, but here on the table is a big stack of her pinhole photos. So I flip through them. And in a corner of one picture I see the left-rear quarter panel of your car."

"You discovered—"

"Yes."

"You sold the RV."

"No shit I sold the RV. Did you really think that thing was inconspicuous? Why not go around fucking my wife in a lime-green Zeppelin?"

"She used it for her pinhole photos."

"Yeah. All of a sudden she was a lot more interested in that pinhole photography project. After I found that picture, I followed her in the RV one day, right to your place, and you climbed in. Jaunty, I thought, very jaunty. I hadn't seen you walk like that before. And then—then all the options sucked. Usually I know what I want to do, but with this thing, trying to decide what to do felt like trying to reach my hand down my throat to grab my liver. I gave up. I figured I'd let you guys figure it out. You seemed to have ideas."

"Is this what you talked to her about, at the golf course?" Ellis asked. "That I didn't tell her to get a divorce?"

"No," Boggs said. "I talked to her about your brother."

"Half-brother," Ellis said mechanically. "If you're depressed, we can—"

"Stop that. I'm not depressed. Do I seem depressed? I'm just tired of thinking."

Boggs glowered at the highway.

"Pig Accident One," Boggs said. "Wounded pigs screaming. Pig Accident Two, they were dead, lumps in the road. But here they were writhing and screaming. Horrible. I've spent some time thinking about those screaming pigs. What does a screaming pig sound like? I imagine it sounds almost human, only a little different, in some unidentifiable way, to make you think, *What in the name of God?* And fog does weird things to sound. The cops wouldn't have been able to see through the fog. You'd have to track the sound of the screams, stumbling around to find screaming wounded pigs, and occasionally you'd hear your partner blasting away, and a scream somewhere stops. Not to mention the fires, the smells of burned vehicles and ham, the body of a man dragged under a semi. What are you to think? What's even the right question to ask? Is it: Who's to blame? Who can be sued? Probably not. 'It changes life forever,' they say. So it's like an inflection point, an instant of chance where the curve of a life changes direction." Boggs joined his hands in an inverted V. "The change of direction is important, but life is what happens before and after. That's the implication. But what if that's wrong? What if what's actually essential is the point of change? The instant when everything is altered: the accident, the collision, the rollover? What if *that's* life? Where everything changes. And if the accident is the essential point, then by looking at those points, I figured I could see something new."

"See something new—" Ellis repeated, amazed. "Let me offer an observation from personal experience. These accidents just make people really unhappy."

"But there must be a kind of compensation. Isn't there a curtain that's pulled aside for an instant? Just at that instant? A glimpse of—of—" Boggs had his hands in front of himself, and he looked at them with predatory intensity, as if he might make a quick movement to bite off his own thumbs. "—meaning? Can you tell me that? Is it tellable?"

He didn't look at Ellis, only his hands. His lips had gone white. Ellis had never seen Boggs like this, never seen his calm fall off him. It was frightening. All their work together had been grounded in factual evidence, they proceeded by reason-based analysis and decision-making, and until now he had presumed that Boggs's actions made some kind of sense in a context of vengeance or a search for something real. But there was no sense here. He looked at Boggs, and Boggs seemed small and curiously childlike.

"There's nothing like that," Ellis said. "Just misery."

"But there has to be an exchange. For every action an opposite reaction."

"No. It's not a solvable system. It's just horrible and that's all."

"A glimpse. The door flutters before it closes again. A horizon beyond the horizon."

"No."

"'Chance and chance alone has a message for us. Everything that happens out of necessity, everything repeated day in and day out, is mute. Only chance can speak to us.' Milan Kundera wrote that. Something like that."

"Kundera was writing about romance! He wasn't talking about getting killed in a car crash."

Boggs sighed.

"Do you believe me?" Ellis asked.

"That this is work has been what I've known, and because it's what I've known I want to see meaning in it that may not exist? That's possible."

"Stop, then. Will you stop? End all this."

"I don't think there's an end to anything, really," Boggs said. "We're always just causing whatever will happen next."

"You're talking like a low-rent philosophy major. We live in the actual world. We have to deal with the actual world."

Boggs shrugged. "Yeah. I'm done driving around."

They sat in silence.

They ate donuts.

Ellis still trembled. The sky was cloudless and depthless and difficult to look at. Over time the wind gathered, and the windmills whirred and made whomp-whomp sounds. Sometimes one windmill or another boomed with aching steel. He worried hopelessly about abandoning the body by the lake. He felt an obligation to it, felt he should have done something differently, although he couldn't think exactly what. Much of the past now seemed this way. He had abandoned Heather and James Dell, too.

Below moved the traffic, always moving. Red car. Black semi tractor and white refrigerated trailer. Green car. Silver SUV. Purple pickup. Green car. When he was growing up in Coil, he recalled, it was next to impossible to see a new car in green; now they were everywhere.

"I saw the two of you embracing," Boggs said. "I knew she was only trying to console you. I knew you were probably only thinking about the man you had hit. But it made it worse, to see you need her so much. And that was it. Nothing had changed in the facts of my life, but I saw them clearly. I couldn't go back to Heather, to you, to work."

Silence again, and Ellis sat weeping. He'd become huge with guilt, as if too obese to move. Time passed and perhaps he slept—was it possible to sleep with eyes open? The scene remained before him, but its meaning changed with the purity of dream. All of it lay under a great bell jar. All of it peered at him and waited. All of it was held in a fog with the noises of the end of the world. All of it fell slowly away.

Suddenly Boggs looked up, startled. And Ellis followed him down the slope of the hill.

As they reached the edge of the road, wind galed off the passing semis, the sun strobed between in the blades of a windmill, and Boggs began talking about putting up little windmills along the interstates to catch the wind thrown off by passing traffic. He said he wasn't sure if the energy captured this way would be negated by an additional wind resistance experienced by the passing vehicles. He raised a hand to shield the sun and talked about the worst gas-station bathroom that he had ever seen. He said something about water. Most of his words were lost in the traffic noise.

Then he turned and stepped into the road.

Ellis, surprised, reached a hand after him, and he felt on his fingertips the air pulsing with the passage of an SUV—

—the SUV that struck Boggs and carried him away.

Boggs flipped over the hood. He bounced off the windshield and roof. He turned heels over head, limbs outstretched, as the SUV passed below him.

He came down on his shoulder. His head bent strangely.

The SUV continued ahead a hundred feet before the brakes locked the tires and they began to cry and the SUV spun in the roadway.

A semi traveling behind had time and space to slow and stop.

Traffic started to back up.

Ellis stared, waiting for something more to happen. Something more had to happen.

Time passed, and he thought, I should understand this now. Someone was shouting. Nothing happened except that people shouted and traffic accumulated in long idling columns.

He went slowly toward Boggs, already sure that Boggs was dead.

Five

Thirty-five

The room—small, oddly shaped, poorly lit—lay at the end of a cul-de-sac hallway, at the place where an older hospital building had been mated to a newer addition, the room itself an architectural afterthought formed by opening some space off the side of a storage closet. It had several corners and one narrow window, and offered barely enough floor space for a single bed, two chairs, and a few pieces of equipment. On the ceiling a fluorescent light box flickered.

"They brought me back to life and then what? Then they put me into a tomb," complained James Dell, his voice a croak.

He sipped from a plastic cup. Water overspilled his lips and fell onto his green hospital gown, where he batted at it. Pale and brightly scarred, he lay in collapse, a pair of eyeglasses with black frames owling his eyes.

Ellis had come here in a state of exhaustion that left him stumbling and half-blind, afraid James Dell would despise him, would refuse him. But Dell seemed hardly aware of him. Instead he worried aloud about money, and because of money he wanted to leave the hospital. Mrs. Dell said he couldn't leave. He said it was a free country. Mrs. Dell said the doctors said he shouldn't leave. He tried to get out of bed but fell back with a shriek and moaned. He said she should help. She glowered and said she would not help him to act like an idiot. He said he would soon be broke. She said he had no choice. He said he would be broke and would have to live under a bridge and cook rats for dinner over a barrel fire. She said he'd never cooked a thing in his life. He said she should have let him die rather than be bankrupted into a life of homelessness and rat-eating, and could she move the pillow under his leg nearer to the knee? Which she did.

Their volume rose and fell; Dell's strength was inconsistent.

Ellis sat in the corner in a plastic chair. He recalled the collapse of James Dell onto the hood and the patter of glass against his own face—and now he sat beside Dell's bed, and Dell complained that there were too many commercials on and changed the channel, and Mrs. Dell hounded him to change it back and leave it, please. Meanwhile the light in the little window over the bed brightened and faded with the passage of unseen clouds.

After Boggs's death, after the police had released him, Ellis had begun driving. He hadn't been sure where he was driving to. He seemed able to see and to recall everything, and this was terrible, and he wished for a catatonic state, a slipping under the waters of consciousness. He ate, he drank, he slept, he went to the bathroom in gas stations and rest stops and Taco Bells. He crossed back through Nebraska, Iowa, Indiana, and then started moving southeast. He came into the foggy, round heaps of the Appalachians and crossed through them into North Carolina and then aimed toward the ocean, until, as he drove a lonesome stretch of two-lane between fields where cotton tufted white like a scatter of snow, the minivan's temperature gauge began to climb. Soon the radiator spit steam.

He had to be towed from the roadside. While a mechanic worked to swap the water pump, Ellis asked what day it was. Almost two weeks had dissolved since Boggs's death.

He went to a phone on a post near the road and, after a minute of doubt, called the hospital.

"He's come out of it," Mrs. Dell exclaimed. "He's really better. I've told him about you, about how you called, about your concern. He wants to meet you."

This—he saw now—was obviously an untruth. But when she said it, he had believed her and glimpsed something. He drove the minivan for a day and a half without rest to reach the hospital.

After listening to them bicker for a while, Ellis excused himself to go to the bathroom.

After drying his hands and stepping back out into the hall, he considered walking out of the hospital and driving away. But he wanted to watch one more time the opening and closing of Dell's eyes, the life of his thin limbs, the sneering of his lips. So he went back.

Dell lay alone in the room, holding up a hand and staring at it.

Ellis said, "I wish I could do more than say I'm sorry."

"Sir." Dell grimaced. "If you apologize again, I'll have them throw you out."

Ellis sat. The overhead light flashed. A passing bed rattled in the hallway.

"I was distracted," Dell said, "and I tried to cross the street where I shouldn't have."

"I shouldn't have tried to pass on the right."

"I've passed on the right a thousand times." Dell's voice guttered with self-disgust. "Nothing wrong with it."

Ellis hesitated, feeling he should apologize, afraid to apologize.

"She went out for some lunch," Dell said. "The bitch."

Ellis stared. "She was here all the time you were in the coma."

"I don't doubt it."

"It was very hard for her, her husband—"

"I'm not her husband. She's not my wife."

"She isn't?"

"Ex. We were unmarried eight and a half years ago. She can go anytime she wants. I don't love her." He wound his sheet on his finger. "I wish I did. It would be something."

Then he sat forward with a jerk and looked around. He complained that she'd been away too long and she was spending money on lunch when she could have just as easily eaten off the tray of food that the hospital gave him.

A short, cushiony nurse came in to fret over the machines.

Ellis rose and excused himself.

He found Mrs. Dell standing in the hallway just outside the door, as if waiting for him, or eavesdropping, or both. She led him a little down the hall, then stopped and looked at the floor. Her skin appeared blue-gray, as if she hadn't been in the sun in years. She said, "He has his own place, but he lives with me. He comes to me crying like a baby, and I take care of him. It's a lot of drama. Eventually, he leaves, then a couple of days later he comes back." She sighed. "I don't know. He says he doesn't love me. I don't know if that's what he really feels."

"I don't know—"

"He often hides what's in his heart. He doesn't have many friends. But I thought there might be a connection between you two."

Ellis stared at her. "But why?"

She said, "Should I give up hope?"

"Not hope," Ellis said.

"Of course I should." she said. "But if I could, wouldn't I have, years ago?"

"Maybe, I don't know— " Ellis cast around for a few words, anything, a cliché. "Maybe a little time apart would help," he said, then regretted having said it. "I'm sorry," he said.

"You should stop saying that. He was running from me."

"In the street?"

"He was trying to get away from me. I had surprised him. I guess I had sort of followed him."

"You weren't going to the play together?"

"No. Oh, no." She shook her head. "Goodbye."

He drove to Heather's house.

Drawing near, he slowed the minivan to a crawl and remembered years before, passing by here in naïveté and embarrassment, while Boggs waved from the garage. The memory roused a sensation that he could not name, although it was excruciating.

A car came close behind him, and he accelerated away. But then through a route of miles he turned and turned back, slowed, turned into the drive, let the minivan idle down its length.

He stood a minute in the driveway. The garage was closed, the windows dark. The grass of the lawn had grown long.

He reached for the doorbell, but then tried the knob instead, and at his touch the door opened. He stood looking at the darkened living room. "Heather?" he called, softly. The walls were worked with innumerable bright colors—images in crayon, water color, construction paper, cellophane, papier-maché, stickers, marker, glued buttons, seashells, bottle caps—pieces of art her students had given her or had simply abandoned. They were stuck up with thumbtacks and filled the walls from floor to ceiling. Their initial effect could be overwhelming, but he had seen them a couple of times before when he picked up Boggs for work trips, and when he lugged in the bookshelf with Heather—he had never again come here alone with her; it had seemed too risky—and he looked at the walls now only to try to detect whether anything had changed. Then he noticed that on the floor lay many objects, scattered or assembled in piles—pens, coffee mugs, silverware, magazines, drink coasters, a tube of Crest, sheets, a bar of soap, wire hangers, a TV remote. He studied these for a while, but could make no sense of them. He toed through to the kitchen, which stood empty, the shades drawn, the refrigerator whirring, a single light under a cabinet illuminating a tub of sugar and a set of knives held to the wall by magnets.

The windowless stairwell was particularly dark. He hung onto the banister as he crept upward. Then the top step lay underfoot, and the guest bedroom stood open and empty. The bed was squarely made and desolate.

The door of the master bedroom stood ajar. It swung under his hand.

The shades drawn, the room lay in dim gray illumination, its objects defined by shadows. After a while he could see Heather asleep in the bed. He felt he could hardly breathe and feared he would inadvertently cry out.

For minutes he stood.

Then he moved into the room, aware of the sounds he made—the brushing of the creases of his clothing, the crackling press of his feet into the carpet, the tiny grinding of his joints. He stood beside the bed, then eased down to kneel on the carpet. She slept on her stomach, her head turned so that the right side of her face pressed into the pillow, exposing the scar on the left side. Her hair spread wild. Her lashless eyelids appeared frail and naked; her face was lined in a way that made her seem tired even as she slept.

He reached toward her, but stopped short. The bed sheets were twisted tight around her. Laundry sprawled at the foot of the bed, and a half-dozen coffee mugs crowded the bedside table. He was glad to watch her sleep and feared that when she woke she would send him away, because he had not saved Boggs, because he had killed Boggs, because he had left her for so long, because to be sent away seemed the least that he deserved. Through parted lips her teeth showed dry and dull white. Her eyes darted under the lids. The scar on her skin seemed more shining and pale than he recalled.

Then her eyes opened; she gazed at him.

Time seemed to condense and fall in tiny droplets while he waited.

"Ellis," she said, unsurprised. "I've been so worried."

"Boggs is dead." His awareness concentrated in a little sphere around her, the rest blurry. "He stepped into the highway."

"They said you were there." She touched his hand. "I thought maybe at the funeral you would come."

"I just drove. For days I didn't know what I was doing. Or I tried not to. I was afraid if I came here you would send me away."

She shook her head. "Why?"

"You'll forgive me?"

"Forgive? There are a thousand things that we should talk about, and I don't even know what you're talking about."

"Heather—"

"I thought about buying an RV like the one my dad had and going out to look for you. The same kind of RV so you would know it was me. But I guessed you would come back." She spoke to the ceiling, turning to him only with glances, as if shy. "Because you had said you would come back when it was over, and you're the kind of person who does what he says he will. Even if you did say you would come back *soon*."

"As soon as I could—"

"If I had a nickel for every excuse."

"The road to hell is paved with nickels."

She smiled a little. "Yes." Then her features suddenly strained, and she rolled away. "It's okay," she said without looking at him. "It's okay."

He moved into bed with her and nestled against her. He tried not to suggest to himself the question of how many times Boggs had lain in this bed.

He wished he had come to Heather's house sooner. He felt impossibly indebted. Here, for now, nothing needed to be explained.

Boggs had been cremated, Heather said, the ashes sent to his parents. She had arranged to have his convertible donated to a charity rather than shipping it back here, but the things piled over the living room floor were Boggs's things, or things that she thought of as his, which she could not bring herself to use or to trash. She asked Ellis if he would do something with them.

So he had a task. When she went to school to teach, he ranged the house, gathering: all the items in the living room, then the shirts and slacks in the bedroom closet—clothing that he had seen Boggs wear many times—and the sunglasses in the dresser, the pocket knives in the credenza in the hallway, the baseball caps on the refrigerator, all into plastic garbage bags that he put on the back patio.

The files of records and financial documents that Boggs had assembled were still stacked on the dining table. Ellis piled them in a cabinet in the spare bedroom.

There was a bookshelf full of audio books on CD. Ellis listened for a while to a scene near the end of the cowboy novel, *Warlock*.

"*There was no sound. One of the barkeepers scurried forward with four white candles. Blaisedell jammed one in the mouth of the whisky bottle, lit it, and placed it beside Morgan's head. He took the bottle from the judge's table and fixed and lit a second, which he placed on the other side of Morgan's head—*"

Then he took the CD out and he scooped all the CDs into garbage bags.

He told Heather what had happened, as best he could, the facts of the event, probably not much different from what the police had told her. The official report, Heather said, had labeled it a suicide. "I don't think he thought it was a suicide," Ellis said. "He didn't look for the car that hit him. He just didn't look to see if there was a car. I don't think he was aware of the car, except as a possibility. He knew there was traffic, which might or might not be able to stop for him. He'd done exactly the same thing a little earlier and got away with it. He took a risk. What do you call a person who does that?" He waited for Heather to say something, but she didn't. He said, "He wanted to feel something, I guess."

He told her that when he reached Boggs and found him dead, he had fallen to the ground and somehow scraped his own face on the asphalt, so he was bleeding freely as the police arrived, and they believed for some time that he had also been involved in the accident.

He labored to raise words. "What's strange is that I have to work very hard to remember the collision," he told her. "As if—as if I can't even feel guilty correctly."

As he spoke, a prickling sensation, like hot sand, had filled him grain by grain until he was choking and could say no more.

• • •

After a couple of days, Ellis was searching through closets for the fourth or fifth time, sorting item by item through drawers, wondering whether Heather would consider a ballpoint from a Hyatt or a stray brown coat button to have been Boggs's.

He also found hidden away in the garage some of Heather's art projects. There were disposable coffee cups that rattled when he lifted them: viewed through a hole in the lid, each contained a diorama—of octopuses hanging from tiny strings, of a dinosaur emerging from an outhouse. He discovered a toy airplane that had been covered with delicately placed feathers and looked like an airplane-shaped chicken. Afraid that Heather might throw it away, he left it hidden where he'd found it.

And then he came on a large box filled with hundreds of pinhole-camera prints, piled and unsorted, a messy heap of images. He sat turning through them one by one, until he came to a photo from the RV's side window that showed a scatter of cars in a wide parking lot, sun coming down from the upper left in a stroke of streaming white, and, in the opposite corner, the rear quarter panel of Ellis's car.

It was the photo that Boggs had discovered, that had triggered the unwinding.

Ellis tried to recall when the photo was taken. It looked like a supermarket parking lot. He couldn't summon a memory of the instant. He wondered if it had seemed idyllic. And then Heather opened the pinhole for a second or two, light struck the film causing chemical changes, and formed an image.

He put the rest of the photos away where he had found them, but he took this one. He carried it to the minivan and put it inside the glove box, where the *airlane* nameplate still rested and reminded him that he didn't know what Boggs had known.

• • •

Heather sat with the TV on and a page before her, doodling dense tangles of lines, craggy, elaborate constructions: leaves, machineries, mazes, branches, flowers, tangles of wire, heaps of rope, blending into one another from edge to edge of the page.

"I feel extravagantly ashamed all the time," she said. "As if I'd been coated with something, plasticky or rubbery, shiny. Minty green. It's strange when no one else seems to notice." She looked at her hand. "Do you still see my scars?"

"I haven't noticed them in a long time," Ellis said. This seemed the only thing to say, even if it was not true.

"I think I'd actually forgotten them. I didn't think I ever would, but then I did. I know because now I see them again."

He watched for her to throw things or claw herself, but she didn't move. He knew something undefined and emotional was shifting between them, and he tried to think through it carefully. But it was like trying to think himself to California.

"About Christopher's accident," he said. Just that, experimentally.

She didn't answer or move.

"You remember—" he said.

"No."

"You don't remember? Or you don't want to talk about it?"

"It's too terrible now."

"Please?" he said. This seemed absurdly inadequate, but when he tried to press on he came only into emptiness and he couldn't think how else to ask or plead. He dared not mention the *airlane* nameplate. She seemed to have a secret, and so he needed to hold onto his own.

"No."

"But don't you—"

"No."

"And if—"

"No."

Thirty-six

The first time he set out, he drove north a few miles, but then turned in at a park that he knew and sat for some hours at the edge of a lake with a swimming area to watch the children scream and splash. Behind him mountain bikes came down a rocky trail with the rattling clatter of rolling typewriters. As the day leaned into dusk, the swimmers started leaving, and soon the water lay smooth, and he sat alone in the bluish light that hovered off the water and recalled the dead man that he and Boggs had left, and who might still, for all that he knew, lie there undiscovered, because in the aftermath of Boggs's death he had never mentioned it to the police.

The second time, he made it to Coil. He circled on the roads, peering at the park, the strip malls, the old buildings in the old center of town, many shut and boarded. Local commerce had shifted almost entirely to a few chain stores and restaurants around an interstate exit several miles to the west. But the high school appeared unchanged, the library likewise.

He stopped in front of a store that sold pet supplies—it stood in the place of a baseball-card shop that he remembered. He sat for a minute, not looking at the intersection where his brother had died, then stood out of the minivan and approached the intersection, looking at the place with his hands in his pockets.

Black-gray asphalt with shallows worn through by the passage of vehicles. Six-inch concrete curbs. Two faint narrow black tire marks angling toward one corner. It wasn't much of a place.

East across Mill Street lay the gas station where Heather had watched the accident, now a green-and-white BP. He studied it with a sense of unease. Whatever it had been back then, he was pretty sure it hadn't been a BP. Catty-corner from where he stood spread the trees and grass of the park that had held his favorite swings. The trees looked older and fewer now, and a weirdly rococo gazebo had been put up to rot. And south across Main Street lurked, presumably, the house where he had once lived; the tall fencing that ran alongside the street had been replaced, now even taller, painted a red-brown. The lane counts on Mill and Main had not changed, but the lights suspended overhead seemed new—and in the years since the accident how many times had the asphalt been resurfaced, the curbs rebuilt, the lane lines repainted? The entire pattern of it could have shifted several feet in one direction or another. The parking lot where he stood had a new curb cut near the intersection. To what extent was this no longer really the place where Christopher had died? To a great extent. But there was no other place.

He didn't want to be doing this work again. It seemed it could only lead him to pain. But he thought of the *airlane* nameplate and went forward. He paced the distances across the lanes, from light pole to curb edge, from curb edge to street sign, measuring a yard with each step, a simple skill that Boggs had made him practice. Boggs had also given him a five-pound sack of sugar and told him to test its weight at arm's length, then gave him a desk lamp, a laptop computer, a brake drum, and asked of each, "More or less than five pounds? Guess the weight?" Soon they descended to the basement garage where Boggs attempted, with loud failures, to juggle wrenches—the memory of the odor of motor oil and sawdust and the riotous clanging of the wrenches became suddenly so vivid that Ellis had to stop a minute and catch his breath.

He ripped a page from the back of the minivan's owner's manual, sketched the intersection in ballpoint, and labeled it with his paced measurements. He added notes on light timing and traffic flow, and amid this work he noticed a new sensation: relief. As if he had swum nearly to the point of exhaustion, but now his feet had found land. This work. How easy it was to move here. The relief unnerved and disappointed him.

Eventually he looked up and saw a woman, in sweatpants and a T-shirt snug enough to show the roll of her belly fat, standing outside the pet-supply store, watching him. She smiled and moved to the side window of the minivan and tapped.

"Ellis Barstow!" she exclaimed as he rolled down the window.

And he said hi, but who was she?

Without provocation she talked about teachers he remembered and some of his friends. She mentioned Christopher, solemnly, and glanced at the intersection. She seemed his own age, more or less, but her weight had bagged into small jowls that exaggerated as she frowned. A spray of curling thin brown hair imperfectly covered her pink scalp. Ellis said little to encourage her, and finally she said, "You don't recognize me, do you?"

He smiled and shook his head.

"Carrie Butters."

Even this did not help. But he said, "Oh, yes, Carrie. Of course." And she still had a look of expectation, so he added, "Wow."

She mentioned more names, one feebly familiar, but it seemed to him he'd never heard of the others. He nodded dumbly. Who *was* she? He tried to subtract the jowls, to thin her face and thicken her hair. But the effort gained him nothing. She talked on, faster and faster, and suddenly she said, with forced enthusiasm, "Well, how about you? What are you up to? What do you do?"

"Nothing," he said. "Nothing right now."

She waited.

"I'm between things," he said. "Between things."

With a little clawing motion she burst into talking about a couple more people. He felt like a disappointment. Soon she looked wildly over to the pet store—Kissing Kritters—as if it had just now appeared there, cast out a farewell, and fled.

He was glad to drive again. While the land streamed by, he worked out a sense that some of the people she had mentioned had been a grade or two below himself, and if she were also from one of the lower grades that might explain how she had been so aware of him while he could not recall her at all. Or perhaps Christopher's death had made everyone aware of him. Nonetheless, he had a feeling of precarious nullity: the place where his brother had died was no longer the place where his brother had died, and Carrie Butters indicated a world that had been his life and yet now, subject to the madness of memory, he hardly recognized it. It was as if a great chasm were opening behind him, and he felt he might easily fall backward into it.

He pulled the minivan into the driveway of Heather's house and watched one of the soda-can birdfeeders spin wildly in the wind. His phone rang, and he took it out and stared at it. Heather had given him a new one, so that she could reach him, and he'd had his old number reassigned to it. He had just stopped in the driveway of Heather's house.

"Fasenden," Ellis said.

"I'd about given up—" Fasenden said.

"My phone wasn't working."

"We're all very upset and sorry. About Boggs."

"Yes."

"Thought you should know—"

"Actually, I have to go."

"You were right, Ellis. About that one with the pigs."

"PA2."

"It was a hit-and-run."

"Well, that was how the physics made it look."

"Yes, right. But, also, a guy confessed."

"Really?" Ellis leaned his head back to the headrest. "Why?"

"Some kid. Nineteen years old. He got drunk one day and told his dad about it. His dad's a cop, and he talked the kid into coming clean."

"I was pretty sure about that one."

"I thought you'd want to know."

"Thanks."

"Truth is, I wanted to touch base anyway. Ellis, you're good at this—"

"No, no."

"What are you doing for work? Are you working? We need your help. We can make it worthwhile."

Ellis laughed. "Can you?"

"Well—" Fasenden stopped and made a little gulping noise. "Ellis, look. I don't want to push. You know me, I'm not pushy. I can't make anyone do anything that anyone doesn't want to do. But if you want to come back—"

Ellis didn't answer.

"Consider it?" Fasenden said.

Ellis hung up.

The next day he drove again to Coil.

The police station had not changed since he was a boy: an almost windowless beige brick building, its function named across the front in aluminum letters. He had entered it only once before, years ago, on a grade-school field trip. The children had been fingerprinted onto souvenir cards, and they peered into a holding cell, which, disappointingly, had no steel bars and was painted pink. "Pink is soothing," said their guide, a woman who normally sat at the reception desk.

He wasn't sure that this wasn't the same woman, now much older, who sat at a desk by the door and nodded and darted glances at him while he explained his purpose. The accident report that he wanted was very old, she said, and it wouldn't be here but at a document-holding facility maintained by the county. She drew a map on the back of an "Emergency Preparedness" brochure, lining roads and highways atop a bulleted list of first-aid items.

Her route took him through the intersection where Christopher had died and onward between two silvered lakes under a vast cream sky, through cow fields, and along the edge of a regional airport where prop airplanes came down and went up with dragonfly noises, to a warehouse with a bank of offices stretched along the front. Its gutters sagged and the appliqué window tints had bubbled. A receptionist sent him to a heavy, balding, mustached, cubicled man in beige pants and a mauve shirt who listened to what Ellis wanted, spent a few minutes peering into an old, DOS-based program on his computer, wrote down a number, said, "Please wait here," and went away.

Ellis studied a photograph on the desk—two fat children grinned before a pull-down backdrop of washed-out blue—until he wanted to smash it.

Finally, the man returned with a manila folder. He said he could xerox the text of the report for ten cents a page, but the photos would have to be sent out for prints, which would take several days.

He went away to copy the report, and Ellis sat with the photos, glossy color prints. He did not look at the photos. He thought of putting them aside, getting up and leaving.

But then, without conscious prompting, his attention settled onto them. The first two photos showed only useless blurs of gray and black; but in the third, shapes could be seen—a lamppost, a portion of a parked police cruiser, and in the middle distance a burned vehicle bellied on the street, light reflecting weakly from the patches of unburned paint on its front end. Between the burned car and the camera lay a blanket-covered shape that was, almost certainly, Christopher.

Ellis experienced a surge of feeling he hadn't prepared for. A ferocious hot pain that rose through his throat and into his eyes.

He set the photos aside and sat with his head in his hands. When the fat man returned with his copy of the report, Ellis gave him a check and asked to have the photos mailed to his apartment's address.

He hadn't been to his apartment since the day after the accident with James Dell. The silent grandfather clock, the shelves of books—everything here held a layer of dust, which obscurely pleased him, and he tried to disturb it as little as possible. He sorted the items piled under the mail slot: junk mail, magazines, catalogs, bills, overdue notices. When he found the photos, he opened the envelope quickly, to preempt hesitation, and turned through the images. But the pain that had caught him the first time he had looked at them did not return.

Christopher's body was visible in just three photos and was never the center of focus, only a thing under a blanket in the middle distance. Ellis looked at it calmly. Why? He didn't know. Was this how he should have felt when he first saw the photo? Or had the feeling before been the true feeling?

But these questions led him nowhere, and he turned from them. He let himself analyze. It was easier to analyze than to follow the circling of unanswerable questions. The evidence in the photos seemed generally as he had expected—short tire marks left by the *airlane*, a point of impact indicated by a spill of fluid and glass in the middle of the intersection, two cars standing at their points of rest, police and fire vehicles scattered around the periphery, everything muddled by the surrounding murk of night. Strange to see how archaic it all looked—the boxy cars, the men with shaggy hair and mustaches, a sign in the background offering a gallon of gasoline for less than a dollar. It had been an Amoco station—so he and Heather had both been wrong.

Working between the photos, the police report, and the measurements he'd made at the intersection, he built a diagram of the scene in his computer. He drew dimensionally correct icons to represent the cars at their points of rest. Then he studied the damage on each vehicle and the tire marks on the roadway to estimate their orientations as they collided and set the icons at the point of impact and at maximum intrusion, with a couple of inches added to account for restitution—his brother's *airlane* striking the left-rear quarter-panel area of the other vehicle at a little less than 90 degrees, the result of both vehicles swerving too late.

When he finished, the diagram showed an overhead view of the lane lines, the curbs, the poles at the corners, the two cars at the instant of impact, and the positions where they had come to rest. This, too, was, in a sense, the place where Christopher had died.

He copied the diagram into PC-Crash, and used the program to create representations of the two cars. He set the simulated vehicles onto the icons at the point of impact, estimated their velocities, steering angles, brake factors, and restitution. Then he ran the analysis and watched as they spun away from the impact toward the rest positions. The *airlane* overshot its mark by a dozen feet; the other vehicle didn't go far enough and ended up facing the wrong way.

He began to make adjustments. Velocity. Steering angles. Brake factors. Restitution factors. Small changes sometimes resulted in large effects in post-impact motion, but after a couple of hours he had refined the model so that the vehicles spun away from the point of impact, scrubbed speed off as they went round, and rocked to a stop exactly where he had marked the rest positions.

He ran the model a few times: again and again the accident enacted itself in shifting pixels, perfectly silent. At impact, the computer calculated, Christopher's car had been traveling at 42.3 mph; the other car at 49.1 mph. By hand Ellis calculated the initial velocity of the *airlane* before it had begun laying down tire marks, and he came up with 46 mph, give or take a couple of mph—a speed not unexpected on that road, a speed that might even be considered cautious, since Ellis had observed many vehicles breezing through at nearly 60 mph.

Had Christopher slowed down because of some distraction?

But one might speculate endlessly about such things. He needed to analyze the data he had.

He couldn't find any hard evidence as to whether Christopher had entered the intersection under a green, yellow, or red light. Witnesses often provided the only available evidence about light timing, and here the witness statements in the police report—from the occupants of other vehicles near the intersection—were all against Christopher. The report mentioned that Heather had been at the scene at the time of the accident and described her injuries, but it didn't include any testimony from her.

He tried to broaden his mindset, to think, What was he gaining from this analysis?

Nothing presented itself. This sort of analysis was needed to make a credible presentation in a courtroom, but he probably could have looked at the evidence and guessed the results to within a few mph beforehand.

Could Boggs have seen something in this that he had missed?

He turned through the photos again. It seemed perhaps the *airlane* had come to a stop a few feet further off the curb than he had represented it in his scene diagram. He moved the point of rest in PC-Crash and began readjusting parameters. It took him an hour to clean up the simulation, but in the end it only made a half an mph of difference.

He went through the photos yet again, and again, until although his eyes focused on the images he seemed not to see anything. He began to believe that by memorizing them completely he might forget them. But then he caught himself and saw this was irrational; it felt like jerking awake just as he started to veer off the road.

He was lying flat on the floor when he heard Heather's car in the drive. Seeing him, she started, then laughed. "You're all right?" She passed through the room, her shoes jarring faintly through the floor into his skull. After a few minutes she returned, barefoot—he couldn't see her feet but knew by the sound.

"Can you get up?"

"It's all right," he said.

"I find you like this," she said, "and I worry that you've been on the floor all afternoon."

"It's only been a moment," he said. "It's not uncomfortable." The sun beat warmly through a window onto his foot and ankle. He monitored the effort of the rise and fall of his chest as he breathed. "It's a very nice floor," he offered.

She frowned, but sat cross-legged beside him.

They said nothing for a while. He felt his heaviness pressing him to the floor; it held him there in a way that gratified him, as if his weight implied his substance, his existence. He thought of the dead man lying beside the lake, the weight of the man's leg in his hands. He was on the point of telling Heather about it, but he caught himself short, doubting.

In hindsight it seemed improbable that there could have been a dead man there. Perhaps it had been a hallucination, or it was a false memory. Boggs had even predicted that later Ellis would doubt the incident had even happened–which seemed dispositive toward the dead man's reality, except that it was exactly the sort of detail a hallucination might incorporate to provide a paranoiac sheen of reality.

He was sure about the memory, but that only made him doubt his mind. And if he extended that logic any further, he would have to doubt every perception.

He pushed himself up—surprising how little effort it took—and put his head in her lap. She stroked the hair at his temples. "You're okay," she said, uncertainly. He closed his eyes and lay there, feeling his weight and her fingers and thinking to himself that he loved her. And he didn't quite trust her. He wanted to ask her about that, but the words too were dense and did not like to rise.

He suspected his own mind. He tried to think of a test, to determine if he retained the scraps of his sanity.

• • •

That night he rose to pace the house. It contained pockets of a faint, nameless smell that Boggs must have carried on his clothes, because at times it sucker-punched him, forcing memories of awful vividness.

He went to the computer and located the municipalities nearest the lake and searched newspapers and records of the last month, but he could find no mention of a dead man found by the lake. It was possible the body still had not been found. But he didn't dare drive all the way out to the lake again to look for the body, didn't dare leave here again.

Instead he looked up the phone number of the police department nearest the lake. Then he climbed into the minivan and drove until he found a pay phone on the outside wall of a gas station. He called the police department and made an anonymous report of a body at the lake.

The day after his call to the police, he sat at the computer and found a small item posted on a newspaper website.

"The County Sheriff's Office is investigating a body found yesterday evening around 7:30 P.M. on the bank of O'Neil Lake. The cause of death is unknown. Lieutenant George Meade says the body has been identified as a missing person, sixty-two-year-old Otis Cleveland Ashe. Meade says Ashe is from Hemingford and was reported missing earlier this year. Investigators believe the body may have been there for more than a week, hidden by tall grass."

He wasn't crazy. He might regret it, but he had his mind. The only thing to do was to continue forward.

He had to see his father.

[illegible]

Thirty-seven

Ellis drove to Coil and then turned west, first following along a river, then down a straight two-lane interrupted here and there by stop signs at the intersections of narrow dirt roads—spanning off to a house, perhaps, or a farmer's field access, a fishing pond, a patch of private hunting preserve. After a signpost indicating the county line, the roadway became an assemblage of patched cracks and potholes that set the steering wheel shaking and panels and joints rattling in bright percussion. He passed ragged houses with missing roof shingles, listing into their foundations, amid lawns ornamented with tires and broken concrete.

He turned onto a dirt-and-gravel road that rolled below the van more smoothly than the patched asphalt had. On either side lay open fields, but the road was lined with oaks and maples that reached overhead so that he seemed to be passing through an arbor. Dust accumulated on his rear window in a brown fungus pattern.

He slowed approaching the driveway, wallowed up to it, turned in.

The only object of any size on the horizon was the house, a two-story clapboard farmhouse, gray neglect gripping its edges. When he stopped at the end of the drive he saw behind the house a long, metal-roofed shed. A little further away, a solitary white toilet sat on the ground. Past the toilet lay a field plowed into parallel furrows and abandoned to low weeds. In the distance ran a trace of fence and low green brush along it, demarcating the next field. The land fell gradually toward the line of the fence and rose again on the other side. Where the land appeared to stop, the sky began with a ridge of clouds black as used motor oil.

He stepped out of the minivan and kicked through untended grass to the front porch—a pair of naked two-by-fours held up one corner of the porch roof, and missing posts gap-toothed the surrounding rail.

When he put his fist to the door, no one answered. His minivan was the only vehicle in the driveway. He sat on the porch steps to wait. He put his head on his arms and dozed a little.

Then he awoke with a jerk as a long Oldsmobile drew up. It parked behind the minivan, and his father emerged: his father with a paunch, shoulders fallen, bagged under the eyes, hair receded and feral, but unmistakably his father, with his father's large hands, his high cheekbones grown even more prominent, his staring dark eyes watery. He wore a button-down shirt of startling white. He crossed half the distance from the car, stopped in the grass, and said, "Is that you?" He raised a hand and pointed at Ellis, as if to clarify.

Ellis felt confused by the question; taken literally, it seemed to allow no negative answer. He stood and opened his hands. "I need to see the car, Dad."

His father came forward with a tight smile, staring. Small, sharp wrinkles rayed from under the lobes of his ears. His arms, above the big hands, were thinner than Ellis remembered. "Boy," he said. "A surprise." He twitched and stepped back and looked around the yard. He laughed. "Let me get you a beer."

His father let him in and passed into the kitchen while Ellis waited in a dark living room. As his eyes adjusted, the furnishings materialized slowly and silently in their places. The room's heavy curtains were pulled, but a vertical slat of light slipped between them, falling over a coffee table and sofa. An unnerving sense of familiarity seized and held him for some seconds before he understood why: he had grown up with this coffee table and sofa, these chairs and end tables, this wall mirror with its thick carved frame, its silver now spotting and browning, holding a distorted version of himself—his aged self examining a mirror where his younger self had once examined himself.

The sofa and the chairs, all in their original upholstery, were dirty, sagging, blackened along the front edges of the cushions and arms. Scratches and stains marked the coffee table. One of the shelves of a low bookcase had been replaced with a plank of particle board that sagged alarmingly under a pair of pickle jars filled with coins.

His father gave him a bottle of beer. Ellis said, "You've kept everything."

His father glanced around. "It's a little old, I guess, but nothing wrong with it." He sat in one of the armchairs, as if to prove it still worked.

"Have you seen a tall bearded man here?" Ellis asked—the same question he'd put to any number of cashiers and clerks, and all at once he was right back in that long pursuit. As if Boggs had arranged things so that Ellis would be pursuing him for the rest of his life.

His father said nothing.

"Have you?" Ellis asked.

"My son died in that car," his father said.

Ellis shook his head. "He didn't die in that car. He climbed out and got himself burned and died in the street. And you had two sons. You might say, 'One of my sons died.'"

"Tell me something," his father said, staring. "About your life."

"Tell me about the big, bearded guy," Ellis said. "I know he was here. I know he looked at the car."

His father didn't answer.

Ellis looked around at the furniture again and hated it, hated the mindless, numb inertia that kept it here. "Did he tell you who his wife was?"

"Why are you here?"

"I need to see the car."

"Why?"

Ellis stood over the coffee table and vaguely tried to recall which of its nicks and scratches had been there when he last saw it. "That's a reasonable question, but it would require a lot of background, and it doesn't really matter. I have a suspicion. That's what it amounts to."

"You mean, to explain you'd have to tell me something about your life."

He reluctantly met his father's gaze. The pouches below his father's eyes sagged as if they stored coins.

"Well, your friend was here," his father said. "He talked for quite a while. Friendly guy. He did tell me about his wife, actually. Had some interesting ideas on this and that. A little full of himself. I showed him the car. He wouldn't tell me much about you, though."

"Can I look at the car?"

A fly noised a circle somewhere overhead. His father shifted and drank. "The other day I ran into someone who knew Heather's dad. At Pep Boys. I was buying lifters for my trunk lid. This guy said Heather's husband is dead. Hit by a car. Is that true?"

"It is. Can I look at the *airlane*?"

When his father only stared, Ellis turned and went to the window and pulled the shade aside. He had to keep a grip on his anxiety and impatience. He felt he might begin to scream. But he sipped his beer.

His father said vaguely, "It's funny."

Ellis looked at him.

"You can look at the car if you'll do something for me. Two things."

Ellis waited.

"Tell me something about yourself. And then listen while I tell you something." A meekness shaded his father's stare.

"All right," Ellis said. "Fine."

A silence.

"Tell you something?"

"Please."

Without intention, Ellis sat. The feel of the chair under himself was familiar. "I hated my brother."

"You didn't really hate him," his father said. He pulled at the sleeve of his strangely white shirt.

"I did."

"Christopher was in a bad position, between myself and his mother, sent back and forth, never able to settle, get comfortable, learn to trust anyone. Maybe he wasn't your friend, but he was your brother. You looked up to him. But he wasn't very generous to you. Which pissed you off, I guess."

"No, he wasn't very generous," Ellis said, low.

"He'd had a hard time, you know. His mother was a very shabby person. He had learned that if he offered something it would give someone else the chance to slap it away. But you didn't hate him. If you think so, it's an idea you've developed since. That's my own fault. I can see it's my fault."

"You're constructing fantasies and blaming yourself for them. I hated him because he was a jerk." Ellis was angry with himself for allowing a conversation he had wanted to avoid. He had always regretted and resented the nature of his relationship with Christopher, but he'd felt that at least he understood it, and he didn't care to open it to questioning.

"I didn't know what I was doing to the two of you. I usually don't know what I'm doing, I guess."

"You have no idea how I felt, Dad." He looked at his father's receded hair, tendriling and floating up and down as he drank his beer. Was this truly his father? His father, certainly, but transformed by years, and so was this in any meaningful way the man he had grown up with? "I'm living with Heather," he said. "I've been involved with her for some time, since before Boggs died. He killed himself. He stepped into moving highway traffic right in front of me."

"Ah," his father said.

Ellis straightened and remembered straightening exactly this way in the same chair long ago.

"I'll tell you this," his father said. "I love you." He examined his shirtsleeve in silence. "But I realize I've never been able to really handle that feeling." Silence. "You were easy to love and Christopher was hard to love. Maybe that was the problem. I over-whatever. Compensated. I don't know. Some years back, I had a girlfriend, this waitress. She has three kids. I meet her, like her, I like her kids. So, after I've been seeing her for a couple of months, she asks if I would pick up the youngest, a boy, from daycare and drop him off at a friend's where he would stay until she gets off her shift at the restaurant. So I do. Pick up the boy, drive him to the friend's house, push him in the door. I'm in the car again when a woman comes charging out, yelling. Couldn't understand her problem at first. Took me a while— What it was, was, I had brought the wrong kid. To look at him, it was plain enough. I knew the kid. I knew what he looked like. I can't really say there was any excuse for it.

"So I take this boy back to the daycare. He's three or four years old, and he's okay. He's just looking around, doesn't seem to mind any of this. I thought it could turn out all right. But when we get back to the daycare, the place is going bonkers—police, a fire truck, my waitress girlfriend, people all running around, yelling. My girlfriend's boy feels bad that he's missed his ride, and he's hiding in a closet, under a pile of blankets. It takes a while to find him. And the father of the boy I took is shrieking at anyone who stands still to listen. He lets me have it. My girlfriend is practically having seizures. A mess. I apologized, sure. But I never saw her again. I thought about it a lot. I realized that I just never learned how to do anything properly. I can't even see things properly. I miss the obvious. It's sabotaged my life."

Ellis waited. He moved his foot and a board creaked; it sounded explosive. He felt sad and heavy and weary and impatient and indifferent—he had heard a number of similar stories from his father, all with the same conclusion, but nothing ever came of them, no change of temperament or behavior. The most surprising part of this one was that his father had managed, however briefly, to find a girlfriend.

In the kitchen, the compressor in the refrigerator kicked on and whirred.

His father finished his beer, stared at him, then stood and led him outside, around the house, and across the yard to the shed where he turned a key in the lock and slid the door aside. It moved with a sound of corroded steel bearings and revealed a space filled high and wall-to-wall with dusty and haphazardly stacked objects, many of them familiar: the brass coat rack, the child-size desk, the crate of board games, the lamp made out of driftwood, the iron headboard, the steamer trunk painted green. As if his father had been preparing and waiting all this time for a reconstruction of the past.

His father heaved out two full garbage bags and revealed the hood of the *airlane*, standing at the center of the clutter like an icon in a shrine.

The two of them stepped over a box of slot-car tracks and squeezed past a cupboard that Ellis recognized from the old kitchen. Leaning into the *airlane*, they pushed it into the daylight. The damaged chassis caused it to move on an arc to the right, so that when they stopped, it pointed toward the toilet standing at the verge of the open fields. Suddenly, Ellis recognized it from his childhood. "You took the toilet."

"The bank got the house," his father said, "so I took out everything. Took the hot-water tank. Would have taken the furnace, but it wouldn't fit through the doorway, and I didn't have time to rip out the doorframe."

"You have our old hot-water tank?"

"Started leaking a while back. It's in the shed there somewhere. Might be useful someday."

"How?"

"Could need a part out of it."

"Why is the toilet out there?"

"Weather won't hurt a toilet. Ceramic. Washes right off."

"You've lost your mind," Ellis said. His father smiled.

Dust on the car's upper surfaces had been disturbed here and there by the brushing and pressing of hands—presumably from Boggs's visit. Wires spilled from the broken headlamp openings. The wheels were overtaken by rust, and the tires were flat and cracked. Looking at the damage across the front, he could see already that the estimate of the angle of impact that he had used in his simulations had been off by a few degrees, although it seemed unlikely to make much difference.

He circled to the other side to check—yes—the *airlane* nameplate was missing.

He retrieved a pen, notepad, and three disposable cameras from the minivan. He borrowed an old retractable tape measure from his father; he couldn't recall if it was the same tape measure they had had when he was a boy. He would have preferred to have several tape measures to establish measurements relative to one another, but his father only had the one. Just inside the shed door, he found a sack of wooden golf tees—he'd never known his father to play golf, but he didn't ask—and used them to mark points in the grass around the car and measured straight lines between them.

He followed the protocol that he and Boggs had developed over the years. He checked and noted vehicle make, model, year, ID number, wheel and tire sizes, transmission type, brake type, overall width, overall height, overall length, axle positions, tire conditions, and brake-pad wear. It was satisfying, doing this work. The vehicle was an indifferent object. The work was methodical and familiar. He knew what he was doing now.

Every six inches, across the front end, he measured depth of crush relative to the rear-axle position—first at bumper level, then again at the hood line. The air was ripe with humidity, and drops of sweat fell on the page as he took notes, glistening in wet blisters. His father stood watching, then went to the toilet and sat facing the open fields, elbows out, as if he might giddy-up the commode into the distance.

Ellis stood fussing with one of the cameras until he realized he was hesitating, unsure he wanted photos of this car. He circled, taking photos from each side and each corner, from low and high, then moved in and snapped close-ups of the wheels, license plates, vehicle ID number, the place where the *airlane* nameplate should have been, the broken headlamps and windows, then focused on the damaged area at the front and took photo after photo at various angles, nearer and further, with and without measuring tape for scale.

A gust of wind ruffled his notes and made the trees along the road silvery and flickering. The oil-black clouds on the western horizon were closing in, rigged with claws of vapor.

He tried the driver's-side door, but it wouldn't budge, so he opened the passenger's-side door and slid over to the driver's side. He had to cram himself into place, thighs nudging the steering wheel, knees into the dash. He sat gripping the steering wheel. Then he took up his pad and noted the mileage, the fuel level, that the gearshift was in neutral. The dash looked largely undamaged, although it was now riven with age cracks. He twisted himself down under the steering wheel to look at the foot pedals, showing a normal pattern of wear.

Wondering whether the headlights were on at the time of the collision, he climbed out but couldn't find either of the bulbs. They might have been lost in the collision, or put into police storage somewhere, or Boggs might have taken them.

He drew out the driver's seatbelt and examined its length and found a transfer marking where the belt had locked and pulled a little plastic off the D-ring during the impact. He took a photo of it, leaned across the front seat, and pulled out the passenger belt, and it also bore a transfer mark.

Ellis stared at it for a long while.

A transfer mark on the passenger's-side belt.

Ellis stared at it, then let the belt run back on its retractor and stepped out of the car. His hands had picked up a layer of grime from the car, and he saw it in great detail—the gray thickest on the pads of his fingers, thinner down through the joints and onto the palm.

A transfer mark on the passenger's-side belt.

He crawled in again, pulled out the passenger belt and examined the mark, then looked away and then re-examined the mark: a small black line across the width of the webbing, almost as if drawn there with a crayon. But it matched the color of the D-ring, and when he pulled the belt away from the D-ring, the impress of the belt into the plastic could be seen there. He photographed both—transfer mark, D-ring.

"Got to put the car back before the rain," his father said behind him.

"A minute."

Sometimes load markings could also be found on the belt-latch plate, but there were none on the driver's side, and on the passenger's side he could only see a very faint marking that might have been a manufacturing effect. Inconclusive.

He crawled into the backseat, which had only lap belts—no D-rings, and therefore no possibility of transfer marks. He checked the latch plates, but there were no indications of loading.

He returned to the front passenger's-side seatbelt and looked at the transfer mark there one more time, felt its texture, turned it in the light. He let the retractor pull the belt back. He stood out of the car. "Dad," he said.

Side-by-side they put their hands on the damaged sheet metal and rolled the car, leaning and straining. His father slid the shed door shut and set the lock, then started toward the toilet. He said, without looking around, "I'm sorry your friend is dead. I liked him."

"I'm going to get going."

"Find what you wanted?"

Ellis didn't answer. His father turned to look. "I need to think," Ellis said.

"You always did."

They watched the weed-infested fields and the sky and the reaching, dark cloud-masses now closing with visible speed. A wind pressed, died, renewed violently.

Ellis put his notes in a back pocket, and as he stood hesitating he could see the rain come across the fields, its leading edge perfectly defined, a curtain in the air with the field below it turning black.

Then suddenly it hit him with heavy cold droplets, and a gust soaked the length of him. He squinted at his father, and his father looked at him through the rain and howled, cheerfully, like an ape.

Startled, Ellis ran. In the minivan he keyed the ignition. He could see his father through the windshield, radically distorted by the water moving on the glass, glowing in his white shirt. He remained atop the toilet, waving his white arm high in the air, like a captain committed to going down with the ship.

When he cleared the rain, traffic was moving densely on the interstate. The afternoon sun, which had stood over his right shoulder in the morning, stood again over his right shoulder.

A transfer mark on the passenger's-side seatbelt. Boggs would have seen the same thing. It meant that a second person had been in the car.

He followed the paired doors of a semitrailer. At a certain distance from the rear of the trailer, he could glimpse the heavy-lidded eyes of the driver in the jittering side mirror.

The police report didn't say anything about a second person in the car.

He realized he'd passed his exit, and for a moment he thought about just going on. To keep driving—to drive and drive and drive—seemed simple and pleasing. Following Boggs, without Boggs. World passing without consequence. But he took an exit ramp and turned back.

On the night of the accident, he'd assumed Heather had been a passenger in Christopher's car, until her father told him she'd been at the gas station.

But if *she* had been driving—

The front seat of the *airlane* had been close against the steering wheel.

He parked beside the house, carried his notes and cameras inside, and went to the computer. He pulled up a reference website: the designed distance between the front and rear wheels of the 1970 Fairlane was within a half inch of the distance he had measured on the driver's side of his brother's car.

So that distance had not been altered by the collision: the dash had not been pushed back toward the seat. Rather, the seat had been slid forward—for a driver shorter than he was, or Christopher had been.

He looked through the police report again, for any suggestion of a second occupant. There was none. The report was signed by an officer whose name Ellis didn't recognize. It did note that Heather's father had been first on the scene. Certainly he'd been there, because Ellis had seen him. Perhaps he'd not been able to author the report because his daughter was involved. But surely he had had input.

Ellis called the police station at Coil. A woman's voice told him that the officer who had signed and filed the report had died a couple of years ago, of a heart attack, just months after his retirement. The woman's voice caught, and Ellis murmured condolences.

He took the police report and his notes and cameras to the minivan and jammed them into the glove compartment and locked it.

Why did he feel so ungainly as he moved? As if the earth were teetering under him? He returned to the living room and sat down.

He tried to think what he should do. Confront Heather? He pulled the idea toward himself like a balloon on a string; then it rose a short distance away again.

He sat in the living room until late, waiting, listening to the air conditioner turn itself off and on. The rain had stopped. The hour when Heather usually returned went by. He checked the windows whenever a car passed.

Eventually he went upstairs to the bedroom. Startled, he stopped—a shape lay in the bed.

At the sound of his step, she shifted a little.

"Love," he said. "You've been here all this time?" he asked. She was silent. "Where is your car?"

"It broke down," she said. "The engine just stopped." Her hand, lying atop the bed sheets, opened and closed. "I got it towed, and then I was late and stressed. I couldn't face school, not another day of it, so I took a taxi home. I thought you'd be here."

He understood that she was frightened of him, and that she had been for some time now.

"Where were you?"

"I've been in Coil," he said.

That night, he lay gathering a hatred of Boggs. He could not believe that Boggs had not envisioned this course of events.

We're always causing what happens next, Boggs once said.

Thirty-eight

He lay beside her until morning. Then he said, "I have to show you something."

Her station wagon had been repaired. They picked it up, then returned the minivan to the house and rode together in the station wagon. She drove; he remembered that she almost always preferred to drive.

The route to the interstate passed through end-to-end suburbs. Tuxedo shop. Liquor store. Laundromat. Starbucks. Church. Chiropractor. Build-your-own-teddy-bear shop. Jiffy Lube. Walgreens. Babies "R" Us. Bed Bath & Beyond. It had been a long time since he'd been in the passenger seat of a car, and it felt unnatural and dangerous, traveling down the roadway without a steering wheel or pedals, without control. Heather wound up the engine and pushed into the interstate lanes.

"Do you still think about Christopher?" Ellis asked.

"Are we going to talk now?" she asked. "Have a conversation?"

"Do you?"

"Of course I do."

"Do you think about the accident often?"

"No."

"You don't."

"I hate to think of it."

"So you just stopped?"

"I'd say it's something I've learned."

"What do you remember?"

"I don't like to remember."

"Why have we never talked about it?"

"There are a lot of things we haven't talked about. Maybe you've noticed." She looked at him, her expression closed.

"Heather," he said, and hesitated, and the two syllables stood empty. They were the last spoken for several miles.

But then he asked, "Please, tell me what you remember about Christopher's accident."

"Why?"

"Heather—please."

"I walked from school to the gas station to buy a Seven-Up and to call my dad for a ride. And I was standing in the parking lot when I heard the brakes and turned and saw one car slam into another." She spoke flatly. "There was an enormous explosion and a fireball. When it had settled down, I saw that one of the cars was Christopher's. I ran to it. By the time I got there, he was already out, and he was going to the other car." She stared ahead. "There were screams and it was hot and Christopher leaned into the burning car and came out with someone. The fire was spreading and he went in again, and the fire and smoke were everywhere, and he was trying to go in even further. He kept trying, and I was screaming at him to come out. Then he just stopped. I tried to pull him, but he was stuck somehow. Someone dragged me away."

"Did you call your dad from the gas station?"

"What?"

"You said that was the reason you were at the gas station."

"I was waiting. I knew he wouldn't be home yet."

"Did you buy the Seven-Up?"

"Yes. I remember the cold of it in my hand when the heat of the explosion pushed out over me."

"How long did it take you to recognize the *airlane*?"

"I don't know. Why?"

"Where was Christopher when you first saw him?"

"This is a strange conversation," she said.

"Did anyone else get out of the *airlane*?"

"Oh God. Ellis—"

"Were there two people in the *airlane*?"

"Did John tell you to ask these questions?"

"Well, there were two people in the car at the time of the collision."

"Did John tell you that?"

"I looked at the car."

"You think I was in there? That's what John thought."

Ellis said nothing.

"I wasn't," she said.

"Who then?"

"Christopher was alone."

"These things are never knowable to one hundred percent certainty," Ellis said, "but the evidence is pretty clear. Someone was in the driver's seat and someone else was in the passenger seat. Both wore seatbelts. When the cars collided, the *airlane* violently decelerated, and the seatbelts locked, and the people in the seats were thrown forward against the belts. The force on each belt was so powerful that the friction of the belt yanking against the D-ring caused the plastic of the D-ring to melt slightly, and a little of the melted plastic rubbed onto the fabric of the belt. This melted plastic is visible on both belts. I think you were in the car. In fact, you were driving. And your dad manipulated the accident report."

She pulled to the side of the road and stopped, tires stuttering on the gravel, and she bent forward and gasped.

"Isn't that right?" he asked.

"I remember watching from the gas station with a can of Seven-Up in my hand."

He breathed shallowly, and she stared at the steering wheel, and time passed.

"Do you want me to drive?" he asked.

She opened her door, stepped out of the car. He thought she might walk away, but she circled the car, and he stepped out and circled the car, and he started to drive.

A boy and an older man, presumably the boy's father, huddled together over something in the lawn—a white-and-red cylinder with tailfins.

"What are they doing?"

"Water rocket."

The father started to work a small hand pump.

"No concrete," she observed.

"You remember."

"Of course."

He wasn't sure if he was simply delaying or if he really hoped to jar her memory this way, but he'd take a small detour to stop in front of the old house, where he'd grown up. The white siding had been replaced with pale blue and—absurdly, he thought—a decorative wagon wheel and ox yoke had been nailed to the wall on either side of the front door. The TV antenna he had climbed was no longer there. A maple tree he had never seen before reached up twenty-five feet or more. Grass had replaced the concrete lawn.

"You remember the joke?" he asked. "Do you know the difference between a cheeseburger and a blowjob?"

"No."

"Great, let's go get lunch."

She glanced at him, but her expression didn't change. "You were afraid of me," she said softly.

"When's the last time you were here?" Ellis asked.

"Before the accident."

"When?"

She sat looking at the house. "I met him here earlier that day, I think."

"You left with him in the *airlane*?"

In the lawn, the boy and his father stepped back, and in a shrill voice the boy shouted, "Ten! Nine! Eight!" At zero, the rocket shot into the sky.

"I don't remember." She frowned. "That ox yoke is ridiculous."

"But you think you got out of the *airlane* at some point and went to the school and then went to the gas station and waited there for your dad to pick you up."

Something crashed just above their heads, and Ellis threw his hands up. Heather screamed.

"The rocket," Ellis said.

"I think my heart really stopped."

The boy and the father came running, and the father took the rocket off the roof of the car, grinning and mouthing *Sorry*.

"But why would you go back to the school?"

"I had friends in choir. Maybe I met one of them. I don't know."

The father and son crouched to prepare a second launch. They stepped back and counted down, but this time the rocket only lifted a foot or so before it flopped over, geysering.

Ellis started the car and drove.

After a time, and a few turns, the road reduced to a cobble of asphalt patchwork. Again he took the dirt road under the trees. Turning in the driveway he said, "This is my father's house."

He stopped behind his father's car.

"The car is here," he said.

Heather was confused. "What car?"

"Christopher's. The *airlane*."

She shook her head with a jerk. "Are you kidding?"

"It's here because my dad is completely nuts."

She followed him to the porch, and as they came up the steps, his father opened the screen door. He let the door slap into his shoulder and his gaze shifted between them. He seemed to be wearing the same clothes he'd worn the day before, with the same or an identical white shirt, clean and pressed.

"Dad, this is Heather."

"I remember, of course."

"Hi, Mr. Barstow. It's nice to see you again."

"We need to see the car, Dad."

"Do you want to?" his father asked Heather.

But she was staring past him. "Is that the same sofa? And chairs?"

His father reached and gripped her shoulder awkwardly, with the fingertips of one hand. Then he turned. "I'll get the key."

He could be heard in the kitchen rattling jars and drawers. Ellis looked again at the living room's wretched objects. Heather pushed a fist into the sofa. Then his father reappeared, holding the key in one cupped hand. He led the way toward the shed, but Heather veered off and stopped near the toilet to look off at the fields while Ellis and his father again slid open the shed doors, slithered through the clutter to the rear of the vehicle, strained to move the car on its rotten wheels into the sunlight.

Ellis then stood beside it, watching Heather. Blue sky topped the open fields, and there rose neither wind nor the sense of imminence that the weather had provided before.

Finally he crossed the open ground and asked her to come. He brought her to the passenger's side and pulled out the seatbelt and showed her the trace of plastic it had pulled off the D-ring, then asked her to lean inside to see the matching impression in the plastic of the D-ring itself.

She looked but said nothing.

Then he asked her to slide over into the driver's seat. "How is the steering wheel?" he asked. "The pedals? Are they too near? Too far?"

"No."

"You see?"

She only sat. He didn't know what to do now, and she said nothing.

After a minute, he climbed into the passenger seat to sit beside her.

"We used to fight in this car," she said. "Christopher did let me drive occasionally. For some reason he always wanted to fight when I was driving."

"What did you fight about?"

"Which party to go to. Dumb things like that. Whose fault it was that we were lost. That was pretty common. We used to drive around paying no attention to where we were going until we had no idea where we were. One time I got out at a farm stand for directions and the woman there talked about all these towns and roads I'd never heard of, and eventually we realized we'd gone almost two hundred miles and had actually crossed into Ohio."

"That seat is set for you. Maybe you were at the gas station earlier on the day of the accident and transposed the memory."

"I remember the heat of the explosion. I remember stumbling on the curb as I ran."

"The collision would have thrown you forward. The belt would have held your torso, but your head would have snapped down, and maybe the next day you had bruising along the line of the belt. Maybe your neck hurt."

They sat facing forward and gazing at the space where the windshield should have been, and it struck Ellis as a terrible arrangement for a conversation. But perfectly common.

"There would have been a flash of light," he said, "and heat through the broken windshield."

"I told John I had nothing to say about it. I don't."

He stood out of the car and looked in at her, then turned and wandered to the house. From the kitchen he looked back through the window. She was still in the car. He found his father in the living room, slouching in one of the chairs, eyes closed, lax, looking dead.

I hate him, Ellis thought.

But the thought passed; it wasn't true. He didn't even dislike his father. His father made him uncomfortable, but he didn't want to let himself develop dislike or hate out of a resentment of discomfort, the proximate cause of which was his father.

"You're not dead," Ellis said.

His father's eyes opened. "Don't think so, but you never can tell." He lifted his head to an awkward angle. "Strange to see her again, isn't it?"

"I've been seeing her for a while."

"Great."

"You don't know anything about it."

"What are you showing her?"

"She says she wasn't in the car."

"So?"

"She was. She was driving."

"Really?"

"Both the driver's and passenger seats were occupied at the time of the accident, and the driver's seat is positioned for a person her size."

His father's eyelids lowered shut again. "It happened a long time ago."

Silence.

"I thought you would have more to say. Christopher was your favorite."

Slack, dead-looking, his father said, "I love you."

"All right."

"You don't believe me."

"All right. I believe you."

"I love you, and I know you know I love you. I guess that must be enough. You love her?"

Ellis turned away and came out of the house. Heather had walked into the fields. He waited for her to turn, so that he could wave for her to come back, but she didn't turn.

The furrowed soil crumbled underfoot. His lungs labored to move the humid air, and he had the feeling that if he tried to shout to her the words would hit the air and fall and writhe on the ground. She stood motionless, looking away, arms hugging herself.

And what did he want from her? He wanted an acknowledgment of the facts. A life without access to facts was like a life without ground underfoot.

"Heather," he said.

"You whisper my name that way," she said, "and I feel like I've embarrassed myself, like I've forgotten to wear pants."

He laughed a little hysterically. She held a dandelion gone to seed, and she was picking it apart, letting the seeds fall down a languid, angled path. He circled to stand in front of her.

"John could have done it," she said. "He could have made a mark like that on the seatbelt."

"Boggs?"

"He would, too."

Would he? Could he? Ellis hadn't thought of such a thing. But he said, "No. It would have been extremely difficult."

"John could do it."

"He couldn't just draw some crayon onto the belt. You saw the D-ring; the plastic had clearly transferred from the D-ring. There would be two ways to do it. One would be to somehow heat the D-ring to the point of melting and then pull the belt over it, and you'd have to experiment with the heat level and practice the movement of the belt to produce an effect that looked right; it would be hard. The other way would be to pull the belt as hard as it would be pulled during a collision. But it's not as if anyone has the arm strength to just reach in and do that. Extreme forces are involved. You'd need to create some mechanical device, an original design and fabrication. And then you'd have to bring it into the car and operate it without my dad ever seeing it. It doesn't make sense."

"It was a used car when Christopher got it. It could have been in some other accident."

"The driver's belt showed only one mark, and it would show two if it had been involved in two collisions."

She cast down her shoulders. "What are we to each other?" she asked. "I don't even know."

"You don't remember the accident at all?"

"I remember it. I remember it just as I told you."

"You don't have any doubt?" He wanted desperately for her to come toward the world he understood.

"It's what I remember."

"But what do you believe?"

"What do you want me to do, Ellis?" She spoke softly. "Tell me. I'll try. What do you want me to believe? That that little black mark is the truth? I'll believe it. Should I tell you that I remember being in the car, the seatbelt on me, my limbs flying, all of that? Then everything would line up for you and that would be that?"

"All I know," he said, "is that one of the first things I learned was to discount witness testimony. We set it aside entirely, if possible, and work from the physical evidence. People will tell you they saw a car shoot a hundred feet into the air like a rocket and flip a dozen times end over end before coming down undamaged on its wheels—stuff that's not remotely possible in the real world. But the physical evidence is objective."

"Physical evidence," she said. Her tone might have been the same if she were echoing the phrases of a gibbering lunatic.

"Verifiable facts and analyzable traces of events as they actually occurred, outside the subjective manipulation of memory."

"You think I killed those people and your brother."

"I'm asking you what you remember. You really don't have any doubt?"

She stepped a little distance from him. "It's like you're asking, *The world ended yesterday—don't you remember?*"

"All right," he said, "what do you want to do?"

She looked at the turned soil at their feet. He awaited the answer with fear.

She said, with exhaustion, "I just want to eat something."

• • •

She drove them back into town—he had a feeling of hurtling down the road with insane speed yet watching it pass very slowly—to DeVito's, an Italian restaurant and pizzeria where his family had sometimes gone. It still stood in its place in the middle of the town's single, central block.

The tables were arranged just as they had been when he was a child. He watched for one of the old waitresses—now in bifocals, short hair, and gaudy lipstick. But the girl who came to the table was only a couple of years out of high school and nervous, touching her ear and trying to smile by straining her lips into a rictus.

Still, the tables and chairs, the wood paneling and green-glass light fixtures, everything but the waitress was as it had been when he was young, when they'd come here on special occasions, and everything seemed fancy and sophisticated. Except now the salad bar seemed classless, and he noticed that the water came in plastic cups, the silverware was cheap, the napkins were paper. Down the center of the ceiling ran a strip of fluorescent lights. It was just a neighborhood restaurant, he saw now, more or less a dive.

They ate quietly.

"Maybe," he said, "if we look at the photos, something will stir up in your mind."

She shook her head.

"If you look at a set of photos long enough, Boggs said, you can always see something new."

"Sounds like John."

He paid, and when he came outside she stood on the sidewalk, looking at the street as if a secret door might open there. A couple of cars floated down the street, lamps glowing in the twilight. The row of buildings across from them stood dark, the windows boarded or hung with For Sale and For Lease signs. Across the railroad tracks and down the street, the True Value remained, the pharmacy, the grocery.

"Will you drive through the intersection?" he asked. "It might bring out some memory. Have you driven it since the accident? Since Christopher died?"

"You want to analyze everything," she said. "Not everything can be solved that way."

"That's not what I'm saying. I'm not an idiot. I know the limits of equations. I read books."

"You read books like a prisoner reads books."

"You're the one," he said, keeping his voice controlled, "who said all you want is to be able to really see things."

She looked at him, then reached forward. Gently, she touched his cheek with her fingers. "All right," she said and turned and stepped down the sidewalk.

He followed. Already she was opening the door of the station wagon. As he approached, the engine ignited, and before he pulled the passenger door closed behind himself she started backing up. "Heather," he said.

She steered into traffic.

"Heather."

She took them west, out of town, the nighttime road streaking under the headlamps. She turned and turned, and soon they drove on unfamiliar roads where cars were scarce. A few houses stood far back from the road, deep in the murk, a window or two glowing. A massive green John Deere tractor tilted on the road shoulder, abandoned. She slowed for an intersection, and low branches groped past the stop sign toward the car.

If the word *accident* was meaningless, if there were no accidents, then somehow he had chosen all of this. He deserved it. But he wanted her to see that she had chosen it, too. He wanted her to see it too.

They had circled, and now Coil lay ahead of them again. They passed an abandoned motel, a used-car lot, a bar called the Best Place. As they heaved and thudded on potholes and patches, Heather leaned forward, right hand flexing.

Two-story houses on festering lawns. A church fronted with a wide parking lot. A low bridge with concrete rails flaking. Most of it looked just as it had when he was a child, returning from the mall in the backseat of his mother's car. They passed the high school.

The road here ran two lanes in either direction, sparsely trafficked. A Buick with red cellophane taped over a broken taillight slowed and turned without signaling.

"How fast was Christopher's car going before the crash?" she asked. "Do you know?"

"Forty-seven, forty-eight, around there."

The lights of the intersection shone a quarter mile ahead. He saw Heather settle the speedometer between 45 and 50 mph. At the intersection, the green light dropped to red. A little white Plymouth rolled to a stop in the right lane, but the left lay open.

A couple hundred feet from the cross street she still held speed, and finally he understood.

He thought of grabbing the steering wheel, but he couldn't see anywhere safe to redirect the vehicle. To reach over to the brake pedal with his foot, he would have to remove his seatbelt. He said, "Heather."

"I want to know."

"I didn't mean this." Although at the same time, he wondered if something might be gained, a more authentic version of the experience.

"I want to know," she said. "Don't you?"

The car bellied into a low place, then rose into the intersection. He felt brightly calm, aware; a passenger, he could do nothing. He started to lift his hands to brace against the dash, but remembered the airbag that would explode from there, and he let his hands drop.

This felt different from the others—from the accident with James Dell, which had moved slowly before him while every detail caught him with surprise, and from the accident that killed Boggs, which came in an instant of distraction and finished even before he understood it had begun. Here he felt no surprise, and as he faced the oncoming event without surprise he thought of how time might be finely subdivided, akin to a process of differential calculus, creating an axis along which his mind could range forward as if all of it were preordained. And maybe it was; probably it could be calculated already.

His left hand, thrown out, came awkwardly against Heather's chest. A green Ford Explorer passed just before them, left to right, the driver peering through his side window, a large bald head with eyes tight, mouth tight, hand risen as if to fend away, and in the window behind him a boy of seven or eight with brown bangs over his eyes, grimacing. Crossing in the opposite direction in the far curbside lane moved a beige Saturn driven by a tall man, his head nearly into the ceiling, watching straight ahead, apparently oblivious, while from the left in the passing lane came a red Chevy pickup. A horn sounded—the Explorer's, although the Explorer had already safely passed by.

As they crossed the first lane, he saw that they would miss the Saturn, but the Chevy pickup would be very close.

Heather hadn't touched the brakes, and in this she had it wrong: the driver of his brother's car had braked. He looked past her profile into the pickup's headlights, incredibly near, as if in the car with them. Shrieking. The pickup braking, shrieking, how long had that noise existed? Heather's profile passed in front of the second headlight. He could not see the pickup's driver, could see nothing past the lamps and the chromed grille. The lamps passed behind the B-, then C-pillars, and the light thrown into the wagon flickered. Perhaps it would slip behind them, by an inch or two, he thought.

But then came the sudden horrendous clash of sheet metal on sheet metal in mutual forced distortion, and the wagon lurched right, and Ellis felt himself twisting, the seatbelt biting into him while his chin slammed down into his shoulder. An instant later the wagon was free of the Chevy, and the noise of the collision ended, replaced by the scream of the tires rubbing sideways and of chassis components smacking into one another. His chin came up, and already he was being pulled in the other direction, toward the door. Lights streaked out horizontally. Objects moved across the windshield—a parked car, a lamp pole, the canopy of the gas station, the fence.

It occurred to him that this was little different from what Boggs had done.

His body hit the door while time subdivided ever more finely, into a desert of sand, and then smaller yet, as if he might approach death atop Zeno's paradox.

A memory came up: Once, after Boggs had made a comment or asked a passing question about Christopher, and he hadn't answered, Boggs had said, "Don't take this wrong, but sometimes I kind of wonder if your brother ever really existed at all." But he did exist, and now he didn't, and that was what had always been incomprehensible, beyond analysis.

The station wagon lurched and heaved as it came into the curb, and Ellis glimpsed a wheel, broken free, rising into the air and away into the dark. The wagon's yawing movement was stopped, but it kept sliding sideways, scraping bare metal over concrete. He couldn't bring his head around to see where they were going, saw only where they had come from. A spectacle of sparks flew up. Heather had her eyes closed.

Another impact pressed him hard against his door. Darkness shuddered up. He couldn't breathe and couldn't see.

Thirty-nine

He touched something warm and human with his left hand.

Heather moaned.

A network of cracks shone in the windshield. Beside him stood a white vehicle, only a few inches from his window—some enormous thing, a pickup or SUV. The station wagon had slapped sideways into it. He looked for his left hand and saw it clutching at the fabric of his own pants. "Heather," he said. He could not get out through his door, because of the vehicle beside it.

"Yes."

"Can you open your door?"

"I thought I would remember," she said. "I really thought I would. I was terrified that I'd remember. But I didn't. I don't. Did you?"

Did he? Did he remember driving Christopher's car into the intersection?

No, he'd never driven Christopher's car. He felt a lurch of nausea. But no. He didn't remember anything like that; there was no evidence of anything like that. That was insanity. The driver's seat of the *airlane*—he recalled—wasn't set for his height.

"No," he said. "No." He unbuckled his belt, leaned across her, opened her door. An excess of adrenaline made objects vibrate. "Can you climb out?"

She did. He crawled over her seat, put his hands on the concrete, and pulled his legs out. Slowly he stood. He examined his right arm where it had hit the door, but there was no blood, only dull pain. Heather didn't appear injured. The vehicle that had stopped their movement was an empty Ram 3500. Ellis smelled faintly the acrid scent of gasoline, and he took Heather by the hand and led her away from it.

The red Chevy pickup that had hit them stood on the road's shoulder, and the driver emerged from it with a cell phone pressed to his head. A couple other cars had stopped. "Are you all right?" someone called.

Ellis nodded.

He felt tremors passing through Heather. He sat with her on the curb. "When the cops come," he said, "tell them you just didn't see the light."

She turned toward him.

"You don't have any idea if it was red or green or yellow," he said. "A lapse of attention. It happens all the time."

"I'll never drive again," she said.

Ellis shook his head. "You can't live in this country without driving."

The traffic started working its way around the pickup, resumed its movements. The lights overhead changed. The air stank of scorched brake pads and smoked rubber.

Forty

The police released her late that evening.

He picked her up in a rental car; she fell asleep in the passenger seat.

He passed the exit for her house and went on. For half an hour he fought exhaustion and drooping eyelids. Then the sense of fatigue faded and he grew alert, open.

He drove on, thinking he'd made a terrible mistake. She knew her story, and who was to say she was wrong? Her story was her story. It formed her. The story could not be unmade without unmaking her. He had committed the horrible mistake of trying to unmake her.

He stopped at 2 A.M. for gas in an island of fluorescent glow, crowded with vehicles and silent drivers. Heather didn't wake. Interstate miles passed. She slept with her head slumped to her shoulder.

Dawn was marshaling when Heather's hands twitched, after which she was still for another ten minutes. Then she groaned and winced as she lifted her head. She blinked at the road. "Where are we?"

The eastern sky, in his mirror, lay awash in shades of pink and lilac. He said, "I'm not exactly sure."

Flat land streamed by. She said, "Pull over."

"Here?"

"Please."

"I'm—"

"Please." She looked decided: the muscles around her eyes relaxed, her lips set—a look that pushed him down like a hand on the head of a swimmer. Reluctantly, he let the car slow and stop on the shoulder.

She stepped out and closed the door. She walked away. Her figure diminished, then vanished, under the blush of dawn light.

He sat and watched the traffic and the road and the landscape. The road ran straight to disappearing in either direction, and on either side the land opened with fallow, weedy fields, trees a distant effect clutching the horizon, except, across the highway, a single old oak, huge, like a thing that would be there forever.

He thought of Heather rushing by him on the swing in the park in Coil. He thought of the stone, the feather, and the bottle cap in her hand.

After a while, he realized he was sweating and rolled down the windows. It alleviated the temperature only a little and brought into the car all the furious noise of the highway.

His gaze drifted to the oak across the highway, to its intricate way of occupying space. A cement truck passed, its barrel striped like a colossal peppermint candy. A lawless unreality hung like a lavender fog at the limit of vision, but flickered away when he turned to it.

For a time he cried out amid the roaring traffic noise. He swore he would wait until he saw her coming. He would wait. He could only wait.

He waited into the afternoon with a headache scraping his eyes.

If he sat here long enough, he thought, he would see an accident occur.

For a long while he watched the oak, its solidity flickered by passing vehicles, and when he turned forward again he saw her.

He held his breath.

Coming out of the quivering distance, beside the flashing traffic. Stooped a little. Limping a little. His mind buzzed, and the air buzzed with traffic, and the approaching figure wavered and separated into a number of advancing figures, then congealed again into one figure that he could see watching him as she came. She was small, but the sun behind her threw out a long, wavering shadow.

When she reached the minivan she opened the door and sat beside him. Smelling of sweat and exhaust and faintly sweet and of herself. Small. Scarred. Without eyelashes. Here.

"Can we go?" she said. "Go find a beach? With sand?"

"Love?" he said, and abandoned all the rest, turned the key, and began to drive again.

Acknowledgments

For helping to keep this story on the roadway: Scott Sawyer, Abe Brennan, Amanda Rea, Tiffany Tyson, Jenny Itell, Don Lystra, Jennifer Vanderbes, Jeremy Mullem, Andrea Dupree, and Mike Henry.

For insight and keeping the faith when most would have given up: Eric Simonoff.

For deep, discerning editing like they say no one does anymore: Cal Morgan.

For teaching me how to reconstruct a vehicle accident: my friends and former colleagues at Knott Laboratory and Kineticorp, especially Nathan Rose, William Neale, and Gray Beauchamp.